Spring 2017

Dear Friends,

On a recent Facebook post, I read a New Year's resolution that said: "I will lose ten pounds this year. I only have fifteen to go." I laughed because that is generally the way my resolutions go. The point being that we all need second chances, a fresh beginning, and that is what inspired this New Beginnings series. *If Not for You* is the third book.

People often ask where I get my ideas for stories. Most often they come from real life. A couple of years ago I met a couple with an amazing story of how they met and fell in love. Vic and Mary Jury inspired me to come up with my own version for Sam and Beth. This is a story of healing, both emotional and physical.

Finishing a book is a bittersweet moment for me. On one hand I'm ecstatic to be finished so I can move these characters out of my brain. I can almost feel the next set clamoring to get inside my head, if they aren't already there. And at the same time it's hard to say goodbye, which might explain why so many of my stories and characters are connected to previous books.

The dedication for this book goes to a high-school friend, Cherie Carlton Thalheimer, and her husband, Robert. Cherie and I have a high-school reunion this year, and it's a biggie—one with a zero in it. We didn't know each other well as teenagers, which I find amusing now because she has become one of my best friends. I finally found someone (outside of my immediate family) who is as nuts about football as I am. The story of our friendship, rediscovering people we knew from the past, is worthy of a book in its own right. Hey, that's not a bad plot idea. I think I'll write that down so I remember . . .

One last note. The poem *The Warning Label No One Reads* was written by my granddaughter Bailey after she broke up with her boyfriend. I found it poignant and bittersweet and with her permission decided to include it in the book. It looks like I might not be the only writer in the family. And the song Sam wrote for Beth was composed by Pete Evick, who is the lead guitarist for Bret Michaels.

If you're familiar with any of my reader letters you know how much I treasure hearing from you. You can reach me any number of ways. The best place to learn about me is from my website at debbiemacomber.com or read my Facebook posts or Twitter. Or you can write me at P.O. Box 1458, Port Orchard, WA 98366.

Now it's time to turn the page and meet up with Sam and Beth and hopefully find a bit of healing in your own life.

Warmest regards,

Debbie Macomber

BALLANTINE BOOKS FROM DEBBIE MACOMBER

ROSE HARBOR INN

Sweet Tomorrows
Silver Linings
Love Letters
Rose Harbor in Bloom
The Inn at Rose Harbor

BLOSSOM STREET

Blossom Street Brides
Starting Now

CHRISTMAS BOOKS

Twelve Days of Christmas
Dashing Through the Snow
Mr. Miracle
Starry Night
Angels at the Table

NEW BEGINNINGS

If Not for You
A Girl's Guide to Moving On
Last One Home

If Not for You

DEBBIE MACOMBER

If Not for You

A Novel

BALLANTINE BOOKS

NEW YORK

If Not for You is a work of fiction. Names, characters, places, and incidents are the products of the author's imagination or are used fictitiously. Any resemblance to actual events, locales, or persons, living or dead, is entirely coincidental.

Published in the United States by Ballantine Books, an imprint of Random House, a division of Penguin Random House LLC, New York.

BALLANTINE BOOKS and the HOUSE colophon are registered trademarks of Penguin Random House LLC.

LIBRARY OF CONGRESS CATALOGING-IN-PUBLICATION DATA
Names: Macomber, Debbie, author.
Title: If not for you : a novel / Debbie Macomber.
Description: New York : Ballantine Books, [2017]
Identifiers: LCCN 2016042032 | ISBN 9780553391961
(hardcover : acid-free paper) | ISBN 9780553391978 (ebook)
Subjects: LCSH: Man-woman relationships—Fiction. | Life change events—Fiction. | BISAC: FICTION / Romance / Contemporary. | FICTION / Contemporary Women. | FICTION / Sagas. | GSAFD: Love stories.
Classification: LCC PS3563.A2364 I35 2017 | DDC 813/.54—dc23
LC record available at https://lccn.loc.gov/2016042032

Printed in the United States of America on acid-free paper

randomhousebooks.com

2 4 6 8 9 7 5 3 1

FIRST EDITION

Book *design by Dana Leigh Blanchette*

To Cherie and Robert Thalheimer,
Seahawks lovers and the dearest of friends

If Not for You

PROLOGUE

It really was a shame. No, not a shame . . . a disappointment, Beth Prudhomme mused, as she sat at the intersection, waiting for the green light. She glanced out the car window at the man her friend had invited her to meet over dinner. Sam Carney was stopped in the lane next to her, also waiting for the light. Again she felt a twinge of regret, knowing nothing would ever come of their evening together.

It'd been silly to put any hope into this blind date. One look at Sam and it was clear they weren't a good match. Beth could just imagine what her parents would say if they were ever to meet Sam. The thought was enough to make her smile. Her mother would have a fit of hysterics. In her mother's eyes, she would view Sam as uncouth, vulgar, and a bane to society. All this because his hair was long and he had a beard. His tattoos would likely send her over the edge. But then her mother had high expectations when it came to the man Beth would one day marry.

It didn't take her long to realize Sam felt the same way about her. His eyes had widened briefly before he could disguise his reaction when they were first introduced. He probably saw her as prim and pristine and oh-so-proper, which she was, thanks to her mother. Beth suspected Sam hadn't been psyched about this dinner date, either, and briefly wondered what had led him into agreeing to meet her. She knew she'd been a big disappointment. The truth was, she'd liked Sam. Although they hadn't spoken much, she felt drawn to his unconventional attitude, which was so unlike her own structured life. It'd been hard to get a read on him, other than when they were first introduced. Beth couldn't help but wonder what he was thinking; he gave away little of his thoughts other than the fact that he seemed more than anxious for the evening to be over. Beth didn't blame him.

She had to admit Sam was handsome, definitely rough around the edges, but Nichole had warned her about that. His shoulder-length hair was tied into a ponytail at the base of his neck. He had nice dark eyes, she'd say that. The color reminded her of warm cocoa. He was tall; she estimated he must be six-two, which was a foot taller than her own petite frame. And he must outweigh her by a good seventy or more pounds. Her friend's description of Sam had given her pause, but her aunt Sunshine had persuaded her to give it a shot.

"Why not? What's it going to hurt?"

True enough, it hadn't hurt, but still the taste of disappointment settled over her.

Sitting in the tall cab of his truck, Sam must have noticed her scrutiny, because he turned his head, looking down at her as they waited for the light to change. Goodness, the truck was so high up she'd need a step stool just to climb onto the seat.

The traffic signal turned green. Offering Sam a brief smile, she stepped on the accelerator and moved forward into the intersection, preparing to make the turn. That was when she noticed the car coming directly toward her, racing through a red light.

In that split second her eyes caught those of the teenage driver in the other car. She had her cellphone in her hand; her face twisted in a look of surprised horror. From that moment forward, everything seemed to happen in slow motion. The girl's mouth opened in a scream. She braced her hands against the steering wheel and slammed on the brakes, but it was too late.

Much too late to avoid a collision.

Knowing what was coming, Beth braced herself, too, but nothing could have prepared her for the impact of the other vehicle slamming into the driver's-side door. The explosive noise of steel crashing against steel was loud enough to burst Beth's eardrums. Despite her death grip on the steering wheel, her arms were jerked free, tossed above her head like a puppet's string as the other car plowed directly into her, spinning Beth and her car around and around.

She opened her mouth to scream, but all that escaped was a gasp of sheer terror and pain, horrific pain.

And then . . . then there was nothing until she heard someone calling her name.

When she managed to force her eyes open, all she could see was Sam.

CHAPTER 1

Beth

"Give Mozart a chance," Beth pleaded with the teenage boy who stared doggedly down at the classroom floor. "Once you listen to his music you'll feel differently, I promise."

The youth continued to avoid eye contact and then chanced a look in the direction of Bailey Madison. Beth had noticed the teenage girl sneaking glances in his direction through most of the class. Before class, both students had asked for transfers, which disappointed her. Beth didn't want to lose either one.

"I like music, but I'm not into that classical stuff," Noah told her.

"But you might be if you gave it a chance," Beth said in what she hoped was an encouraging voice. Noah Folgate sat through the entire class period with his arms folded and his eyes closed, except when he took peeks at Bailey.

"Besides, the only reason I signed up for the class was because my girlfriend, I mean my ex-girlfriend, did."

"You can stay in the class," Bailey said. "I'm dropping out."

Beth motioned for Bailey to join them. Noah's gaze narrowed and he crossed his arms and refused to look in the other girl's direction.

"Bailey, why did you register for the class?" Beth asked.

Clenching her books to her chest, Bailey shrugged. "I'm in band. I like anything to do with music."

"Are you and Noah friends?"

"We . . . used to be."

"Would you like to be again?" Beth asked.

Noah stared at the teenage girl. Bailey nodded and her voice trembled when she said, "More than anything."

Noah blinked as though her words had shocked him.

Beth knew better than to get caught in the middle of teenage angst. She really did, but she'd watched these two closely through class and suspected that whatever had happened between them was what prompted them to ask for a transfer.

"Noah, would you be willing to give the class another week?"

The high school junior shrugged.

"Bailey, what about you?"

"I suppose that would be all right."

"Great." Beth rubbed her palms together. "We'll talk again next Friday, and if you both feel the same way, I'll do what I can to help you find another class."

"Can I go now?" Noah asked.

"Of course."

The boy shot out of the class, but Bailey lingered behind. "I know what you're doing, Miss Prudhomme. I don't think it'll help. Noah thinks I cheated on him. I didn't, but I can't make him believe me. I don't know that I can be with someone who doubts me and has trust issues. I'll give it another week, but don't expect Noah to change his mind. If he doesn't, it will be far too painful to be in class with him and see him every day."

"Of course," Beth said sympathetically. She hoped they could work it out. She'd done what she could; the rest was up to them. She really hated to see them drop out of the class for personal reasons, especially when by their own admission they were both musically inclined. Unfortunately, they had little understanding or appreciation of the depth and beauty of classical music. Given the chance, she believed they would come to love it as much as she did. Noah and Bailey were exactly the kind of students she enjoyed most. The challenge, of course, was to keep the two of them from dropping out of class.

This was Beth's first teaching experience, but she'd had some success convincing her private piano students to give Schubert, Bach, and Beethoven a try. Once they'd learned about the great composers and played their music, her private students had been hooked. Beth hoped to hook these high school students as well.

Feeling like she'd made headway, Beth straightened her desk. It was Friday at the end of a long week of classes and she was more than ready for the weekend, not that she had any big plans. As a recent transplant from Chicago, the only person Beth knew, other than a few teachers, was her aunt Sunshine. She was making friends, though, at church, where she volunteered for the choir, and in her apartment building.

Sunshine was the best. Just thinking about her eccentric, fun-loving aunt produced a smile. Beth didn't know what she would do without her. Her aunt had given her the courage and the encouragement to break away from the dictates of her family. Beth loved her parents, but they, especially her mother, had definite ideas about whom she should marry, her career, her friends, and just about everything else. Until she moved, her mother even accompanied her when she bought clothes, not trusting Beth to choose her own wardrobe. Without realizing what she was doing, her mother was strangling her. She had to break away or suffocate.

She had saved money from teaching piano and was prepared to leave in the middle of the night rather than argue. Her family wasn't holding her prisoner; she was free to go. Sunshine was the one who'd invited Beth to move to Portland, Oregon. Looking for employment, she went online and saw an opening for a music teacher in a local high school. Beth wanted that job in the worst way and was determined to get it, to live her own life instead of the one her mother saw for her.

Before following through with her escape plans, Beth decided to tell her father. He was by far the more reasonable of the two. It'd been a good decision. Even now Beth didn't know what he said to her mother, but whatever it was had been life-changing for her. The next morning Phillip, her father, told her she had his word that Ellie, her mother, would not visit or interfere in Beth's life for six months. No visits to Portland. No tearful phone calls. No tossing guilt. Any contact would be instigated by Beth herself.

She was basically free; well, at least for the next six months. Before her mother could change her mind, Beth loaded up her car and left that very day. Her mother had stood on the lawn and wept as Beth backed into the street and started on her way.

When she arrived in Portland, she stayed the first few days with her aunt, scheduled interviews, and was over the moon when she was hired at the high school. As soon as she had the job, she found an apartment she could afford and for the first time in her twenty-five years she was on her own.

Weeks earlier she'd had no hope, but now, after breaking away, hope had found her. When she was settled in her own apartment, Beth called her parents and told them she was set. The conversation had been awkward, and when her mother had sniffled softly, her father made her get off the phone. Beth knew the tears were about more than the fact that she'd left Chicago. It hurt her mother that Beth was in the same city as Sunshine. The two sisters had never gotten along. Whatever had caused the rift between them was a mystery to Beth. She hoped that at some point Sunshine would explain what it was that had put such a heavy strain on their relationship. Once in her youth, Beth had asked her mother, but her mother had said it was something that happened a long time ago and wouldn't explain further.

Beth collected her books and purse and was heading down the hallway when she heard her name.

"Beth," Nichole Nyquist, a substitute English teacher who'd be-friended her, called out from behind her.

"Hey," Beth said, smiling as she turned around, happy to run into her friend. It'd been a couple days since they'd last con-nected. They'd met during the first week of classes and struck up an immediate friendship. After the birth of her second son, Nich-ole had given up her full-time position and currently worked only as needed. Seeing Nichole was a treat, as she hadn't been at school all week.

"Do you have a minute?" Nichole asked.

"Of course."

"I wanted to ask you to dinner tomorrow night."

"Oh." The invitation came as something of a surprise. She'd been to Nichole's house once and briefly met her husband, son, and stepdaughter. Kaylene was also a senior at the high school. Nichole and Beth ate lunch together in the teachers' lounge when they could, but those times were rare.

"I know it's last-minute. I wanted to connect with you earlier but didn't, and the next thing I knew it was Friday. I've been think-ing about this awhile; I hope you can come."

"I don't have any plans," Beth said, a bit wary of this sudden bout of chattiness from Nichole. "You've been thinking about what?" Nichole had left that part suspiciously blank.

"Ah . . ."

"Is there something you aren't telling me?"

Nichole scratched her ear and then let out a long sigh. "Actually, there is. Rocco is inviting his best friend, Sam Carney, to dinner. I wanted the two of you to meet."

Beth held the textbook closer to her chest. So that was it. Nichole planned on setting her up with Rocco's friend. Normally that wouldn't be a problem. She'd gone out to dinner and a movie with Tyler Crowley, an English teacher. He was divorced, lonely, and a little too eager to get involved in a relationship. Beth turned him down for a second date when he'd asked her again. He got the message after that.

Nichole paused as though hesitant, and Beth knew there was more to the story. "Tell me a little about Sam."

Nichole slipped her purse strap over her shoulder and clung to it as if she wasn't sure where to start. "He's a great guy and he isn't bad looking either."

"Divorced? Single?"

"Single. Never been married. He's a mechanic, and from what Rocco tells me, he's one of the best in the city. Apparently, he can fix just about anything."

If nothing else, Beth would know where to go if she experienced car trouble. Still, she sensed there was something else Nichole wasn't telling her. "And . . ." she prompted.

"And, well, Sam probably isn't like any other guy you've ever dated."

Seeing as her dating experience had been limited to an approved list from her mother and that one date with Tyler, that was probably true. Still, she felt obliged to ask. "Different in what way?"

Nichole glanced down the hall as if looking for someone. "It's hard to explain."

Beth waited, giving Nichole time to collect her thoughts.

Her friend sucked in a deep breath. "When I first met Sam, he was . . . I'm not sure how to explain it. Let's just say he was a bit unconventional . . . still is, for that matter."

That was a curious way of putting it. "How so?"

"He swore a lot."

"Not good." Beth got enough of that from her students in the hallways. She found it to be in bad taste and a sign of a poor vocabulary.

"It's better now," Nichole was quick to add. "Owen makes Sam give him a dollar for every swear word he uses." She struggled to hold back a smile. "The first few months I was convinced he was going to pay for my son's college education."

Owen was Nichole's son from her first marriage. "Good for Owen."

"I can't say what Sam's language is like now, but when he's around the house his descriptive phrasing isn't as picturesque as it once was. Rocco and I don't get out as much as we once did, so we don't see Sam socially a lot anymore. He stops by the house a couple times a week, though. He's crazy about Matthew. I've never seen a man take to a baby the way he has. He's perfectly content to hold him, and he isn't averse to changing a diaper, either. Just not a messy one."

So he liked babies. That was good. The swearing was troublesome, though. Sure as anything, her parents would balk at the thought of her dating a mechanic, but then she'd specifically moved from Chicago to get out from under their thumb.

"Anything else you care to tell me about Sam?" she asked, undecided. Frankly, this dinner didn't sound promising and could end up being a disaster.

Nichole held her gaze. "Actually, I think it would be best if I didn't say anything more. You should make up your own mind about Sam. All I can tell you is that he's a really great guy. I had my doubts when I first met him and you might, too. Just give him a chance, okay?"

Beth nibbled on her lower lip. "Let me think about it. Can I get back to you either tonight or first thing tomorrow morning?"

"Sure. I know it's a last-minute invite . . ."

"It's fine, Nichole. Thanks for thinking of me. I'll let you know soon. Promise."

They left the building together, and by the time Beth reached Sunshine's studio she'd decided against meeting Sam. It would be a waste of time on both their parts. From what little Nichole had said, it didn't appear they had anything in common. The music teacher and the mechanic.

Not a good match.

Not a good idea.

Sunshine was busy painting, her long, thick, salt-and-pepper hair hanging straight and loose, reaching all the way down to the middle of her back. Beth couldn't ever remember seeing her aunt in anything other than long skirts and Birkenstocks. She'd remained a flower child who never outgrew the 1960s. Concentrating on her work, her aunt apparently didn't hear Beth enter her studio.

Standing back, Beth waited and watched. Her aunt was a talented artist. Her work was highly sought after and hung in galleries all across the country. What fascinated Beth was the prices she got for a few squiggly lines. It was between those lines where Sunshine's talent came to life. In that space was intricate artwork, cleverly hidden at first glance. It often took Beth several minutes to see the full picture.

This current project displayed rows upon rows of blooming poppies, their color vibrant against a backdrop of what appeared to be random strokes of red paint. She stared at it for several minutes until she saw it. A school of fish. Unbelievable. Beth couldn't help being mesmerized.

Her aunt released a deep breath as if she'd been holding it in and then relaxed, stepping back to consider her work, and nearly tripped over Beth.

"Beth, how long have you been here?" she asked, setting down her paintbrush.

"Not long."

Sunshine apparently followed Beth's eyes and cocked her head to one side. "You like?"

"It's brilliant." As far as Beth was concerned, there was no other word for it.

Sunshine tossed back her head and laughed, the sound bubbling up from her like champagne fizz. Beth loved hearing her aunt's laugher. It had a magical quality that never ceased to amuse her. Just listening to it made her want to laugh, too. She resisted the urge to close her eyes and store it in her memory bank for times when she was low and struggled with worry or frustration.

"You say that every time, you know?"

"Because it's true."

Sunshine walked over to the tiny refrigerator, similar to the one in Beth's college dorm room, opened it, and took out a bottle of water. Handing one to Beth, she grabbed another for herself. "To what do I owe this pleasure?"

Beth felt a little silly turning to her aunt for advice. "I have a question for you."

"Fire away." Stretching out her arm, Sunshine saluted her with the water bottle.

"A friend asked me to dinner tomorrow night and . . ."

"Male or female?"

"Female, but it's a setup. She wants me to meet a friend of her husband's, though technically he's her friend, too, I guess." Beth felt a little funny talking about this, but the fact remained she was a novice when it came to men and relationships. She'd dated some in high school and college but had never been in a serious relationship.

"And the problem is?"

Beth leaned against the edge of the table, unsure how to explain.

"To hear Nichole tell it, my dinner date is a bit coarse, what my mother would term *uncivilized*."

"You've mentioned Nichole before, haven't you?"

Beth took a sip of water and nodded. "Yes, she was one of the first teachers to welcome me at the high school. She's great. I have her stepdaughter in one of my classes."

"So the problem is . . . ?"

"Sunshine"—Beth sighed—"I can only imagine what my mother would say if she heard I'd agreed to have dinner with a mechanic."

Sunshine set her water bottle aside and cupped Beth's face with both hands, staring deeply into her eyes. "My dear girl, that is your problem in a nutshell. You are living your life to please your mother. This guy—"

"His name is Sam."

"Sam could be the most wonderful man you're ever likely to meet. You haven't even met him and you're already judging him, deciding he isn't worth knowing because he wouldn't get your mother's approval! My dear girl, take a chance." She lowered her hands and gave an expressive sigh. "I knew a Sam once, and fell instantly in love with him. He was an artist, unconventional, crazy talented, married, but I didn't learn that until it was too late and he'd stolen my heart."

"Oh no." Beth had never heard her aunt talk about anyone named Sam. But then there'd always been men in and out of Sunshine's life. No one man seemed to last for long. It was as if her aunt was looking for something elusive that continually escaped her.

"I have no complaints. When we were together it was glorious: a time I treasure. We were equals, in tune with each other. All we talked about were art and wine." A wistful look and a smile stole over her, as if she was caught up in the memory of her love affair.

"Is he the reason you never married?" Beth hadn't dared to ask the question before.

"Because of Sam?" She shook her head. "Not at all. He was a

passing fancy, nothing more. It was a good thing he was married; otherwise, we would have grown to hate each other—our personalities were far too similar. But while it lasted . . . it was heaven."

"Do you really think I should agree to this blind date?"

"Beth, my beautiful, beautiful child, of course you should. Let go of your inhibitions, live free, fall in love; make the most of this opportunity. Who knows, this Sam could end up being the man of your dreams."

Beth managed to suppress a giggle. "I doubt it." Even Nichole seemed uncertain that she was doing the right thing.

"Why not? You'll never know unless you try. Be positive, throw away your doubts, and pretend you're meeting a prince."

From the meager description Nichole had given her, Sam sounded nothing like royalty. Still, her aunt was right. She needed to give him a shot. No harm, no foul.

Beth kissed her aunt's cheek and left wearing a smile. Fact was, she couldn't ever remember leaving Sunshine without smiling.

As soon as she was home, Beth sent Nichole a text.

Count me in.

Not more than a minute passed when she got a return text.

Great. See you at six.

Beth knew it was a mistake to feel the least bit optimistic about this blind date. She'd heard about these kinds of setups from her friends often enough to know they rarely worked out.

Even with all her doubts, she spent Saturday morning filled with happy anticipation, a sense of excitement. She had two piano students in the morning, which left her afternoon free.

When the time came to get ready, it took her nearly an hour to decide what to wear. She didn't want to appear too formal in a dress or skirt, nor would she be comfortable dressed casually in jeans and a sweater.

Before long she had nearly her entire closet laid across the top of her bed. In the end, five minutes before she was scheduled to leave, she decided on black leggings and a white linen top. Instead of heels she wore ballet flats. Giving herself one final inspection, she drew in a deep breath, gazed at herself in the full-length mirror in her hallway, and decided this was about as good as it got. The look was a little like Audrey Hepburn in *Breakfast at Tiffany's,* although she wasn't nearly as beautiful.

As she left her apartment complex, Sunshine's words rang in her head.

This Sam could end up being the man of your dreams.

Beth was ready to meet that special someone.

So very ready.

CHAPTER 2

Sam

"Nichole wants to invite you to dinner."

Sam looked up from the engine he was tinkering with in the driveway of his house. He grabbed the pink rag that was tucked in his back pocket and wiped his hands clean while he mulled this over. He'd eaten with Rocco and Nichole any number of times, but never with a specific invitation. Most times he was at the house around dinnertime and Nichole threw an extra plate on the table. No biggie. This sounded suspicious.

"What's up?" Sam asked skeptically.

"Dinner," Rocco said, shrugging off the question.

"Why are you asking me like this? There's a catch, isn't there?"

"No catch."

Okay, he'd play along. "When?"

"You available tonight?" Rocco asked.

The handwriting on the wall was coming into focus, and he didn't like what he saw. "Short notice, isn't it?"

"You got any other plans?"

A beer in front of the Seahawks preseason game was about as social as he intended to get this Saturday night.

"Didn't think so." Rocco didn't wait for an answer. He walked around to the other side of his truck.

"You need to come," six-year-old Owen insisted.

"Why is that?"

Rocco grinned and ruffled the top of Owen's head. "He's looking for you to fill his jar full of dollar bills."

Sam snickered; the kid had cleaned him out more than once.

"Only have to pay if you use bad words," Owen clarified. "You need to come because Mom's been cooking all morning and she's got a special friend coming."

Now they were getting somewhere. Slowly straightening, Sam glared at Rocco, who avoided eye contact. "A special friend?" he repeated. "Of Nichole's?"

Rocco frowned down at his stepson as if to scold the boy.

So this was a booby trap. "How special?" Sam said again, focusing his gaze on his best friend. Sounded like there was a price to be paid for said dinner.

"Another teacher," Rocco said with a shrug as if this was a small thing. They both knew it wasn't.

"Male or female?" Although he already knew the answer.

Rocco thrust his hands into his back pockets and cleared his throat as if something had got caught in his windpipe. "Female."

"And exactly when were you going to mention the invitation also included this *special* friend of Nichole's?"

Rocco walked around to the other side of Sam's truck. "I was getting around to that."

"Sure you were," Sam muttered. "You know I don't do blind

dates." Or relationships. Better than anyone, Rocco knew Sam's history with women, all of which was negative.

"I know . . ."

"She's not blind, Uncle Sam," Owen inserted before Rocco had a chance to speak. "It's like a date and Mom said she's perfect for you."

"Right." His gaze didn't leave Rocco's. This sneaky invite wasn't like Rocco. "What's the deal?" he asked, continuing to wipe his already clean hands.

Rocco continued to look ill at ease. "Nichole's got her heart set on this. She really likes this teacher."

"You've met her?"

"Once, briefly."

"Her name is Beth," Owen rushed to add.

Sam waited for Rocco to enlighten him. "And?" he prompted when his friend remained suspiciously quiet.

"Beth came to the house shortly after she met Nichole. I was there, but for the life of me I don't remember much about her."

Apparently, she wasn't memorable. He didn't know Rocco to lie, but Sam wasn't convinced his friend was telling him the full truth.

"I remember her," Owen popped up excitedly. "She's nice; she's not ugly or anything."

That was an underwhelming endorsement. Bending over, Sam went back to working on the engine of the classic 1967 Dodge R/T. "Like I said, I don't do blind dates."

"Sam," Rocco said and groaned.

"You gotta come," Owen insisted. "Mom's making homemade chicken cordon bleu, and she baked her special applesauce cake."

"No thanks."

"She's even using the china we got from Grandma."

Sam still wasn't convinced. "Knowing Nichole, she's got a backup plan. She can invite the next unsuspecting guy on her list."

"Nope." Again it was Owen who spoke. "She said you're the one."

"He's telling you the truth," Rocco said.

Sam groaned and slumped his shoulders. It was just his luck that Nichole would pick on him. "Why me?"

"Beth is the music teacher at the high school."

"What kind of music?"

"Classical stuff: Mozart and Bach and a whole bunch of those old guys. You play the guitar, she plays the piano. You have a lot in common."

"Like I listen to Mozart," Sam muttered, shaking his head. He didn't need to meet this teacher friend of Nichole's to guess they were about as ill-suited as any two people were likely to get.

"She likes other kinds of music, too," Owen said. "She knows Uncle Kracker and Bruno Mars."

Owen was doing the talking. Seeing how silent Rocco remained made him all the more suspicious.

"She ever listen to the Oak Ridge Boys? What about George Strait, David Allan Coe or Carrie Underwood?"

Owen frowned. "I don't know, but you can ask her."

Sam didn't plan on it, seeing that he had no intention of showing up for this dinner. He glanced at Rocco. "You're not saying much."

"This wasn't my idea."

Thankfully, Rocco understood where he was coming from. "Thank God for that."

"Did he use God's name as a swear word?" Owen asked Rocco.

"No." Both Rocco and Sam chimed in together.

"You coming or not?" Rocco pressed.

"Not." No good would come of this blind date.

Even with his head bent over the truck engine, Sam saw Owen's face fall. "Mom's not going to be happy."

Sam managed to suppress a smile. He straightened and eyed his friend. "I want to know how Nichole managed to rope you into this?" Rocco was the one person who knew him best. He was well aware of the way Sam felt about friends setting him up.

"I love my wife," Rocco said, exhaling slowly. "You have to know this wasn't my idea, but Nichole has her heart set on you meeting Beth. The hell if I can refuse her."

Owen grabbed the sleeve of Rocco's shirt and jerked it. "Hell's a swear word."

"I am not paying you a dollar for *hell*," Rocco muttered.

"You said it again. That's two dollars."

Rocco groaned. "It's in the Bible, and any word in the Bible can't be considered a swear word." Glaring at Sam, he said, "See what you've done? You're the one who started this."

"And I've paid through the nose."

"You can use other words instead of bad ones," Owen helpfully supplied.

"True, but do you know the looks I get when I swear saying mother-forklift?"

Rocco burst out laughing.

"You think it's funny, do you?" he asked, but he smiled himself. These days he'd gotten inventive when it came to swearing. He had Owen and that glass jar of his to thank. The jar now stuffed full of his dollar bills. And actually, Sam didn't mind. He'd gotten into the habit of letting swear words fly without thinking. It'd taken Owen calling him to task for him to notice.

"Please come," Owen pleaded.

"It's important to Nichole," Rocco added. "You know I wouldn't ask you otherwise."

Sam angled his head toward the sky. He didn't like this. Not one bit. "You owe me for this."

"I'll make it up to you," Rocco promised.

Rocco would make it up to him. Sam would make damn sure he did.

Oh damn . . . he wondered if he owed Owen a dollar if he swore in his thoughts.

After Rocco and Owen left, Sam immediately regretted agreeing to this blind date. He wouldn't do it for anyone other than Nichole. But when the time came, he showered and combed his shoulder-length hair back and tied it at the base of his neck. He hated getting his hair cut just about as much as he hated shaving, which is why he wore a beard. Examining his reflection, he noticed his beard had gotten a bit scraggly looking. He reached for a pair of scissors and he trimmed it back. Sam sincerely hoped Nichole appreciated all the trouble he was going through for this dinner idea of hers.

Shuffling through his closet, he chose a shirt with a button-down collar and put on a clean pair of black jeans. This was about as fancy as he got. If this teacher was looking for some suave dresser, then she was out of luck.

One thing Nichole did right was cook his favorite dinner. He was a sucker for her applesauce cake and he'd never tasted a better cordon bleu than what Nichole made. To be fair, hers was the only homemade cordon bleu he'd ever tasted, but he suspected few would compare. Being single, he frequently ate out and his meals usually consisted of something he was able to pick up at a drive-through on the way home from the car dealership. Either that or tavern food he got at The Dog House, where he often hung out. Not as much now that Rocco had married. Sam had other friends, but none as close to him as Rocco was.

Sam arrived at Rocco and Nichole's place at around five-thirty. He had a few questions he wanted to ask Nichole before this teacher friend of hers arrived. Besides, he'd volunteer to hold the baby while she put the finishing touches on dinner. Knowing Nichole, she'd be fussing over every detail.

He sincerely hoped she wasn't putting any stock into something developing between him and this teacher friend of hers. From the little bit he knew about . . . what in the world was her name again? Brenda? Brittany? Something like that. For the life of him, he couldn't remember. No matter what her name was, he already knew it wasn't going to work. He had no intention of getting involved in a relationship.

Owen had the front door open by the time Sam had climbed out of his truck. "Hi, Uncle Sam."

"How ya doing, kid?"

"Good." Owen held the screen door for him.

Sam ruffled the top of his head as he entered the house. Right away a mixture of delicious scents greeted him. If nothing else, he was getting a home-cooked meal out of the deal. Otherwise, it was destined to be a complete waste of his time and this teacher's, too.

"Sam," Nichole greeted him as she came out of the kitchen dressed in a pretty pink blouse and black slacks. She looked good. The baby fat had disappeared or was cleverly disguised. He didn't know which. She kissed his cheek and held on to his forearms. Her eyes were warm and full of gratitude. "Thank you."

"Don't thank me yet. I hope Rocco told you I'm not interested in having friends set me up." Usually it turned out to be a huge disappointment on both sides.

"I know. I know. Rocco wasn't happy about it, either, but I swear you're going to like Beth."

Beth, that was it.

"Owen said she's into classical music."

"She loves all kinds of music."

He rolled his eyes.

Nichole slapped his upper arm. "Get rid of the attitude. You're going to have a lovely evening."

Sam sincerely doubted that, but saying so would only irritate Nichole. He liked his friend's wife. He hadn't been sure about the two of them when Rocco first brought her around. It wasn't long, though, before she'd managed to worm her way into his heart, not that he was in love with her or anything. She'd won him over because of the way she loved Rocco. The changes in his friend were huge after Nichole came into his life.

There was a time when Rocco had been pretty wild, boozing it up and getting into scrapes with the law. He'd been free and easy with women, too, which was how Kaylene had come into his life. Hard to believe Kaylene was eighteen now and a high school senior. Everything changed for Rocco when he got custody of his daughter. That was when he settled down and became a responsible citizen. Eventually he took over ownership of Potter Towing. It was through the towing company that he'd met Nichole, when he pulled her out of a ditch.

It didn't take Sam long to realize how strongly Rocco felt about Nichole. She had him hook, line, and sinker almost from the first day they met. It surprised Sam that a classy woman like Nichole would marry Rocco. Far as he could see, they were still head over heels about each other. Sam doubted there was anything Rocco wouldn't do for his wife. She brought Owen into the marriage and now they had Matthew, and from what Rocco said, in a year or two Nichole wanted to have another baby. Good for them. Sam enjoyed being an adopted uncle. He'd always loved kids.

"You ready to meet Beth?" Owen asked.

"I'm ready to settle down in a rocking chair with Matthew," Sam said, seeing that the infant was asleep in the fancy baby contraption set up in the living room.

"Not now," Nichole warned. "I just fed him and got him down. With luck he'll sleep through dinner."

Sam was disappointed, but there'd be plenty of opportunity later. "Need any help?"

"You can help me with the wine," Rocco said, coming out of the kitchen with a bottle of chardonnay in his hand.

"I'd rather have beer."

"We're having wine tonight," Nichole informed him.

"I can't have a beer?" He didn't bother to hide his disappointment.

"Later," Rocco mouthed.

Sam managed to hide a smile and winked back at his friend.

Nichole braced her hands against her hips. "We're serving wine with dinner."

"Sounds good to me." Sam knew better than to argue with the woman of the house.

The doorbell rang and automatically Sam stiffened.

It was about to start: the awkwardness, the polite exchange of chitchat. She would look him over and he would check her out. Not that he was interested in knowing anything more about her than he already did. Him and a classical music teacher. Not happening.

"I'll get it," Nichole said, automatically heading for the front door.

Rocco stood next to Sam and placed his hand on his shoulder. "Relax," he breathed. "How bad can it get?"

Sam stiffened. "I think we're about to find out."

Nichole let her friend into the house and then with a smile she gestured toward Sam. "I'd like to introduce my friend, Beth Prudhomme. Beth, this is Sam Carney."

This was even worse than he thought. Her gaze shot to him and her eyes widened. He had much the same reaction. She was exactly what he'd expected, what he dreaded most. Everything about her— from the way she stood, shoulders and back straight—spoke of education and breeding. He saw it in how she moved, how she carried herself, in her clothes.

He'd met her type before, women who brought their cars into the dealership who hardly looked at him because he was the mechanic and far beneath their social status. Maybe he wasn't being fair, but he saw the look in her eyes and suspected they reflected the look in his. This would never work. Just as he'd feared, this evening was already doomed and it hadn't even gotten started.

"Beth," he said, dipping his head.

Like Owen claimed, she wasn't ugly. She was no raving beauty, either. In a word, she was ordinary, more on the plain side than beautiful. Small breasts. Skinny legs. Nothing to make her stand out in a crowd. He could only speculate what there was about her that made Nichole think they would ever be compatible. Looking at Beth, he couldn't see a single thing. Her eyes told him she thought the same thing about him. No way.

"Hello, Sam." Her voice was cultured and educated as she stepped forward and offered him her hand. Her touch was light, delicate, the same as she was.

"You remember my husband, Rocco," Nichole continued.

"Hi, Rocco." Beth turned away from Sam and looked at Rocco, offering him the same polished smile.

Oh yes, this was going to be a l-o-n-g evening.

Very long indeed.

CHAPTER 3

Beth

The start of the evening hadn't gone well. Everyone seemed to be on edge. Beth did her best to pretend everything was fine, although she knew otherwise. Nichole tried, too, speaking animatedly.

"Why don't we all sit down," her friend suggested.

Sam pulled out the chair at the dining room table as if he was more than eager to get this dinner over with as quickly as possible.

"I was thinking we'd sit in the living room first for appetizers and conversation," Nichole suggested, looking expectantly toward her husband to rescue her.

"Yes, good idea," Rocco said, sounding overly enthusiastic as he headed for the other room as if he couldn't get there fast enough.

Sam looked like his best friend had just stabbed him in the back.

"Now, Mom?" Owen asked, looking expectantly toward his mother.

"Now would be perfect," Nichole told her son as she gestured toward the living room, ushering Sam in that direction.

Beth hadn't been in the house ten minutes and already she could tell this evening was going to be torture. For her and for Sam. How foolish she'd been to put any stock in this night. No one needed to tell her Sam had been an unwilling victim. Everything he said and did told her he would give just about anything to have escaped this farce. While Beth appreciated her friend's efforts, surely Nichole could see this wasn't working.

It demanded restraint not to lean over and whisper to Sam, "You want to get out of here and pretend this never happened?"

She didn't, of course, but the temptation was there.

Nichole took the chair by the fireplace. Rocco hesitated and then sat down in the chair on the other side, which left the sofa open for Beth and Sam. Sam sat down first, at the farthest end possible, almost as if he would be infected with Ebola if he strayed too close to her. If it wasn't so ridiculous, Beth would have given in to a fit of laughter.

Nichole glared at the other man.

Sam glared back.

While he'd obviously agreed to this dinner, he felt compelled to let Nichole and Beth know he was here under protest.

Beth resisted sitting as far from Sam as she could. Again, her upbringing came into play, and she sat in the middle of the cushion, her hands primly folded in her lap. Her back was as straight as a light pole. She felt like a grade-schooler called into the principal's office to be reprimanded. This evening seemed like punishment and she was sure Sam felt the same.

"Beth recently moved to Portland, isn't that right?" Nichole said once everyone was seated.

Beth nodded.

Silence.

"Where did you move from?" Rocco asked, glaring at Sam. Apparently Nichole's question was Sam's cue to pick up the conversation.

"Chicago."

"Why here?" Sam asked in a way that sounded like *Why me?* His question suggested he would have been saved this awkward dinner if she'd chosen some other city.

"I'm close to my aunt and she lives here. Sunshine was the only one I knew in town before I started teaching at the high school."

Owen appeared, carrying a cheese platter with thin slices of cheese and crackers. Rocco leaped to his feet as if his chair had sprung him upward. "I'll get the plates and napkins."

Beth guessed he would have done just about anything to escape the tension in the room.

Nichole's husband returned just as Kaylene bounced her way down the stairs. The teenager had dyed her hair purple and she wore matching colored sneakers and a bright smile. "Hi, Sam," she said, hurrying over to kiss him on the cheek.

Beth watched as Sam relaxed and smiled back at the girl. It was nice to know he could smile. The truth was he was attractive when he did. Beth regretted that she wasn't likely to see one of those smiles directed at her. Her one hope was that he understood she had been an unwilling victim herself.

Nichole gestured toward Beth. "You remember Beth, don't you?"

"Sure. I'm in one of her classes. Hi, Miss Prudhomme."

"Hello, Kaylene."

Rocco returned with the plates and napkins, and paused when he saw his daughter. "Be home by midnight."

"Yes, Dad," she returned in a singsong voice.

"And call if you leave Maddy's house."

"Okay, okay." She rolled her eyes. "He forgets I'm eighteen and will be away at college next year."

Kaylene looked to Beth. "Nice to see you, Miss Prudhomme."

"You, too."

With that the teenager was out the door. As if he'd been practicing all day, Owen stepped forward with the cheese plate. "The yellow is cheddar cheese and the white is Monterey Jack," he announced.

"Good job, Owen," Nichole said, praising her son.

Owen went to Beth first, holding out the platter as if he were offering her a fine delicacy. She accepted the small plate from Rocco and selected one slice of the Monterey Jack and a Ritz cracker.

Owen moved to Sam next and he took no less than ten crackers and about six slices of cheese. She was about to comment that he must be hungry and then decided better of it. Anything she said would sound judgmental. He was a big guy and probably had a big appetite.

Owen went to his mother next and then to Rocco.

"The cheese is made locally," Nichole said, clearly looking to generate conversation.

Silence.

"I told Sam that you like Mozart," Owen supplied, as if he felt it was his responsibility to stir the conversation. "He asked me if you'd ever heard of George Strait."

"I have."

"What about Carrie Underwood?" Owen asked.

"Her, too." She glanced toward Sam and struggled not to smile, but one twitched at the corners of her mouth. He probably saw her as a prissy music teacher like Marian, the librarian in the musical *The Music Man.*

Their eyes met and held for the briefest of moments before he blinked. She saw some of the tension leave his shoulders.

"I want to learn how to play the piano. If I take lessons, will you be my teacher?" Owen asked.

"I'd be happy to," Beth said.

Seeing that Owen was dominating the conversation, Nichole spoke up. "Why don't you see if anyone would like more cheese?"

"Okay."

She stood. "I'll check on dinner."

"I'll help." Eager to make her own escape, Beth followed her friend. She did feel slightly better. That one moment of nonverbal communication between her and Sam had helped. That didn't mean, however, that she wanted to be left alone in the room with Sam and Rocco. From the look the two men exchanged, they were just as glad to see the women go.

As soon as Beth and Nichole were in the kitchen, Nichole whirled around. "Beth, I am so sorry. I want to slap the two of them."

"It's fine." Still, she was curious. "What did Rocco have to do to coerce Sam into coming to dinner?" The poor man looked absolutely miserable.

"Is it that obvious?"

"I'm afraid so." Frankly, Beth felt much the same. If she had more experience with this sort of thing, she might be able to pull it off and find a way to extricate them both from this uncomfortable situation.

This evening was vaguely familiar. Nearly every date Beth had ever been on had been arranged by her mother. At least the men Beth had previously dated hadn't been pressured into meeting her—not that she knew of, anyway.

"I so hoped this evening would work out," Nichole said, her shoulders sinking. "Sam is such a great guy."

"Does he date much?"

"I . . . I don't know. He's never introduced me to anyone, if that's what you mean, but I've seen him with women. There's one in particular, Cherise, I think her name is. She hangs around The Dog House—that's a tavern Rocco and Sam stop by every now and

again. I've seen Sam with her a time or two, but it's nothing serious."

"What made you think I'd be a good match for Sam?" Beth
couldn't help being curious. Anyone looking at them could see how
ill-suited they were.

"I like Sam," Nichole said, "and he needs someone like you in
his life. Owen loves him, and you should see him with the baby.
He's so natural with them both. I thought . . . I hoped if he met the
right woman that he'd . . . oh, I don't know what I thought."

"Nichole, please, don't worry about it."

"It isn't you, I promise," Nichole insisted.

Beth wasn't convinced. "Not everyone is going to feel attracted
to me; I accept that, and clearly Sam isn't interested."

It looked as if Nichole wanted to argue, but then she apparently
changed her mind. "I feel terrible."

"Don't, please. We'll muddle through the rest of the evening
and then put it behind us. Deal?"

"Deal," Nichole echoed. "You're a good sport."

"Thanks. Now let's have dinner so Sam and I can both escape
with our egos and dignity intact."

Nichole grinned and then gave her an impulsive hug. "Thank
you."

"No problem."

"I'm vowing to never try this matchmaking business again."

Beth smiled, disappointed for her friend and at the same time
relieved.

While Nichole took dinner out of the oven, Beth mixed the salad
and dished it up. Together they carried the salad plates into the
dining room. Rocco and Sam had moved to the table and Rocco
had poured the wine.

Thankfully, dinner was a little less awkward. Beth complimented
Nichole, although she barely tasted the food. She sat directly across

from Sam and wished she knew how best to reassure him that she
held no aspirations toward furthering the relationship.

He seemed a bit more at ease, too. The conversation wasn't as
stilted, but it wasn't lively, either. Sam mentioned the Seahawks and
seemed surprised that she knew a fair bit about professional football. It was comforting to have scored points with him.

About halfway through dinner, Owen glanced from one to the
other and said, "You should tell Sam the story you told me about
Mozart," he suggested.

Beth chanced a look at Sam. "Would you like to know something about Mozart?" she asked.

"Of course he would," Rocco answered for him.

Sam shot his friend a look that clearly said he could answer for
himself. "Sure, why not," he said.

"I'll tell it," Owen said, excitedly. "Mozart started playing the
piano at age three and was composing at age four."

"That's cool," Sam said, clearly unimpressed. "I wonder if Carrie Underwood started singing around that age."

Owen frowned. "I don't know. Do you?"

"Nope."

The remainder of dinner passed quickly, with Nichole and
Rocco carrying most of the conversation. Every now and again
Sam would glance at Beth and they'd share a look. She hoped he
understood she was as much a casualty as he was. He didn't give
any indication what he felt, and that was fine.

As soon as the dinner dishes had been cleared, Nichole said, "I
made applesauce cake for dessert."

"I swear I couldn't eat another bite," Beth said, planting her
hands on her stomach as if she was about to explode.

Sam scooted back his chair and pantomimed her action. "Me,
neither."

"In fact, I should probably be heading home," Beth added.

"I should, too."

Both Beth and Sam got to their feet as if they couldn't leave fast enough.

"Are you sure?" Owen asked Sam. "I thought applesauce cake was your favorite."

"He's sure," Rocco said. "I'll save some for you later," he assured his friend.

"Thank you for the lovely meal," Beth said, reaching for her purse on her way to the door.

"Yes, thank you," Sam added.

They reached the front door and in a comedy of errors both tried to go through it at the same time. Beth looked up at Sam and smiled; he chuckled and held the door open for her. Neither one of them was willing to stay a minute longer than necessary.

Beth climbed into her car and drove away first, with Sam right behind her in his monster truck.

They pulled up to the intersection at the same time. Beth was in the turn lane and Sam was right next to her.

She looked over at him, and after a moment he glanced at her. If she'd had the nerve she would have mouthed the word *sorry,* knowing he'd been as miserable as she'd been.

The light turned green and Beth drove into the intersection.

And that was when she saw the vehicle come barreling toward her and knew there was no way to avoid a collision.

No way to escape.

CHAPTER 4

Sam

Sam watched in horror as the car raced directly toward Beth's vehicle. Instinctively, he shouted out a warning, as if that would do any good, but it was too late.

The sound of the impact was explosive, sending Beth's vehicle spinning like a toy top. Several cars screeched to a stop, looking to avoid any further collisions. Sam was the first one out of his vehicle, racing toward Beth's car, his heart pounding so hard it felt as if it was about to explode inside his chest. Thankfully, he wasn't a man given to panic. Adrenaline shot through him and he saw that his hands were shaking, not knowing what he would find.

As he ran past, he noticed that the other car, the one that hit Beth's, looked to be in much better shape. The front end was smashed and steam rose from the dented hood. The young girl inside was moaning, but he ignored her, eager to do what he could to help Beth, who had taken the brunt of the impact.

He was the first one to reach her. The driver's-side window had shattered, and the air bag had discharged. Glass had spilled on the inside, and he saw that she had several lacerations on her face and hands.

"Beth," he said gently, wanting to reassure her, "it's Sam. Are you badly hurt?"

Slowly she opened her eyes and blinked at him, her eyes locking with his as she groaned. He could see she was going into shock and grabbed his cell and immediately dialed 911.

"What's your emergency?" the woman on the other end of the line requested.

"Multiple car accident, corner of Sandy Boulevard and Sixteenth Street," he shouted into his phone. "Looks like one woman is badly hurt, minor injuries to the other."

A moment passed. "Dispatch has been notified."

"Hurry," he pleaded. "I'm pretty sure the woman is going into shock."

"Dispatch has been notified." Before he could cut the connection, the 911 operator asked for his name and number, which Sam quickly supplied. As soon as he was off the phone, he leaned toward Beth. "Help is on the way," he assured her. "You're going to be okay."

All she seemed to be able to manage was another moan.

He heard someone screaming hysterically behind him and glanced over his shoulder to see the other driver had climbed out of her vehicle. "My father is going to kill me."

"If he doesn't, I will," Sam shouted back at her, furious with the teenager.

"My brakes failed," she insisted.

Sam knew it was a lie. Just before the crash he was convinced he saw the girl's phone in her hand. He'd stake his next year's pay on the bet she'd been texting.

Other drivers had stopped and someone tried to calm down the hysterical teenager. Sirens could be heard in the distance. *Thank God.*

Beth continued to groan, and he noticed that her breathing had gone shallow and she was drifting in and out of consciousness. Not knowing what else to do, he reached for her hand and held it gently in his own. "The medics will be here any minute," he reassured her softly. "Hold on. Everything will be better once they get here."

She tried to speak, he noticed, but seemed unable to form words. Her eyes were intently focused on him.

Sam picked a piece of glass from her hair and then brushed another from her forehead. Blood marred her face. He would have given anything to comfort her, but he didn't know what more to say or do. Holding her hand seemed lame, but under these circumstances he didn't know what else was possible. Her gaze held his, as if fixing on him gave her what she needed to endure the pain.

The fire department arrived and a team of men raced toward Beth. One of the men asked Sam to stand back, which he did, albeit reluctantly. Beth groaned loudly in protest when he released her hand.

Sam could hear them speaking to one another, and although he couldn't understand all the medical jargon, he knew enough to figure out that she had suffered multiple fractures. Thankfully, the airbag had deployed, which saved her from greater injury.

He waited while the firemen pried open the badly dented door. Police arrived and began asking him questions. His heart continued to pound as he watched the team work to free Beth from the tangled vehicle.

"You witnessed the accident?" the officer asked, pad and pen in hand.

"Yes. I was stopped at the red light. Beth entered the intersection when the signal turned green."

"You know the victim?"

"I only met her tonight."

"Are you sure the light was green?"

He glared at the police officer. "Positive. The other driver was texting."

"You saw that?"

"No, but if I were you I'd check her phone."

The cop nodded. "I'll do that."

The girl was being attended to by a medic and continued with hysterics, claiming her brakes had failed. Thankfully, she admitted she'd run a red light. Her sobs echoed into the night. She seemed far more worried about her father's reaction to the accident than about the fact that her carelessness had badly injured Beth. Sam wanted to shake some sense into her but knew anything he said or did wouldn't be appreciated. The questions went on for what seemed like an eternity. Even while being interviewed, he couldn't take his eyes off Beth. Once the door was removed and she was lifted from the vehicle, she cried out in what could only be excruciating pain. Sam grimaced and glared once more at the teenager who'd caused the accident. Beth was placed on a gurney. He tried to see her as the medics placed her inside the emergency vehicle. As best he could tell, she was now unconscious.

"Where are they taking her?" he demanded.

The traffic cop looked up from the pad on which he was writing. "Most likely Providence. It's the closest."

"Can you find out for sure?"

"No." He seemed agitated that Sam would interrupt his questioning.

"Then I'm following the medics. She's new in town and only knows a few people." He wasn't sure where this protective attitude was coming from, but it consumed him. For whatever reason, he felt it was important that Beth not be alone. Conscious or not.

"Is there someone you can call for her? A relative? A friend?"

Of course. Nichole. He hadn't thought of her until that very moment. He reached for his phone and hit the number for Rocco. His friend picked up on the third ring.

"Okay, Sam, I know what you're going to say—"

"There's been a car accident," he said, cutting off the other man. "Beth is badly injured. I saw the whole thing."

"What?" Rocco asked, seemingly stunned.

"Beth was in a car accident," he repeated. "Some kid was on her phone and ran the red light, slamming into Beth, hitting her broadside. She's hurt, Rocco, badly. She's being rushed to the hospital . . . cop thinks Providence."

Rocco didn't answer him and then his friend shouted for Nichole. He heard the urgency, and Nichole must have, too, because Sam heard her ask, "What is it?" This was followed with a few short, sharp sentences as Rocco repeated what Sam had just told him.

They, too, had a short discussion. "We're going to the hospital. Nichole is contacting Leanne to see if she can come stay with the kids. We'll get there as quickly as we can."

"I'll meet you there," Sam said, his voice filled with resolve.

Rocco hesitated. "You sure you want to do that? You barely know Beth."

"Yes," he shouted, hardly understanding it himself. "I'll see you soon." With that, he disconnected the line.

The investigating officer held him up for an additional twenty minutes, with repeated questions that put Sam on edge. He'd already told the officer everything he knew. For reasons he would be hard pressed to explain, he felt this compelling need to get to Beth. At this rate Rocco and Nichole would make it to the hospital before he did.

When he was finally able to break free, he raced to the medical facility, driving ten miles above the speed limit. If he wasn't careful he'd be in an accident himself. Parking wasn't convenient, and he ended up in the garage on the sixth floor. By the time he made it to the emergency room waiting area, he was breathless.

He didn't see Rocco or Nichole, so he hurried to the front desk, hungry for information.

"I'm here to find out about the car accident victim? She was brought in no more than thirty minutes ago."

The woman whose name tag identified her as Susan McNeil asked, "Name?"

"Sam Carney." As soon as he spoke he realized she was asking about Beth. "Sorry. I'm Sam. The woman who was brought here by paramedics—the victim of a car crash. Her name is Beth."

"Last name?" she asked, punching a few computer keys. When he didn't immediately answer, the nurse glanced up.

Sam was no help. For the life of him, he couldn't remember. Nichole had mentioned it when she made the introduction, but it was completely out of his mind now. Fact was, Sam hadn't paid that much attention. He didn't expect he would ever see her again. "Sorry, I don't know."

"You're not a relative?"

"No." That much should be obvious. This was like talking to the police officer all over again. He got little information while he was repeatedly asked questions he found difficult to answer.

The sliding glass doors leading in from the outside opened and both Rocco and Nichole came rushing into the waiting area. They immediately joined Sam at the front desk.

"She's asking for Beth's last name," Sam said.

Nichole supplied it.

"Are you a relative?" Susan McNeil asked.

"No, I'm a friend."

Susan nodded. "Do you have the contact information for any relatives?"

"No, sorry. Beth is going to be all right, isn't she?" Nichole's voice trembled with concern.

"Sorry, I'm not allowed to give out information," Susan said.

"Beth was just at our home for dinner. She left about forty-five minutes ago." Nichole was visibly upset. "I can't believe this has happened."

Sam felt unsettled as well. Witnessing the accident had shaken him. When he'd left dinner, he hadn't had feelings toward Beth one way or another. She seemed nice. Nothing special but pleasant.

He'd gotten her message and she'd gotten his. As soon as he realized she'd been finagled into this the same as him, he'd relaxed. They'd both been in a rush to escape, nearly knocking each other over in their eagerness to get out the door. He'd smiled about it at the time, but he found little amusing at the moment.

"Beth hasn't lived in Portland long," Nichole was explaining to the woman at the desk, breaking into Sam's musings.

The hospital employee made a notation in the computer.

"I know she has an aunt living in the area," Nichole supplied. "Her family all lives in Chicago."

"Do you happen to know the aunt's name?"

Nichole exhaled as if rummaging through the filter in her brain. "I believe it's Sunshine."

Susan McNeil glanced up and narrowed her gaze. "Sunshine is her given name?"

"I . . . don't know, but probably not."

The questions continued, with Nichole answering as best she could. One thing was clear, the three of them were the only ones waiting for word on Beth's condition.

Once the hospital had collected as much information as they could from Nichole, the woman manning the desk said, "If you'd like to wait, I'll let you know about your friend as soon as any news is available."

"Thank you," Nichole whispered and turned away from the desk.

Rocco and Sam followed her into the crowded waiting area.

They were fortunate to find three seats in close proximity. Rocco and Nichole sat together and Sam took the chair across from them.

As soon as they were seated, Nichole leaned forward. "Tell us what happened."

Sam relayed the details once again.

"How badly injured was she?" This came from Rocco.

"Bad. My guess is she has fractured ribs, and I suspect her hip is broken as well. I heard the paramedics mention a collapsed lung."

"Internal damage?" Rocco asked.

Sam nodded. "It's possible."

Nichole released a soft gasp. "She's going to live, isn't she?"

Sam didn't feel qualified to answer. "I can't say."

"Was she conscious?"

"Partly. I spoke to her, but I don't know if she heard me or not. She was in a great deal of pain. I could see she was going into shock. I was the one who called for help."

"Did she say anything?" Rocco asked.

"No." All Sam could think about was the way she'd locked her eyes with his as if holding on to him, as if he would be the one to pull her through this crisis. In thinking about it, Beth had remained remarkably calm. Sam wasn't sure he would have reacted the same.

When they first sat down, Rocco and Nichole had been full of questions. As time wore on the conversation dwindled until there was nothing left to say.

An hour passed. Rocco bought them coffee out of a machine. Sam took a sip, grimaced, and let the rest grow cold.

He didn't know why it was taking this long. He got up to stretch his legs and strolled past the front desk. Susan McNeil glanced at him and gave a gentle shake of her head as if to answer his unspoken question. She had nothing to tell him.

When he returned to his seat, Rocco studied him as if he had something to say. If that was the case, it went unsaid.

Sometime later, Sam glanced at the time. It'd been almost two hours since the accident.

"There's no need for you to stay," Nichole told him.

"You can leave if you want," Rocco reiterated. "Nichole and I will let you know in the morning what we hear."

"No." Sam's response was adamant. He wasn't leaving. No way. He wasn't sure why he felt so strongly about it, but he did. He wouldn't desert Beth now, not after the way her eyes had held his. He had to know if she was going to survive this.

When the doctor appeared, the physician paused and looked around the waiting area. "Is anyone here for Beth Prudhomme?"

All three hurriedly rose to their feet. Right away Sam noticed the physician wore a brooding dark look.

Nichole spoke first. "How's Beth?" she pleaded, holding Rocco's hand in a death grip.

Sam studied the doctor, trying to read his eyes but seeing nothing.

"She's in surgery with internal injuries. She has four fractured ribs and a fractured hip that requires surgery."

Sam had guessed as much.

"She'll need to be in the hospital several days and then will be transferred to a rehab facility for the remainder of her recuperation."

Nichole sagged against her husband as if the news was almost too much for her. "Oh poor Beth."

"You're her friends?"

"Yes," Nichole said.

He looked from one to the other, nodded, and said, "Good."

Good?

Sam could only speculate what the other man meant by that. If he were going to read anything into it, the other man was telling him Beth would need her friends now more than ever.

CHAPTER 5

Beth

Beth woke and blinked, having trouble focusing. She knew she was in the hospital, because the nurse had told her so when she'd regained consciousness in the recovery room following surgery. Amazingly, she hadn't felt any pain. Not then. The pain had come later, and thankfully, she was given medication that immediately put her to sleep.

She sensed someone was with her. Turning her head, she found Sunshine sitting in the chair beside her bed. She seemed to be deep in thought but noticed right away that Beth was awake.

Sunshine stood and brushed the hair from Beth's forehead. "Hey, Sleeping Beauty, glad to see you're awake."

Beth managed a weak smile.

Sunshine's worried gaze revealed her concern. "This is a fine predicament you got yourself into."

"Sorry," Beth said, but her voice was no more than a whisper.

"Don't apologize, Sweet Pea."

"How'd . . . you find out?" She hadn't expected to see anyone in her room.

"The hospital called. Someone must have told them I was your aunt. They found my number in the contact list on your phone."

"Oh." Beth briefly closed her eyes. "Sam," she whispered.

"Sam?" Sunshine repeated, apparently unable to follow Beth's line of thought.

"He was there." She remembered very little of the accident itself. What did come to mind was Sam. He'd held her hand and spoken softly, assuring her that help was on the way.

"At the accident scene?"

"Yes." At the time she was convinced she was going to die and had peace about it, and then Sam came and told her she was going to be all right. For whatever reason she chose to believe him. She would survive. This wasn't the end, her life wasn't over, at least not yet.

"Who's Sam?"

"The man."

"Sam the man," Sunshine said with a widening smile. "That explains everything."

"Nichole and Rocco's friend."

"Ah," Sunshine said, her eyes brightening with understanding. "Your dinner date. How'd that go?"

"It was a disaster."

"Sweet Pea, the car accident was a disaster, not dinner."

Beth made an effort to smile. "True. Sam must have called Nichole."

"Makes sense."

"She knows you're my aunt." That must have been how the hospital was able to contact her. As soon as she connected the dots, she gasped. No doubt her aunt had gotten in touch with Beth's parents.

"Honey, what is it?" Sunshine asked, immediately worried. "Are you in pain? Should I call for the nurse?"

"No." Beth felt like she was about to hyperventilate. "Did you let my parents know?"

Sunshine hesitated. "Not yet."

"Thank . . . God." Her relief was instantaneous, tension draining out of her. No doubt her mother would use the accident to come rushing to her side and insist she return to Chicago for her recuperation. This was all the excuse Ellie Prudhomme would need to dig up the tender root of Beth's independence.

"Before I call your parents I thought I should talk to you," Sunshine explained.

"Good . . . don't say anything, please . . . please." With effort she raised her arm and reached for her aunt's hand, giving it a gentle squeeze. The last thing Beth wanted or needed was her mother rushing to her deathbed, crying, telling Beth that she'd made a terrible mistake in leaving Chicago.

"You don't want me to tell your parents about the accident?"

"Don't . . . don't tell them."

"Oh Sweet Pea, they need to know. You were seriously hurt."

Beth pleaded with her aunt. "Mom . . . will make a big deal out of this."

"Honey, it is a big deal."

"I don't care. I don't want Mom rushing to Portland." Her mother would blame Sunshine and make Beth's recovery miserable, more miserable than it was destined to be already.

As if a heavy weight had been pressed against her shoulders, Sunshine sagged into the chair she'd scooted close to Beth's hospital bed. "I have to tell them something."

"Okay, tell them . . . tell them it was . . ." She found it hard to speak. "Tell them it was minor."

"Minor?" she repeated and shook her head. Sunshine was far too honest to willingly lie.

"Okay, an accident," she whispered, struggling to swallow.

As if sensing her problem, Sunshine lifted a glass of water with a straw and directed it to Beth's mouth.

She managed a single sip before she was able to continue. "Don't tell them . . . how badly hurt I am." These few words exhausted her, but Beth had to be certain her aunt understood.

Sunshine shook her head. "You know your mother is going to ask."

"Be . . . evasive."

"Baby girl, I don't know . . ."

"Then I'll call Mom."

"And then your father will call and drill me with questions," Sunshine said, her brow furrowed with a frown.

This was worse than Beth imagined. No matter what her parents said, she refused to move back to Chicago. As it was, it'd taken her far too long to break away. As their only child, Beth had been the light of their lives. They wanted her happiness, and unfortunately her mother had a clear picture of what that should be. A view that often clashed with Beth's wants. Her mother didn't trust her to make her own decisions, and she seemed convinced that the moment she broke away Beth would fall flat on her face, which apparently she had.

"I'll make the call," Sunshine said, reaching for her phone.

Depressed and discouraged, Beth swallowed tightly, already knowing it was going to be a complication she didn't feel strong enough to handle in her weakened state. "Okay."

Sunshine left the room and was gone for eleven minutes. Beth knew because she watched the clock and counted off every one of those minutes, struggling not to fall back asleep.

When her aunt returned to the room, Beth immediately made eye contact. "Well?"

"Rest easy. Thankfully, I was able to reach your father."

That in itself was a surprise, because he was so involved in his work that he often left his phone at the house. "I told him about the accident and assured him that you didn't want your mother booking the next flight to Portland. He's going to talk to her and explain that she gave her word to leave you be for six months no matter what."

Hope flared briefly, and then she realized her father must be the one coming. "Dad?"

"No. We discussed that, but I told him I was afraid if he flew out Ellie would insist on coming as well. I managed to convince him I had everything under control. I suggested they let you handle this on your own with my help."

Beth could barely believe her good fortune. "Eleven minutes."

"Eleven minutes?" Sunshine repeated.

"You did . . . all that . . . in eleven minutes?"

Sunshine's blue eyes twinkled with delight. "My dear girl, you underestimate me."

It went without saying that Sunshine had been insistent and per-suasive. Her father appeared to be handling the news of her inju-ries well. Beth paused and realized she didn't know the extent of everything herself. She recalled the doctor briefly talking to her and explaining that she was about to have surgery. From what she re-membered of the conversation, her spleen was being removed and then there was something about her hip being fractured along with a number of her ribs. That helped explain the ghastly pain she felt.

"Rest, Sweet Pea," her aunt advised, gently brushing the hair from her forehead. "All is well. Your mother has a mah-jongg tour-nament this weekend and your dad promised to downplay the ac-cident. You're off the hook. Just make sure you connect with them and pretend all is well."

"I will . . ." Sleep called to her. "Thank . . . you." Her aunt had always been her biggest champion.

"Sleep now."

Beth didn't think she could keep her eyes open another second and fell into a deep slumber. Knowing her parents weren't rushing to her bedside helped ease her mind. That assurance was all she needed to float easily into the land of happy dreams.

Beth woke with the sound of someone entering the room. She assumed it was a nurse. It seemed they were constantly in and out, checking her vitals, giving her meds, or doing one thing or another. The staff had been wonderful and caring, and she didn't feel she could complain.

When she turned her head, instead of one of the hospital personnel she found it was Sam. It took her a moment to identify him because he wore his hair down and he was dressed casually in jeans. He had a single red rose she was certain he must have picked up in the hospital gift shop.

"Hey there," he said, coming all the way into the room. "I thought I'd stop by and see how you're doing." He set the flower down on the stand next to her bed.

"Better," she whispered.

"Certainly better than the last time I saw you."

Beth managed a smile.

"You remember I was there?"

She nodded and wondered if he knew how much he'd helped her.

He came to stand next to the bed. It seemed he wasn't sure what to say next.

"The . . . girl?" Beth asked.

"What girl?"

"In the other car. She okay?"

Sam frowned. "She seemed to be. I'm sure she had a few scrapes and bruises but nothing serious. Her biggest concern was what her father was going to say because she'd wrecked his car."

Beth closed her eyes and swallowed. "Good."

"Good?" Sam repeated, sounding angry. "I wanted to shake her. She didn't even ask about you. I hope she loses her license over this. It's what she deserves."

His indignation amused her and she managed a smile. Sounded like the teenager's father would probably see to that.

"You're mighty forgiving," Sam said. "I don't know that I'd feel the same."

"Being upset won't help."

"True," he admitted, albeit reluctantly.

He looked away and Beth felt he was probably ready to leave. She wanted him to stay, had things she wanted to tell him, but she was too weak yet. Even talking tired her out.

"I should probably go." He took a step back from the bed.

Beth extended her hand to him. "Before you go . . . thank you," she whispered.

"Oh sure." He glanced toward the rose. "It's nothing. I wanted to check in and see how you're doing."

She closed and opened her eyes. "Not for the flower . . . for being there. I . . . I thought I was going to die."

"Hey, so did I; you scared the crap out of me." He smiled. "Wonder if Owen would consider that a swear word. If he does, then I'll owe him another dollar."

Beth smiled. "I won't tell him."

"I appreciate it," he said, grinning now.

He was handsome when he smiled, which didn't appear to be something he did nearly often enough.

"You being there helped me. You said I was going to be all right and I believed you."

He nodded. "I probably shouldn't admit it, but I was pretty shaken up myself."

"You were hit?"

"No, no, just seeing how badly hurt you were got to me."

It was more than his assurances that helped. "You held my hand."

"Don't suppose you noticed how hard it was shaking?"

"No. Your touch, it grounded me." She wondered if he'd noticed how tightly she'd clung to him.

He shook his head. "Truth is, Beth, I think we were basically holding on to each other."

"You called Nichole and Rocco?"

"Right away. Has she been here?"

Beth had been out of it most of the day. "I don't know."

"She said she would."

"I've been asleep . . . I can't seem to stay awake long."

"Last night we were all here at the hospital, worried and anxious for an update on your condition. It took hours before we learned anything."

Sam was full of surprises. "You came to the hospital?"

"Would you rather I hadn't?" His question had a defensive note.

Unexpected tears welled in her eyes. "I . . . I didn't expect that. Thank you." She took a breath. "You thought I was going to die, didn't you?"

His grin transformed his face. The laugh lines that fanned out from his eyes told her he probably had a good sense of humor. His eyes were dark and bright as they smiled down on her. She liked his beard and briefly wondered what it would be like to kiss a man with a beard. It was bound to be a pleasant experience and one she wouldn't mind.

She wasn't herself. Beth didn't look at a man and wonder what it would be like if he kissed her. They'd said more to each other in the few minutes since he'd entered the room than they had through the entire dinner party.

"Nichole and Rocco were here as well," Sam added.

"I'm sorry you had to wait so long."

"I couldn't imagine being anywhere else." He looked a little embarrassed and shrugged one shoulder. "I wouldn't rest easy until I knew you were going to be all right."

"Are you assured I'll recover now?"

"Seems you will."

"So I'll live to torment another poor, unsuspecting blind date."

A short laugh burst out of Sam. "I'm sorry, Beth."

"Me, too."

Sam dismissed her apology. "Nichole was ready to skin me alive if the looks she sent my way were any indication."

Beth grinned. "I don't think she was happy with me, either."

"I doubt she'll play matchmaker again."

"Why'd you agree?" She'd suspected almost immediately that Rocco had somehow coerced him into meeting her.

Sam relaxed. "Rocco's a good friend—the best. He said it meant a lot to Nichole, and there's little I wouldn't do for the two of them."

"I thought Rocco was holding you hostage."

Sam tucked his hands in his back pockets. "What about you? Why'd you want to meet me?"

She remembered her own hesitation. "Nichole asked me. I wasn't keen, but my aunt convinced me I should go. She said . . ." It seemed silly to tell him this, but she did, anyway. "She said you could be the man of my dreams."

Sam frowned. "Bet I was a sorry disappointment."

"No more than I was to you."

His face sobered. "Actually, you weren't that much of a letdown."

Beth guessed she should consider that a compliment. "You, either."

"I avoid relationships," Sam explained. "Don't want you thinking it was anything personal."

That was reassuring.

Then he was quick to add, "Decent women unnerve me."

Beth blinked up at him, unsure what he was telling her.

He looked slightly embarrassed. "That didn't come out right, did it?"

"What kind of women are you comfortable with?" she asked.

He shrugged. "I don't know," he said, as if no one had ever asked him that before. "The kind who hang out at The Dog House, I guess."

That was the tavern Nichole had mentioned. For sure it didn't sound like the name of a tearoom.

"You know what I mean, right? Women who play pool and drink beer. The kind who don't mind if I say a four-letter word every now and again."

"Ones who won't charge you a dollar when you do," she said, struggling to hold back a smile.

He grinned. "Yup."

"What about Nichole? Isn't she decent?"

"Nichole," he repeated slowly, as if he hadn't considered how he felt about her before Beth had asked.

"Does she go with Rocco to The Dog House?"

"She used to before Matthew was born."

"Play pool?"

"Taught her myself," he boasted.

"Drink beer?"

"She prefers wine, but when she's with Rocco she has beer. It isn't her favorite, though."

"I'm glad you made an exception for her."

"It wasn't hard. Nichole is great and Rocco is crazy about her. Before Nichole, all he thought about was work and being a good dad for Kaylene. The responsibility weighed on him. Then he met Nichole and everything changed. I hardly know him any longer. She turned his world upside down."

"Did you like the changes?" she asked.

A frown briefly appeared. "At first I thought she was playing him. A classy woman like that with a tow truck driver. It didn't add up. I warned him once and he nearly snapped my head off. They split for a while, something to do with her ex-husband, and I don't think I'd ever seen Rocco more depressed. I might have said I told you so if I hadn't been afraid he'd rip off my head."

Sam seemed lost in his thoughts. "I didn't mean to rattle on like that," he said, shaking his head.

"I'm glad you did. I like them both."

"They're good people."

Beth suspected Sam was good, too. Unfortunately, it was unlikely she'd have the chance to find that out for herself.

CHAPTER 6

Sam

Sam had a busy day Monday. But then every day was busy at the car dealership. As head of the service department, Sam took his responsibilities seriously. The owner once said that Sam was the best mechanic he'd ever known.

Sam had been with the GMC dealership for ten years and made a decent living. Not that he was going to be buying a yacht anytime soon, but then he was more interested in cars than he was in boats. At last count, he owned three vehicles, a truck and two classic cars that he tinkered with: a 1967 Dodge RT and a 1965 Chevy Impala. In addition, he did plenty of work on the side. He understood engines far better than he ever did women. Friends came to him with car troubles. There wasn't a vehicle he couldn't get back into running shape with the right parts. Even as a kid, he liked nothing better than to disassemble whatever he could find and then put it back together.

He finished up with his last car, handed the keys off to the owner, and closed down his station for the night.

Thinking of women, and the complications they brought into a man's life, Beth came to mind. Actually, she'd been in his thoughts most of the day. For someone who'd recently had major surgery, she'd been remarkably alert. He hadn't meant to stay more than a few minutes, and they'd ended up talking for the better part of an hour until she'd fallen asleep from exhaustion.

Sam couldn't remember having that long of a conversation with a woman in . . . well, forever. Okay, not while he was sober, anyway.

It surprised him that she remembered him holding her hand at the scene of the accident until the medics arrived. Even then her eyes had followed him, silently pleading for him to stay with her. He wanted to, but the paramedics had moved him out of the way. He understood it was necessary, but he'd hated leaving Beth; hated letting go of her hand. Surprisingly, he'd felt the same reluctance to leave her while visiting her at the hospital.

He wondered how she was doing. He knew she was in a lot of pain, and the thought of her suffering troubled him. He'd heard the medical staff wanted her up and moving, which shocked him. That didn't seem right. Forcing her to get up on her feet with a fractured hip and ribs made no sense to him. But then, what did he know?

Nichole had said she was going to stop by and check on her. Walking toward his truck, Sam reached for his phone and scrolled down his contact list until he found Nichole's number. He wasn't completely sure he had it and was grateful when he saw he did.

He hit the connection and waited for her to answer.

"Sam?"

Apparently, his name showed on her phone screen. "Hey, Nichole, how's your friend?"

"Beth?"

"Yeah. You went to see her today, didn't you?"

"I didn't," she returned, her tone filled with regret. "Matthew was fussy all morning and was running a fever, so I ended up taking him to the doctor. I spent a good part of the afternoon there and then I had to run to the pharmacy to get the prescription."

Sam loved that baby and was immediately concerned. "What's wrong with him?"

"Ear infection."

"Damn." Sam had those as a child and still remembered how badly his ear had ached. He ended up having tubes inserted after repeated infections.

"Don't let Owen hear you say that," Nichole teased.

"Tell him I owe him a dollar." The way these dollars were adding up, Owen would have enough money to buy his own car by the time he was ten.

"Matthew's on antibiotics and is sleeping now, but it's been a rough day for us both."

So Nichole hadn't been in to see Beth.

"Did you call her?"

"No. I couldn't, Sam, not with Matthew demanding all my attention."

He hated the thought of Beth being in the hospital without visitors. She must be miserable, and the pain would feel all the more intense when she was alone.

"You could go see her," Nichole suggested.

He could, of course, but Nichole didn't know that he'd been up to visit once already. "I suppose."

"If you do go, let me know how she's doing and explain why I haven't been by."

"If I go," he repeated.

"It wouldn't hurt. She isn't going to wrestle you to the ground and demand you marry her."

"Very funny." He tried to sound sarcastic, but he couldn't keep the smile out of his voice. What he found amusing was that he discovered he actually liked Beth. She wasn't anything like he expected. When he first met her she seemed plain, a little too vanilla for his liking and ever so proper. He didn't view her that way after their conversation. She had a good sense of humor and was a caring person. He suspected there weren't many people who would ask about the well-being of the other driver.

"I'll find out what I can," he said, giving in.

"You mean you're actually going to the hospital?" Nichole sounded shocked.

"Don't make a big deal out of it."

"Okay, but thanks."

Now that he thought about it, he wouldn't mind making a return visit. If he was looking to make an impression, which he wasn't, he'd go home, shower, and change out of his work clothes. He decided against it. He'd run in, check and see if she needed anything, and then report back to Nichole. That would be the end of it. The visit would put Nichole's mind to rest and his own, too.

"I'll be in touch," he promised before he ended the call.

The hospital was out of his way, and it took him thirty minutes in traffic in what would usually take about twenty. All during the drive he berated himself, unsure why he was going. He was no Florence Nightingale. Normally he avoided hospitals, and other than this situation with Beth, he couldn't remember the last time he'd voluntarily set foot in one.

He didn't want to get involved or lead her into thinking he cared. Bottom line, he decided, he felt responsible for her. That was hard to explain, because there was no logical reason he should feel that way. He wasn't the one who'd hit her. Just because he happened to be at the scene of the accident, he felt obliged to look after her. Didn't make much sense, but it was what it was.

He found decent parking and made his way into the hospital.

When he arrived on her floor, her door was closed. He stood outside, wondering what to do, and then decided to knock.

"Come in," Beth called. Her voice sounded stronger than it had the day before, which was a good sign.

He opened the door and took a couple steps into the room, stopping abruptly. A woman stood on the other side of Beth's bed. She looked like a poster child for Haight-Ashbury in the late 1960s with her tie-dyed skirt and her long, straight, salt-and-pepper hair.

When she saw him, the woman's face lit up into a huge smile.

"Sam," Beth breathed, clearly surprised.

"This is Sam?" the other woman asked.

Beth nodded.

Before he could acknowledge either woman, the older one hurried around the bed and enveloped him in a bear hug. "I am so happy to meet you," she squealed, as though this was one of the greatest honors of her life. She gave him another squeeze before she released him enough to where he could breathe again. She leaned back, keeping hold of his upper arms. "I don't know what Beth would have done without you," she said, sounding close to tears. "She's told me everything."

Sam's gaze shot to Beth, wondering what she could have possibly said to warrant this over-the-top greeting.

"How precious of you to come see her," the woman gushed.

"Sam," Beth said, gesturing toward the other woman, "this is my aunt, Sunshine."

"Sam," he said unnecessarily. "Carney," he added.

Gripping hold of his hand, she kissed the back of it. "Thank you. A thousand times thank you."

"Ah . . . sure." He fully intended to drill Beth and learn what all the gratitude was about.

"So you've come to see Beth. I was just leaving." She turned back to her niece, kissed her forehead, and then swept out of the room, taking a dramatic exit, blowing them both kisses on her way out.

"That," Beth said, "was my crazy, wonderful aunt Sunshine."

"Wow, she fills up an entire room, doesn't she?"

"She does."

"Exactly what did you tell her about me?"

"Only that you helped me at the scene." She swallowed. "Don't get your nose out of joint."

He widened his eyes. "My nose out of joint."

She attempted a smile. "That's something my dad says."

He felt he should explain why he'd stopped by a second day in a row. He tucked his hands in his back pockets and remained where he was just inside the door. "Nichole sends greetings. She wasn't able to get away. Matthew's got an ear infection and she spent the day at the doctor's office."

"Poor Matthew. I had those as a kid, too."

He felt awkward, the way he had when he'd first arrived the day before, bringing her the rose. That had been a last-minute decision. When he came into the hospital he saw someone carrying flowers. Thinking it might be expected, he felt bad knowing Beth probably didn't have anyone to bring her flowers. A minute later, he saw the flower display in the window of the gift shop and bought the rose on impulse.

"I told Nichole I'd check in and see how your day went and report back," he said, as a means of explaining his visit.

She shifted and grimaced. "It's been a long day, but last night was the worst."

"How so?"

"It's so dark and quiet. The pain seems to be more cutting then. I slept in fits and starts most of the night. I don't think I slept more than an hour at a time."

"Hasn't the doctor prescribed pain meds?"

"Oh yes, but I'm only allowed to take them every four hours and they hold me to the minute." She grimaced for the second time.

"Are you in pain now?"

She moistened her lips and nodded.

"How long before you're due for another pill?"

Her eyes went to the clock on the wall. "An hour."

Sixty minutes can feel like an eternity when in pain. "Is there anything I can do?"

She met his gaze as if determining how serious he was. "Yes."

"Name it." Whatever it was, he'd find a way to help her.

"My aunt brought me my Bible. Would you read to me from the Psalms?"

The request shocked him and he raised both hands as if she'd pointed a rifle at him. "You want me to read to you from the Bible?" What had he gotten himself in for? "Sorry, babe, I don't think so. I open that book and fire and brimstone will rain down from the heavens."

Her face fell with disappointment. "You're joking."

He waved his hands. "Afraid not."

She exhaled and he could tell she was utterly miserable. Closing her eyes, she gave him a sad smile. "Okay, I understand."

Sam felt her frustration as if it were his own. He couldn't believe he was actually considering this. Feeling guilty, he reached for the Bible, which was on the stand next to her bed. "Where do I look for the book of Psalms?" he asked, completely unfamiliar with the Bible.

She opened her eyes, which widened with surprise when she saw he'd taken the seat next to her bed.

"Open the book to the middle and you should be in Psalms."

He did as she suggested, and sure enough he landed in Psalms. "Any particular one you want me to read?"

"Just start reading where you are."

"Okay." Sam drew in a breath and relaxed against the chair. "Psalm 5. *Give heed to my words, O Lord. Consider my groaning.*" He continued to read, finishing that Psalm and then going on to another. "A guy wrote these?" he asked, and noticed Beth was asleep.

He continued reading silently and found the answer to his question. At the top of the Psalm it read *A Psalm of David*. Sam didn't know a lot of Bible stories but distinctly remembered hearing about David and Goliath. He wondered if this was the same David who'd written these Psalms. He started flipping pages and eventually happened upon the passage with a little help from the footnotes. He turned to First Samuel and silently read of when David defeated the giant, losing himself in the story.

When next he looked up, he found that Beth was awake and studying him, her look curious.

"My reading put you to sleep," he said, a little embarrassed to have her finding him still reading her Bible. He'd found several places where she'd written notes in the margins. He didn't know people did that sort of thing. It was like he'd flipped open the pages of her diary.

"Your reading relaxed me. Thank you."

The nurse came in with her pain meds. Beth swallowed them down with a glass of water and let out a deep sigh.

"I happened upon the story about David and Goliath," he said. "There were a lot of details there that I didn't know."

"Like what?"

Sam grinned. "Like King Saul wanting David to wear his battle armor. I could just picture David trying to walk in all that cumbersome gear. It sort of cracked me up. He was young, too."

"A teenager."

"Brave of him, but then he was promised the daughter of the king if he succeeded."

"Good incentive, don't you think?" she teased.

"Depends on the daughter," Sam returned.

Beth laughed softly. "I guess it would."

"Did David ever get his prize?" He was curious to know if the Bible mentioned that.

"He did. Saul kept his word and gave David his daughter Michal, but, you know, those arranged marriages don't always work out." She held his look for a moment and then smiled. "It's sort of like being coerced into meeting a strange woman at a friend's house for dinner."

Sam barked a laugh. "True."

"Thankfully, you weren't stuck with me for life the way David was with Saul's daughter."

"A terrible fate for sure."

"Really?" she asked, mocking him. "What about poor Michal, who didn't have any choice in her husband?"

"Yes, poor girl forced to marry a hero. It must have been tough."

"You have no idea."

Sam resisted the urge to smile. He'd rarely had a time with a woman like this. A woman like Beth. He enjoyed their banter.

"Can I do anything else for you?" he asked when he saw that the pain pills were kicking in and her eyes were growing droopy again.

"Nothing, thanks."

"I'll call Nichole," he said, making his way to the door.

"Tell her not to worry about coming to visit."

"Will do."

He headed for the door when Beth stopped him. "Sam."

He turned, finding he was reluctant to leave her.

"Thank you. Really, thank you. I'm glad you came back."

"My pleasure, my lady." He raised his hand to his forehead and saluted her as if he was a troubadour.

"Sam?"

"Yes."

She hesitated. "Would you . . . ?"

"Would I what?"

She shook her head and looked embarrassed.

"What is it? Do you need me to bring you something?" He'd do whatever it was she needed and be happy to be able to help.

"Do you think you'll come back again?" Her gaze held his, as if she was afraid of his answer. "I shouldn't ask you that . . . please don't feel . . ."

"I wouldn't mind at all."

"You're sure?"

He nodded. It was the truth. He actually looked forward to it.

CHAPTER 7

Beth

Beth eyed the single red rose on the stand next to her hospital bed and thought about Sam's latest visit. In a moment of weakness, she'd asked him if he wouldn't mind stopping by again. Somewhat to her surprise, she found that she liked Sam and enjoyed his visits. He'd impressed her with his willingness to read her Bible even when it made him uncomfortable. His subtle sense of humor amused her.

The contrast between Sam and the men her mother found suitable was striking, and by more than appearances. He was genuine and honestly cared about her. He'd stayed with her at the scene of the accident and had gone to the hospital and had visited her not once but twice. She couldn't imagine any of the pretty boys she'd dated doing any of that. Certainly not Kier, who lived off a healthy trust fund and had never held a job, something he seemed proud of. Beth viewed these prospective husbands her mother pushed her to date as weak and spoiled. She couldn't understand why her mother saw any one of them as a good match for her. As for her father, he seemed oblivious to what was happening. Not until their talk before she moved to Portland did she realize how unaware he actually was. Beth knew she would never find happiness with any of the men her mother pushed her into dating. Ellie Prudhomme was Kier's staunchest advocate. Beth cringed at the thought of the self-centered, egotistical man. Even now she couldn't understand what her mother saw in him.

Beth was reluctant to admit that when she'd first met Sam she'd seen him through her parents' eyes. And yet Sam was everything Kier would never be. She liked that he was strong physically and that his strength didn't come from working out in a fancy gym. There didn't appear to be a spare ounce of fat on him, and while he could be a bit gruff and unconventional, she'd seen a gentle side to him at the accident and then again last evening when he'd sat by her bedside and read to her.

Knowing Sam intended to visit again helped her through the long, tedious hours being hospitalized. Although it was early afternoon, she was already looking forward to seeing him. He'd been the bright spot in her day on his last visit, staying until she was so tired she could barely keep her eyes open.

If she was surprised by how much she enjoyed him, she assumed he felt much the same. They certainly hadn't gotten off to a promising start. Even if nothing more developed than these few visits, she would always appreciate everything he'd done for her.

On Tuesday midafternoon, Nichole stopped by. Beth was pleased to see her friend and regretted that she was weak and unable to hide her discomfort. The doctor said she would probably be moved to the rehab center the following day. It looked like she would be at that facility two or three weeks and perhaps longer. Sunshine had offered to let her recuperate at her house, but that wouldn't work. Beth didn't want her aunt to play nursemaid to her, especially when she needed to be at her studio. Besides, Sunshine was often out of town, traveling to art shows all around the country. The last thing Sunshine needed was to be driving Beth back and forth to physical therapy every day.

"How's Matthew?" Beth asked as soon as Nichole arrived.

"Much better. He slept most of the night, which was a relief. Leanne's watching him now."

Beth knew Leanne was Nichole's former mother-in-law. The two were tight. A bit unusual but the relationship worked. Leanne considered Rocco and Nichole's children her own grandchildren and treated them as such. She was married to a Ukrainian man who baked the most delicious bread Beth had ever tasted.

"Sam called to let me know you'd had a rough day," Nichole said as she came around and set down a crossword puzzle book she'd brought with her. Her gaze fell on the single red rose. "That's lovely."

Beth felt a warm happiness gazing at the rose. "Sam brought it."

Nichole's head whipped around. "Sam Carney?"

"Yeah, when he stopped by Sunday afternoon."

Nichole's eyes widened. "Sam has been up to see you twice?"

"Yes." Beth didn't know why Nichole looked shocked. She didn't think it was meant to be a secret. If he didn't want her to mention his visits, then he should have said so earlier.

As though stunned, Nichole sank into the chair. "Wow, that's great."

Beth felt she needed to explain. "Now that Sam and I have had a chance to get to know each other a little, I find I like him. He's good company. I don't think he has any idea how funny he is." She repeated part of their conversation that made her smile, especially his definition of "decent women."

Nichole groaned and rolled her eyes. "He's definitely one of a kind."

"He said he'd be back."

Nichole's eyes widened. "Sam did?"

Beth felt she had to let her friend know the truth. "I . . . I asked him if he wouldn't mind visiting again and he said he would."

Nichole looked as if she wasn't sure what to say.

Beth didn't want to appear overly curious, but she did have a few questions she hoped Nichole could answer. "You mentioned he's a mechanic."

"One of the best, according to Rocco. And a good friend, too. Owen loves him."

"With good reason, if that jar of dollars is anything to go by."

Nichole relaxed against the back of the chair and smiled. "It's more than that. I told you before that he's super with the kids. Even Kaylene. It was Sam who took her out driving when she first got her learner's permit. Rocco only drove with her once. I don't know what happened, but Kaylene returned in tears and Rocco said he was through. Sam stepped up and showed the patience of a saint. Even with driver education classes, I don't know if Kaylene would have gotten her driver's license if it wasn't for Sam."

Further proof that there was more to the man than met the eye.

"Owen thinks of him as the best uncle ever. My two sisters live in Washington state and we don't see them often, so the only men in his life are Rocco and his father. My ex-husband tries, but he has trouble understanding the needs of a six-year-old. It's Rocco and Sam who taught Owen how to ride a bike and throw a softball. Sam has attended every one of his T-ball games along with Rocco."

"You mentioned how good he is with Matthew."

"He's amazing with the baby. That's the reason I wanted the two of you to meet. Like I said earlier, Sam's a bit of a character and he seems to have trouble with meaningful relationships with women, but with a little patience I think he could be a real catch."

After all he'd done to help her, Beth found she was willing to be open-minded about Sam, something she hadn't been earlier. "What's his problem with relationships. Did he have a bad experience that left him bitter?"

Nichole released a slow breath. "Before I put together the dinner, I asked Rocco about that very thing. He said as far as he knew Sam had only been involved in one serious relationship, and that was years ago. I'll see if Rocco will give me a few more details. I know Sam's not currently involved; if he is, he doesn't talk about it and I've never met her."

Beth couldn't help wondering. "He told me he didn't do relationships."

"That's the impression I get, too. But seeing how great he is with our family and how much the kids love him, I felt I had to try. My romantic heart believes he would make a wonderful husband and father."

"I appreciate that you thought of me, but I don't know if I'm up to taking on this grizzly bear of a man. Plus, there's no indication he has any feelings for me. Well, other than pity."

A smile blossomed in Nichole. "Au contraire. I've never known Sam to buy a woman flowers."

"It's a single flower," Beth reminded her.

"A rose," Nichole said, as if that was of major significance. "A *red* rose."

"From the hospital gift shop. They probably only have red roses."

"Still, Sam isn't the kind of guy to buy a woman flowers. He did for you, though."

Beth smiled, remembering how he quickly set it down on the table, as if holding it had burned his fingers. He'd felt awkward with it. At the time she hadn't fully appreciated the gesture.

"Did Sam say when he was coming back?"

"No . . . but I assume it's tonight, as I'm being transferred to the care facility sometime tomorrow."

Nichole frowned.

"What?" Beth asked.

Lifting her arm, Nichole gently brushed Beth's dark hair from her forehead.

It didn't take Beth long to understand what her friend was too kind to put into words. "I look terrible, don't I?"

Nichole smiled.

"My hair is a mess. I don't have any makeup here." She was definitely at her all-time worst. If there was anything to be grateful for it was the fact that she hadn't seen herself in a mirror.

"I know just the thing." Nichole's eyes brightened as she spoke. Hurrying to her feet, she reached for her purse.

"Where are you going?"

"I'll be back."

Before Beth could say another word, Nichole left, a woman on a mission.

Thirty minutes later she returned, her cheeks flushed with excitement. She set a plastic sack from a local chain drugstore down on the foot of the bed. As if unveiling a work of art, Nichole withdrew each item from the bag one at a time. "Dry shampoo." She placed that on the tray in front of Beth. "A brush and comb," followed by a curling iron.

"Nichole!" Beth couldn't believe anyone would do this.

"I'm just getting started." Next came a bevy of cosmetics. It appeared her shopping trip had yielded everything Beth would need and more to help her feel more like a woman again.

Pleased with herself, Nichole giggled like a teenager. "I swear Sam isn't going to know what hit him when he stops by this evening."

An hour later, Beth felt a hundred times better. Her hair was styled, and while these weren't her normal choices when it came to makeup, Nichole surprised her with how well she did matching up colors to complement her skin tone.

"You'll let me know what happens when Sam sees you?"

"I will," Beth promised. She'd been miserable and in awful pain the last two days. She hadn't complained while Nichole fussed over her, but by the time her friend left, Beth was both exhausted and exhilarated. She rested for the remainder of the day, counting down the hours until she would see Sam again.

At five-thirty, she wondered if he'd come directly from work the way he had the day before. Wanting to look her best, she sat up in bed despite the discomfort.

At six-thirty she realized he'd probably gone home to shower and change clothes. Perhaps he felt he wanted to look his best for her, too. The thought pleased Beth, although it was probably silly to put any significance into the timing.

At seven-thirty she started to grow concerned.

At eight-thirty she realized he hadn't said *when* he intended to return, only that he would. She was the one who'd made the assumption it would be that night.

By ten she was depressed, miserable, and fighting self-pity. Sunshine hadn't been able to stop by, as she'd left town for a gallery event. She hadn't wanted to, but Beth had insisted her aunt go. Beth's hip ached, and the incision where her spleen had been removed was a constant source of discomfort, not to mention the terrible ache in her ribs.

Struggling to hold back tears, Beth was furious with herself for putting stock in a few careless words Sam had said on his way out the door. Embarrassed that she'd asked him to visit, she resisted covering her face with her hands. Her cheeks burned with regret.

Beth had to accept that her move to Portland had turned into a disaster. Her mother was right. She was naïve and gullible and needed the protection of her family. All Beth wanted was to make her own way, her own decisions, and, most important of all, her own choices when it came to her life. Now it looked like she would be out of work for months, going through rehab. For the next several weeks she would be dependent on the charity of others. Her first taste of freedom and she'd royally screwed up. The temptation to pull the sheet over her head and sink into a pit of despair was almost irresistible.

Sleep was impossible. She sniffled and would have kicked some sense into herself if it wasn't so painful to move her legs . . . to move at all. Shooting pain from her cracked ribs stabbed her every time she shifted in bed, and her hip throbbed with a constant dull ache despite the pain medication. She was a physical and emotional mess.

It must have been close to midnight and she was wallowing in depression, listening to music on her phone in an effort to ward off sinking any deeper into self-pity. When the door to her room opened, Beth assumed it was the nurse and, not wanting to talk, she turned her music off and kept her eyes closed.

"Beth?"

Her eyes shot open. "Sam?" He'd come at midnight! The man was nuts. She pulled the earbuds free and blinked at him in astonishment.

"Did I wake you?" he whispered. He stood just inside the doorway with his guitar in hand.

For a long moment all she could do was stare at him, convinced she was hallucinating. "What are you doing here this time of night?" she whispered back when she was able to talk.

He walked over to her side and set his guitar on the end of her bed. "You said the nights were the worst and you had a hard time sleeping."

She blinked up at him in the dim light.

"I thought I'd sing you to sleep."

Beth really did feel like weeping then. "Oh Sam," she whispered, nearly choking on her words. "I thought . . . I thought . . ." She couldn't make herself say it.

"What did you think?" he asked, his gaze warm and gentle.

"That you weren't coming."

"Wouldn't miss it," he returned. He seemed surprised that she'd doubted him. "I told you I'd be back."

"But it's late and you have to work in the morning and . . ."

"Babe, trust me, I've been up far later than this and still managed to work the next day. Even hungover, I'm a good mechanic."

She didn't question his work skills. From everything she'd heard from Nichole and Rocco, Sam knew his way around an engine.

He paused and his gaze narrowed as he studied her. "You look different."

So he'd noticed her hair and makeup.

"I like it."

Beth couldn't have quelled her smile had she tried.

Sam pulled out a chair, sat down, and balanced his calf across his knee, then dug a pic out of his jacket pocket. "What were you listening to?" he asked, noticing her phone and the earbuds.

" 'Bravery' by G. P. Telemann. Ever heard of him?"

"Can't say that I have." He strummed a few bars and then glanced up at her.

"Are you taking requests?" she asked.

"Don't know Mozart or Telemann, but I do a mean Rascal Flatts."

Beth's smile was so big that her mouth hurt.

"I'll play for you a bit." He strummed a chord or two and then picked up the rhythm. The music was wonderful and it surrounded her, filling her up. Her playlist had helped. Sam helped a lot more.

"You sleepy yet?" he asked.

Not in the least; not with Sam sitting next to her bed, guitar in hand. "Nope."

"Settle back and close your eyes," he suggested.

Relaxing as best she could, Beth leaned back, wincing at the pain in her ribs. "Know any cradle songs?" she asked.

"No."

"Didn't think so," she teased. "Johannes Brahms."

"I should have guessed." He grinned at her. "I can do a little Garth Brooks, but that's about as close to a lullaby as you're gonna get out of me." Sam chose a song she didn't recognize and sang softly. His voice was deep and melodic; Beth was mesmerized. An hour earlier she'd been ready to pack her bags and return to Chicago with her tail between her legs and admit defeat. Now she was riding high, overwhelmed by the man sitting by her side. She'd mentioned ever so briefly that she hadn't been able to sleep well, and now here he was, playing and singing to her. No one had ever done anything like this for her before. No one.

He sang her two songs, then paused, his hands poised above the guitar strings. "Are you sleepy yet?"

She wasn't about to waste a moment of his visit by sleeping— not if she could help it. "Keep singing—that will put me to sleep."

"It'd help if you closed your eyes."

"Not happening." Then, because she had to know, she asked, "Do you play in a band?"

He grinned. "Nah, I'm not that good."

"You underestimate yourself, Sam. I'm a music teacher. I know *good* when I hear it."

"Whatever," he said, continuing with another song, clearly unwilling to believe her. When he finished he looked up. "If you aren't sleepy, are you in pain?"

She had to stop and think about it, and surprisingly, she wasn't. "Not at the moment. An hour ago I was miserable, fighting off tears."

His mouth tightened. "How long before you can have another pain pill?"

"My last pill was at ten."

"You mean to say you were close to tears even after the pain meds? They need to up the dosage."

"It wasn't physical pain," she clarified. "I was depressed and overwhelmed with everything that's happened. I don't want to leave Portland and move back to Chicago, but I may have to."

"I don't see why. You have friends to help you. And what about your aunt? Rainbow, wasn't it?"

"Sunshine."

"Right. I'm sure she doesn't want you to move away."

"Probably not, but I don't want to be a burden and that's what I see myself becoming."

"Not to Nichole and not to me."

"Oh Sam." Her throat thickened and she was at a loss about what to say. "I don't know what I would have done without you. I think you might have saved my life." At the time of the accident, she was convinced she was going to die. He'd been there, maintaining eye contact, grounding her, reassuring her. His presence had meant everything in those agonizing moments before the Aid Car had arrived.

Again he brushed off her compliment. "Come on, Beth, don't give up so soon. I came here to help."

She felt tears of gratitude fill her eyes and quickly blinked them away.

"I'll be back," he promised. "If you want, I'll stop by tomorrow to see how you're doing."

Her disappointment was almost impossible to hide. "I won't be here. I'm being transferred to the rehab facility."

"Where?"

She gave him the name but didn't know the address. Setting aside his guitar, he reached for his phone and found it. "I'll come visit you there. Deal?"

"Deal." It was hard not to show how pleased she was.

"Now close your eyes. If this doesn't put you to sleep, then I've made a wasted trip."

To satisfy him, Beth lay back and obeyed.

"Good girl," Sam whispered and continued to play.

Beth thought it would be impossible to sleep, but Sam's voice softened and before long she felt her body relax as she started to drift off. She fought sleep, but it did little good. The pain meds and the fact that her body needed rest in order to heal eventually lulled her into dreamland.

When Beth was half asleep, Sam gradually stopped playing and singing. If he didn't need to work in a few hours she might have pulled herself out of the near sleeping state. She didn't want him to go, but it would be selfish to hold him up any longer.

When he scooted the chair back, it made a light scraping sound. She'd waited all day for him and had to admit he'd been worth the wait.

Then something happened. Something even more unexpected than his midnight visit.

Sam leaned down and brushed the hair from her forehead and kissed her there. His mouth was soft and warm against her skin.

Oh yes, he'd been well worth the wait.

CHAPTER 8

Sam

Sam was busy looking at the electrical system on a 2011 Cadillac when he saw Rocco pull into the garage towing a vehicle. It wasn't unusual for his friend to deliver a car to the dealership, but it wasn't all that common, either.

Straightening, Sam grabbed hold of the rag tucked in the back pocket of his overalls and wiped his hands clean. While he worked to keep his nails and cuticles free of grease, it was an endless task. He thought about Beth's hands so perfectly shaped, soft and small. He marveled that she could play the piano with hands that delicate. Funny thing, he barely knew her, but she never seemed far from his thoughts. It'd been a long time since a woman had stayed in his mind the way Beth did.

Rocco handed the paperwork off to one of Sam's crew and then approached him.

"Hey," Rocco said.

"Hey." He responded with their traditional greeting.

"How's it going?"

Sam continued to wipe his hands. "Good. You?"

"Good. You got a minute?"

"Sure. What you need?"

Rocco walked over to the coffeemaker and poured himself a cup. He motioned toward Sam, silently asking if he wanted one.

Sam shook his head. "No thanks." His friend didn't seem himself and looked uncomfortable. Sam noticed how Rocco glanced around as if to be sure they had privacy.

"You sure everything is okay?" Sam asked, curious now. "Matthew's ear infection over?"

"Yeah, yeah, all's well." Rocco leaned against the counter and sipped his coffee. He seemed to find something interesting to look at in the cup.

Knowing him as well as he did, Sam figured his friend was gathering his thoughts. Rocco's frown thickened as if he wasn't sure where to start.

Sam waited, thinking if he gave Rocco enough silence the guy would eventually get around to what he wanted to say.

Rocco straightened and looked up. "Nichole mentioned you've been up to see Beth every day since the accident."

Sam stiffened slightly. "Yeah. What of it?" He didn't mean to sound defensive, but realized he probably did.

"You like her?"

"Not going there for the ambiance," Sam returned sarcastically.

Rocco grimaced. "Right."

"Beth's great," Sam said, unsure where this discussion was leading. At this point he wasn't sure what Rocco's intentions were.

"You feel sorry for her?"

"Of course I do. The only relative she has in town is her aunt."

"Ever met the aunt?"

"Yeah. Her name's Sunshine; found out she's an artist. From

what Beth tells me, her work sells for big bucks. Never heard of her myself, so I went online; she's good, real good. Guess no one would pay that much for one of her pieces if she wasn't."

"When did you meet the aunt?"

"Second time I was there. Beth's coming along nicely now. The staff have her up and taking steps with a walker. Hard to believe they make her walk so soon after the surgery." Sam was proud of her; it hadn't been easy, and it was clear walking was more than a little uncomfortable for her.

Rocco nodded and looked down at his feet. "I have to tell you I'm worried."

"You? About Beth?" Right away Sam wondered if Rocco knew something about Beth's condition that he didn't. Perhaps she'd hidden something from him regarding her injuries. It seemed her progress was slow, but then he was no medical expert and he wasn't sure what to expect as normal. "She's healing the way she should, isn't she?"

"Far as I know."

"Then what's wrong? Is it something to do with her job? The school hired a substitute teacher to cover for her. Beth told me she can have her job back once she's able to return to work."

His friend refused to meet his gaze. "It's not about her job and it isn't about her family, either."

"Then what's the problem?" Sam wished his friend would get to his point instead of hedging. If there was a problem, then he wanted—no, he needed—to know what it was.

Rocco inhaled a deep breath and then blurted out, "I'm concerned you're visiting Beth because you feel sorry for her."

"I do feel bad for her. So what?" He had a whole plethora of feelings for Beth. He liked her a whole lot more than he ever expected he would. He loved watching her face light up like a Christmas tree the instant he walked in the door. A couple times he hesitated before coming into the room, anticipating that smile, wanting to hold on to it for a few extra seconds. Her smile did amazing things to his heart. Just seeing it made him happy, but he wasn't telling Rocco that, or anyone else, for that matter.

"What about when she's recovered and her life is back to normal?" Rocco asked.

Sam crossed his arms, disliking these questions. "What about it?"

"How are you going to feel about her then?" the other man asked, more to the point.

Sam shrugged. "How do I know? We aren't there yet."

Rocco's eyes narrowed slightly, as if he was unsure how to respond.

This was getting a little too personal and Sam took exception. He wasn't entirely sure what Rocco was trying to say and found himself getting irritated. Rocco might be his best friend, but he was crossing the line.

Rocco looked about as uncomfortable as Sam could ever remember.

"The thing is, Sam, this isn't like you."

"So?"

"So," he said, raising his voice, "don't lead her on, okay?"

"I'm not leading her on. The most I've done is kiss her forehead when she was asleep."

"That's just it, buddy. Beth is at a vulnerable point, and here you are, her white knight, bringing her roses and—"

"One rose," he interrupted, bristling. "I brought her one fricken rose."

"And it was red," Rocco returned just as quickly.

"So it was red, big deal. It was the only color the gift shop had." Now that he thought about it, maybe there'd been other colors. That rose just happened to be in the front of the case and the one he reached for.

"And now here you are paying her all this attention. Beth stuck in the hospital—"

"Rehab facility," he corrected. "She was moved there this afternoon."

"Whatever," Rocco muttered. "You get my point. She's a captive audience and I'm afraid once Beth doesn't need you any longer you'll conveniently forget about her." Rocco exhaled slowly. "Trust me, I didn't want to have this conversation. You're as good a friend as I've ever had. I know you practically as well as I know myself."

Rocco did know him, no argument there.

"You told Beth you don't do relationships and I haven't seen you in one since—"

"I get the point," Sam said gruffly, cutting him off. He didn't need any reminders of Trish and his last disastrous affair.

"I didn't want to have this conversation, but I felt I had to even if it meant butting into your business. It's your life and I feel like crap even mentioning it. Nichole thinks I should stay out of it and she's probably right. From what you said, it sounds like this isn't anything beyond friendship for you. I'm afraid it's becoming more for Beth."

"In other words, you're suggesting I cool the visits?"

"That's up to you. I said what I had to say, the rest is your call."

"Got it." Sam exhaled.

"We good?" Rocco asked, his gaze holding Sam's.

He didn't respond right away, thinking about what his friend had said.

"Listen, Sam, if I've offended you—"

Sam cut him off. "We're good."

Rocco left soon afterward and Sam was left deep in thought. He returned to the Cadillac with the electrical problem and stared at it for several minutes until one of the other mechanics came to ask him a question and broke him out of his trance.

When he sat down with his lunch, he took a seat outside away from the rest of his crew while he mulled over his conversation with Rocco. Hard as it was to admit, it was time he came to his senses. He didn't know what the hell he was doing. Sam liked Beth; she was surprisingly good company. He did feel bad about her situation, but he was no superhero ready to leap in and save the day.

From what little Beth had told him, she'd downplayed her injuries to her parents and Sunshine was out of town. Reading between the lines, he suspected they had been suffocating her for most of her life. He wasn't entirely sure what was going on between Beth and her parents, but what little she'd mentioned said a lot.

He reached for his phone and was about to send her a text. He typed it out, and then for reasons he couldn't explain even to himself, he decided to phone instead.

"Sam?" Beth answered, and he could hear a smile in her voice, although it felt a bit anxious. "Is it your lunch break?"

"Yeah."

"I'm glad you phoned."

Sam exhaled slowly, feeling foolish. Rocco was right. The last thing he wanted or needed was emotional entanglements. "I thought I should let you know I've got something tonight and I won't be by."

A short pause and then, "Okay, sure."

Now he was the one who was disappointed. While he'd never admit this to Rocco, he'd been looking forward to surprising Beth. He planned to bring her a thick vanilla malt from his favorite mom-and-pop stand in celebration of her release from the hospital.

"You understand, right?"

His words fell heavy between them and hung there for a long moment. Beth finally spoke.

"Of course," she assured him. She didn't sound quite like herself, though.

Sam feared there was something she wasn't telling him. "Everything's okay?"

"Of course." The words sounded strained, as if she was having trouble speaking.

He exhaled, worried now that she hadn't taken the news well.

"It's fine, Sam," she assured him softly. "Really."

He was going to miss seeing her. "When you being released?" he asked, in order to keep her on the line.

"I . . . I don't know yet. Soon, I suppose."

Maybe he'd just space out his visits moving forward. "I'll stop by the rehab center sometime . . . maybe later in the week."

"Sure, that would be great."

They said their good-byes and Sam slipped his phone back into his pocket. He set his half-eaten sandwich aside and, deep in thought, he leaned forward. If Rocco was going to worry about anyone getting hurt in this relationship, or non-relationship, or whatever the hell was happening between him and Beth, his friend should be more concerned about him.

Sam got through the rest of the day and noticed his crew went out of their way to give him space. Apparently, they recognized his mood wasn't the best. Filling out the last of his paperwork, Sam headed home and then decided what he needed was a beer at The Dog House. He hadn't been by his favorite watering hole since Beth's accident.

He found parking on the street and Al, the bartender, raised his hand when he saw Sam.

"Hey, where you been?"

"Around." Sam slid onto a stool, not looking for conversation.

Al didn't bother to ask him what he wanted to drink. Sam was a good enough customer that the bartender already knew. Within a couple minutes of his arrival, Sam had a mug in his hand. He looked up at the big-screen television above the bar and listened to the commentator analyzing the previous weekend's preseason football games. Sam liked football about as much as he did beer, and normally what the pros had to say riveted his attention.

Not so this evening. Again and again, Sam's thoughts went back to Beth in that care facility, listening to her iPod. Before he'd left, Beth had told him the title was *Courage*. He didn't remember the composer's name, but apparently it was one of those classic compositions she liked so well. Definitely not his thing. Though that was unfair, seeing that he had never heard it.

Cherise slid onto the stool next to him. "Sam, been missing you," she said and slid her arm down his back. She hung around the tavern and liked to think he had feelings for her. Sam didn't.

"You working too hard, baby?" she asked.

He ignored her. "Not in the mood," he muttered, doing his best to ignore her.

"I can make it better, you know I can."

Sam shook his head, and despite himself, he smiled. "Not this time."

"You sure?"

"Positive." The contrast between her and Beth was night and day. Beth was clean and fresh like springtime. Cherise was the last dregs of winter, her beauty fading, her appeal melting. His stomach tightened. He'd been away from Beth for less than twenty-four hours and already he missed her. All morning he'd been looking forward to her smile.

Cherise slid off the stool and rested her chin on the curve of his shoulder. "You call me if you need me, okay?"

He nodded, but he wasn't going to. He knew what he needed and that was seeing Beth.

Cherise drifted over to the pool table and started up a conversation with another of the regulars.

The thought of Beth sitting in the convalescent center alone, putting on a brave front, twisted his gut. He didn't know where this relationship was going, but he was determined to be careful. Nichole was right to be worried. Sam had to be sure he wasn't leading Beth on when he had no intention of getting romantically involved with her. He had to make sure she didn't get emotionally attached to him. If necessary, he'd talk to Nichole himself and reassure her.

His phone rang and he saw that it was Nichole. He didn't answer. Having her jawing at him held little appeal. After a few rings it went to voicemail. She didn't leave him a message and he was grateful.

A minute later, Nichole sent him a text. Call me ASAP.

Sam stared at the message for several seconds before he typed back. Problem?

With Beth.

Again he studied the message, growing more irritated by the moment.

What kind of problem?

Call from aunt. Complication—life threatening.

Sam wasn't sure what Nichole was telling him, but he wasn't taking any chances. He punched the button that would connect him with his best friend's wife. Nichole picked up on the second ring. Matthew was screaming in the background.

"What's going on?" he demanded. "Is Beth okay?"

"I don't know."

"What do you mean you don't know?" Sam demanded. "What's wrong?"

Matthew's wailing was making it difficult for Sam to hear Nichole, let alone make sense of what she was saying.

"Sunshine reached out to me about Beth."

"She's been released to the care facility, hasn't she?"

"No," Nichole explained. "That's just it."

Her words came jerky, as if she was bouncing Matthew on her shoulder in an attempt to comfort him so she could talk.

"Sunshine got word a blood clot has developed in Beth's lung."

"What?" Sam was stunned and nearly speechless. "I spoke to her earlier this afternoon and she . . ." He hesitated. He remembered she hadn't sounded like herself and he'd assumed it was disappointment. Twice he thought he might have heard her take deep breaths, but at the time he hadn't given it a second thought.

"It's a dangerous complication, Sam."

Sam leaped to his feet. He slapped a few dollars down on the bar and started toward the door.

"I'm on my way."

"I can't leave. Matthew is running a fever again and Rocco's at work. I didn't know who to call."

"You did the right thing. I'm on my way."

"If you'd rather not go . . ." Nichole said, sounding uncertain.

"What part of 'I'm on my way' don't you understand?" he shouted.

Nichole sighed. "Thank you, Sam. Once you see her, will you contact Sunshine? She's worried sick."

"Will do," he said and disconnected.

Sam probably broke every driving law in the books getting to Providence Hospital. Once he arrived he hit the door with both hands, slamming it so hard he was surprised the glass didn't shatter. He raced toward the elevator and repeatedly stabbed the button. When it wasn't fast enough to suit him, he headed for the stairs, taking them two at a time until he reached the floor where Beth's room was. By then his heart pounded like a locomotive and his breath came in pants. He needed to be sure Beth was all right, barely understanding why it felt as if his own life was in danger.

CHAPTER 9

Beth

"Sam." Beth breathed his name, unable to hide her surprise. He'd said he wasn't coming and now all of a sudden he was here. He looked as if he'd run the entire way, his shoulders heaving with exertion.

Closing her eyes, Beth wanted to hide beneath the sheets. She looked and felt dreadful. When he'd phoned earlier to tell her he wouldn't be by as planned, she was almost relieved. Something was wrong, but she didn't know what. He must have sensed it, too, because he made a point of asking her if she was okay. It was later after the call that everything had taken a turn for the worse.

"What happened?" he asked, coming close to the bed. He reached for her hand, holding it tightly in his own, pressing it against his chest. She could feel his racing heart and tried to reassure him with a soft smile.

The oxygen tube in her nose was uncomfortable, but it helped to ease her breathing, which had become painful and difficult. "I have a pulmonary embolism," she said, and because she didn't know what that was when it was first mentioned, she added, "That's a blood clot in my lung. Apparently, it isn't uncommon when someone has a hip fracture."

"This pulmonary thing is dangerous?"

"So they say." Actually, she'd looked it up on Safari on her phone and learned more than she cared to know. She was being treated now and closely monitored, but this complication was likely to add four additional days to her hospital stay.

"I sensed something was wrong this afternoon when I called," Sam said. "You seemed to be having trouble breathing."

She lowered her eyes. "Yeah, but no one knew why, at least not right away. My oxygen levels dropped significantly and the nurse in charge phoned my doctor, and then everyone started rushing around. I had a number of tests, starting with a chest X-ray and then an electrocardiogram."

"Do you feel better now?"

She hesitated before she answered. "No."

Sam raised her hand to his mouth and kissed the backside. It was such a sweet, reassuring gesture that tears gathered in her eyes. She rapidly blinked them away, embarrassed by the display of emotion. He was practically a stranger, yet he'd been her rock from the moment of the accident.

"Who told you?" she asked.

"Nichole. Apparently, the hospital notified Sunshine . . ."

"Oh no." Beth groaned. "And now she's probably freaking out."

He grinned. "Probably. I know how I felt when I heard. Nichole sent me a text on my way to the hospital. Sunshine is flying back as soon as she can get a flight."

"Oh dear. I didn't want her to do that." Beth's shoulders sagged with regret. This art show was important to her aunt, and she hated the thought of Sunshine cutting it short because of her. "I wish she wouldn't."

"Beth, come on. Of course she's coming. She's worried about you." He hesitated, his hand tightening around hers. "For that matter, so am I. What can I do?"

He'd been so good to her, and in her weakened state it demanded every shred of control she possessed not to break into tears.

Sam apparently noticed her struggling with her emotions. "Would you like me to read you another Psalm? I'll do it if it will ease your mind. Actually, I might do it anyway to ease my own."

Despite the tears crowding her eyes, Beth smiled. "I wish you'd stop being so wonderful."

He chuckled. "That's not a word most people would associate with me."

"I do." It shocked her how quickly he'd come to mean so much to her. It'd been only a few days and it was as if her entire day revolved around him and his visits.

"My guitar is in my truck. Would you like me to play for you again?"

Of all the things Beth missed most during her hospital stay, not being able to play the piano topped the list. Yes, she could listen to music, which she did every day, but it wasn't the same. Nothing compared to being able to sit down at the piano with her own hands running over the keys. The sound pulsed through her fingertips, the music swirling around her, lifting her above whatever was troubling her mind, lifting her higher and higher until her problems dissolved into thin air.

Sam released her hand and she immediately felt the loss of his touch. "I'll be back in a jiffy." He took two steps in retreat before turning and hurrying out of the room.

Before he'd arrived she'd been feeling low, wondering why all this was happening to her. The instant Sam walked in the room,

Beth felt better both emotionally and physically. She didn't want to become dependent on him, so when he phoned to say he wouldn't be by she'd thought it was probably for the best. Then here he was, and she was doing an imaginary happy dance knowing that as soon as he'd heard he'd rushed to the hospital to stand at her side.

Within a few minutes, Sam returned with his guitar.

"Thank you," she whispered when he pulled out the chair next to her bed and took out his pick.

He smiled up at her. "I'm taking requests."

She smiled. "How about a little Bob Dylan. His music soothes me. It always has."

"Me, too."

Resting his hands on the strings, Sam played a gentle melody. The notes whirled around her, and she sighed as if he'd wrapped her in a warm blanket. Sam glanced at her and smiled and she swore the connection between them in that moment felt almost physical. One unlike anything she'd ever experienced before. He played two or three songs before the door to her room opened and one of the nurse's aides came in to take her vitals and test her oxygen levels. Over the course of the last few days, Beth had gotten to know the nurses, who were wonderful, and the aides, too. Jazmine was one of her favorites.

Jazmine glanced shyly at Sam as she made a note of Beth's temperature and blood pressure.

When she'd finished getting what she needed, she hesitated and then asked, "Would you mind if I cracked the door open? Several patients have asked. We'd all like to hear the music."

"I don't mind." Beth looked at Sam for approval. Her gaze held his and she smiled, letting him know how much she appreciated his playing. "I'm not the only one you're soothing," she whispered.

Jazmine left and Sam continued to play. As she had the night before, she struggled to remain awake, not wanting to fall asleep when Sam was visiting. Twice her eyes drifted closed, and she forced herself to open them again.

"Sleep," he urged. His voice was low and rough, and as odd as it might sound, gentle at the same time.

After a restless and uncomfortable afternoon being dragged from one test to another, Beth was exhausted. It felt as if she'd run a marathon. Lulled by the music and Sam's presence, she felt her eyes drooping closed. She wasn't sure at what point she fell asleep. All she knew was that when she woke, Sunshine was on the other side of her bed.

"Oh my dear, precious girl."

"I'm so sorry," Beth whispered.

"Sorry?" Sunshine repeated. "What in the name of heaven do you have to be sorry for?"

"Your art show."

Sunshine made a sweeping gesture with her arm. "Oh, for the love of heaven, there are art shows every other day. Don't you worry. I was foolish to have left you when I did. If anyone has regrets, it should be me. I hated the thought of you going through this alone."

Beth glanced about the room, and then realized it was morning. Sam must have left when she fell asleep. Try as she might, she couldn't keep her eyes open any longer. "Sam stopped by."

"Yes, I know."

"You know?" The two of them must be communicating.

Sunshine looked amused. "He was sound asleep in that chair when I arrived."

Beth nearly gasped out loud. "He spent the night here . . . at the hospital?"

"Apparently. His guitar was propped against the wall and he'd slouched back, legs stretched out in front of him and his arms crossed. On my way to your room I swear I could hear him snoring."

"You did not!"

Sunshine laughed, the sound girlish and irresistible, making Beth want to laugh along with her. She could be in a room with a hundred people speaking at a high volume and be able to pick out her aunt simply by the sound of her laughter.

Sunshine grew serious then. "I'm going to need to talk to your parents about this latest development, Beth."

"No," she cried, instantly alarmed. This was the last thing Beth wanted. Knowing her parents, especially her mother, this complication was sure to bring them rushing to her side as if she were on her deathbed. Before she could protest further, pleading with Sunshine to reconsider, her aunt raised her hand to stop her.

"Don't get your panties in a wad."

"What?" Beth cried.

"You heard me. I'll handle this. Your mother has already booked a ticket to come visit. I'll do what I can to reassure her, but it wouldn't surprise me if she leapt on a plane the minute she hears about this."

"Mom's coming?" The weight of the news fell heavy on Beth. This was the last thing she wanted to hear.

"I did my best, Sweet Pea, but you know your mom. She's worried. I wasn't going to mention it until it got closer to the time, but with this latest development I can't guarantee that I can keep her away. It was hard enough to convince her to give you a couple weeks before she flew out."

If her mother came, then there was a good possibility she'd meet Sam. The mere thought was enough to make Beth go cold inside. That would not go well. She could just imagine what Ellie would have to say about her precious only child associating with a man with long hair, tattoos, and a beard. And associating with Sam was definitely in Beth's plans. Even now, thinking about him produced an immediate smile. That he'd stayed by her side through the night was above and beyond anything she could expect. Knowing he'd done that for her made Beth go all soft inside.

"Whatever you say, don't let Mom catch the next plane to Portland." Beth's biggest fear was that once her mother met Sam, Ellie would do whatever she could to sabotage the relationship. Beth refused to let that happen.

"Beth, girl, I can hardly stop her. I'll do my best to delay her as long as possible, but no way is she going to stay in Chicago when her baby girl is experiencing complications. I'll do what I can to give you time to regain your strength, but you need to accept that she's coming."

Beth's shoulders sank with defeat. Her aunt was right. This latest development was all the excuse her mother needed. It was nothing short of a wonder that Ellie hadn't shown up thus far.

"Do what you can," she pleaded. Her one ace was the fact that Sunshine and her mother didn't get along. They avoided each other whenever possible. Beth knew some disagreement had happened in their youth that had caused this rift, but whatever it was remained a well-kept family secret. When Beth questioned her mother, Ellie refused to discuss it. As a teenager Beth had asked her aunt; Sunshine said it was over something that had happened so long ago she'd completely forgotten about it. Beth didn't believe her but hadn't pressed the issue. Whatever happened was clearly a sore spot between the two sisters.

"Rest now," Sunshine urged her. "You're going to need every bit of strength you possess when facing your mother."

"You know I'm going to be worried the entire time." Beth made a show of placing the back of her hand against her forehead. "The undue stress is sure to cause even more stress and complications."

Sunshine burst out laughing. "Are you sure you weren't a drama major?"

Beth waved her away. "Do what you've got to do to convince my mother I'm going to be whole and healthy without her sobbing at my bedside."

Grinning, her aunt asked, "You need me to get you anything while I'm out?"

"Yes," she cried. "Get me peace of mind by keeping my mother as far away from me for as long as you can."

"On it," Sunshine promised, smiling on her way out the door.

After Sunshine left, Beth sat up and reached for her phone to text Sam.

You spent the night?

She waited several minutes before she got an answer. She giggled when she read his response.

Not on purpose.

Her phone rang almost right away. Her smile grew even bigger when she saw it was Sam calling.

"Morning," she greeted.

"Yeah, well, it isn't exactly a good one. I've got a crick in my neck and my eyes burn and my fingers are too big to try to text. I figured I'd call. You feel better today?"

"I do." While breathing was much easier, it was the mental aspect that had taken a swing for the better. Seeing Sam, knowing he'd been by her side the entire night, had elevated her spirits into the stratosphere.

"Good, then it was worth it."

"I know you're tired, so don't worry about stopping by today," she said. She made the offer knowing she would sorely miss seeing him.

"You don't want me to come?" He sounded more than a little offended.

"I do . . . more than anything, but I think it would be better if you went home and got a decent night's sleep."

Her suggestion was met with a short pause. "The thing you don't realize is that I enjoy spending time with you."

Beth closed her eyes in order to soak in his words. "Oh Sam."

"Don't know how it happened. Not even sure it's a good thing—"

"It is," she interrupted him. "It's a very good thing."

"Been warned already."

Her immediate fear was that her mother had somehow gotten word that she was seeing Sam, which was ridiculous. It wasn't like her mother had hired spies to check up on Beth and report back her activities. As for her and Sam, they hadn't gone out on a single date. Yet in the last few days, they'd spent countless hours together and had even spent the night together, although it was completely innocent.

"Warned? By who?" she asked.

"It's not important."

"Who?" Beth insisted.

"Rocco. He's afraid I'm leading you on."

"Oh." This was interesting. Beth wondered if Nichole knew about this.

"Didn't do much good, though, did it?" he teased.

"Glad it didn't."

Sam made a noise that sounded like a deep yawn. "I need to get off the phone."

"You at work?" she asked.

"Not yet, but I'm telling you things I normally wouldn't. Blame it on the fact I had about an hour of sleep the entire night."

Beth relaxed against the pillow. "If the lack of sleep is responsible for this conversation, then I'd like to suggest you go without more often."

She thought she heard him chuckle, but she couldn't be sure. One thing she did know: Her smile was so wide her mouth hurt.

CHAPTER 10

Sunshine

Sunshine stood in the hospital hallway outside of Beth's room with a growing sense of dread. Talking to her sister was never pleasant. Their relationship had been strained for years and had grown even more so since Beth's move to Portland. She'd spoken to Ellie more in the last three months than she had in the last five years. This rift between them started back in her college days when Sunshine was in art school.

Immediately Peter came to mind, and with his memory a flash of pain. The sharpness had receded through the years. Thoughts of him no longer crippled her as they once had. Time does that, she reasoned, dulling the razor edges of disappointment and loss.

As much as Sunshine would like to delay talking to her sister, she couldn't. Beth was anxious and the added stress wouldn't help the healing process. She scrolled down her contact list and hit the button. Her heart pounded in her ear as she waited for her sister to pick up. Sunshine would have much preferred to speak with her brother-in-law. Unfortunately, Phillip was sure to have left for the office by now.

"Yes?" Ellie answered, her voice clipped and short. "What is it this time?"

Stiffening, Sunshine noticed that her sister avoided saying hello because she had caller ID. It was Ellie's less than subtle way of letting Sunshine know she didn't welcome the call. She sighed and repressed the urge to tell Ellie she wasn't keen to talk to her, either. Not a great way to start what was certain to turn into an unpleasant conversation. Come to think of it, they hadn't shared a friendly chat in more than thirty years. Sad as that was to admit.

"Hello, Ellie." Sunshine did her best to remain calm after the rude greeting.

"Hello, *Louise.*"

Sunshine disliked her given name, which was one reason she'd changed it. She gritted her teeth and waited several seconds until she could speak calmly. "I thought I'd give you an update on Beth."

"I hear from my daughter. I don't need you to act as a go-between."

Maybe it would have been best to let her niece handle this. "You're right, of course."

"Nice of you to admit it, *Louise.*"

Again she was forced to silently count to ten as her sister pointedly tried to irritate her. "After a small glitch in her recovery, Beth is doing better." She avoided finishing the sentence, avoided explaining. *And technically Beth was doing better than yesterday.*

"I'm coming to check on her myself. Now, why is it necessary for you to disrupt my morning? I have a lot to do before I leave."

Sunshine started to respond, but before she could speak, Ellie continued.

"Just because my daughter chose to move to Portland, you seem to think it's your duty to fill me in on matters that are none of your concern."

"I was only—"

"Looking to rub it in my face that Beth chose to live close to you."

Biting down on her inner cheek, Sunshine forced herself to not retaliate. "Ellie, please—"

"My point," Ellie said, slowly releasing her breath, "is that Beth is my daughter and I don't need you to update me on her condition."

"I agree," she said, in an effort to keep the peace. "This time, though, Beth asked me to contact you."

Her announcement was met with silence.

"What's wrong?" The change in Ellie's attitude was immediate.

"It's a small complication."

"What kind of complication? Never mind. I'll cancel my luncheon and catch the next flight out."

"Don't, Ellie. Please. Keep your original flight. Beth is fine and she wants to do this on her own. I'm here as a backup should she need anything. I realize my being close to her upsets you and I'm asking, begging, you, really, to give Beth a chance to spread her wings without either of us standing guard over her. I can appreciate how difficult that is, especially now. Wait, please, give her some breathing room, and when you do arrive, I promise to stay out of your way."

Ellie's breathing evened out, and Sunshine could see that her sister was taking her words to heart. She hesitated, as if weighing her options.

"I'm in charge of a charity luncheon this week. Perhaps it would be best if I kept my original flight."

Again she paused, and Sunshine could almost hear her sister chewing on her bottom lip as she considered her options.

"You're sure Beth doesn't need me to come right away?"

"Positive."

"I don't know . . ." Ellie whispered.

Time to draw her big gun. Phillip. Beth's father had become his daughter's greatest ally. "If you don't trust me, then talk it over with Phillip before you change your flight," Sunshine suggested.

"And if I don't, you'll call him yourself."

"Yes." Without hesitation.

"Have it your way, then," Ellie said stiffly. "I love my daughter and I refuse to let you or my husband keep me away from her."

"No one is keeping you away from your daughter. Beth specifically asked that you not come rushing to her side now. Listen to her, Ellie. It's what she is asking of you. Don't you care about what Beth wants?" Sunshine asked.

"My daughter needs me."

"For what?" Sunshine asked. "To buy her clothes, to decorate her apartment, to introduce her to men you consider a good match for her? Just whose life is this? It doesn't sound like Beth's. It sounds like yours. For the love of heaven, Ellie, don't you realize you're smothering the poor girl?"

"You're as bad as Phillip."

Nicest compliment Sunshine had gotten all week.

"All right," Ellie said grudgingly. "I'll keep my original flight, but if I hear one more thing about Beth and this accident there is no way anyone is going to keep me away from my daughter." The words and the way she spoke told Sunshine further arguments would be useless. Her sister's mind was made up and there was no changing it.

"Beth will be out of the hospital soon and well on her way to recovery." She didn't mention that Beth would be transferred to a rehab facility. Sunshine would let her niece explain that.

"Thank you, Ellie. I know Beth will appreciate your restraint."

Ellie didn't say anything for a long moment, and when she spoke next her voice was less brusque. "Is my baby hurting?"

"She was in the beginning, but she's getting better day by day."

"Thank you," her sister whispered, sadness fusing with her words. "I'd like to say it was a pleasure, but alas, it never is with the two of us, is it?"

"No. I wish it was different, though." Once again Sunshine extended a hand to Ellie. It was up to her sister to reach for it.

Her words were met with silence and then "Good-bye, Louise," Ellie said as she cut the connection.

One final dig.

It saddened her that they couldn't let go of the past. This matter with Peter stood between them as wide as the Grand Canyon. And it didn't look to be shrinking anytime soon.

Sunshine remained in the hospital hallway for several minutes, mulling over her conversation with her sister. It hadn't always been like this between them. As teens they'd been close, trading each other's clothes, telling each other secrets. Naturally they squabbled now and again. What two sisters didn't? They decided early in their teen years to attend the same college. That was the start of all the problems, although they would never have guessed it at the time.

A year ahead of Ellie, Sunshine was a junior when she met Peter. The two of them dated exclusively. A few times they even doubled up with her sister. It was all so perfect, so wonderful. Peter loved her and she loved him. Loved him still.

Ellie liked Peter, too, and repeatedly told her how lucky Sunshine was to have him in her life. Young as she was, Sunshine hadn't realized how fragile love could be.

Sunshine swallowed down the sense of hurt and betrayal just as she had so many times before. The two people she had loved most in the world had betrayed her; they might as well have ripped her heart out of her chest and stomped on it. The pain had lessened with the years. She refused to allow herself to wallow in it again. It served no useful purpose; nothing positive would come of dredging up the memories that had the power to torment her.

Once more Sunshine reminded herself all that was in the past. She had a good life, friends, a career she loved, and she made enough money from her artwork to live comfortably. What she didn't need was the strife and angst of her emotionally needy sister.

Yet here they were again, and the prize this time was Beth.

The phone conversation with her sister had shaken her. It took several minutes to calm her nerves. Once her head and her heart were settled, Sunshine returned to Beth's hospital room.

Her niece looked up, her eyes and face full of anxiety as she waited to hear. "How'd it go?"

"I should have talked to your father."

"Mom answered the phone?" Beth tilted her head back and stared blankly up at the ceiling.

Sunshine didn't need to explain further. It'd been an error in judgment to hope Ellie could put their differences aside when it came to Beth, seeing that they both loved the young woman.

"Is she rebooking a plane ticket as we speak?" Beth asked, nervously rubbing her palms together.

"She says she isn't, but only time will tell."

Beth looked miserable. "I suggested she discuss it with Phillip. My guess is your father will talk her out of it. She did have something important on her plate this week, so that works in your favor."

"Dad might think she should come, though."

"Maybe, but I doubt it." Sunshine felt bad. "She said she didn't need me to act as a go-between and that you've been talking to her."

Beth rubbed her palms together and looked away, but not before Sunshine saw the look of guilt.

"Beth?" Something was definitely up. "You have been talking to your mother, haven't you?"

"Yes . . . sort of."

"What does that mean?"

"I haven't lied," Beth rushed to add. "I couldn't even if I tried.

Mom would see through that in a heartbeat. I haven't been telling her the full truth is all. She might . . . you know . . . assume things."

The way her sister had kept Beth under her thumb was just plain wrong as far as Sunshine was concerned. Her niece was an adult and her sister insisted on treating her daughter as a child. Little had pleased Sunshine more than the day Beth announced she was moving to Portland. The fact that Beth had chosen to live in the same city as Sunshine had rubbed salt in Ellie's wounded pride.

Beth was smart. Smarter than Ellie gave her credit for. Sunshine loved her niece and they were tight, but Beth chose to live in Portland because she knew her mother wouldn't be inclined to visit often, for obvious reasons.

"What assumptions has your mother made?" Sunshine asked.

"You know . . . that the accident wasn't nearly as bad as it was," Beth reminded her, and bit down on her lower lip.

Sunshine nodded.

"I did tell her it would be awhile before I returned to work and I might have let her assume all I needed was a few days to rest up."

They both knew it would be weeks before Beth returned to teaching, possibly even months. Beth was in for a long haul of physical therapy due to the rod in her hip. She'd been up and walking, but it was difficult and painful for her. The doctor had scheduled her for intensive physical therapy until she'd gotten the blood clot in her lung. Now her rehabilitation had come to a standstill.

"Do you still call your mother every day?" Sunshine asked. That was one of the stipulations Ellie had made when Beth chose to leave Chicago.

"I did in the beginning," Beth admitted. "Now it's every other day. I'm weaning myself away from her."

"Good for you." Sunshine was happy to see her niece make the break. It was long overdue.

Beth looked down and avoided eye contact. "Unfortunately, Mom isn't taking it so well. If I don't call her, then she calls me."

There was more to this, and Sunshine waited for Beth to explain.

"I let her calls go to voicemail."

A smile crept across her mouth as she struggled to hold back her amusement.

"I explained I can't be at her beck and call while teaching. I have a life, and really it's ridiculous. I'm twenty-five years old, not fifteen. Mom asks the most outrageous questions."

No doubt. Ellie's real fear was that Beth, given her own choice, would steer away from the life path she had chosen for her daughter. It astonished her how little her sister knew Beth. Again and again Sunshine had been impressed with her niece's kind heart, her passion, and her insights into the teens she worked with at the high school. Beth was wonderful, and her sister didn't seem to appreciate or understand her own daughter, nor did she trust her.

"How's that working for you?"

"Up until now, fairly well. Mom isn't controlling me, and it's like her main purpose in life has been taken away from her."

"It's time, Sweet Pea."

"Past time."

Sunshine more than agreed but didn't say so. Beth had been smart enough to figure this out on her own.

"Now, about your young man—"

"He isn't mine," Beth cut in, her cheeks flushing pink.

Sunshine held back the giggle as best she could. "My dear girl, I know your mother has controlled most of your social activities from the time you were old enough to date. You should know no man spends the night in an uncomfortable chair if he doesn't have a strong interest in a woman."

Beth's shoulders tensed. "If you're going to make an issue of the fact that he isn't someone—"

"Hey, hey." Sunshine did laugh then. "I like Sam. He's good for you."

Beth's eyes smiled, although Sunshine could tell she struggled to hide her feelings for Sam. "I think he's good for me, too."

Before Sunshine could comment, Beth continued.

"We're not dating or anything . . ."

"Yet."

Beth did smile then. "Yet," she agreed. Almost right away the smile faded and her eyes grew dark and serious. "I know Mom will be here soon, and I'm worried."

"About her meeting Sam?"

Beth nodded. "You and I both know Sam isn't someone my mother would consider suitable for me. Which in my mind is ridiculous. What about character? What about being a man of his word? Those are qualities I consider important. Okay, I know all about The Dog House from Nichole, but—"

"The Dog House?"

She snapped her mouth closed as if she wanted to yank back the words before she quickly added "Never mind."

"Beth, you don't need to defend Sam to me. I'm on your side."

Her niece's shoulders visibly relaxed. "Good, because I like Sam . . . a lot."

"I know you do, and that's great."

Sunshine left the hospital shortly afterward and headed to her studio, eager to get back to her latest project. Often, when she returned from a business trip or a few days away, her head would swim with ideas. She could barely wait to get to the studio and get a paintbrush in her hand. Not so this day. Once in her studio she found she couldn't paint. This was what Ellie did to her. She'd allowed her sister to steal her joy. So many times over the years, Sunshine had wished for a better relationship with Ellie. It hurt that they couldn't be sisters, couldn't be friends.

After an hour of fussing around her work area, Sunshine drove home. Agitated, she cleaned her house and scrubbed the stovetop until she wore a hole through her rubber gloves. Then she set to work in her yard, clearing the flower beds despite the threat of rain. It was necessary to do whatever she could to take her mind off the sadness that made her heart ache for the sister and the friend she might have had in Ellie. This lifelong tug-of-war that had left them divided and wounded. Sunshine couldn't help wondering if it would ever end.

CHAPTER 11

Sam

Beth's doctor said he wanted to keep her an additional three days in the hospital. With this latest scare, Sam decided he didn't care what Nichole or anyone else thought. He fully intended to keep seeing Beth. She let him know she looked forward to his visits, and the truth was he liked spending time with her. Thursday night, however, was his poker night with the guys. He never missed. It was ritual. Him and the guys. All his friends were married and they faithfully attended unless it was a family emergency. Usually Sam was the first to arrive and the last to leave.

This Thursday was different. As always, Sam joined his friends, but his mind wasn't on the game. It was on Beth, wondering how she was doing, if breathing had gotten easier for her, if she was regaining her strength. Worries for her circled his mind. He missed her and his concentration wasn't on the game. He lost his money early, and much to everyone's surprise made an excuse to leave.

"Already?" Alex asked, not bothering to hide his surprise.

"What's the rush?" Charley wanted to know. Charley was a high school friend of Rocco's and had become a friend to Sam, too.

Even Rocco looked surprised. "It's not even nine-thirty."

Rather than explain, Sam grabbed his jacket and headed for the door. He knew even as he pulled away from Charley's house that he was heading to the hospital. By the time he arrived it was after ten.

Sure enough, Beth was awake. The minute he walked into her room, her smile nearly blinded him. It was as if she reached out and grabbed hold of his heart. Try as he might, he couldn't explain his reaction. No woman had ever affected him this way.

"I had a feeling you were going to show," she said and stretched out her arm to him.

Gripping her hand, Sam kissed her knuckles and felt mildly guilty. "You should be resting."

"I couldn't sleep. I just had this feeling you were coming."

"Yeah, I did, too," he admitted. Beth got to him in ways that should make him run for the hills, yet he remained rooted to the ground, unable to stay away. He wasn't sure where this relationship was going. Hadn't taken time to consider the future, and knew he probably should. He didn't want to think about anything but the present. He was living one day at a time with Beth, and while he fully expected this to blow up in his face sometime in the future, he didn't care. He'd deal with it when the time came.

"Did you have a good day?" he asked, and noticed she no longer needed the oxygen tube to aid with her breathing. That was an improvement.

"I'm anxious to get out of here. People die in here."

Sam snickered at her joke.

"What about you?" she asked. "How was your day?"

They'd texted back and forth a few times and talked over his lunch break. "Best parts were talking to you."

She smiled again, her eyes bright and warm. "For me, too."

"Are you being transferred tomorrow?"

"That's the word."

He saw the fine lines etched between her eyes in a soft frown. "You worried about something?" he asked, and realized he was getting to know her well enough that he could tell when something troubled her.

"What makes you ask?"

Sam waved his finger at her like a pendulum. "You can't answer a question with a question. That's breaking the rules. Now answer the question."

She sighed, her shoulders sagging slightly. "I talked to my mother this afternoon."

"And?"

"She's arriving next week."

"This worries you why?" He'd heard scant little about her family. He'd noticed that every mention of her mother produced a frown.

"She'll meet you, Sam, and she's going to—"

"Going to what?" he asked, his grip on her hand tightening.

"Judge you."

Sam held her gaze. "And that bothers you?"

She didn't meet his gaze. "Yes, because I'm afraid she'll scare you off and you won't have anything more to do with me and that would devastate me."

"Beth, babe. Listen. Your mother might be a dragon lady, but she isn't going to run me off."

"You haven't met my mother."

"Beth, listen to me." He tucked his index finger beneath her chin and raised her head so she couldn't avoid looking at him. "Your mother isn't going to influence my feelings for you one way or the other."

Hope widened her eyes. "Promise."

"Promise." Sam hated the thought of Beth stressing about this.

Leaning forward, their foreheads touched and Beth whispered, "I'm holding you to that promise, Sam."

"You do that." The temptation was to kiss her. He thought about it often enough; in fact, it'd been paramount on his mind for several days now. Slightly lifting his head, he rubbed his nose against hers and then, because he couldn't resist a second longer, he pressed his mouth to hers. It seemed Beth, too, had been waiting for this moment with the same eagerness as Sam had. As soon as their lips met, she released a low groan and parted her lips, welcoming him. Sam wound his hand around the back of her neck, his fingers tangling with her hair as he slanted his head slightly. She placed her hands against his chest and then gripped hold of the fabric of his shirt, clinging to him.

Delicate as she was, he didn't dare kiss her the way he wanted to. The hunger was there, the need, the desire, but he restrained himself, lightly brushing his mouth over hers so they were barely touching. Gradually he pressed more firmly, rubbing the slick moisture back and forth until he swore he'd never experienced a more erotic kiss in his life.

When he broke away, his breathing was irregular and harsh. He held her for several heart-throbbing seconds while he regained his composure. It took him that long to find his voice.

"I better go." He continued to hold her, finding releasing her harder than ever.

"Okay." She, too, continued to cling to him. Expelling her breath, she eased away and whispered, "That was nice."

"That was more than nice," Sam said, and kissed the top of her head as he pushed back. "It was wonderful."

Beth's eyes remained closed. "I've been wanting you to kiss me forever. What took you so long?"

Sam grinned. Good question. "The hell if I know. All I can say is that it was worth the wait."

Her smile widened. "Yes, it was."

———

Friday Sam knew Beth was scheduled to be discharged from the hospital and transported to the rehab facility. Sam wished he'd taken the day off so that he could be with her, which didn't make sense. Sunshine was sure to go with her. Still, he remained distracted, concerned about Beth. The kiss changed things between them. He found it impossible to stop thinking about Beth and wanting to kiss her again and again. All he knew was that within a matter of a week she had become important to him. More important than was logical or reasonable.

Despite all their differences, he was drawn to her in ways that he hadn't been to a woman in longer than he could remember. Okay, he could remember, but that was a relationship he'd prefer to forget.

Her smile was part of the attraction, he knew. Her entire face lit up with happiness whenever he came to visit, as if she'd been waiting all day for just that moment. The irony of it was he'd been the one who could barely wait to get to her. Her smile had a way of hitting him square in the chest. God help him, he could live a year on one of her smiles.

They also shared a love of music. Sam had none of the formal training she'd received. He'd taught himself how to play the guitar and mostly played by ear, although he'd learned to read sheet music by watching YouTube. Her knowledge was extensive, but she'd never made him feel inferior or like less of a musician. He felt a certain sense of pride knowing his playing relaxed her enough to help her fall asleep.

Leaving her was hard. Often he stayed as long as an hour after she'd drifted off, doing nothing more than studying her. Yup, he had it bad. For most of his adult life, Sam had avoided relationships, or ones that lasted more than a few days or, more accurately put, nights. Everything was different with Beth. He was different with Beth. She was concerned about him meeting her mother. Well, he wasn't turning tail no matter what. He didn't know what the future held, but he was fairly certain Beth would be part of it.

Irrational as it seemed now, when they'd first met he hadn't noticed or appreciated how beautiful she was. Her beauty wasn't classic, with high cheekbones and perfectly shaped facial features. Hers was subtle and delicate, which helped explain why it took him longer than it should have to notice. He was touched that she clearly made an effort with her hair and makeup for him. It wasn't necessary. All he saw was Beth, and it didn't matter to him if she had on lip gloss or if her hair was combed.

Even the guys in the shop had noticed the change in him. Sam blew them off and shrugged off their good-natured ribbing.

"Going to see your girlfriend tonight?" Bob Unger asked as they started cleaning their stations at the end of their shift on Friday.

"Who says I got a girlfriend?" Sam demanded.

"Hey, Sam, we're your friends. You don't need to hide anything from us."

"Yeah, Sam. I see you sneaking off during lunch and talking on your cell."

"When we gonna meet your girl?"

Grinning, Sam ignored them. He dug his truck keys from his pocket and headed out of the garage. "Have a good weekend."

"You aren't joining us for a beer?" Bob asked, his mouth hanging open in surprise.

Sam had been the one to instigate the Friday-night beer time with the guys. "Can't tonight," he called over his shoulder as he climbed into his truck. He was in a rush to get to Beth.

"Yup, it's a woman. Only time any of us miss a Friday night is when a woman's involved."

Sam didn't answer. No need. His friends had him pegged.

Once back at the house, Sam quickly showered and changed clothes, anxious to get to Beth. This was a big day in her recupera-

tion process and he wanted to be sure the transition to the rehabilitation center had gone smoothly.

As soon as he found her in her room her eyes lit up, followed by
that beautiful smile. That did it to him every time.

"Sam."

"Hey." He stood just inside the door, drinking in the sight of
her. He walked up to the bed and took hold of her hand, marveling
once more how dainty it felt in his much larger one. Hers was soft
and perfectly shaped, delicate against his callused, grease-stained
fingers.

"I'm glad you're here."

"I am, too." And it was the honest-to-God truth. He badly
wanted to kiss her and leaned forward to plant a soft kiss on her
cheek.

For half a second she looked disappointed, and then, in a rush,
she asked, "You have your guitar with you, don't you?" It was as if
she couldn't get the words out fast enough.

He'd kept it with him nearly all week. "It's in my truck."

"Wonderful. Would you mind carrying me into the foyer?" She
lifted her arms, waiting for him to lift her off the bed.

Sam hesitated. "Shouldn't you be using your walker?"

"Probably," she agreed, lowering her arms, "but it would take
me twenty minutes to get from here to the lobby, and by then I'd be
too tired to play."

"Play?"

"The piano. Didn't you see it on your way in? There's a piano
against the wall to the right of the door, and, Sam, I *need* to get to
that piano. I can't tell you how much I've missed playing."

Sam couldn't have disguised his smile if he'd tried.

She raised her arms a second time so Sam would take the hint
and lift her off the bed. Asking him twice wasn't necessary. Other
than holding her hand a few times and that one kiss, he hadn't held
or touched her. Sam was willing to admit these were unusual cir-

cumstances. Never in all his thirty-six years had he spent this much time with a woman and have their relationship be completely innocent. He had to admit he'd given a lot of thought to what it would be like to have her in his bed. Being a healthy male, it was only natural for his mind to wander in that direction.

Lifting her from the bed, he was surprised by how light she was. He'd carted tools heavier than this woman. Her arms automatically went around his neck as he held on to her, bride-style.

She smelled like roses and he had to assume it was her perfume. He resisted the urge to bury his face in her neck and breathe in the scent of her. Having her this close was everything he'd imagined. More. His heart beat at a furious pace when her fingers tangled with the hair at the back of his head. He swallowed a groan when her hands rested against the nape of his neck. This small intimacy was enough to nearly undo him. He wondered if she had any idea what she was doing to him, and he doubted she did.

Now that she was in his arms, Sam didn't move. He remained immobile, standing next to her bed, savoring the simple pleasure of holding her in his arms.

"Am I too heavy?" she asked.

He laughed for the simple reason he found it difficult to speak. When he found his voice, he said, "I'm thinking you need to walk for me after this." He wasn't sure he had the willpower to hold her again and resist kissing her with a need and hunger that would shock her.

He carried her out of the room, down the long corridor, and into the foyer, where the piano sat. In his rush to get to Beth, he hadn't noticed it earlier.

"You want me to walk for you?" she asked, resting her head against his shoulder. This woman. He swore she was going to be the end of him. "I need incentive," she told him, staring at him with a look that immediately roused his suspicions.

"What kind of incentive?"

She pressed her index finger against her lips, as if needing to give his question sufficient consideration. "A reward."

"You got it. Anything you want within reason."

"What I have in mind is reasonable. Do we have a deal?"

He was suspicious but willing to play her game. "Deal." He carefully set her down on the piano bench.

Beth smiled up at him and lovingly placed her hands over the familiar keys as if caressing a lover's face. The piano was an old upright, and all Sam could do was hope it was in tune.

"Did I ever mention I was born with perfect pitch?" she said. "My father's mother taught me to play and she picked up on it right away."

"One of your many gifts, no doubt," he said, loving the joy he saw in her as she began to play.

She must be wondering about the piano the same as him. He'd never known anyone with perfect pitch but understood that if a key was even the slightest bit off it would grate against Beth's ear like nails down a chalkboard. After testing the scales, her fingers bounced, striking chords. Just the way her hands moved showed respect and love for this musical instrument. Beth was in her element and he saw a side of her he'd never known before.

When she finished she looked at Sam. "Would you get your guitar?"

"If that's what you want."

Nodding eagerly, she said, "Please."

After making sure Beth was settled, Sam left through the double glass doors, walking swiftly toward the parking lot. He'd meant to bring his guitar into the facility when he'd first arrived. His only excuse was that he'd been in too much of a hurry to get to Beth.

Sam returned to hear her playing a tune he didn't recognize. He froze as her hands were a blur over the keyboard. When she noticed he was back, Beth's smile was huge.

"Oh, how I've missed this," she said with the softest of sighs. It was the same sound Sam made when he stepped into a hot shower after a long day of physical labor. "Do you realize how long it's been since I played?" she asked, although it was a rhetorical question. Her fingers literally flew over the keys with a skill and knowledge that left him speechless.

"What's that song?" he asked, scooting out a chair and sitting next to her.

"It's an *Étude* by Fredrick Chopin."

Sam had watched many people play a piano, but never had anyone done it with such feeling and joy as Beth. His mouth must have been gaping open, because Beth gave him an odd look.

"What?" she asked.

He scratched the side of his head. "Wow. That was incredible."

"It's a lovely piece; one of my favorites."

Sam was in awe. "It sounded like a bubbling brook flowing over a waterfall. I don't think I've ever heard anything like it. I've certainly never seen anyone play like that before."

"It was going through my head earlier today and I wanted to play it in the worst way."

"It got my attention."

Sam pulled a chair up closer. He placed the guitar on his lap and leaned forward, waiting for her to play more.

"Your turn," she said.

"Ah. No way." Sam shook his head.

"Sam, please. You and that guitar are the only things that got me through this last week."

When she put it like that, how could he refuse? "Will you play with me?" he asked.

She agreed with an eager nod.

Sam righted his guitar and reached for his pick. "You know any Johnny Cash?"

"No, but I'll pick it up."

Sam strummed a few chords, studying her while he played.

"It sounds familiar but I can't name it."

" 'I Walk the Line,' " Sam supplied.

It didn't take Beth long to pick up the melody and the rhythm. The piano quickly joined the guitar, the two instruments blending together as if they were one piece.

After a few minutes Beth glanced at him. "We sound good together."

"We do," he agreed, his smile so big his face ached. "Really good."

Sam started another song, and again all Beth needed were a few bars before she was able to join in. He was convinced she'd never heard this Macklemore number, but it didn't matter. After two or three such songs, he noticed a small group of staff members had gathered to watch and listen.

They must have played for forty minutes or more before Sam could see that Beth was tiring out. "That's enough for tonight," he said, and immediately sensed her disappointment.

"Just a few more songs. I'm loving this."

The thing was Sam loved it, too. It would have been easy to give in, the temptation was there, but in the end he shook his head. "We'll do it again. You're going to be here awhile." It'd been a big day for her, and Beth was exhausted. Sam wondered if she'd done too much.

"You two been playing together for long?" one of the aides asked, stepping closer to the piano.

"Not long," Sam answered, sharing a smile with Beth.

"Well, you're amazing, both of you." She started to leave, then turned back and asked, "Do you want me to get you a wheelchair, Beth?"

"No," Beth insisted, smiling up at Sam.

He knew what she wanted. What he wanted. He carefully lifted Beth into his embrace the same way he had earlier. Again her arms went around him, her fingers smoothing the hair that fell at his neck. She laid her head against his shoulder. He loved the warm feel of her so close to him.

"Back to the room?" Sam asked, and, unable to resist, he kissed the top of her head.

"Back to the room," Beth echoed.

He felt her staring at him as he carted her down the wide hallway. It was as if she were memorizing his features. Briefly she ran her fingertips over his beard.

"Something wrong?" he asked.

"Nope. I was just thinking that you look more like a lumberjack than a mechanic, especially with your beard."

"Does it bother you?"

She shook her head. "Not at all. I like it. You keep it trimmed and neat." She wove her fingers into the coarse hair and rubbed her palm down one side. "I've never kissed anyone with a beard before. I had no idea it would be so good," she said, and immediately looked away as if she hadn't meant to say the words aloud.

"Did it tickle your nose?" he asked.

"A little. It's not as prickly as I thought it would be."

Sam didn't say anything when her fingers explored his beard until they were in her room.

"You like?" he asked.

"Very much," she said and grinned, before tearing her gaze away from him and pointing toward the other side of the room. "Get me my walker, okay?"

"Not tonight, babe, you're tired."

"We had a deal," she hurried to remind him.

Still, Sam hesitated. "I don't want you to wear yourself out."

"I won't."

He wasn't convinced.

"A deal is a deal. Now, how far do I need to walk before I get my reward? Don't make it too easy for me, either."

"Beth, no."

"Please."

Sam doubted he could refuse this woman anything.

"I want to show you what I can do."

Frowning, Sam glanced down the long corridor. "To the nurses' station and back." It was only a few feet away. He didn't want her collapsing.

"I can walk farther than that."

"Do you want your reward or not?" he asked.

"Okay, okay," she said with a laugh.

Sam helped her to her feet and noticed how she held the walker in a death grip. This was a bad idea and he regretted agreeing to it almost immediately.

Beth's first few steps looked unsteady and were little more than a shuffling of her feet. On edge, Sam remained close to her side, at the ready in case her legs gave out or she needed assistance.

Her progress was slow and methodical. Each step was a determined effort.

"You're doing great," Sam told her.

She bit into her lower lip. "If you knew what I wanted for my reward you might want me to crash and burn."

"Not happening, babe," he promised. "This is far enough. Turn around."

She paused and looked up at him. "Have I mentioned how much I like it when you call me that?"

"Babe?"

"Yeah."

She hit him with another of her megawatt smiles and Sam was forced to look away before he did something they would both regret. "Time to head back to your room."

Her legs looked like they were about to give out on her by the time she made it past the nurses' station.

"Hi," one of the nurses' aides called out to him. "You can come play your guitar for me anytime you want."

Sam ignored her as if she hadn't spoken.

Beth faltered slightly and Sam's arm automatically went around her waist. "You look beat," he said.

She nodded. Sam glared at the aide, a pretty blonde who was about his own age. He didn't appreciate that she was blatantly flirting with him, especially in front of Beth. She didn't need that.

Although the distance wasn't far, by the time Beth returned to her room, she was barely able to shuffle her feet. Sam was convinced she was close to collapsing and gripped hold of her waist. A gasp of relief escaped her as she sagged against him. Right away Sam lifted her into his arms and gently placed her on her bed.

Beth fell back against the pillows and released a deep sigh, briefly closing her eyes.

"You okay?" he asked.

She nodded rather than responding verbally. He noticed that the muscles in her thighs and calves quivered with the strenuous effort.

"You should have listened to me when I told you to stop," he chided, doing his best to hide how strongly seeing her in pain affected him.

"It will be worth it. Give me a few minutes and I'll be ready for my reward."

At this point he was willing to get her just about anything. "All right, what's your desire, Your Highness."

She stared at him, her eyes warm pools of longing. "What I want more than anything is for you to kiss me again." She sounded breathless and her eyes locked onto his.

"A kiss?" Sam repeated, unable to suppress his delight. "I think I can manage that; I just don't know that I'll be able to stop with just one."

Tired as she was, Beth laughed. "I was hoping you'd say that."

CHAPTER 12

Beth

Beth had spent most of the day thinking about the kiss she'd shared with Sam the night before. He'd claimed it'd been wonderful. That was for sure, and it fed her eagerness for more. She'd dreamed about him kissing her and was disappointed that it took him nearly a week. She understood his restraint. She was pathetic being in the hospital, hooked up to IVs and tubes. It seemed wrong for their first kiss to take place in such a clinical, antiseptic environment. The rehab center wasn't much better, but she was past caring.

As soon as she mentioned she wanted him to kiss her again Sam's gaze dropped to her mouth and lingered there. His eyes rounded and his beautiful mouth curved upward in a gentle smile. Oh yes, this was what she'd been waiting for, the look in his eyes that said more than an entire library of books. He wanted this, too, and was as impatient as she was.

Leaning forward, Sam slipped his hand around the back of her neck and eased her forward, his hold firm, determined. When he pressed his lips to hers, Beth released a sigh that felt as if it came straight from her center. She'd waited all day for this moment, and she wasn't going to rush through it now.

His mouth was soft, gentle against hers, moist and warm. She'd been so enraptured by his first kiss that she'd barely paid attention to his beard. It tickled her now and she smiled slightly at the feel of it against the tender skin of her face. This was good. So good, and she was determined to hold on to every detail, cataloging them in her mind, wanting to put them to memory.

When Sam opened his mouth slightly, she followed his lead, and then it was Sam who groaned. She wasn't sure how long they continued to kiss. It seemed all too brief, not nearly long enough to satisfy her or keep her from wanting more. With his mouth over hers, the tip of his tongue outlined her lips in a slow, sensual perusal. It was all Beth could manage not to melt in his arms.

When Sam eased away, she made a moaning protest and buried her face in his chest while she gathered her wits, which had completely deserted her. All she could think was *Wow*. She was convinced that until Sam had kissed her she'd never really been kissed before. She didn't want him to stop, but he had pulled back and his breathing seemed harsh and labored.

"I should go," he said, gently releasing her. "You're exhausted."

Beth wanted to protest and stopped herself. He was right. Her day had been full and she was bone weary. She slowly lay back down so that her head was against the pillows. "Thank you," she said, shocked at how low her voice was. "For everything." She longed to tell him how much his kisses had meant to her but was unable to find the words. She had no idea kissing could be that wonderful or feel that good.

Sam hesitated, then took her hand and raised it to his lips, kissing her fingertips as though he had a difficult time leaving her. "I'll be by tomorrow afternoon."

"Sure."

"I'd come sooner but I've got sh— stuff I need to take care of."

"Of course. Sam, please, I don't want you to feel obligated to visit every day." It was important he understand it wasn't his duty to keep her entertained. Her stomach tightened at the thought that he'd felt seeing her was some unwritten requirement because he'd been at the scene of the accident.

He kissed the back of her hand. "Truth is, Beth, I don't think I could stay away."

It was his parting words that stayed in her mind the rest of the night. Sleep didn't come easy. Every time Beth closed her eyes, she could almost feel Sam's kiss against her lips. All that feeling and the emotion that went along with it overwhelmed her. She wondered how long it would be before he kissed her again, and she prayed it would be soon.

Sunshine arrived midmorning.

"How's it going, Sweet Pea? You digging your new digs?"

Beth smiled. "I've already been up and walked the hallway twice."

"Great. No PT today?"

"Later. It's a lighter load on the weekends."

"Cool." Her aunt scooted the chair closer to the bed. "Have you heard from your mother?"

Frowning, Beth sighed. "Yes, briefly. The conversation went okay. She arrives on Monday." Despite Sam's assurances, she couldn't help worrying what would happen when her mother met him. Already she could hear her mother's objection to Beth dating a man like Sam. Even knowing a confrontation was sure to follow, she refused to hide their relationship, refused to make apologies for him when none were needed. Nothing her mother said was going to influence the way Beth felt about him. All she could hope was that Sam's feelings for her were equally strong and that he not be influenced by her mother.

"It's going to be fine," Sunshine told her, gently squeezing her arm.

"You'll be here, right?" she pleaded.

Her aunt's silence was answer enough. "I promised your mother I'd give the two of you alone time."

Beth struggled to sit up straighter. "Sunshine. No, please, you can't do this to me. I need you."

"Baby girl, you're stronger than you realize. How long is your mother intending to stay?"

"Two days."

Her aunt looked relieved. "That's no time at all. It'll go by so fast you'll hardly know Ellie was in town."

"You're joking, right? My mother will find a way of making sure the entire facility knows she's arrived. She'll make more of a production than Hannibal crossing the Alps." Beth could envision it now. Her mother was sure to make a huge scene worthy of an Academy Award. She dreaded Sam viewing any part of that.

"I have a feeling you're more worried about what will happen with Sam than you are about seeing your mother."

Beth didn't deny it.

Her aunt's gaze softened. "You like Sam, don't you?"

It would be useless to lie. "Yes . . . so much. We had such a good time last night, making music together. He says he plays the guitar for his own pleasure, but you know what? He's talented. I could have played with him all night, but I didn't have the stamina. Sam enjoyed it, too."

"That's great. Don't you worry, Sweet Pea, I might not know Sam all that well, but my guess is he won't be scared off by your mother. If he is, then he isn't worth fretting over."

"But he has no idea what she's like," Beth argued. "We've only known each other a short while and—"

Her aunt stopped her. "Trust me, you have nothing to worry about," Sunshine insisted. "You've completely unbalanced that poor man. He's nuts over you."

Beth wasn't convinced. "I hope you're right."

"I am. Now relax."

Beth did worry, though; she couldn't help herself. She stewed and fretted and mulled over every negative scenario of what could happen once her mother met Sam. And then Ellie Prudhomme arrived. Predictably, once she saw the extent of Beth's injuries, she burst into tears loud enough to echo through the entire facility. "Oh Beth," she wailed. "I had no idea."

By now the majority of Beth's bruises had yellowed and the cuts on her face had mostly healed. Sitting at Beth's bedside, Ellie dabbed at her eyes with a tissue, all the while demanding to know why Beth hadn't let her know how serious the accident was.

"Mom, please," Beth cried. "You want to know why? This is why." She gestured toward her mother. "You're making a scene. It isn't like I'm on my deathbed. I'm doing just fine."

"You could have died."

"But I didn't."

"I should never have agreed to let you move away." Her mother paused to daintily blow her nose. "I knew from the beginning that it was a mistake and I was right. But your father wouldn't listen to me and now look what's happened. I absolutely insist that you return home with me. It's where you belong; I'm making the arrangements myself. I'll—"

"No, you're not," Beth said, cutting her mother off. This was exactly what she'd feared most. She was stronger now, though, and she wasn't about to give in to her mother's demands. "I am not leaving Portland."

At the ferocity in Beth's voice her mother's eyes narrowed with surprise. "This is Sunshine's doing, isn't it? Don't bother to lie to me. She's the one who put you up to this."

"You seem to think Sunshine has this powerful pull on me and you couldn't be more wrong. She has done nothing but encourage and support my decision, which is something my own mother hasn't done."

Her mother bit into her lip and blinked back tears. "I can't believe you'd talk to me like this, Beth. Everything I do for you is rooted in love."

"I know that, Mom, but I'm not a teenager. I'm an adult, and right or wrong, I need to make my own decisions and live my own life. You can plead and insist all you want, but I'm not changing my mind. I signed a teaching contract. I fully intend to keep my job and, God willing, accept another for next year if it's offered."

Her words were met with stunned silence.

It took Beth a few minutes to realize why. Sam stood in the doorway to her room, his gaze focused intently on her. Knowing her mother was due to arrive, he'd cleaned up, and wore fresh jeans and a button-down shirt. He looked great and Beth welcomed him with a warm smile, grateful he'd arrived when he did. The conversation with her mother was about to get heated.

"Mom, I'd like you to meet my friend Sam Carney."

Sam came into the room and extended his hand. "I'm pleased to meet you, Mrs. Prudhomme."

Her mother continued to stare at Sam, which seemed to be the only response she was capable of making. It took her an awkward moment to realize he held out his hand, but thankfully, manners insisted that she respond.

Ellie looked at her daughter. "Sam is your . . . friend?"

"He's much more than that," she said, not breaking eye contact with Sam.

He walked around to the other side of the bed and stood next to her.

"Sam was at the scene of the accident," Beth explained. "If not for him, I think I actually might have died. We both owe him a great deal."

"Thank you," her mother said, although it sounded a tad begrudging.

Beth held her hand out to him, interlacing their fingers.

Her mother cleared her throat. "So the two of you are . . . involved romantically?"

Sam tore his gaze away from Beth long enough to answer. "Not quite yet."

"Sam," Beth protested. "Yes, Mother, we're involved romantically." She refused to let him downplay their relationship in order to soothe her mother's ruffled feathers.

"I see," Ellie said, slowly giving the word strong emphasis. "So Sam is the real reason you refuse to return to Chicago."

"One of the reasons," Beth admitted. "An important one."

Her mother forced her gaze squarely on Sam. A lesser man would have folded at the intensity of it. "What do you do for a living, Sam?"

"He's a mechanic," Beth replied between gritted teeth.

"Babe, I can answer for myself," Sam said. "I work for Bruce Olsen GM dealership as a mechanic. I'm the head of the department."

Her mother straightened. "A mechanic, you say." She made it sound like he picked up trash on the side of the road for a living.

"Mom," Beth protested softly.

"Did you attend college?"

"Mother, please." Her voice was stronger the second time.

"A couple years at a community college and I decided I was better cut out for trade school."

Her mother took a moment to soak in the information and was about to ask another question when Sam spoke.

"Before you say anything more or ask any other questions,

there's something you should know. I care about your daughter a great deal, Mrs. Prudhomme. I'm sorry if you disapprove of me, but that isn't going to change the way I feel about Beth."

"Nor is it going to change the way I feel about Sam," Beth said, in order to make sure her mother knew where she stood.

"I'm beginning to get the picture here," her mother said slowly, thoughtfully.

"I hope you do, Mom."

Ellie nodded and sighed as her shoulders sagged forward. "I was afraid something like this would happen."

"Something like what?" Beth challenged.

Her mother shook her head. "Never mind."

And that was exactly what Beth intended to do.

CHAPTER 13

Sam

Early on, Rocco had warned Sam to treat Beth with care. It took kissing her and meeting her mother to convince him that he might well be in over his head with this woman. He'd met her mother only the one time, and frankly that was enough to last him a lifetime. He loved the fierce way Beth stood up to the woman, defending him at every turn. She made sure Ellie Prudhomme knew she wasn't backing down in any way, shape, or form when it came to living her own life. Sam couldn't have been more proud of her.

As the days progressed, Sam discovered he wanted to kiss her more than he wanted to breathe. Every time she was in his arms and his lips were on hers was better than the time before, better than he could have ever imagined. His feelings for her intensified each day until she was all he thought about. He'd heard about besotted men who walked around with their heads in the clouds. He remembered Rocco acting that way when he'd first met Nichole.

He never thought it would happen to him, and yet here he was, every bit as dopey as his friend had been.

Sam remembered a half-drunk Rocco telling him about Nichole. It wasn't a good time in their relationship. It looked like the two of them were about to split and in fact might have. Rocco had been drowning his sorrows in beer and started mumbling under his breath. Sam had the feeling his friend had forgotten he was even there. Rocco muttered something about kissing Nichole and feeling the earth move like a friggin earthquake. At the time, Sam had grinned, amused. That sounded like lyrics to a Carole King song. He wasn't smiling now. That was exactly how he felt when he kissed Beth. There'd been a quake, all right. One that registered high on the Richter scale. It felt like the floor beneath his feet had started to heave and buckle and all they'd done was kiss. He couldn't begin to imagine what would happen if things had gone any further.

Nichole was right to be concerned. She might have introduced Beth to him, but apparently, now she had doubts, and frankly, Sam didn't blame her. Getting emotionally involved with him wasn't the best option for Beth. She was refinement and innocence, educated and smart. He was none of that.

And yet . . . Sam found he was addicted to her the way a heroin addict needed a fix. He couldn't go twenty-four hours without seeing her. At the end of the workday, he rushed out of the garage and was home only long enough to shower and change clothes. The one exception was his poker night, and even then Sam was eager to leave as soon as he could, needing his Beth fix.

Thankfully, Beth's recovery was coming along nicely. Walking remained difficult for her. Within a short amount of time she'd advanced from the walker to a cane. They often ate dinner together, and then it was off to the piano. He loved their jam sessions. Sam could easily play for hours with Beth. It'd gotten so the staff and half the residents of the rehab center came to listen in.

She chatted with the crowd and took requests. If he didn't know the tune, like Beth, he was able to pick it up easily enough. Several times a few brave souls would sing along. Beth's talent moved him and she'd managed to convince him that he wasn't half bad. They entertained the facility for a couple hours every night and would have played longer if Beth had more stamina.

She was regaining her strength little by little. He could see an improvement even if she couldn't. He understood her frustration and knew she was eager to get back to teaching and her life. The thought worried him some. Once she was released, their relation- ship was sure to shift. It was inevitable. He just didn't know how or what it would mean.

He wasn't sure what it would look like once she was back to the schedule she'd kept before the accident. Their nightly jam sessions were sure to end. It did no good to worry about it now, although Sam had a fatalistic attitude. He had to be willing to let her go, and while it would gut him, it would probably be for the best. Sam, however, refused to let his thoughts wander down that unwelcome path.

Saturday morning, three weeks after the accident, Rocco needed Sam's help getting a new dryer installed onto the small back porch that served as their laundry room. As always, Sam was happy to lend a hand. It'd been a week or longer since Sam had connected with Rocco and Nichole. As soon as they were finished, he'd head off to the rehab center to see Beth. It never felt right to be away from her for long periods of time. When he left her, his thoughts would automatically calculate how long it would be before he could see her again.

Getting the dryer through the narrow doorway was going to be tight. There were only a couple inches of room, and Sam had al- ready bitten off a few swear words as the two men struggled to get the dryer on the porch. As they lifted the appliance up the steps and eased it through the opening, Owen was at the ready, his money jar in hand. Sam scraped the back of his hand as they moved the dryer through the narrow doorway, lifting away several layers of skin. He swallowed a cuss word, thinking that later he'd let Beth kiss it and make it better. He was sure to get a healthy dose of sympathy from her. Thinking about her sweet lips kissing his hand produced a smile. He might be able to convince her his lips ached, too. At that thought he chuckled.

"What's so funny?" Rocco groaned, bent over, as they lifted the heavy machine.

Sam hit his hand again and this time it really hurt. "Son of a . . ." He bit off the last word and could almost feel Owen's disappointment.

Once they manipulated the dryer through the door, Rocco and Sam stepped back and exhaled. Thankfully, it took only a few minutes to hook it up.

Disappointed, Owen returned to the house to deposit the money jar in his room. When his stepson was out of earshot, Rocco said, "Got a bit of news about Nichole's ex."

"What's going on?" Sam had never met the other man, but over the years he'd heard plenty. Before Nichole and Rocco were married, Jake had basically blackmailed Nichole into breaking up with Rocco, threatening to take her to court for custody of their son if she continued the relationship.

"He's going through his second divorce. Wife number two caught him cheating. Seems he didn't learn his lesson with Nichole."

"Doesn't look like he can keep his zipper closed," Sam muttered. Jake had been a lucky man with Nichole and blew it. Some guys never learn. Although Rocco didn't mention it, Jake wasn't much of a father figure, either. The parenting plan called for him to have Owen every other weekend, but the majority of the time Jake was busy. Owen saw his father once a month if that. To the best of his knowledge, Jake hadn't attended a single one of Owen's T-ball games. Rocco was more of a father to the six-year-old than Jake would ever be.

"It hurts Nichole that Jake is mostly absent for Owen."

Sam knew what he was saying. "That choice is his." But Nichole wasn't the only one who felt bad for Owen. Rocco did, too, and worked hard to be a positive role model and stepfather to the boy.

"It's a good thing Owen's got Leanne and Nicolai."

Sam knew that the older couple spent a lot of time with Owen and with the baby as well, showering the newborn with love and attention.

The door off the kitchen opened and Nichole appeared, wearing one of the apparatuses that carried the baby in the front, pressed against her chest. Matthew was sound asleep, his head resting against his mother's breast. Sam reached out and cupped the baby's small head. He enjoyed seeing Rocco with a young family, and his heart ached for all the might-have-beens in his own life.

"Lunch is ready," she said.

Both men moved into the house, where Nichole had set the table.

"How's Beth?" Nichole asked as she set a tray of sandwiches in the center of the table.

"Improving a little more every day." Sam was proud of the progress she'd made. He didn't try to hide his smile, which came to him whenever someone mentioned Beth's name. Sam noticed Rocco watching him and frowning.

"What?" Sam demanded.

"You falling for her?" Rocco asked.

"Maybe." This wasn't a discussion he wanted to have, especially now in front of Nichole. He turned his attention to the plate of sandwiches and said to Nichole, "Beth mentioned you were by recently."

"Yeah. Shawntelle and I came for a visit the other day. Now that she has a piano close at hand she's resumed teaching piano lessons. A couple of her students were there at the same time. Kids from the high school have stopped by, too. Beth has improved a lot since the last time I was up to see her."

Sam knew Shawntelle was Rocco's bookkeeper and a good friend to Nichole.

"We arrived when she was arguing with the physical therapist about getting in the pool."

Sam snapped to attention. He didn't know anything about this. "What'd you say?"

"Beth didn't want to get in the pool even though the physical therapist said it would help her."

"Why not?" he demanded. He'd kept close tabs on her treatment and was surprised she hadn't mentioned anything about water exercises.

"I don't know why she refused," Nichole admitted. "You'll need to ask her."

"I will." He would definitely find out what was holding her back.

Rocco frowned. "What's the deal? Is she afraid of the water?"

"I don't know," Nichole said. "Shawntelle and I only heard the end of the conversation. I don't think we were supposed to hear what we did. All I can tell you is that the therapists said it would help her, but Beth refused."

This didn't make sense. Beth was one of the bravest women Sam had ever met. He couldn't imagine her backing down from anything.

Owen appeared and sat at the table. "Mom baked brownies this morning and she let me help."

"You want to be a chef when you grow up?" Sam asked.

"I do if I can bake brownies."

Grinning, Rocco walked over to the refrigerator. "You want a beer or a soda?"

"Soda." Sam pulled out a chair and sat down next to Owen. Nichole had set out plates along with a big bowl of potato chips and sliced apples.

Sam reached for a ham-and-cheese sandwich and studied it as if analyzing its contents. Finally, curiosity got the better of him. "Don't suppose Beth mentioned me?"

Nichole laughed. "Your name was every other word. It was Sam this and Sam that. Listening to her, one would think you walk on water."

Holding back a smile would have been impossible.

"She said the two of you have been entertaining the patients and staff every night with your music."

Rocco reached for a sandwich. "You two are playing together?"

"Yeah." He could see that his friend was amused but unsure why.

"What's so funny?" Sam asked Rocco.

His buddy shrugged. "Nothing. I just never thought I'd see the day."

"See what?"

"You," Rocco said, lifting the bowl of chips and emptying a large portion onto his plate.

"What about me?" Sam had a feeling he should let this go, but he couldn't make himself do it.

"You," Rocco repeated, "hung up on a girl."

"I'm not hung up on Beth." He was. He so was, and he had no clue why he would deny it.

"Would you two stop," Nichole interceded. "You're beginning to sound like kids on the playground."

Sam was happy to drop the subject. This thing with Beth was new and he had yet to fully take in what it was exactly, that they had other than a shared love of music and a connection he would be hard pressed to explain to anyone, even himself. And of course her addictive kisses.

Hearing that she didn't want to get into the pool for her physical therapy puzzled him, and he was anxious to talk to her about it. As soon as he finished with his sandwich, he made his excuses.

"I best head out," Sam said, scooting back his chair.

"You didn't eat a brownie," Owen announced, as if Sam had decided against sampling nectar from the gods.

"Next time, kiddo." Sam ruffled the top of the boy's head, raised his chin at Rocco, and hugged Nichole. "See you."

"Thanks for the help," Rocco called after him.

"Anytime," Sam returned as he headed out the door. He didn't hesitate and drove directly to the rehab facility.

When he found her bed empty, he did a search of the hallways, knowing she was probably walking the corridor. She used every excuse to stay out of bed, walking until the pain was too much for her or she grew weak.

It didn't take him long to find her. Watching Beth walk, he was once again amazed at the progress she'd made in such a short amount of time. Seeing her without her being aware, Sam felt a tug against his heart. She made him proud, knowing every step brought her pain. Sheer resolve was what drove her. Her concentration was keen as she purposefully moved one foot in front of the other. Several times he saw her grimace, and it was all he could do to keep from rushing forward, lifting her in his arms, and carting her back to her room. If it were possible, he would gladly take on that discomfort himself rather than see her suffer.

Sam never expected such strong feelings for another woman. The depth of his attraction stunned him. It was like his heart reached out to her, willing her health and happiness, even if that meant it wasn't with him.

No, that wasn't true.

Just thinking about Beth with another man and his jaw tightened. He'd be lying to himself if he said he didn't want her with him. That on its own was a surprise, seeing how he felt when they first met. Beth, sweet and proper; him being his irreverent self. It'd taken the accident for him to discover how much they had in common.

As if sensing his presence, Beth glanced up. Immediately her face broke into a smile, her eyes widening with inexplicable joy.

"Sam. When did you get here?"

"Just a few moments ago."

She started toward him, nearly stumbling in her rush to reach his side.

Sam lunged forward, wrapping his arms around her before she had a chance to lose her balance. "Hey there, one step at a time."

"I'm glad you're here."

"Me, too." He hugged her and kissed the top of her head. He wanted to really kiss her, the way he normally did when they were together. Prying eyes prevented him from doing something he knew would embarrass her.

"You got the dryer moved for Rocco and Nichole?"

"We did. Nichole dutifully fed me lunch and now I'm here." He released her and she apparently noticed his injured hand.

Her eyes lit up with alarm. "You hurt yourself."

"It's nothing," he said, dismissing her concern, loving that she'd noticed.

Frowning, she tenderly rubbed her thumb over the back of his hand. "It looks painful."

"It isn't, but if you want to kiss it and make it better . . . just saying."

She laughed as he knew she would and pressed her lips over the small injury.

"Better?"

The question fell gently from her lips. He loved hearing the tenderness in her voice. "Much." Although it wasn't necessary, he kept his arm tucked around her waist and kept her as close to him as possible.

He waited for a few moments, letting her set the pace as they walked, then asked, making the question as casual as he could, "What's this I hear about you refusing to do water therapy?"

"Who told you that?" Her voice held more than a hint of defensiveness, the subtle change in her obvious.

"Does it matter?"

"Yes . . . no, I guess not. It's no big deal. I'd rather not do it is all."

"Why not?"

She shrugged. "I like the beach and everything, but I'm not a good swimmer and—"

"It'll help, babe."

"Sam, please, I've listened to all the arguments. No one is more eager to get back to my life than me. I'm not convinced it will do much good, and I don't want to put myself through the anxiety of getting into the water. It's not a big deal."

He went still, preparing an argument.

Beth interrupted his thoughts by punching him playfully on his forearm. "Stop calling me babe."

He frowned, taken aback by her request. "I thought you liked it."

"Generally I do, especially when you say it in that sexy tone of voice. One look into your eyes and I'm ready to dive into the deep end of the pool."

"Good, that's what I want to hear."

"But not when it sounds like you're disappointed in me. Then it sounds like a chastisement."

"You're afraid?" He suspected that was the case.

Her beautiful eyes looked up at him. "I'm not much of a water person and—"

"Would it help if I got in the pool with you?"

Her eyes widened, as if she wasn't sure she'd heard him correctly. "You'd do that?"

"If it would help you, of course."

She appeared stunned. "I . . . I don't know."

"If you're worried about getting in, I'll lift you so you won't have to climb down the steps."

"It isn't that."

"Then what's the problem?"

"It shouldn't be a big deal—"

"Something happened, didn't it?"

She sighed and after a moment nodded. "I was eight and the son of a family friend held my head underwater. He was older and he thought it was funny. I thought I was going to drown. I've been uncomfortable in water ever since. It's silly, I know."

"It isn't silly." Sam didn't know the name of the boy who'd frightened her, but if he ever met the jerk he was determined to make him pay for terrorizing Beth.

"It's time I got over this, isn't it?"

"You can do this, Beth."

"You'll come in with me the first time?"

"Said I would, didn't I? I'll come more than once if you need me to."

She looked at Sam with such adoration that he thought his heart would quit beating. What she didn't know was that he'd be willing to walk over hot coals if she asked it of him. Hot coals, sharp knives, anything. She was that important to him.

Yup, he was in big trouble.

CHAPTER 14

Beth

Beth was convinced it was a mistake to let Sam talk her into getting into the pool for her physical therapy. This phobia of being in the water was completely irrational. It wasn't like someone would leap into the pool, grab her, and hold her head underwater. She wasn't a kid any longer.

As a young girl Beth had been terrified of drowning. The ocean didn't bother her nearly as much as an enclosed swimming pool, even though a pool with lifeguards and people around was actually much safer than the potential for disaster in a vast ocean. Still, little soothed Beth more than spending time on the beach. She'd gone several times as a youth with Sunshine to Seaside, Oregon, and had loved every minute. Their time at the seashore held some of her favorite childhood memories. But an enclosed pool terrified her.

Monday morning, Beth hoped Sam would forget all about his promise. It meant him taking half a day off work. That was a lot to ask even if he had volunteered. She'd tried to talk him out of it, claiming it wasn't necessary, but Sam had insisted. She hated that he would need to be away from the garage because she was afraid of the pool. It embarrassed her to be weak. Repeatedly Sam had assured her it was nothing. She knew otherwise.

Beth kept a close eye on the clock, dreading the physical therapy. When Sam hadn't shown up by the time the therapist arrived, she felt a certain relief. And an equal measure of dread. Unfortunately, the pool time had been set. As much as she would have liked to get out of this, there was no backing out now.

"It's going to be fine," Cassandra, the therapist, assured her. "We'll go nice and slow. If you get uncomfortable, let me know and we'll make other arrangements."

"You promise?"

"Of course, but I know you're going to be just fine."

Beth didn't find her confidence reassuring, especially since Sam seemed to have been delayed.

Which surprised her. Usually Sam was punctual; being late was unlike him. A hundred excuses ran through her mind. He might have gotten unexpectedly called in to work or he'd gotten delayed in traffic. Perhaps he'd changed his mind and decided it was time for her to put on her big girl pants and face her fears. None of that added up, though. If he'd been delayed or something unexpected had come up he would have sent a text. Now she had two concerns on her mind. The pool and Sam.

Cassandra glanced at her watch. "I'm afraid we can't wait for your friend any longer."

Beth swallowed against the tightness in her throat and squared her shoulders, determined to make the best of it. "Okay. Let's do this."

By the time they got into the pool area, her heart was palpitating at an alarming rate. The pool was booked for the hour and

Beth did her best to delay as long as possible, taking off her robe, pulling back her hair.

Unable to put it off any longer, Beth let Cassandra help her into the water. Although it was a welcome eighty-three degrees, the shock of it caused Beth to gasp. She stood on her tiptoes and hugged her arms close to her sides.

"You'll warm up soon enough," the therapist assured her.

Beth offered her a weak smile, struggling not to hyperventilate from the cold and the ever-present fear of actually being in a pool.

"How are you doing?" Cassandra asked.

Unable to answer verbally, Beth nodded, certain all the blood had drained from her face. Thankfully, Cassandra had a tight grip on her hands, steadying her.

"We'll be finished before you know it."

"Good."

The door to the pool opened and Sam came inside. Beth's grip on the therapist's hands instantly loosened.

"Sam." She didn't bother to hide how happy she was to see him. She was about to say more when she noticed the somber look about him.

"Sorry I'm late." He looked decidedly uneasy and his gaze just managed to avoid meeting hers. Something had happened, and while she wanted to ask him what, it wasn't a conversation she wanted to have in front of her therapist.

After a moment, he looked her way and offered her a weak smile. That was all she needed to relax. Having Sam with her was enough to soothe her fragile nerves. Her fear didn't completely vanish, but with him in the room, it became manageable.

While they waited, he quickly divested himself of his jeans. He had on his swim trunks. Beth noticed his long legs and the dark hair that covered them. He started toward the steps leading into the water when Cassandra stopped him.

"You'll need to remove your shirt."

Sam hesitated. "I can't keep it on?"

"No. Street clothes aren't allowed to be worn in the pool."

After several uncomfortable moments, Sam grabbed the T-shirt at the back of his neck and jerked it off, tossing it carelessly aside. He was in the water in quick order, almost as if he couldn't get in fast enough.

Beth didn't understand. His naked torso instantly captured her attention. He had washboard abs and was a fine specimen of manhood. There wasn't a spare ounce of fat on him. Certainly there was no reason for him to be self-conscious about his body. Then she noticed the tattoo over his heart.

Lucinda.

He had a woman's name tattooed there in a flowing French script with curves and swirls that were artistic. As she repeated the name in her mind, it sounded almost poetic.

They hadn't discussed his past loves. The subject had never come up in casual conversation. It was clear, however, that Lucinda was someone special to Sam. This helped explain why he was late and why he'd wanted to wear the T-shirt into the water. He hadn't wanted Beth to see the tattoo or to know about this woman.

She didn't understand what the problem was. It was understood that he had been involved in other relationships. Perhaps not recently, but in the past. And really, why should it matter? But apparently it did to Sam.

Beth remembered when Nichole first mentioned her meeting Sam. Her friend told her it had been awhile since he'd been involved with anyone. At the time, Beth hadn't given it a second thought, and really, why should she? That night at the dinner, Beth never expected they would have any kind of relationship.

On the positive side, seeing the other woman's name etched on Sam's chest like a banner helped distract her from her fears as she went through the therapy exercises. With Sam next to her in the water, it helped quiet her fears. He ignored the question in her eyes.

Cassandra started to run Beth through a series of movements, but with Sam at her side, it was becoming a major distraction.

"Pay attention, babe."

"I'm trying," she muttered under her breath. Her head was buzzing. First off, looking at Sam and his muscular body filled her with longing. She wanted nothing more than to run her hands up his bare chest. It was more than his body that kept her preoccupied. Seeing another woman's name tattooed over his heart filled her head with questions.

"Beth," Cassandra said, causing her to jerk away from Sam's hold.

As if guessing he was causing a problem, Sam moved behind Beth and placed his hands on her waist in order to help her maintain her balance. If he thought he was helping, he wasn't. Having him stand this close, his breath fanning the back of her neck, caused an eruption of goosebumps.

Sam noticed. "Is the water too cold?" he whispered close to her ear.

Doing her best to concentrate on the exercises, Beth madly shook her head. "No . . . it's fine," she said, not wanting him to know what he did to her.

"You're doing good, babe," he said, talking under Cassandra as she counted out the numbers of repetitive movements as Beth exercised the muscles that would aid coordination and speed up the healing process.

As best she could, Beth did what was asked of her, but her focus was on Sam instead of the exercise routine. Try as she might to pay attention to Cassandra, Beth couldn't help being aware of Sam's close proximity. When her foot slipped and she started to go under, Beth gasped, fear paralyzing her. Before a scream could escape, Sam's arms were around her, holding her upright.

"No fear, babe, I've got you." His arms held her tight around her middle, pulling her against his torso. Beth closed her eyes, savoring the feel of his warm skin rubbing against her own. She felt dizzy and disoriented and it had nothing to do with nearly having her head go under the water. It was all Sam.

"Beth." Cassandra joined her. "You okay? Are you having a panic attack?"

"Sorry . . . no, I'm fine. I slipped . . ."

Sam's hold on her hadn't loosened. If anything, he seemed to keep her closer than ever. Beth saw Cassandra's gaze clash with his as if the physical therapist was letting him know he had become more of a distraction than a help. Sam reluctantly released her.

Cassandra exhaled. "I think that should be enough for today."

Beth's gaze shot to the clock on the wall and she noticed it'd been only thirty minutes. Not that she was complaining.

Now that Sam was in front her, Beth's gaze repeatedly skimmed over the tattoo.

Cassandra seemed to sense the two of them needed time alone and made an excuse to head into the locker room. "I'll be back in a few minutes," she said, getting out of the pool and reaching for her towel.

"Okay," Beth said, her eyes centered on Sam.

As soon as the door closed, Beth offered him a weak smile. "I appreciate you coming."

He shrugged, discounting her gratitude.

She wasn't good at ignoring the elephant in the room, or in this case the alligator circling them in the water. "You didn't want me to see this tattoo, did you?" She slid her index finger over Lucinda's name, letting it linger there.

He didn't answer. He kept his hands on her waist as if afraid she might slip again.

Beth glanced up, hoping to make eye contact, but Sam's gaze

was focused on something on the other side of the pool. "Clearly this woman is someone you loved in the past."

"No," he corrected. "It's someone I love now."

"Oh." She blinked at the shock of the words. Although she'd known Sam only a few weeks, she knew in her heart it wasn't in him to be involved with two women at the same time.

"Oh Sam, I'm sorry. Did she die?"

"No."

Beth was more confused than ever. "Oh." She wished she could think of something more to say other than a stunned response.

"I'd rather not talk about it." He dropped his hands and started for the edge of the pool, leaving her standing in the water while he grabbed a towel and started drying off. He kept his back to her, ignoring her as he dried and hurriedly dressed.

Beth tried to think of something to say that would break the tension between them. Some joke they could both laugh at, but nothing came to mind.

Thankfully, Cassandra returned. By the time Beth was out of the water, Sam was dressed and had the beach towel bunched up in his arms.

"I need to get to the garage."

"Of course. I appreciate you coming."

"No problem. You did great."

Overwhelmed as she was, Beth doubted she'd done anything more than make a fool of herself, the way her mind had been focused on Sam.

"You've proved you can do it. You won't need me again, right?" Sam said.

It wasn't really a question. This was his way of letting her know he had no intention of getting back in the water with her.

Sam started for the door.

"You're leaving?"

"Yeah. Work, babe."

He couldn't seem to get away from her fast enough. "Thanks for coming," she called after him.

He looked back and nodded. "Later."

"Later," she echoed. But Beth had the feeling it might be awhile before she saw Sam again.

And she was right.

CHAPTER 15

Sam

It'd been a mistake to get into the pool with Beth. Now Sam was placed in the unenviable position of deciding what to do next. He knew it was coming, knew there was no avoiding telling her about Lucinda. If their relationship had any kind of future, he would need to explain.

Two days later, Sam got a call from Rocco. He wasn't surprised and actually wondered why it took that long.

His friend was never one to beat around the bush. Without any form of greeting, he said, "Nichole asked me about Lucinda."

"Figured that was bound to happen." Sam exhaled as he sat in front of his television and crossed his ankles on the coffee table. "Beth must have called Nichole."

"You have a crystal ball or something?"

Sam ignored the question. "What did you say?"

"Said it was your story to tell. How'd Beth find out about her?"

When he'd agreed to get in the pool with Beth, Sam had completely forgotten about the tattoo on his chest. It was such a part of him now that he no longer noticed or even thought about it.

Only on Monday morning, when he put on his swim trunks, did he realize there was no way to avoid Beth getting a full view of her name. He wasn't ready to let Beth open the door to that cesspool, but there was no avoiding it once he was required to take off his shirt.

"She saw my tattoo," he told Rocco.

"You walking around that hospital without a shirt these days?" The question was half tease, half serious.

"First off, it isn't a hospital, and second, no. I helped her with her PT in a pool." In his mind it was either break his promise to Beth or reveal the biggest heartache of his life.

"You gonna tell her?"

Sam figured he didn't really have a choice. The fact that he hadn't gone to visit her in two days weighed heavy on him. He'd missed being with her. He'd missed seeing her face light up when he walked into her room. And he especially missed jamming with her. His evenings had taken on an entirely new purpose. Making music with Beth had given him joy, the kind of joy that built up inside, fueling him like tinder to a fire. Those hours with her fed his soul. He'd been out of sorts for the last two evenings not being with Beth; not sitting at her side, strumming his guitar as she played the piano.

He'd felt hollow.

Lost.

Alone.

He wasn't sure when it happened, when Beth filled the empty spaces of his life. All he knew was that he was listless and bored without her, and the knowledge chewed away at his conscience.

He was an idiot. The one he was hurting most was himself. He was miserable, which was stupid because he knew how to fix this. Knew what he had to do to make this right.

"I've got to go," Sam said with a sense of urgency.

"What are you going to do?"

"Talk to Beth. To explain."

"Sam, are you nuts? It's after ten. She's probably asleep."

Sam doubted that. He hadn't slept well in two nights and he suspected she hadn't, either. Without bothering to argue, he cut off the call, grabbed his jacket, and headed out the door. Filled with impatience now, he drove directly to the rehab center. Although it was closing in on eleven, Sam expected Beth would still be awake.

He was wrong.

The door to her room was closed, and when he carefully opened it, he found it dark inside.

He hesitated and then whispered, "Beth?" The light from the hallway bled inside the room and he could see she was lying on her side facing him, her eyes closed. Slowly they opened. For an elongated moment, they stared at each other, saying nothing.

Beth spoke first in a soft whisper. "You don't have to tell me."

Sam came into the room and slowly released the door so it would close, encasing him in the darkness. It took a moment for his eyes to adjust to the lack of light. He actually preferred the anonymity of the dark. It would make it easier if she couldn't see his face. Slipping into the chair next to her bed, he reached for her hand, claiming it between his own. Then, needing her to know how much she meant to him, he brought it to his mouth and kissed her palm.

"I've missed you," she whispered.

"Missed you, too. Couldn't stay away any longer."

"You didn't need to stay away."

"I know. I was an idiot." He kissed her hand again in apology. Then, drawing in a deep breath, he said, "I figure you deserve to know the truth. I met Trish when I was in my early twenties and knew almost immediately that she was my soulmate. I was crazy in love with her."

"Sam, please, you don't need to explain," she said. "Trish? Who is Trish?" she added, clearly puzzled.

"Patience, babe."

"Okay," she whispered with a sigh so adorable it took all his restraint not to reach for her and kiss her senseless.

"Trish and I hit it off right away. She was divorced and a few years older than me. I thought I'd been in love before, but I'd never felt like I did with Trish."

Beth's hand tightened in his and Sam doubted she realized she was squeezing his fingers. Truth was, it would make him uncomfortable to hear about a man she'd once loved, and he didn't expect it was any easier for her.

"We played Russian roulette with birth control and it was only a few months into the relationship that she told me she was pregnant." This was the hard part and his chest tightened with the memory.

"You have a baby?"

"I'm getting to that."

"Sorry," she whispered.

"The pregnancy was something of a shock, but it shouldn't have been. The more I thought about being a dad, the more excited I got." He could feel it even now, the anticipation, the excitement. Being a typical man, he'd yearned for a son, but would have been happy with a daughter, too. "Right away I started buying baby toys," he said, and paused because the memory brought up pain he longed to keep buried. Even speaking of that time in his life hurt, and he feared his voice betrayed him.

"Sam," Beth whispered, "my hand. You're hurting my hand."

He immediately relaxed his grip. "Sorry, babe." He hadn't realized he'd tightened his hold.

"What happened?" she asked when he didn't immediately pick up the story.

"I learned that Trish wasn't divorced after all. She was still married and had only been separated from her husband."

"Oh no." The shock in her voice was a fraction of the blow he'd felt when he'd discovered the truth.

"If that wasn't surprise enough, I then learned that the two of them had been discussing a reconciliation."

"But—"

"I know," he said, stopping her. "One of the reasons I was happy to learn about the pregnancy was that I'd felt Trish emotionally withdrawing from me. I didn't want to lose her, and in my twisted thinking the baby was sure to keep us together." What a fool he'd been.

"She told her husband about your affair?"

"Yes, and soon enough he learned about the pregnancy. As you can imagine, he wasn't happy about it, but like me, he loved Trish, and he was willing to stay married." Again he paused and swallowed against the tightness in his chest. "With one stipulation." Sam inhaled sharply. "Ron, her husband, didn't want Trish to have any link to me. He was afraid I would use the baby as an excuse to continue our relationship and the truth is he was right."

He paused to let his words sink in. He wasn't sure Beth understood what he was telling her.

"You really loved her, didn't you?"

Beth had no idea. Sam would have died for Trish, and in some ways he had. For the last fourteen years he'd avoided relationships. He didn't date and found it hard to trust women.

"Yeah, I really loved her." The words grated against his throat, making it difficult to speak.

"Oh Sam," she said softly and pressed her hand to the side of his face, cupping his bearded jaw as if to ease the pain. Her gentleness touched him and he leaned into her hand and briefly closed his eyes. It took a moment before he was able to continue.

"Trish came to me in tears," he said. "She wanted to save her marriage. In order to do that, I had to relinquish all rights to my child. She begged me, Beth, saying if I had any feelings toward her whatsoever that I would give up my child. She wanted me to stay completely out of both of their lives. That was the only way her husband would agree not to file for a divorce."

Beth made a mewling sound, as if she understood the agony of his decision.

"Trish told me how much she loved her husband. She needed me to surrender all parental rights so the baby would be raised by her and Ron. So the three of them could be a family. I argued that I couldn't, wouldn't, do that. I vowed to take her to court and fight for my child and I meant every word. I wanted the baby to be mine in every way. Then Trish crumbled, sobbing and begging me to agree to Ron's terms, but I insisted. And she said that even though it would kill her, she would give me the child to raise.

"The baby was a tiny fetus, but I already felt this incredible love. Knowing the importance of a mother, I wasn't sure I had it in me to take him or her away from Trish. If I agreed to what Ron wanted, it meant that I would have no contact with Trish or my kid ever again."

"So you agreed?"

It'd been the hardest decision of his life. Sam had seriously considered raising the child on his own, but he'd seen the struggle Rocco had caring for Kaylene only part-time and he realized how difficult it would be for him with an infant. He couldn't bear what this would do to Trish, either. It was an impossible situation.

"Yes, I agreed," he said simply, rather than review the angst of the decision.

"The baby's name is Lucinda?" she asked.

He nodded and then realized she probably couldn't see him.

"Yes. I've only heard from Trish once since she reconciled with her husband, and that was shortly after the baby was born. She sent me a text message and said she'd had a girl and named her Lucinda Marie. Lucinda had been her grandmother's name."

"You've had no other contact since?"

"None." It nearly killed him a little every time he thought about his daughter. "She's thirteen now." Hardly a day passed, even after all these years, when his daughter didn't make her way into his thoughts. Her name was over his heart and it would remain there as long as he drew breath.

Beth didn't say anything for a long time. Finally she kissed the back of his hand and then held it against the side of her face.

"Later, shortly after I gave up all rights to Lucinda, Rocco got full custody of Kaylene. He made it work. It wasn't easy having a kid around, especially without a lot of family support, but he managed. Right or wrong, I realized I would have found a way had I taken the baby."

"Trish is the reason you don't do relationships, isn't it?" Beth asked.

"Yes. But you need to know I haven't been living the life of a saint. There've been women, Beth. I'm not proud of the way I've used them in the last several years. I haven't wanted to risk my heart until you."

He didn't realize what he'd said, and by then it was too late. Still, he didn't regret that Beth knew how important she'd become to him in the last few weeks.

"Sam," she whispered. "Oh Sam."

Not kissing her wasn't an option. Emotion filled him and the need to hold and love her nearly overwhelmed him. For the first time in memory, he felt free of the burden of his decision. Slipping his hand around the base of her neck, he brought her mouth to his. The kiss was warm and wet, urgent and needy on both their parts. It felt as if he was giving away a piece of his soul as he twisted his mouth over hers, wanting to give her everything he'd withheld from every woman he'd touched since the split with Trish.

Soon kissing her wasn't enough. Not even close to being enough. He wanted more. Needed more. Standing, he wrapped his arm around Beth's back, dragging her upright, all the while kissing her with a hunger and desire that nearly consumed him. He didn't know what would have happened if she hadn't given a small gasp of pain. In his desire, he'd forgotten her injuries.

Immediately Sam released his hold and buried his face in her neck. "Sorry, baby," he whispered. "I didn't mean to hurt you."

Beth wound her arms around his neck and held him close. Several moments passed before she spoke. "Thank you for telling me about her," she whispered. He appreciated that she understood what it had taken for him to peel back the scab and reveal his wounded heart.

Only a chosen few knew about Lucinda. Not even his parents realized he had a daughter. Rocco had been his friend since just after high school and had lived through that emotional time with him. He hadn't advised Sam, feeling the decision was his and his alone. When he told Rocco what he'd decided, his friend hadn't said a word. None was necessary.

"I'm glad you know."

He brushed the hair from the side of her face and tucked it behind her ear.

"Can I ask you something?" Beth said.

"Anything." There was little he would withhold from her.

"Are we in a relationship?"

He grinned and kissed her temple. "You tell me. I text you first thing in the morning when I wake, I spend my lunch hour talking to you, and at night as soon as I'm off work I rush home and shower so I can spend as much time with you as possible before you're too tired. That's the closest thing I've had to a relationship in more years than I can remember."

He felt her smile. "What about later, you know, after I'm out of here and back in my apartment?"

"What about it?" Although he asked the question, he'd wondered the same thing himself. He was eager to hear her thoughts. He would follow her lead. If she wanted to end it, while it would hurt, he'd walk away, no questions asked.

"Everything is bound to change," she said.

"Probably," he admitted.

"I won't be here any longer."

"Which is a good thing, right?"

"Right. Oh Sam, you have no idea how much I want to get back to my life again."

"No, I don't suppose I do." Then it dawned on him that she might be trying to tell him something. "Does this mean . . ." He hesitated and then started again. "Are you saying you'd rather not see me once you're out of rehab?"

"What?" she asked, and sounded shocked. "I'll answer that question the same way you answered mine. You're the first person I think about when I wake. I grab my phone and look for your text messages. I don't eat lunch or take a nap until I've talked to you at noon, and then after my last physical therapy session I count the minutes until I see you at night. These last two evenings I felt empty when I sat at the piano because you weren't with me. In fact, one of the aides said it sounded like I was playing for a funeral."

Sam laughed and hugged her closer. "I'm crazy about you, Beth. Head-over-heels crazy. Yes, things will change when you're back to your regular life, but the change will be for the better."

"The better," she repeated.

"We'll figure everything out together."

And they would. Sam was determined that they would.

CHAPTER 16

Beth

Soon after Sam told Beth about his daughter, she noticed a shift in him. His smile came easier and he seemed more lighthearted, teasing and joking with her. It was as if sharing his past had lifted a heaviness from his shoulders. He'd always been gentle with her, tender and caring. In the days after his late-night visit, his eyes shone bright and clear without the cynical gleam she'd noticed in him the first night they'd met. After their talk it seemed his cynicism disappeared altogether. It was as though sharing what had happened with his daughter had cracked the wall he'd built around his heart so that healing could begin.

She continued with the pool therapy, and just as Cassandra had promised, Beth made remarkable progress. Sam didn't go into the water with her again, as it wasn't necessary. She'd conquered her fear for the most part, and every day it got easier until she was forced to admit she actually enjoyed her pool time.

The last week of her rehab, Beth was walking steadily, leaning on a cane. She was due to be released at the end of the week and she couldn't wait.

Her aunt came to visit early Tuesday morning. As soon as she walked into the room, she announced, "I've talked to the head of the facility and I'm taking you out this evening."

"Out?" Beth had to wonder what her aunt had planned. "You mean *out* of the building?"

"Yes, love. What did you think I meant?"

"I don't know." Beth tensed as she mulled this over and realized she didn't feel ready. "I don't think I can . . ."

"You can and you will. Everything's already been arranged. We're going to dinner at a funky Mexican place I discovered that serves—"

"But Sam is expecting me to be here." Thankfully, Beth had a good reason to refuse.

"Tell him you've got plans for the evening," her aunt suggested, immediately dismissing her excuse.

Although she tried, Beth couldn't think of a way to roadblock her aunt. It took her a few moments to realize how silly she was being. One would think she'd want to get away for a short while. It'd been a month since she'd last been anywhere. This was crazy. More than anything, she wanted to get back to her everyday life, teach her classes, get involved in the activities she'd only begun to do.

It was then that Beth had an epiphany. It came to her that the rehab center had become her safe place, a cocoon where she was comfortable and could hide from life. All her needs were met without her having to do much of anything. Worries, concerns, fears were on the other side of the glass door.

Lost in her thoughts, Beth took a moment to realize her aunt was talking to her. "You aren't going to disappoint me, are you?"

"No, I'm not," she said, gathering her resolve. "Sam will understand. It's time to par-tee."

Sunshine laughed and floated about the room. "You've been cooped up in here far too long. It's time you got reintroduced to the world."

"You're right, it is."

"It's going to be fun," her aunt promised, gripping hold of Beth's hands and squeezing her palms together. "We'll have fish tacos and tostadas and drink shots of tequila."

Beth smiled. It'd been far too long since she'd had good Mexican food.

"I'll be by to collect you around five-thirty."

"Perfect."

Her aunt left soon afterward. Beth was impatient for Sam's call at noon.

"Sunshine is taking me out of the facility tonight," she blurted out as soon as they connected.

"That's great, babe."

"At first I didn't want to go and I didn't understand what was wrong with me. I'm dying to get back to normal, to reconnect with my students and back to the classroom. And yet I found myself looking for excuses not to go."

"Babe, that's crazy."

"I know. Then I realized I feel safe here . . . leaving means getting into a car again. Because the rehab center is next door to the hospital, an aide wheeled me over. I haven't been in a car since the accident. Then I thought what if I'm in another accident? What if—"

"Beth," he said, interrupting her. "Stop. It's only natural to be afraid after everything you've been through."

"I think I should see a shrink."

"What you're feeling is only natural. If you need to talk to someone, then talk. Don't let fear paralyze you."

"You think I should see a professional about this?"

"Do what you need to do. You can't stay at the rehab center the rest of your life."

"I know," she murmured, but now, when she was days away from leaving, she felt the unnatural fear of going back to her life the way it once was. She'd grown accustomed to the routine of the facility, the orderliness, the structure. Once she walked out those doors, her life would change. That was what she wanted, right? What she'd hungered for.

"You've gone quiet again," Sam said, drawing her attention back to the present. "What's going through that beautiful head of yours?"

"It's more than getting in a car, Sam," she admitted, her voice dropping.

"What's on your mind, babe?"

"Us," she whispered. "I'm afraid what will happen to us once I'm released. It's all going to change and—"

"I had no idea you were such a worrier," Sam said, cutting her off. "Nothing will change the way I feel about you, Beth, I can promise you that. Not a single damn thing."

Relaxing, she leaned back and smiled. "I think you owe Owen a dollar."

"I'm pretty sure *damn* is in the Bible," Sam argued. "You're missing the point. What we have is real. I'm not letting anything get between us."

"My mother . . ."

"We've already crossed that bridge and we're still together," Sam reminded her.

Her mother had remained suspiciously quiet after her short visit, which wasn't the least bit reassuring. Beth was convinced Ellie Prudhomme was working behind the scenes and had something drastic planned. She didn't know what it could be, but like Sam said, she'd cross that bridge when necessary.

"You think I should go with Sunshine?"

"Of course, and be prepared to have a good time. I want you to have fun, to remember what it is like to laugh again."

"I laugh with you," she reminded him. It was one of the things she loved about him most. Sam had a quick, easy laugh that made her want to laugh herself whenever she heard it.

"And you'll laugh with me again."

Beth felt better after talking to Sam. Nothing he said was profound, but he made sense. It wasn't like she could avoid riding in a car the rest of her life, or driving one, for that matter. Sooner or later she would need to face that demon and swallow down her fears. Funny how once she admitted to one fear, two or three others immediately leaped into the fray. They were like balls bobbing to the surface of her consciousness, shooting up so fast they zoomed into the air before she could beat them down.

Stiffening her resolve, she said, "I'll go and I'll have a wonderful time."

"That's *my* girl."

She smiled, happy to be considered his girl.

CHAPTER 17

Beth

Just as she'd promised, Sunshine showed up at five-thirty to collect Beth. She was dressed and ready, both physically and emotionally prepared to face this fire-breathing dragon. To her surprise, once they were on the road, she didn't experience any more than a slight twinge of panic. It was going to be okay. She was going to be okay. The realization reassured her.

Sunshine drove them to an upscale Mexican restaurant, and as promised, she ordered fish tacos and tequila.

"These are the best fish tacos I've had in years," her aunt told her, closing her eyes as she savored her first bite of her soft-shell taco. "There was this hole-in-the-wall place in Chicago I loved years ago that served the most wonderful food." As though transfixed, she released a sigh of absolute pleasure. "The food was authentic and cheap. I was a starving art student at the time. Peter was as poor as I was, and yet we scraped together enough to eat out every Friday night. For six dollars we could share an order of spicy fish tacos and a bean tostada. Can you imagine, for six dollars?"

"Peter?" Beth asked. "I don't remember you ever mentioning him. Was he another of your artist friends?"

As if caught up in her memories, Sunshine stared back at her and a strange look came over her. "Yes," she answered finally, a smile frozen in place.

Beth set her taco aside. Her aunt often spoke of the men in her life, the ones she had loved and lost, the adventures they'd shared, the sweet sorrows of letting them go. As far as Beth could see, there'd never been anyone her aunt had loved heart and soul.

"Tell me about him," she urged.

Seemingly lost in thought, her aunt reached for her margarita. "Another time," she said after a long pause.

In that moment, Beth knew this man, Peter, wasn't a casual flame but someone important in Sunshine's past.

"You loved him," Beth said.

Sunshine grew still and quiet, and the light in her eyes dimmed. "Oh yes, I loved him like I have never loved before or since."

Suddenly everything became clear to Beth. "He's the reason you moved out here." As a child, Beth remembered hearing her mother mention that Sunshine had childishly escaped to the West Coast. The comment had been casual, but the word *escape* had stuck in Beth's mind. Right away she wondered what her wonderful, fun-loving aunt was fleeing from. In her childish imagination, Beth had concocted a wild story of dragons chasing after her.

Her aunt attempted a smile but failed. Sadness rimmed her eyes. "Stop me before I get all maudlin. Peter Hamlin is history. We haven't spoken in over thirty years."

Peter Hamlin. Beth stored the name in her memory bank, determined to find out what she could about this man her aunt had loved and clearly loved still.

"What would you say if I told you I think I'm falling in love?" Beth ventured.

The change in her aunt was immediate, and her entire face brightened as though grateful for a different topic of discussion. "Sam, no doubt."

Beth lowered her gaze to her plate and nodded. Her aunt's laugh caused her to glance up. "You're amused?"

"Oh yes. I'm dying to hear what your mother had to say about him."

"Actually, she said very little."

"Ellie managed to contain her opinion?" Sunshine sounded shocked.

"She did. I expected a full repertoire of questions and concerns before she left. It didn't happen, so I've been waiting for the other shoe to drop. Knowing my mother, she's probably having a full background search done on Sam, going back two or three generations."

Sunshine laughed. "That sounds like something she'd do."

"She's planning something; I know she is."

"Then be ready for it."

That was good advice. "I already know she considers Sam all wrong for her precious daughter. The thing with Mom is that she doesn't see Sam the same way I do. Sadly, she looks at family connections and a bank account more than the content of one's character."

The smile left Sunshine's eyes and she nodded. "It's a shame, really. If she had the chance to know Sam, she'd feel differently."

"Something else Mom is forgetting," Beth said. "This is my life. I'm twenty-five and fully capable of making my own choices, dating whomever I want."

"Yes, you are," Sunshine said, agreeing with her. "How did you ever cope with the way she controlled you?"

"Music has always been my escape," Beth confessed.

Sunshine nodded in understanding. "As art has been mine."

"When I felt as if my mother was burying me under the weight of her expectations, I'd sit at the piano and immerse myself in music. Sam is a musician, too." Although he hadn't mentioned it, she wondered if it was when he relinquished his daughter that he took up playing the guitar. Music must have helped him deal with the burden of his choice. Playing together, they had found a common language, a way of communicating that went beyond words. They had learned to read each other through a shared passion.

"Stick to your guns when it comes to Sam," Sunshine advised, and smiled as she said it. "I don't have any idea of what sticking to your guns has to do with anything, but it sounds good."

"I will," Beth said with determination. "I'm not giving Sam up . . . unless he gives up on me first."

Sunshine looked surprised. "Is that likely?"

"I'm a little afraid of what will happen once I'm on my own again. He doesn't seem to see a problem, but I'm not so sure."

"Oh?"

The comment invited a response.

"Things are bound to change," Beth said, uncertain of how best to share her fears.

"In what way?"

Beth had yet to give voice to her concerns and she needed a moment to think matters through. "Sam has been my guardian angel through this ordeal. I fear he sees himself as my protector. I don't want or need him to be that. I don't need a guardian, but I'd be grateful to be his friend."

"And lover?" Sunshine arched her brows suggestively with the question.

Beth was afraid her cheeks filled with color. "When the time is right, yes." It didn't take much to imagine Sam as her lover. He was a man of passion, and she found it easy to believe that same hunger for life would translate well into lovemaking.

"I like Sam," her aunt told her. "I have from the first. If he has a problem being overprotective, set him straight. He's a smart guy, he'll catch on fast enough."

"And if he doesn't?"

Her aunt cocked her head to one side with a knowing look. "I've seen the way Sam is with you. That boy is smitten. He isn't going to do anything to risk what he's found in you."

Smitten. What a lovely word that was, and one Beth hadn't heard in a long time. "What do you think he's found in me?" she asked, curious to hear her aunt's thoughts.

"Renewed hope," she said without even the shortest of pauses. "That first time we met, shortly after the accident, he seemed shiftless, lost. True enough, he was concerned about you, worried. Even after a short acquaintance I realized that below the surface there was more to him than meets the eye. Almost immediately I recognized something in him . . . something we share. I sensed that he had given up."

"What have you given up on?" Beth felt compelled to ask.

"I'll get overemotional, so I'd rather not say."

Beth speculated that it had something to do with the name she'd mentioned earlier. *Peter Hamlin.*

"What do you think Sam has given up on, then?"

Sunshine shrugged. "I couldn't say, and even if I could it wouldn't be my place. My point is that over the last six weeks I've noticed subtle changes in Sam. I've witnessed this transformation. I'm guessing this time with you has been a welcome surprise to him. I doubt he ever expected to meet someone like you."

Funny Sunshine should say that, because Beth was the one who felt she'd received a gift by knowing Sam and making music with him.

CHAPTER 18

Sam

This was the day, and Sam refused to miss it. Beth was being released from the rehab facility after three weeks of intensive physical therapy. Sam couldn't be more proud of the work she had done and the improvement she'd made in such a short amount of time. She was able to walk without the cane now, although she tired easily. He took the day off work so he could be there when she walked out the door.

Sunshine arrived before him to pick her up and drive Beth to her apartment. As a surprise, Sam waited outside the rehab facility with a bouquet of flowers and five big, colorful balloons. They'd both eagerly anticipated this day. Beth could finally get back to her real life, to teaching her students the music she loved, to everything she'd managed to build in the short amount of time she'd been in Portland.

It started to drizzle rain as Sam stood outside, impatiently waiting. He glanced toward the sky and sighed. His head was buzzing with small concerns—big ones, too. Beth had talked about her own worries, fearing what was only natural for someone in her situation. Sam had a few of his own.

They hadn't talked much about the sure-to-be changes in their relationship once she was discharged. Inevitably it would shift. No doubt there. He didn't know how or what the future held, and dwelling on it did nothing good for his digestion. Sam felt a stronger connection to Beth than he had to any other woman since Trish. That alone offered its own set of qualms. He understood that Beth was nothing like the other woman, but at the same time he remained reluctant to risk his heart a second time. Yet he'd found it impossible to maintain his guard.

He'd never enjoyed time with a woman the way he did with Beth. Their nightly jam sessions had been some of the happiest times he could remember in years. The fact they could laugh together and tease each other had been foreign to him. They'd bonded over the music and had agreed to return to the rehab center at least twice a week and play for the patients and the staff, as much for their own enjoyment as for others'.

This thing with Beth was unchartered territory for him. He hoped they'd be able to move forward, to continue as a couple, but he was prepared to let matters fall where they would.

The misty rain continued, typical of autumn in the Pacific Northwest. Discharging Beth was taking much longer than he'd expected. He'd assumed when Sunshine went inside that it would be only a matter of minutes before she appeared with Beth. Not so. It'd been fifteen minutes already and he saw no signs they'd be coming out anytime soon.

Another fifteen minutes passed when Sam caught sight of Beth and her aunt. The sliding glass doors parted and he stepped forward.

As soon as Beth saw him with the flowers and the balloons, her face lit up with joy. "Sam," she cried, "you're here."

"Wasn't going to miss seeing my girl walk out of that facility."

She headed straight for him with her arms wide open, her smile as bright as a summer's day. She bubbled with laughter as she tossed her arms around him.

Sam hugged her back, the balloons and flowers tangling. Every doubt and worry he had fled the instant she was in his arms.

Beth rode with Sunshine, holding on to the flowers while he dealt with the balloons and followed behind in his truck. They went directly to her apartment, which was close to the high school. It was a one-bedroom place with an impossibly tiny kitchen. The apartment was like Beth, bright and cheerful. He felt her warmth the moment he walked inside. Knowing she came from money, this must have been quite an adjustment from what she was accustomed to in her Chicago home. But it was hers, and just the way she paused and breathed in the atmosphere, Sam knew she loved it. He wasn't the least bit surprised that the first thing she did was walk over to the piano and run her fingers over the keys.

"How are you feeling?" Sunshine asked, once the array of flowers was deposited in a pitcher. Beth apologized that she didn't have a vase.

"Wonderful. I want to throw out my arms and twirl around. I'm home at last."

Sam couldn't have held back a smile had he tried.

"I've loaded you up with groceries and the sheets on the bed are fresh. You need anything else?" Sunshine asked.

"A hug," Beth said, reaching for her aunt. "Thank you for everything."

Sunshine hugged her back. "I'll check in on you later." She hesitated and then suggested, "You might want to call your parents."

Beth rolled her eyes. "Okay, I will, but later."

"Do it."

"I will, I will," she promised.

Sunshine left. As soon as she was out the door, Beth was in Sam's arms. "I can't believe you took the day off."

"Wouldn't miss it, babe. What do you have on your mind? Anything you want to do? Any place you want to go?"

"Out," she returned instantly. "Take me out."

"Anywhere in particular?" Her request didn't surprise him after being trapped for more than a month in two different medical facilities, first the hospital and then the rehab center.

"No, just out where I can breathe the fresh air and soak in the freedom of being alive and with you."

That sounded perfect to Sam. They spent the rest of the day together and it couldn't have been more wonderful. Sam drove her out to view Multnomah Falls. Beth insisted he park so they could get out and view the site even in the rain. He stood behind her, hands on her shoulders, looking for any excuse to keep her close. They ate thick sandwiches and drank coffee at a diner. Beth talked nearly nonstop, full of glee and joy. Sam drank it all in, savoring each moment, praying it would always be like this for them.

And knowing it wouldn't.

Beth returned to teaching, and while both Sam and Sunshine wished she'd have started off more slowly with half-days, she chose otherwise, too eager to get back to her students. Sam had met a few of the teenagers she taught and she'd told him about several others until he felt like he knew half of her classes himself. He loved her enthusiasm and was fairly certain the teenagers were drawn in by her joyful spirit. He understood that classical music wasn't the most popular elective, but he didn't doubt for a moment that Beth made it fun and exciting.

By Friday, the first week she was back, as he feared, Beth was exhausted. Sam checked in on her that evening, not intending to stay long.

"You overdid it," he chastised gently.

"Maybe. Are you going to say I told you so?" she asked, her eyes wide and beseeching.

"Nope." He stood, looking down on her.

"Why not?" she asked on the tail end of a yawn. "You were right."

"Having you admit it is reward enough." He glanced at his watch.

"Sit," she said, and patted the space next to her.

Sam shook his head. "Think I should head out."

She blinked back her surprise. "Already?"

"Yeah, you're tired and I've got things to do."

"Okay." She didn't bother to disguise her disappointment. "Is everything all right, Sam?"

He shrugged. "Why wouldn't it be?"

"You didn't answer my question."

He scowled at her. "It's fine."

"Stay," she said softly, "just a few minutes more."

Reluctantly he sat down on the sofa next to her. Beth leaned against him and reached for his hand, intertwining their fingers. "It's been over a month now," she said.

"Since the accident," he said, remembering that first evening they met. He never would have guessed Beth would become this important to him.

"Since everything," she added. "I've seen you nearly every day."

"True."

"I've spent more time with you than I have anyone in a long time."

"True again."

"The thing is, Sam, after all that time together, I've come to know you, know your moods. I know without you even having to tell me when you've had a good day at the garage or when you're disgruntled with one of the guys."

He didn't know he was that transparent, but it didn't surprise him. Beth seemed to have the ability to see straight through him.

"Did you call your parents?" he asked, wanting to change the subject.

"Sam!"

"Did you?"

"Yes, and we had a . . . decent conversation. Now stop and let me finish what I was saying."

He nodded, although he wasn't keen to continue.

"Something's troubling you."

He shrugged. This was the very subject he'd been hoping to avoid.

"Do you want to talk about it?" she asked in that gentle way of hers.

"No."

"I'm a good listener," she reminded him.

"Not your business," he snapped.

She sucked in a soft breath in an effort to hide her surprise. "Okay."

"Can we drop it?"

"If that's what you want, and apparently it is."

"Good. Now tell me how the conversation went with your parents." That should be a safe enough subject.

She hesitated and then said, "Not your business."

He blinked back his surprise, snickered, and let go of her hand. "Think it's time I left." Not waiting for her to respond, he headed for the door. Beth didn't stop him, which was fine by him. The sooner he left, the better. As it was, he might say something he'd regret later, and he didn't want to do that.

Sam got all the way to where he'd parked and hesitated and then looked to the sky. Beth was right. He was out of sorts, upset and on edge. With good reason. He hadn't meant to be gruff and regretted the way he'd handled the situation. Beth had no idea what day this was. He had a knot in his stomach and knew he needed to make this right. He looked back up at her building, wondering if she was stewing the same as he was. Heaving a sigh, he returned to the apartment complex and rang her doorbell.

Beth answered, and for a moment all they seemed able to do was look at each other.

"It's Lucinda's birthday," he said, looking down.

"Your daughter," she whispered, and immediately reached for him, hugging him. "I'm sorry, I didn't know."

She couldn't have known, couldn't have guessed. "I'm the one who needs to apologize. I should have told you sooner." Beth was everything good in his life and he wasn't willing to risk losing her because he was in a sour mood.

"If you don't want to talk about it, that's fine. I understand."

"I'd rather not."

He kissed her, needing her warmth and her gentleness in an effort to let go of the regret, the pain of never knowing the daughter who was his own flesh and blood.

Later they sat in front of the television sharing a bowl of freshly popped popcorn and watching a movie on Netflix.

Out of the blue, Beth asked, "I wonder how many Peter Hamlins there are in the world?"

"Who's Peter Hamlin?"

"A man."

"I got that much. You're looking to find him?"

"Yup, and I'm determined."

He didn't like the sound of that and made an effort to appear disinterested when he definitely wasn't. "Do you mind telling me why?"

She grinned up at him. "Are you jealous, Sam?"

"Should I be?" He arched his brows with the question.

Her eyes sparkled with renewed life. "Nope." She entwined her fingers with his and raised his hand to her mouth for a kiss. "Sunshine mentioned him when we were at dinner. She still loves him after thirty years."

"What happened?"

"I don't know, but I'd like to find out."

Sam exhaled slowly. "Are you sure that's wise?"

She took her time answering. "I don't know. I saw the look in Sunshine's eyes when she mentioned him. It was a slip of the tongue. I'm convinced she never meant to say his name aloud. Whatever happened between them devastated her. I have a feeling my mother knows, but I'd rather not ask her."

"Why not? That might save you a lot of trouble."

Beth released a sigh, her shoulders rising and lowering with the release of her breath. "Sad to say, I'm not sure I can trust her to tell the truth. I suspect she'll brush off the question. Besides, I do everything I can to avoid talking to my mother."

Sam knew the two had a prickly relationship. "Sunshine didn't tell you anything more about him?"

"Nothing. As soon as I asked about him, she shut up tighter than an oyster."

"Maybe your aunt doesn't want you to know. Didn't you say all this happened thirty years ago? Sometimes it's better to leave matters as they are, especially if the other person doesn't have a clue you're stirring the waters."

To her credit, Beth appeared to give his words serious thought. "Maybe, but I'm curious. You know Sunshine has never married. I always thought it was because she was a free spirit. Now I'm not so sure. I think the reason she's remained single all these years is because of this man and whatever happened between them."

Sam still had reservations. While Beth seemed to have strong feelings on the matter, he feared she could be sticking her hand in a snake hole. "Are you sure your aunt wants you meddling in her past?"

Again she took a moment before she spoke. "No, but I can't help thinking that if Sunshine still loves him after all these years, just maybe he feels the same way about her. What if he does and my finding him is what clears the path for them to reunite?"

Sam tightened his hold around her shoulders. "I had no idea you had such a romantic heart."

"I want Sunshine to be happy."

"She's happy. That woman is brimming with joy."

"Sure, she's fun and quirky, but deep down I have to wonder."

Sam mulled this over. "You realize Peter Hamlin is probably married and a grandfather by now," he said.

"Maybe, and if that's the case, then so be it."

Sam remained unconvinced. "Your aunt is a famous artist, right?"

"Right. So?"

"So if this man she loved was so inclined, he wouldn't have a problem seeking her out on his own, don't you think?"

Beth groaned. "I hate it when you argue with me."

"Are we arguing?" he joked.

"No, but you're being reasonable and I don't want to hear it. I'm determined to find him, Sam, and if I have to ask my mother I will, but only as a last resort." She sighed again. "Are you going to say 'I told you so' if this blows up in my face?"

"Nope. Don't think I'll need to if that happens."

"Probably not," she agreed. "You've given me something to think about, though, and while I agree with most of what you said, I still want to learn what I can. Sunshine doesn't need to know what I'm doing."

Sam wasn't convinced this search for her aunt's lover was a good thing, but he had to admire her spirit.

———

Rocco groaned when Sam contacted him by phone Saturday morning about helping him with one of his vehicles. "You've got to be kidding me," his friend complained. "An engine must weigh a ton."

"Yup." Sam didn't argue.

"I could easily come up with a dozen excuses why it would be impossible for me to help you."

"You could, in which case I have one word for you."

"One word? All right, lay it on me."

"Dryer."

Silence followed before Rocco muttered something under his breath that would have cost Sam a good ten bucks if he'd said it in earshot of Owen.

"What time do you need me?" Rocco asked.

"I'm free all day. Let me know what works best for you."

"How about next year?"

"Very funny. You'd do it if it was Nichole asking you, right?"

"Right. And it'd be the same with you if Beth asked you for something. You'd do it, right?"

"Most likely," Sam agreed.

"Thought so. You gonna buy me a beer afterward?"

"I'll think about it."

"I'm not doing it without the promise of a cold one."

Sam laughed. "Okay, it's a deal."

Apparently, Rocco wasn't done complaining. "This is what I don't understand," he muttered. "How is it that two strong-willed men have found women who have the ability to twist us around their little fingers?"

Sam didn't have an answer for him. "Can't say."

"Me, neither, but I know if Nichole asked me to pack up the house and move to the moon, I'd seriously look for a way to make that happen. Makes no sense whatsoever, but because she asked, I'd do it."

"I know what you mean," Sam agreed. Crazy as he was about Beth, there was very little he wouldn't do to make her happy. "The thing is . . ."

"Yeah?"

"If you asked Nichole the same thing, she'd do it for you, too. That's love, my friend."

"Oh, and when did you become such an expert on the subject?"

"Guess it must be close to six weeks ago now?" Sam admitted.

Rocco chuckled. "Personally, I'm glad to see you take the tumble. I never thought it'd happen."

"Truth is," Sam repeated, "I didn't, either. Meeting Beth . . . man, I owe you."

"Not me. You owe Nichole."

"Right, but you're the one who conned me into that dinner."

"And you were so happy to attend," Rocco teased.

Sam laughed.

"About as happy as I am to be lifting an engine out of that old car of yours," Rocco grumbled.

After they finished Saturday morning, Sam kept his promise and treated Rocco to a beer at The Dog House. A cheer rose when the two men walked into the tavern. It used to be that Sam spent the better part of his nights at his favorite spot. In the weeks following Beth's accident, he'd stopped by only a couple times.

"Sam." Cherise called out his name as soon as he sat down at the bar. "I've been worried sick about you," she said, wrapping her arm around his neck and leaning her head against his. "Where have you been keeping yourself?"

She smelled of smoke and rancid oil, which he didn't think was supposed to be her perfume. Funny, he'd never noticed that about her before. He removed her arm from around his neck and hoped she got the hint.

"Hardly ever see you anymore, either, Rocco."

"There's a reason for that," Rocco reminded her. "I have a woman now and she takes up my time."

"Same here," Sam said.

"You, too?" Cherise sounded shocked. "I thought, you know, that the two of us . . ."

"Sorry, Cherise, but it wasn't meant to be." It'd been a mistake to get involved with this woman, even on a casual basis. Fool that he was, Sam knew it and he'd done it, anyway. She was another of the several regrets he lived with. Well, he was on another path now and he was glad of it.

The two men drank their beer, chatted with a few of their friends. Sam was surprised to find he didn't have nearly as much in common with the guys as he once did. Someone suggested a pool game, something Sam and Rocco used to enjoy. Sam probably would have agreed if he wasn't so anxious to see Beth.

She'd spent part of her day relaxing and getting ready for the next school week and had promised him dinner. He didn't want her overworking herself and was eager to get to the apartment. He'd written a song he wanted to play for her. It was his first attempt at writing music, and he'd spent hours working on the lyrics. He wasn't a great wordsmith and had struggled to put his thoughts down on the page and then match them with chords on his guitar. He was interested to see if Beth, with all her musical talent, would be able to pick up the tune on the piano.

Sam and Rocco left The Dog House no more than thirty minutes after they arrived. The tavern didn't hold the same appeal it once had, and they both seemed to recognize it. Their lives had moved in other directions and that suited Sam. He realized his friend felt the same.

Sam's Song for Beth

I've been broken
For such a long time
And love
Wasn't much a friend of mine
It took everything I had to give
But God
Must have had sympathy
And suddenly
God gave Beth to me

CHAPTER 19

Sunshine

Sunshine had been in a blue funk ever since her dinner with Beth. She blamed the fish tacos. She knew better than to order them. Her memories of Peter were invariably tied to their favorite Friday-night date at the Mexican restaurant. The plate came with three tacos, she recalled. Peter would eat two while she ate one. Even after all these years, she could still taste the delicate spice-coated white fish served on warm homemade corn tortillas with finely chopped onion, tomatoes, and cilantro. The little café never charged them extra for sharing a plate. She ate the rice and Peter loved the refried black beans. Their food was none of the Tex-Mex that was so popular these days. This was as authentic as it got.

As authentic as their love.

Peter was in art school with her at Columbia College Chicago; his medium was sculpture. He was gifted beyond anyone she'd ever known. He was as passionate about his art as she was about her own. The difference was that Sunshine had her family's love and support. Peter didn't. He'd defied his father, who had refused to finance his schooling. Peter's father was a corporate attorney and expected his only son to follow in his footsteps. When Peter chose art school over his father's objections, it caused a rift in their relationship that rivaled that of the Grand Canyon. The only way Peter was able to attend was due to his mother, who funded his schooling. She'd returned to the workforce as an art/history teacher in order to pay his expenses. The marriage was on tentative ground because she'd stood up to her tyrannical husband.

Sunshine first saw Peter at the campus library, and he immediately piqued her interest. He sat at the table across the room from her. Her immediate thought when she laid eyes on him was that he was gorgeous. His dark brown hair was long and always in his eyes. He constantly brushed it aside. In retrospect it was probably the motion of his hand as he pushed away the curls from his face that first attracted her attention. He looked up then and their eyes met. His were as blue as an Alaskan glacier. Dark hair. Blue eyes. She was lost.

Embarrassed to be caught studying him, she quickly looked down and dutifully continued her research. When she glanced up again a few minutes later, he was gone and her heart sank.

She returned the next night and Peter was there, too, sitting one table closer to her. They eyed each other several times. Then, as he had the night before, he left before she did, and again she swallowed her disappointment.

By the third night she decided if he didn't make a move, then she would. Sure enough, he was at the library when she arrived. She wasn't nearly as bold or as outgoing then as she was now. Wanting to meet him and tired of waiting for him to do something, she plopped her books down on the table next to him and pulled out her chair.

———

"I'm Louise," she said.

"Peter."

"My friends call me Sunshine."

"What should I call you?"

"What would you like to call me?"

He smiled and it felt as if someone had turned up the lighting in the library. The entire area seemed to be brighter, sunnier. "I'd like to call you for a date."

Sunshine had laughed, garnering glares from other students.

They pretended to study. Sunshine's assignment had been finished the first night she saw him. The only reason she'd returned to the library was with the hope of seeing Peter again. Instead, they passed notes to each other.

Caught up in the memories, Sunshine made herself a cup of tea and ventured into her art room, finding comfort there as she remembered Peter. After all these years, everything was still fresh in her mind.

They fell in love quickly. He was her first love, and in reality her last. Her heart had never completely belonged to another. It was always Peter and it would forever remain so. They did everything together. They met in the mornings, walked each other to classes, and studied together. They rode their bikes around town, as neither could afford a car. Sunshine repeatedly reminded Peter that he was talented and he shouldn't give up on his art to satisfy his father's plans for his life. He needed that reassurance, and she was happy to supply it because it was the truth.

For her entire senior year, they were together nearly every day. Then Sunshine had the opportunity to study for three months in Italy and had been thrilled. Peter had been invited as well but couldn't afford to go. He wanted her to give up the trip and she refused, which was the first serious disagreement they'd ever had.

She thought he was being selfish and he said she was being insensitive.

They were both right.

They were both wrong.

For six months they'd lived in their own world, and Sunshine
was convinced nothing would ever be strong enough to penetrate
it. They'd talked of getting married as soon as they graduated and
found work that would support them. Because she was young and
naïve then, she believed the power of their love would see them
through anything. How wrong she'd been. How foolish.

*"Peter's cute," Ellie said when Sunshine brought him home to meet
her family. Ellie had spent a year abroad, so this was the first chance
her little sister had to meet him. Sunshine had written plenty about
him to Ellie in the year she was away in France.*

*Peter rarely visited his family home, which had become a battle-
field. For his mother's sake, he avoided confrontations with his father.*

*"I think so, too," Sunshine agreed, a bit wary of Ellie's interest in
Peter. And his in her sister. Sunshine saw the looks the two exchanged.*

"You two serious?" Ellie asked.

"Very. We're going to be married," Sunshine told her sister.

"Really?"

"We're talking about it," Peter said.

Sunshine should have known then. Should have suspected.

*"We're in love." She looked at Peter and saw his gaze was on her
sister. "Right, Peter?" she pressed.*

"Right," he echoed.

Ellie was beautiful, but Sunshine wasn't concerned.

She should have been.

———

When Sunshine left for those three months, she was convinced that their love would remain solid. By this point she'd been dating Peter for nine months. She'd met his mother but not his father. His mother, Anna, was a delicate woman with refined tastes. She was close to her son and nurtured his desire to support himself with his talent as a sculptor. His father wouldn't allow any of Peter's work to be displayed in their home. Sunshine appreciated how difficult it was for this sensitive, brilliant young man to stand up to his overbearing father. Despite his talent and passion, Peter suffered serious doubts when it came to his art and was in constant need of validation. Sunshine tried not to worry what would happen while she was away, but it was only three months. Surely he'd be able to be without her for that long.

Ellie promised to be there for him, and in the weeks before Sunshine left, she became their shadow. As a joke, Sunshine started calling her Mary after the nursery rhyme "Mary Had a Little Lamb." Because wherever she and Peter went, Ellie was sure to go.

Peter and Ellie went to the airport with her. Even now Sunshine could remember waving to them as she went through security. Both promised to keep in touch. To be fair, Sunshine had her doubts. Peter had seemed more and more withdrawn, and she'd assumed he remained upset that she had this wonderful studying opportunity in Florence and he didn't.

The first week they wrote each other every day. Sometimes two and three times a day. She shared with him what she was learning, sent photos and notes, and counted down the days until her return. His responses continued but were short in comparison. Then gradually they came infrequently.

At the end of three months when Sunshine returned home and saw them, she knew. No one needed to spell it out for her. Peter and Ellie were in love. They each felt guilty, were remorseful, begged her forgiveness.

——

"*Sunshine, listen, please,*" *Peter begged her.* "*I'm sorry, so sorry. Neither of us planned this; it just happened.*" *She'd been back from Italy less than twenty-four hours when they sat down with her. They held on to each other and faced her together, both with sad, mournful eyes.*

"*We're in love,*" *Ellie said, and to her credit her sister did look contrite. If Sunshine didn't know her sister better she might have believed her. But Ellie had always wanted whatever Sunshine had, and this time it was Peter.*

Peter looked down, unable to meet her gaze. "*I'm sorry.*"

"*Do you want Ellie?*" *Her heart was breaking just asking the man she loved this question.*

Peter remained silent.

"*Answer me,*" *she cried out, holding back the tears that burned like sulfur.* "*For the love of heaven, have the decency to at least answer me.*"

Apparently, Peter didn't know.

The tears came then, and Sunshine swiped them from her face as she turned and walked away.

The next time she saw Peter and Ellie she made the decision for him. "*I . . . I'm going to attend graduate school in California. I have an offer . . . I wasn't going to accept, but it seems that would be for the best.*" *Remaining in Chicago and seeing him with her sister would have killed her.*

"*No,*" *Peter protested.* "*You have an offer here, too . . .*"

Sunshine shook her head, unwilling to even consider his plea. "*Do you seriously think I could remain here with the two of you?*"

"*Let her go. It's for the best,*" *Ellie advised, tightening her grip on Peter's arm.*

"*Yes,*" *Sunshine agreed, as she turned away.*

———

Three months later Sunshine was in California. She'd left without a word and shunned all contact with them. She buried herself in her studies and her painting, and after a year had a show in a well-known gallery. The first piece that sold, created in a frenzy of pain, anger, and emotion, was titled *Betrayal*.

The oil painting showed a loving couple walking with their arms around each other with a lamb following closely behind. On closer examination the eye would eventually see that the lamb wasn't so lovely or innocent. Cleverly woven into the walkway were thin lines of twine wrapping around the man's legs like vines, securing him to the lamb. In the man's hair was another face looking back longingly at the lamb. It was the first painting she did with a picture inside a picture that told a story beyond initial impressions. If Sunshine had anything to thank her sister for, it was inspiring her to try this technique.

A few months after she landed in California, Peter wrote, but she returned his letter unopened. She didn't speak to her sister again until her mother begged her to make peace for the sake of the family.

Six months after she was in California, Peter phoned. The only way he could have gotten her phone number was from her mother.

"You returned my letter."

"Yes."

"If you'd opened it, you would have learned that Ellie and I broke up. She's dating someone else now."

It probably wasn't the most forgiving thing to do, but Sunshine laughed. "I didn't need to read your letter to figure that out. The only reason Ellie wanted you was because I loved you."

"*Past tense?*"

"*Why are you surprised?*"

"*Your sister—*"

"*You don't need to tell me anything about my sister that I don't already know, Peter.*"

Dead air said more than if he had shouted across the line. Finally he spoke. "*I was a fool.*"

"*Yes.*" *He wouldn't get an argument from her.*

"*I love you, Sunshine.*"

She bit down on her lip so hard she tasted blood. "*I love you, too,*" *she whispered, broken,* "*but it's too late. I'll never get over what you did. You might as well have stabbed me in the heart. I should have known the minute I told Ellie I wanted to marry you . . .*" *She stopped talking. It was useless to continue, useless to relive the pain of her sister's treachery.*

"*I was human,*" *he argued.*

"*Well, I'm human, too,*" *she returned heatedly.* "*You should know I'm dating someone else now.*"

Her words appeared to stun him, as though he found it hard to believe she could have feelings for anyone other than him. It seemed he knew her better than she realized.

"*Do you love him, too?*" *he asked after another tense silence.*

She lied because she wanted to hurt him the same way he had hurt her. "*Yes,*" *she said,* "*very much.*"

He didn't say anything for a long moment. "*I see . . . I want you to be happy, Sunshine.*"

"*I am . . . I'm very happy.*" *She forced a cheerful note into her voice.*

"*I appreciate that you answered the phone.*"

She smiled at that. Had she known he was on the other end of the line, she would never have picked up. "*Sure. No problem.*"

"*You're a wonderful artist, Sunshine. I have no doubt you're going to be a huge success.*"

At the time she'd been working on that first painting that caused such a sensation. "If I am," she said coolly, "I have you and Ellie to thank. I paint with passion now, something my teachers once said I lacked."

He didn't comment. "Good-bye, my love."

It was on her lips to remind him she was no longer his love, but she decided against it and silently ended the call.

Using a number of excuses, Sunshine refused to return to Chicago for the holidays. It was better that she remained in California, and her mother begrudgingly accepted that she was right.

A year passed before Sunshine heard anything about Peter again. A Christmas card arrived from his mother. At the bottom of her holiday greeting, Peter's mother wrote a single line.

Peter is in law school.

Sunshine's chest tightened, and for a moment she found it impossible to breathe. He would hate every minute of it. For days afterward she moped around her tiny apartment, restless, agitated, and overwhelmingly sad.

A year later Anna sent her another Christmas greeting with another line, one equally devastating to Sunshine.

Peter is engaged to the daughter of my husband's law partner.

Sunshine never got another Christmas card from Peter's mother after that, and frankly she was relieved. It hurt too much to know he had given up the one thing in his life that brought him joy.

The two of them were more alike than she was willing to admit, because she, too, had given up the one thing in her life that gave her joy and love. She gave up Peter.

CHAPTER 20

Beth

Noah Folgate waited for Beth after school on Friday afternoon. She was pleased to see he'd taken her advice and hadn't dropped out of the music class. Neither had Bailey.

"Ms. Prudhomme?"

"Yes, Noah?" she said as she gathered books and papers off her desk. She glanced up and saw him standing just inside the room. "I wanted you to know that I'm glad you're back."

"Thank you. I'm glad to be back."

"Do you remember that you asked me not to drop this class?"

"I do remember. I asked you to give it a week."

"I did. The only reason I even signed up was because of Bailey, and then we broke up and I thought, you know, classical music wasn't really my thing. I didn't know Bailey had asked to drop the class, too. When we heard about your accident, Bailey and I talked and I asked her to homecoming and she cried, she was so happy. We stayed in your class and I'm glad we did. You were right. I liked learning about Mozart. He was one cool dude. I've learned a lot and now I . . ." He paused as if he was embarrassed. "I want to thank you."

"Noah, I'm the one who should be thanking you. You made my day."

He lowered his voice, as if he was afraid someone might be listening. "You're a better teacher than Mr. Englehardt."

"If you don't mind, I won't tell him you said so."

Noah smiled. "Yeah, it's probably best that you don't."

They walked out of the school together. Beth was almost to her car, one Sam had helped her choose, when her phone rang. Thinking it was Sam, a happy feeling came over her. On Friday afternoons he spent an hour or more with the guys from the garage and he usually didn't phone until he was home. The number that showed wasn't one she recognized, though.

"Hello," she said tentatively. She'd gotten several solicitation calls lately and was wary of getting more.

"Beth. It's me, Kier."

"Kier," Beth repeated and groaned inwardly. He was one of her least favorite people and he epitomized everything she disliked about the men her mother pushed on her. Everything came easy for him. He'd never had to work to prove himself. One time she'd been out with him when his car got a flat tire and he'd thrown a fit, kicking his BMW as if to punish the car for inconveniencing him. Owen would have made a mint off Kier.

"I'm in town. Let's get together."

"I'm busy this weekend." A small white lie but forgivable, not that it would do any good. Kier was far too accustomed to getting his own way.

"Your mother asked me to check up on you."

No doubt she had.

"You know she won't let me hear the end of it unless I give her a full report."

"Right." Six measly months. Her parents had agreed to give her these six months. They'd already broken their word. To be fair, she had been in a bad car accident, but still . . . Was six months so much to ask? Naturally, her mother would find a way around their agreement. If she put Kier off, Beth could guarantee Ellie Prud-homme would be on the next flight to Oregon, making Beth's life miserable. Ellie had already let her feelings be known when it came to Sam. He wasn't the man for Beth. He wasn't suitable. Lowbrow. The list of subtle and not-so-subtle complaints mounted with every conversation, which is one reason Beth's calls home were in-frequent at best.

"Let me take you to dinner," Kier said. "I know a great place downtown. Not that it can compare to anything Chicago has to offer, but it will do in a pinch."

It wouldn't do any good to argue. His comment about the res-taurant showed what an arrogant jerk he was. "When?" she asked, accepting defeat.

"Seeing that you're busy all weekend"—he knew she was lying and his tone said as much—"it will have to be tonight."

She might as well get it over with. "Okay. I'll change my plans."

"I thought you'd manage to squeeze me in."

"I'll meet you at the restaurant," she suggested. "Give me the address—"

"No way," Kier argued. "My mother raised me better than that. I'll pick you up at your apartment. I'll be by at six."

"My address is—"

"Already got it," he said, cutting her off.

Of course he did. Her mother would have seen to that. "All right, then," she said, unable to hide the defeat in her voice. "See you at six."

"We have a lot to catch up on," Kier said, which was another way of telling her it was going to be a long night.

Closing her eyes, Beth leaned against the side of her car, dreading this dinner. She had tentative plans with Sam for later. He and Rocco had something going on, but she didn't know what. Telling him she was going out with another man wouldn't sit well with him.

She climbed in her car and heaved a giant sigh before she reached for her phone again.

Sam answered almost right away. "Hey, babe."

"Hey," she returned. "I'm going to need to bow out of anything tonight."

"Oh?" Sam didn't bother to hide his surprise. "What's up?"

She could tell by the timbre of his voice that he suspected something wasn't right. "A friend is visiting from Chicago." Her heart was pounding, hoping he heard the regret she felt about not spending her evening with him.

"Bring your friend along," he suggested. "Nichole and Rocco invited us to Rock and Bowl. Several of Rocco's crew are going to be there, and I was thinking we could—"

"That won't work." She would love to see what her mother would say if Beth told her she went bowling with the crew from a towing company. It was comical enough to make Beth smile. Her mother would probably have a coronary.

"You didn't let me finish," Sam said.

"I know. I'm sorry. My friend has already made other plans, but I'd much rather be with you."

Sam didn't say anything for a long moment. "Have fun. We'll connect . . . whenever."

Beth hated to end their conversation like this. She hoped he understood how disappointed she was. "Do you want me to call once I'm home?"

He paused and then said, "Not necessary."

That stung, and she blinked back the hurt. "You don't want me to call?" she asked, unsure of his mood. "I told you I'd rather be with you. This is a friend of my mother's, and if I don't meet with him she'll fly out here herself and it won't be pretty."

"*Him*, Beth? Your friend is a he?"

"Yes." She'd wanted to avoid this, but now that was impossible. "His name is Kier and he's the son of a family friend."

"I notice you didn't invite me to join the two of you."

She stiffened. Sam was right; she hadn't once considered including Sam in this dinner date. "I . . . should have, I know, but . . ." She let the rest fade.

"But what?"

Beth pressed her hand against her forehead. "Can we please talk about this later?"

"No," he objected. "We can't, because I know what's going through that head of yours. I'm an embarrassment to you, Beth, you don't need to spell it out. I get the picture. If you're looking for me to apologize for who I am, you'll have a long wait."

"That is so not true."

"Coulda fooled me. It's fine. Go out with this family friend, enjoy your evening. Can't say I blame you. Fancy dinner in a posh restaurant versus Rock and Bowl. Guess I should be grateful you want anything to do with a guy with grease underneath his fingernails."

"Stop," she insisted. "That's ridiculous and you know it."

"Can't say I do." With that Sam ended the call.

Beth was angry and her hands shook as she tossed her phone back into her purse. Leaning forward, she pressed her forehead against the steering wheel. This was their first big fight and it was a doozy. She didn't know how to prove that she wasn't embarrassed by Sam. The fact that he worked with his hands and that he was good at what he did made her proud.

Back at her apartment, Beth dressed for dinner with a heavy heart. She toyed with the idea of calling Sam back, but pride wouldn't let her. He was being obtuse and unreasonable. It wasn't like she was at his beck and call. They didn't have any set plans that night. Everything had been up in the air.

Typical of Kier, he left her waiting fifteen minutes, and when he finally arrived at her apartment he kissed her on both cheeks. "You're as beautiful as ever." He glanced around, taking in her apartment and frowning as if it was far below his standards. It was hard not to remind him that she lived on what she made teaching music and wasn't living off a trust fund. Instead, she bit her tongue and did her best to pretend she didn't notice his censure.

"Home sweet home," Kier said with a fake smile.

Beth resisted suggesting he take pictures in order to give a more accurate account to her mother. In her current mood, it was hard to hide her feelings.

It came as no surprise that the evening was dreadful from beginning to end. Kier chose a restaurant she had never heard of before, a place that offered only one seating a night. The menu was pretentious and the waiter even more so. It was as if he felt obliged to detail each ingredient used in the making of every dish.

"The mushrooms were grown in the shadow of the Washington rainforest, hand-picked by altar boys."

Well, it went something like that. Beth had to use her linen napkin to disguise a smile while Kier absorbed the description and asked a number of asinine questions. She'd suspected it was going to be a long evening, and she was right.

It was after eleven by the time Kier dropped her off at her apartment. Standing outside her door, he seemed to wait for an invitation to come inside. He wasn't getting one and it took several uncomfortable minutes for him to figure that out. Before he left, he braced his hands against her shoulders and looked deeply into her eyes. "It was good to see you, Beth."

She could lie and say she felt the same, but she didn't. The best she had to offer was a weak smile in return.

"We'll have to do this again."

Not if she could find a way out of it. "Give my mother my best," she said.

"Will do," Kier promised. Then, when she least expected it, he leaned forward and gave her a moist, openmouthed kiss.

It took every bit of restraint she possessed not to wipe her hand across her lips. The evening was even worse than she'd anticipated. As soon as she was inside her apartment, she leaned against the door and grabbed her phone, praying Sam had left her a text message or called.

He hadn't, and it felt as if her heart had sunk to the level of her ankles.

After a sleepless night, Beth made her decision. She should never have gone out with Kier. Her heart had been with Sam and their friends the entire night. As ridiculous as it sounded, she'd gone because she'd wanted to please her mother. What was she, five years old? Beth's life was her own and it was time she started living it. Deep down there was a small child, looking to make her mother happy. Well, no more. Beth was finished. She was cutting the umbilical cord.

Now all she had to do was tell Sam how sorry she was. Before her first piano student arrived, she called Sam's cell, ready to do whatever was necessary to make things right between them.

Her call went immediately to voicemail, which told her he'd turned off his phone.

Beth had three piano students from nine until noon. When the last one left, a twelve-year-old who showed real talent, Beth couldn't stand it any longer. She grabbed her phone and tried Sam again.

Same thing.

He wasn't going to make this easy.

Beth left her apartment and drove to Sam's house. She saw he was working on one of his old cars. He was bent over the engine, and if he noticed when she parked at the curb, he gave no indication. She walked up his driveway.

Sam glanced up, saw it was her, and then returned to whatever he was doing as if she wasn't there.

Beth knew that she'd hurt him, and she was sorry. The best thing to do was address it head-on. "I came so you'd know I'm not ashamed of who you are or what you do, Sam."

He looked up a second time and said nothing.

"It's true. Please don't be like this."

"Like what? Like a mechanic?"

Frustrated now, she wanted to stomp her foot. "I had no idea you could be this stubborn."

"Don't think you know me at all, babe."

"That's not true," she argued.

"I knew I was going to regret getting involved with you."

"Would you stop? You're being ridiculous. I'm the same Beth you cuddled with in front of the television two nights ago. Nothing has changed except that I had this stupid obligatory dinner I felt I had to attend. I hated every minute of it. Every single minute. Why do you find that so hard to believe?"

"Then why did you?" he demanded.

"My mom's involved . . . It's complicated."

"No doubt." He straightened and moved away from the car, tucking his hands into his back pockets.

"Did you have a good time last night without me?" She needed him to give her something, anything that would crack this granite wall he'd erected that she couldn't seem to navigate.

"Peachy," he told her.

"Did . . . did you take anyone else?"

Sam didn't answer. Instead, his face broke into an easy smile. "Don't think you're the only woman I know. We aren't exclusive. You go out with other guys . . ."

"One guy who I don't even like."

"Whatever."

"So . . . you?" She couldn't finish the question when he'd basically told her he'd gone with another woman. For a wild moment she was convinced her heart stopped beating. She swallowed hard, and when she could breathe again she somehow managed to smile back.

"Oh." She took two steps in retreat, praying he would stop her. He didn't. She turned and started toward her car when she changed her mind. No way was she giving up on him, on them. No way.

Whirling around, she saw that he was watching her. She walked straight back to him and thrust her arms around him, hugging him close around his middle, uncaring if she got grease or anything else on her clothes. He stumbled back at the strength of her hold. She clung to him as if they were free-falling off a cliff.

"I can't bear to fight with you. This is killing me."

His hands were in her hair as he crushed her against him.

"I'm sorry, so sorry, Sam. You're right. I should never have gone with Kier. I did it because I was looking to appease my mother, and that was wrong. I'm through. Done with it. Finished."

Sam kissed the top of her head and rubbed his chin over her crown. "I was so jealous I hated myself."

"I'm jealous, too. I can't stand the thought of you with anyone else."

He snickered softly. "I stayed home last night."

"You did?" She stepped back enough to be able to look him in the eyes. "You stayed home?"

"And stewed."

"I didn't sleep well."

"Me neither," he confessed.

"We can't do this to each other, Sam. I hurt you and I'm sorry."

"I'm an embarrassment to you."

"No," she cried, desperate for him to believe her. "I wouldn't care if you dug ditches."

"As it happens, I did that one summer after high school." He grinned and covered the hand she pressed against his cheek.

"What matters to me is you."

"You matter to me, too, babe. So much."

He hugged her until it hurt to breathe, but Beth didn't care. She was in his arms, and that was exactly where she wanted to be.

CHAPTER 21

Sam

Matters had smoothed over with Beth, and Sam was glad they were back on an even keel. A couple weeks passed and the October rains hit in full force. One Sunday afternoon while Sam was busy doing wash, he got a call from Rocco. "Remember how you said you owed me one?"

Curious question. "When?"

"Don't be cute. Just recently. I was the one who introduced you to Beth, remember?"

"Yeah. So?"

"So do you have any plans with her today?"

Sam didn't like the sound of this. "Why do you ask?"

"Need a favor."

"One that involves Beth?"

"Yup."

Sam had the feeling he wasn't going to like this. "What do you need?"

"It's Nichole's birthday and I want to take her out for the evening. We haven't had a night with just the two of us in months. Owen is spending the weekend with Leanne and Nikolai and they're taking him to the zoo and dropping him off in the morning. Kaylene is out with friends. We had a sitter lined up, but she called and has come down with the flu."

"Let me see if I get this straight," Sam said. "Are you asking Beth and me to babysit Matthew?"

"You got it."

Sam rubbed a hand down his face. "Never done anything like this before."

"Didn't think you had. Figured the two of you could manage. We won't be gone long, just dinner and a movie."

"Dinner and a movie?" he repeated. "That's what? Three, four hours?" A lot could happen in that amount of time.

"Call if you have problems and we'll come home."

Sam loved the kid, but he wasn't a babysitter.

"Can you do it?"

He remained uncertain. "You can't get anyone else?"

"You weren't my first choice."

"All right, all right. I'll call Beth and get back to you."

At five-thirty Beth and Sam pulled up at Rocco and Nichole's place. Beth didn't seem any more confident about this than Sam was, but she was game. Neither one of them was willing to disappoint their friends.

"Just how much trouble could one baby be?" Sam asked.

"Right," she said with more enthusiasm than warranted. They looked at each other and burst out laughing.

"You babysat as a teenager, right?"

Beth hated to disillusion him. "Not really. A little, I guess, but all the kids were older. No babies."

Sam groaned. "I have the feeling we're both in over our heads."

"I've never been around babies much," she confessed, and seemed as nervous about this as Sam was.

"You think I have?" he asked.

The front door opened and Rocco stepped outside and onto the porch. "You two going to sit in the car all night or are you going to come inside?" He looked pointedly at his watch. "Dinner reservations are at six."

"Guess we can't put it off any longer," Beth said.

"Looks that way," Sam agreed.

Nichole was holding Matthew in her arms when they stepped inside. She'd written out a list of instructions and phone numbers in case they had any trouble. Sam took the tablet and read over the first page. Looked to him like the history of the Roman Empire would be a shorter read.

Beth took the baby from her friend. Thankfully, he was asleep.

"I really appreciate this," Nichole whispered.

"We're happy to do it," Beth told her, looking down at the baby.

"Hey," Sam said, frowning at Rocco. "Speak for yourself."

"Don't listen to him," Beth said, smiling. "He loves Matthew."

"No way am I changing a poopy diaper. I want to make that clear right now."

"Honey, come on," Rocco urged. "We're going to be late."

"I already said I'd handle the poop," Beth assured Sam. She looked at Nichole and said, "Go. We've got this. And happy birthday. Enjoy tonight with your husband."

Nichole hesitated and Rocco brought her coat and, before she could make an excuse to linger, ushered her out the door.

When it clicked shut, Sam stiffened. It sounded to him like a jail cell closing.

Beth sat down with Matthew. Looking at her with the baby asleep in her arms did something funny to his heart. For a long moment all Sam seemed capable of doing was staring at her. He didn't think he'd ever seen her look more beautiful, and that was saying something.

"You don't need to hold him," Sam said, forcing himself to look away before his heart turned to mush. "I can put him down in that contraption he sits up in if you want."

Beth looked up, her eyes smiling at him. "I enjoy holding him."

Sam sat down next to her. "Thought you said you've never done anything like this before."

"I haven't. Doesn't take much skill to hold a sleeping baby, Sam."

Needing to touch her, he placed his arm around her shoulders. "You look good with a baby in your arms."

She turned to smile at him again and he couldn't resist kissing her. Sam doubted he'd ever grow tired of kissing Beth. She angled her head toward him and soon they were making out like no tomorrow. Sam wove his hands into her hair, and their breathing grew heavy as the lengthy exchange continued. When they broke apart, they were both nearly panting.

"You make me forget the baby," Beth whispered.

"What baby?" he asked, leaning his forehead against hers.

Beth giggled softly. "Your kisses are addictive, you know that, right?"

"That's what all the girls say," he teased.

She playfully slapped his upper arm and Sam laughed. Apparently, he was louder than he thought, because Matthew jumped as though startled and let out a wail. With panic-stricken eyes, Beth looked to him. "What should I do now?"

"Gently bounce him," he suggested, although he was unsure.

She did, but that only seemed to infuriate Matthew.

"Maybe he's hungry," Beth said. She reached for the list of instructions Nichole had left. She flipped through the first few pages and announced, "It says here he usually eats dinner around this time. It needs to be heated. Here," she said, and passed off the wailing baby to him. "I'll go heat up his baby food."

Sam took Matthew and gently tucked him against his side. "Hey, little man, what's the problem?"

Whatever was bothering him, the kid wasn't giving it up. Not knowing what else to do, Sam followed Beth into the kitchen. She'd located the jar of baby food and had it open and was dishing it up to set inside the microwave.

"Hey, look, dinner," Sam said, pointing it out to the baby. "Oh yum, peas. Bet you love peas."

Matthew kicked and cried even louder. "I don't think he's overly fond of peas," he told Beth.

Her eyes filled with concern. "Do you think I should look for something else? This is what Nichole left out."

"No. Let's go with the peas."

Beth reached for the tablet a second time. "Nichole's note says we need to change his diaper before we feed him. Do you want me to do that?"

Sam weighed the question. Beth was busy getting Matthew's dinner ready. He should be able to handle changing a simple diaper. That sounded doable.

"You finish up here. I'll take care of the diaper." He took the baby into the nursery and set him down on the changer. Thankfully, Nichole had a stack of disposable diapers close at hand.

Once Sam managed to unsnap the kid's pants, Matthew started squirming, twisting around so that his butt was halfway in the air.

"Hey, buddy, I need a bit of cooperation here." At least Matthew had stopped screeching.

"How's it going in there?" Beth called out.

"Not good," Sam shouted back. "Could you give me a hand?"

"On my way."

As soon as Beth was in the room, he instructed, "You change him and I'll hold him down."

"Okay." She didn't sound all that confident, but she didn't argue.

Sam changed places with her so that he was at the head of the changer. As soon as Matthew's belly was exposed, Sam bent down and nuzzled him, blowing on his stomach, making a loud noise. Matthew kicked up his legs and laughed.

Beth quickly cleaned his bottom and lifted up his legs in order to get the fresh diaper under him. "Nichole manages to do this all on her own and it's taking the both of us."

"He likes to squirm."

With some difficulty, Beth managed to get the diaper on him and re-snap his pants. Tugging gently on his arms, Sam got Matthew to a standing position and lifted him into his arms. "Okay, little man, it's dinnertime."

They returned to the kitchen, and while Sam got the baby strapped into the high chair, Beth washed her hands and then brought out the peas and the peaches.

"You lucky boy. Look here," Sam said, pointing to the peaches.

Matthew gleefully slapped his hands against the tray.

"You feed him," Beth suggested.

"Me?"

"You do the peas and I'll do the peaches."

"I'll do the peaches. He hates peas."

Matthew continued to slap the tray. "All right, all right," he agreed. "I'll do the peas."

Sam sat down in front of the high chair and dipped the coated spoon into the peas. "Open up," he instructed the baby. Instead, Matthew grabbed hold of the spoon, spilling the peas all down his front.

"I forgot the bib," Beth cried, and raced to get it. She brought a washcloth back with her, but by then Matthew had managed to get peas all over the front of Sam's shirt.

Beth gasped. "How'd he manage that?"

"He flung a spoonful of peas at me."

"Try the peaches," she suggested.

It didn't matter what Sam fed the kid, Matthew wanted to feed himself. The spoon made it into his mouth about one out of five attempts. By the time the dish was empty there were peas and peaches in a two-foot radius around the high chair and a good majority of it was on Sam as well.

Beth planted her hands over her mouth. "Oh Sam."

Peas and peaches were smeared all over Matthew's tray, and the kid looked like he wore half of his dinner on his face and hair. The baby couldn't be happier, though. It was as if his sole mission had been to see how much food he could get on Sam and himself.

Beth returned with a clean washrag and handed it to Sam. "I can't believe what a good sport you are about this."

"Doesn't look like I had much choice," he said, wiping the wet cloth over his face and beard. "I have to say I had no idea dinnertime would be quite this adventurous."

"Me, neither," Beth agreed as she wiped Matthew's hands and face. "Do you think we should give him a bath?"

"Don't think we have much choice. I'll run the bath water while you keep him entertained."

Matthew was in high spirits and ran his hands over his tray, smearing the food that remained there as if he was an artist creating a masterpiece.

Sam went into the bathroom, ran the bathwater, and returned in time to see that Beth had managed to clean off the high chair and Matthew. The kid's hair stuck straight up with a mixture of green peas and peaches. When he saw Sam, he lifted his arms, ready to be set free of the contraption that held him in place.

"I'll be right in to help," Beth told him. "Nichole says as soon as he's eaten dinner we need to change him into his pajamas and feed him his bottle, then put him down for the night."

"Sounds good." Sam carried the baby back into his bedroom and again needed Beth's help getting him undressed. Who knew a kid this little would have moves Houdini couldn't manage?

Bathtime was fun, although Sam ended up getting as much water on him as he had Matthew's dinner. The kid loved being in the water and took delight slapping his hands and splashing water in every which direction. More than once Sam had to reach for a towel to dry his eyes.

While he washed the baby, Beth got out Matthew's pajamas. It took both of them to dry and dress him. Sam bounced him against his hip while Beth heated his bottle. She was about to take him from Sam when he smelled something bad.

"Do you smell what I smell?" he asked Beth.

She sniffed near Matthew's butt and then raised her eyes to his and nodded. "Poop."

Holding Matthew away from him, Sam handed her the kid. "He's all yours."

"Sam!"

"I draw the line at poopy diapers, Beth. Said so earlier."

"Okay, okay, but I'm going to need help."

Together they managed it, but it wasn't pretty. Sam kept his head twisted away while Beth cleaned the baby. "Rocco should have supplied a gas mask for this," he complained.

Beth laughed. "Oh come on, it isn't that bad."

Matthew was in good spirits. As soon as Beth settled down in the rocker with his bottle, the baby reached for it with both hands. She gently rocked him as he eagerly drank his milk.

Sitting across from her, Sam took in the sight and smiled. She might have been nervous about this, but she was a natural with the baby. He'd enjoyed holding Matthew, but it was always when either Nichole or Rocco was around. This was the first time he'd been responsible for the tyke, and he was grateful Beth was there to back him up.

Matthew closed his eyes and was soon asleep. He finished the bottle and Beth gently removed it from his mouth, placed him over her shoulder, and burped him. "I'm afraid to move," she whispered, "for fear of waking him."

Sam reached for the pad Nichole had left them and flipped through the pages until he found instructions for getting the baby to bed. "It says here seven-thirty is his regular bedtime." Sam twisted his wrist in order to look at his watch. "Seven-twenty-five. We're right on schedule."

"Okay, I'll hold him another five minutes and then we can put him into bed."

Their plan worked. Sam gently lifted Matthew out of her arms and noiselessly walked into the baby's room and placed him in the crib. They stood looking down on him for several minutes, wanting to be sure he was fast asleep. Tiptoeing out of the room, they gently closed the door and then collapsed onto the sofa.

"I'm exhausted," Beth said, leaning against Sam.

"Me, too."

"Who knew taking care of a baby could be so demanding?"

Sam shook his head. "To think Rocco and Nichole do this every day, and from what I hear, Nichole is hoping to get pregnant again soon."

"Are they nuts?" Beth asked.

"Apparently." He tucked his arm around Beth, who snuggled up close to him.

"You were wonderful, Sam," she said, yawning. "You're going to be a great dad one day."

Sam kissed the top of her head. She didn't know what she was saying, didn't know that he would have given anything to be a father to his daughter. He wouldn't remind her, but he couldn't help thinking it.

Beth fell asleep leaning against him, but Sam remained wide awake with thoughts of his daughter in the forefront of his mind.

He put an end to all the might-have-beens before they overpowered him. Instead, he focused on Beth. Right away tension tightened his belly.

Beth. Sweet Beth. Who did he think he was kidding? This thing with her, whatever it was, had gotten well ahead of him. Everything was happening too fast. Watching her with Matthew and all of a sudden he was looking into the future, thinking about babies and everything that went along with being a family man. That wasn't him.

Sam wasn't looking to change his life. His enjoyed his freedom. One thing was for sure: He didn't want his future tangled up with responsibilities. He liked the way things were pre-Beth.

Years ago, after Trish, he'd made the decision not to get involved in another relationship, and here he was with his arm around Beth and his heart and head tangled up in knots. He'd known the first night they'd met it wasn't meant to be. They were completely wrong for each other. Beth's mother knew it, too. One look at him had told Ellie Prudhomme what Sam already knew. He and Beth were all wrong together.

Yet here he was.

Something had to change and quick before he got in too deep, if he wasn't there already.

CHAPTER 22

Beth

"How are things going with Sam?" Sunshine asked, as Beth and her aunt strolled the wide aisle of an indoor antiques market. Her aunt loved looking at things from the past, and Beth enjoyed accompanying her. Sunshine was a study in contrast. Her art was cutting edge and modern, and at the same time she savored reclaiming, restoring, and making new what was once discarded and old.

"Sam's great." Beth watched as her aunt walked over to a display of buttons. He had quickly become her everything. It frightened Beth sometimes when she thought about him. Their relationship seemed perfect, and instinct told her that perfection wouldn't last. Soon they would hit a curve, and at the speed in which their relationship was progressing, they would either crash and burn out or find they could adjust and accommodate.

"First loves are special," Sunshine commented, picking up a button and examining it. "They are the ones that mark us."

Her aunt gave no further indication about her own first love, so Beth posed the question. "We never forget our first love, do we?"

"Never," Sunshine agreed. She replaced one button and reached for a cloth-covered one, holding it in the palm of her hand. "I once read that during the Civil War women of the south would soak these cloth buttons in perfume and then sew them into the collars of their men's shirts. That way the scent was a constant reminder of their loved ones waiting for them at home."

"That's so romantic." Her mind automatically went to Sam and how dreadful she'd feel sending him off to fight with an uncertain future. Sewing one of her perfume-soaked buttons in his collar would mean as much to her as it would to him.

"Who was your first love?" Beth asked, venturing closer to the subject on her mind. She hadn't given up the idea of finding Peter Hamlin, although she hadn't pursued it as of yet. Sam's words of caution had stayed with her.

Her aunt paused and a dreamy look came over her before she gently shook her head and then laughed, brushing off the question with a lighthearted response. "I had several."

"Sunshine! Certainly there was one who stuck out in your mind more than anyone else."

Her aunt increased her pace. "Of course there was," she agreed, and then marched off, leaving Beth no choice but to pick up the pace in order to follow her.

Not once during the entire afternoon was she able to get Sunshine to bring up Peter's name, but Beth knew it was him. It seemed that even now after all these years the subject of this man she'd once loved was too painful to discuss. Beth didn't know what role her mother had played in what had happened between her aunt and Peter Hamlin, but she suspected it was major. Something had caused the rift between them, a subject neither one seemed willing to discuss.

"What about the man you mentioned that night we had dinner?"

"What night?"

She ignored the question. "His name was Peter."

Her aunt grew suspiciously quiet.

"Did my mother have anything to do with what happened between you two?" she asked.

Her aunt's eyes grew sad. "Listen, Beth, some subjects are best left alone. This is one of them."

In that moment, Beth was convinced that her mother did have something to do with whatever had happened with Peter. Now more than ever she was curious to find out what she could.

Beth had found several Peter Hamlins on the Internet but deduced that the one living in Chicago was the man she sought. He was an attorney and worked in a prestigious law firm in the heart of the city. Of all the Peter Hamlins she'd found, this one matched up age-wise, as well. No guarantees, though. The only way to be certain was to contact him and ask. Facebook was no help, as his site was strictly professional.

Sam cautioned her when she told him what she'd discovered. "You could be stirring up a hornet's nest."

"Maybe, but I feel that at least I have to try." Sunshine had done so much for her that if Beth had even a small chance of bringing her beautiful, loving aunt happiness it would be wrong to let it drop.

It took Beth several days to build up her resolve to make the phone call to his Chicago office. She had to do it on her lunch break. Not wanting other staff members to overhear the conversation, she sat in her car. Her finger shook as she punched out the number.

"Hamlin, Wilkens, and Bower," the receptionist answered.

"I'd like to speak to Peter Hamlin," Beth returned in her most professional voice.

"Do you have an appointment?"

"No." She was afraid her voice might have trembled as she answered.

"Would you like one?" the receptionist returned.

"No, this is a personal matter. I'm calling from Oregon."

"From Oregon," she repeated, "and you say this is a personal matter?"

"Yes."

"I'm sorry, but Mr. Hamlin is in court this afternoon."

"Oh . . . I hadn't considered that," Beth said, thinking out loud.

"Would you like to leave me your number for Mr. Hamlin to return your call?"

Beth considered that and realized that wouldn't work. "I'll be in the classroom the rest of the day."

"Can I tell him what this is in regard to?" the woman pressed.

Again an internal debate waged inside her. "No," she decided quickly. "I'm not sure this is the same Peter Hamlin I need to speak with."

The woman grew hesitant. "Perhaps I can help you. My name is Sondra Reacher and I've been with the firm for nearly forty years. Technically, I'm retired, but I can't seem to stay away, so I come in two days a week."

Beth was tempted, but she didn't know enough about Peter Hamlin to ask the right questions. "This might sound silly, but does he enjoy fish tacos?"

The receptionist got another call and Beth was put on hold. She waited what seemed like a long time, but it was only a couple minutes before the woman returned.

"Where were we?" she asked.

"Fish tacos."

"Yes, I remember now. I've known Peter from the time he joined the firm and his father before him, too, as well as the other partners. As I recall, Mr. Hamlin does like Mexican food. I can't remember what he orders, though."

"That's encouraging. I think I might be on the right track."

"Won't you give me your name?"

Beth hesitated. "It would mean nothing to him."

"Try back again, and in the meantime I'll mention your call to Mr. Hamlin."

"Thank you," Beth said.

As soon as Beth disconnected she contacted Sam. His lunch break coincided with hers and they often spoke as they had when she was hospitalized. He answered on the first ring, as if he'd been anticipating her call.

"So how'd it go?" he asked right off.

"He wasn't there, but the receptionist was as helpful as she could be. She urged me to call back."

"Are you going to?" he asked.

"I suppose I will. I think this lawyer is the one."

Sam didn't approve of her plan, but thankfully he did nothing more than offer his advice. "Think carefully before you do," he urged.

"I have been giving it a lot of thought. I want to do this for Sunshine. It might go nowhere, but the least I can do is make the effort." The more she thought about it, she knew Sam might be right. She could be opening a can of wriggling worms and the ramifications might well bleed into her entire family. The hostility between Beth's mother and Sunshine was as thick as lava, and adding to it was sure to cause even more problems. The two sisters were rarely in the same room together, and when they were, the tension was often unbearable. Beth loved her aunt, and more than anything she wanted do what she could to help Sunshine to find the happiness she deserved.

———

Beth tried again on Tuesday afternoon. A different receptionist answered and blew her off like she was a fly on her pizza plate. Wednesday it was the same thing. The most she could get out of the woman was the time for an appointment, the soonest of which was in December. The woman urged her to take it, as Mr. Hamlin was in high demand. Although she never expected to actually make the appointment, she booked it, anyway.

On Friday Sondra Reacher, the older receptionist, was back on duty. "It's me again," Beth said, hoping the woman recognized her voice.

"Ah, yes, I remember you."

Beth was relieved. "Please tell me Mr. Hamlin is in his office today and not in court." She didn't mention that she'd called four times that week already.

"He's in," the woman said.

"Can I speak to him?" Beth asked, her excitement growing.

"Let me put you on hold. I'll check with him. You'd better give me your name this time."

"It's Beth. Beth Prudhomme."

The woman repeated her name, asked for the spelling, and then lowered her voice to say "I'll do my best. No promises."

"Thank you."

Beth was put on hold and her heart raced the entire time she waited.

"This is Peter Hamlin." His voice was sharp and impatient, as if she'd interrupted an important meeting. "I understand this is a personal matter?"

"Yes, yes, it is," Beth said, her mouth going dry.

"In regards to what?" he demanded.

"I'm wondering if you're the same Peter Hamlin who once knew my aunt. Her name is Louise, but her friends call her—"

"Sunshine," Peter finished for her, his voice instantly softening.

"Yes. So it is you?" Happiness and relief bubbled up inside her. "I was making an educated guess and—"

"What does she want?" He returned to the clipped gruff voice he'd used earlier.

Then, before she could answer, he asked another question.

"Is she okay?" He made the questions sound like she was on the witness stand for the opposing side and any response was to be treated with suspicion.

"She's in good health . . . now, if you'd give me a chance to explain."

"Then she wants something." The hostility made her stiffen.

"No, not at all. My aunt doesn't want anything. She doesn't even know that I've contacted you. I haven't told her . . . she mentioned you and I could tell that you'd been important to her at one time and decided to try to find you."

He was silent for several heartbeats. "Then what do *you* want?" he asked, sounding less angry now but not overly pleased.

"I want my aunt's happiness."

"She's a successful artist and—"

"So you've followed her career."

He didn't answer right away. "Yes."

"Then you know she never married?"

Again the slight hesitation. "Yes."

"Did you?" Beth ventured. She had this romantic picture in the back of her mind that she would bring these two people who had once loved each other back together again. There would be roses and champagne and they would still be madly in love after all these years.

"I did. Are you Ellie's daughter?"

"Yes."

"Listen, Beth Prudhomme, I'm a busy man. I have a client waiting. I don't know what you expect from me, but I want none of it.

I made my choice, your mother made hers, and so did Sunshine. Let's leave it at that."

Before Beth could say another word, the line was disconnected. Beth sat in her car, staring at her phone, unable to believe her aunt could have loved a rude, arrogant man like Peter Hamlin.

"He was awful," Beth told Sam later that evening.

"Babe, what did you expect?"

"Not that," she admitted as she tossed together a salad for their dinner. Sam had offered to take her out, but Beth wasn't in the mood. She wanted to vent, and doing it in a restaurant wasn't the best idea.

"I'm sorry you're disappointed."

"I had this fantasy built up in my mind of the two of them reconnecting and discovering their love had never died."

"That's in the movies, Beth. Real life is different."

"I can't believe my aunt could love such a jerk."

Sam tucked his arms around her waist and nuzzled her neck. "They fell in love years ago. Time changes people."

"I know." Inwardly, she prayed it would never change the way she felt about Sam.

"What does Sunshine have to say about him?"

"Nothing. Every time I ask about her first love, she changes the subject. The most information I've gotten out of her is that he likes fish tacos."

"You did your best."

Beth tried, but she couldn't help being disappointed.

Hours later, as she tossed and turned, unable to sleep, she couldn't accept that this bad-tempered, unfriendly man was the same one her aunt had loved. And from all outward indications, Sunshine loved him still.

Saturday morning Beth waited until after her three piano students had come for their lessons before she reached out to her aunt. She wouldn't tell Sunshine what she'd done, but she had to know more about Peter if she was going to make this work. There was a missing piece in this family drama—actually, there were several such pieces missing—and Beth was determined to lock it into place.

She brought Sunshine lunch at her studio. Her aunt had always made Beth feel welcome and special.

"What did you bring me?"

"Hummus and fresh cut-up veggies, a hard-boiled egg, and a huge peanut-butter cookie."

"Perfect. That's a well-rounded lunch. Let's start with the cookie."

Beth couldn't contain her smile. "We always ate dessert first when I was a kid, too, remember."

"I'm not likely to forget."

"Do you remember the time you wanted to take me on a picnic and Mom wouldn't let me go because she said I had hay fever?"

Sunshine rolled her eyes. "Which time?"

Beth pretended not to hear the question. "We ate under the dining room table."

"And your mother had a fit."

"We got crumbs on the carpet," Beth reminded her.

"A federal offense for sure."

They both laughed. Beth took care peeling away the plastic wrapper around her cookie. "I've never asked why you and my mother avoid each other."

"It's a long story, honey, and best left as it is."

"Perhaps," Beth agreed. "Still, I'd like to know."

"Have you ever asked your mother?"

Beth had years ago, after a short visit with Sunshine. Her aunt was appropriately named. Her visits were like scattered rays of beaming light that came into Beth's life when she seemed to need it most. She often wondered how Sunshine knew the best possible time to visit.

"I did ask Mom and she brushed me off and said I should ask you and then warned me against it."

Sunshine laughed. "That sounds like something she would do."

"She means well," Beth said. She did, too, and hoped she wasn't about to make a fool of herself. "Won't you tell me?" Beth asked, growing serious.

Her aunt waited a few moments before she answered. "I'm thinking this isn't the time or the place. I will, my love but not now. Another day."

It was hard to accept but she agreed. "Answer one question; that's all I'll ask for now."

"Okay, ask away," Sunshine said, with a classic wave of her hand.

"Was whatever happened between you over a man?"

Sunshine's gaze shot to hers and her eyes widened. "Yes," she whispered.

"Is his name Peter?"

"You said one question."

"This is part B."

"That's two questions."

"Louise, tell me the truth." To the best of her knowledge, this was the first time Beth had used her aunt's given name.

"Yes," she whispered, her eyes filling with sadness. "His name was Peter."

"And he loved fish tacos?"

"And sculpting, and, oh my, he was talented. He loved to laugh and sing songs he'd composed in my honor, and read aloud to me until I fell asleep in his arms. We connected on every level. I never loved anyone the same again," she whispered, lost in the perfect love in her past.

This was the same Peter Hamlin Beth had spoken with over the phone? It didn't sound like she'd found the same man at all.

CHAPTER 23

Sam

Sam had been in a sour mood all week without any real reason that he could name. Everyone noticed, not that there was any hiding how he felt. This wasn't like him, and he felt he owed his entire staff an apology.

It took him until Thursday to figure out what was bugging him when it should have been obvious. It was Beth. He hadn't been able to think straight since their stint babysitting Matthew. Their being together was all wrong. He knew it then but didn't know what to do about it and so he'd pushed the thought out of his mind. Not that it'd done any good. He'd made excuses to avoid her ever since that night—well, other than the two nights they performed together at the rehab center.

Beth had tried to talk to him, but he was having none of it. After a while she gave up and he was grateful. Everyone was entitled to an off day, or, in his case, an off week.

Friday afternoon following work Sam asked Rocco to join him and his crew. As was their habit, Sam and the other mechanics met at a nearby tavern for a cold draft beer and downtime. They were just finishing off the last of their beers when Rocco strolled through the door.

Sam was slouched over his mug, his mind whirling with his dilemma. He was glad to see Rocco and hoped his friend would help him sort through his thoughts. He lifted his beer, silently inviting Rocco to join him.

"Sup?" Rocco asked, as he slid out the stool next to Sam.

"Not much," Sam answered.

Rocco gestured toward the bartender and asked for a beer. He had his own mug within minutes.

"Been thinking," Sam said, and kept his gaze focused straight ahead.

"About?"

"Been troubled all week," Sam admitted. "Ever since you had Beth and me watch Matthew."

"About what?"

"Beth."

Rocco was silent for a short moment. "You two have a falling out?"

"A minor spat, easily settled. And that's just it, we should have had a big one by this time and we haven't."

"You looking to fight with your woman?"

"No," he said, getting flustered. He tensed. Even Rocco considered Beth to be Sam's woman. He swallowed tightly, unsure how best to explain his feelings. "I expected things to change after she got out of the hospital and they haven't. We talk every day, see each other four or five times a week. It's like overnight my life revolves around hers and hers around mine. It's too much."

"Not following you, buddy. You're not fighting and you think that's a bad thing?"

"No. Okay, yeah, we get along and that's cool. It's everything else, Rocco." Sam wiped a hand down his face and wished he could explain himself in a way that made sense. Problem was, he wasn't sure he could put it into words. "Did you know she's not talking to her parents?"

"What's that got to do with anything?" Rocco asked.

"A lot. I met her mother; it didn't go well. She wasn't in my face or anything, but I got the message and so did Beth. I'm not good enough for her daughter. Later the mother sent this guy she wants Beth to marry to town to check up on her."

"The night of the Rock and Bowl?"

"Yeah."

"Heard she isn't interested in him."

"She isn't."

Rocco glanced his way. "So what's the problem?"

Sam exhaled a long, slow sigh. "Beth and I had a great time with Matthew, and I have to tell her it scared the crap out of me."

Rocco raised his hand, stopping him. "We were talking about the mother."

"That's part of it."

"What's Matthew got to do with Beth's mother?"

"Not a damn thing. Hear me out, will you?"

Rocco shook his head as if to clear his thoughts. "Am I going to be able to follow your line of thinking?"

"Hope so," Sam confessed. "That night with Matthew I saw Beth holding your son and all at once I'm thinking that could be the two of us, and Rocco, I got to tell you that shook me. Not until later when Beth fell asleep with her head on my shoulder. I was walking through a field of daisies holding Beth's hand and suddenly I realized this is not me. I got caught up in this romantic dream and it shook me up good. Everything is happening too fast and I need to put the brakes on before this relationship gets out of hand."

"Okay," Rocco said slowly, reluctantly.

"You don't get it, do you?" Sam said. He sipped his beer, but it tasted bitter on his tongue. He was confused and unsure and needed his friend to help ground him before he got lost in that field of daisies.

Rocco's deep frown cut through him. "Are you saying you want to end it with Beth?"

"No." That was one thing he was confident about. "Not at all. I'm crazy about her."

"And it's scaring you to death."

Sam laughed because his friend had it in a nutshell. Beth had him scared out of his wits. "This isn't me. I'm not interested in making a commitment and she's the kind of woman that is going to want one."

"Has she said anything along those lines?"

"Not yet." It was coming, though. As sure as the autumn rains, the day was fast approaching when Beth would want more. A lot more, and no way was Sam ready.

"What are you going to tell her?"

If he knew that he wouldn't have asked Rocco to stop by for a beer. "Don't know yet, that's the problem." He rubbed his hand down his face. "She told me not long ago I was her first serious relationship."

"She's serious and you're not."

He was serious, but he was leery of what that would mean. "Beth has barely dated. Her parents have kept close tabs on her nearly her entire life. The men she dated before me were all Mommy-approved. She looks at me like some kind of hero and we both know that's bogus."

Rocco snickered as though amused.

"What's so funny?" Sam demanded.

"You remember when Nichole broke up with me? Her ex threatened to take her to court for custody of Owen because he found me an unsuitable role model."

"Not like I can forget." Those days had been bleak ones for his friend, who acted like a wounded animal, and not just any animal but a grizzly bear. No one got close without fear of losing an appendage or being cut wide open by a sharp tongue.

"I was angry and bitter."

"No kidding, Sherlock." Sam had been on the receiving end of his friend's anger more than once.

"But deep down I figured Nichole was right to break it off. I wasn't near good enough for her and I knew it. Actually, it didn't come as any big surprise when she wanted to call it quits. It was what I'd been expecting all along."

"You not good enough for Nichole? That's bull and you know it."

"You're wrong. No way did I deserve that woman loving me. Got history and most of it isn't good. You know that better than anyone. I did my best to make up for it, being a tax-paying citizen, raising my daughter as best I could. But Nichole and me? She deserved better."

"She wanted you, though."

"She did, and I thank God every day for whatever it was that I did to deserve her." Rocco paused and took a swallow of his beer.

"You saying that's what is going on with me?"

"Can't say, Sam. You're the only one who can answer that."

He mulled it over for several moments. "It's more," he admitted. "Beth has a way of getting to me like no one else, not even Trish."

"She knows about Trish and the baby."

"That's a perfect example." He gestured with his hands, nearly spilling his beer. "Never told any other woman I was seeing about Trish, but Beth knows. She even knows Lucinda's birthday, and it didn't take much for me to spill out all that pain, either. I get around Beth and my emotional filter disappears."

"And watching Matthew is what drove you over the edge."

"Basically, yes." He hated to admit it, but the bottom line was this: "I'm not the marrying kind, Rocco. You know that."

"Can't say that I do."

Sam let out a bark of laughter. "You're like one of those guys who gives up cigarettes after twenty years of smoking. All at once you become the poster child for not smoking and you're talking to everyone about giving up their smokes."

"We talking about cigarettes now?"

"No, we're talking about falling in love. You love Nichole and all at once you see unicorns and rainbows for everyone else."

Laughing, Rocco snorted beer out of his nose. "Unicorns and rainbows?"

"Yeah. That sh— ain't for me."

"You owe Owen a dollar."

"Don't, either. I stopped myself in time. More to the point, you're so caught up in what you have with Nichole you think it's for everyone and it's not."

"I didn't set you up with Beth. Nichole did."

"Okay, fine, but it's the same thing. You're both looking at life through rose-colored glasses. You expect everyone else to feel the same way about love as you do."

"That's not such a bad thing, is it?"

"It is for me," Sam said and straightened. Talking to Rocco hadn't given him any answers; he felt more confused than ever.

"So how are you going to explain all this to Beth?" Rocco asked.

If he knew that he wouldn't have asked Rocco to meet him. This weighed heavy on his mind. "I'm not sure yet."

"If I'm hearing you correctly, you want her to date other men."

"Yes. Makes sense she should. Even if we were to get more serious, which I'm not willing to do at this point, I'd feel better if she had some experience under her belt. She sees me as this shining knight. No way can I continue to live up to her hero worship. She needs to date other men, get a taste of the world, before she ties herself to me."

Rocco nodded as if he understood. "You going to suggest that to her?"

"I should, don't you think?"

"Well, yeah, but I'm wondering . . ."

"What?" Sam demanded when his friend didn't continue his thought.

"You still want to continue to date her yourself, though, right?"

Sam needed to think that through. Going cold turkey would be hard. Beth had become an important part of his day, of his life. Too important, which is what prompted this entire debate. She was the reason for his crappy mood all week. Well, not Beth personally, but the way he felt about her.

"Yeah, I would like to continue seeing her." He hesitated to use the word *date*. Sam didn't date. He'd made certain she understood that weeks earlier. If she wanted to call their occasional dinners out dates, then that was on her.

No way would anyone refer to their music sessions as dates. That was nothing more than entertaining a few people a couple times a week. Most definitely that wasn't dating. Okay, fine, he was willing to admit he stopped by her place once or twice a week and they'd watched television together. He'd seen more movies in the last three weeks than he had in the last three years. Chick flicks, even. Stuff like that should have knocked some sense into him. This relationship continued much longer and he'd be watching the Hallmark Channel.

"Are you thinking to suggest the two of you be friends?" Rocco asked.

"Yeah, friends." Sam brightened, relieved. Telling Beth they should be friends was the perfect solution. It wouldn't be that much different. He already considered Beth a friend.

Rocco snickered into his beer.

"What?" Sam demanded.

"Good luck with that."

"What's that supposed to mean?"

"You tell Beth that you want to be just friends and see what happens."

Frowning, Sam studied Rocco. "Why do I feel like this is a joke and no one is letting me in on it?"

"Don't go the friends route," Rocco suggested.

"Why not?"

"She won't take it well."

"But I mean it."

Rocco shook his head as if pitying Sam. "All I'm saying is that trying to friend-zone this isn't the best idea. Trust me."

"Okay." Rocco would know better, although Sam didn't understand why.

Rocco slid off the stool. "Time I headed home. Nichole's waiting."

"Appreciate the talk."

"Let me know what happens," Rocco said and slapped him across the back.

Sam nodded. He sat for several minutes, then decided the sooner he had this conversation with Beth the better. He reached for his phone.

She answered before the end of the first ring, as if she'd been expecting his call.

"Hey," he said.

"Hey," she returned enthusiastically. "You in a better mood?"

"Yeah."

"Great, because I've got all kinds of things to tell you."

She sounded like she was taking a stroll on cloud nine. Sam hated the thought of bursting this bubble.

"I'm hungry."

"Want me to fix us something?"

He bristled. She was already acting like a wife. "No. Want to meet me at Red Robin for a burger?" he asked. This wasn't a date. If he was asking her out on a date he'd go and pick her up.

"Sure."

His shoulders sagged with relief. "Give me thirty."

"Sounds great. I've missed you this week."

CHAPTER 24

Beth

Beth was in a great mood. She'd had a defining conversation with her mother in which she'd made herself crystal clear.

"You stepped over the line, Mom," Beth had told her mother.

"What do you mean?" Her tone was defensive.

"Kier." All it took was one word to explain what she meant.

"Well, Sweetie—"

"You don't need to say anything. I know why he was in town. You're concerned about Sam and me."

"Yes, S-a-m," her mother drawled out his name. "Sweetie, surely you recognize—"

Beth cut her off again. "What I recognize is that you're trying, once again, to manipulate my life, and Mom, as much as I love you, I'm not going to allow you to do that."

"I'm only doing what I think is best for you."

"What *you* think is best," Beth said pointedly. *"You."*

"I'm older and wiser. No one knows you better than me."

"Mom, listen, because I'm only going to say this once. *This is my life*. I will date who I want. I will make my own decisions. I will make my own choices. If you can't let me do that, then there's nothing more for us to say."

Her mother gasped softly. "You don't mean that."

"Yes, Mom, I do. With every fiber of my being I mean it."

Her words were followed by a long pause.

"Are we clear, Mom?"

Her question was followed by a deep, reluctant sigh. "Yes, we're clear."

"Good."

After she disconnected, Beth felt like standing on her balcony and pounding her chest like Tarzan. She had taken control of her life. No more Kier. No more control issues. Beth had made it clear. THIS WAS HER LIFE.

Sam had been in a pissy mood all week, not really wanting to talk or spend much time together. But maybe he was over it, since they were having dinner together. She'd missed him. And she had news to share with him. Good news. Exciting news.

By the time she arrived at the restaurant, Sam had their name on the list, and no more than five minutes later they were escorted to a booth. Sam liked hamburgers and she did, too. She considered them comfort food because she'd so rarely eaten them while living at home. Actually, she and Sam shared a lot in common when it came to tastes.

Once seated, the waiter took orders for their drinks and their meal as well. As soon as he left the table, Beth, who was all but bursting with excitement, said, "I had a conversation with my mother this morning."

Sam arched his thick brows. "I thought you weren't talking to your mother."

That was true. Beth had been upset about Kier's visit and wanted to make sure her mother understood she wasn't going to allow her to manipulate her life choices. Ellie Prudhomme had phoned countless times and Beth had refused to answer.

"I've been ignoring her calls ever since she sent Kier to check up on me. But then she sent several texts, threatening to fly to Portland if I didn't take her call." Beth had been surprised. She didn't think her mother even knew how to text.

"Guess she took the option away from you."

"Well, I certainly didn't want her visiting me again."

"So how'd it go?"

Sam leaned back and crossed his arms. Beth read that as a defensive measure, certain she was about to tell him how much her mother disliked the fact she was dating him.

"Actually, it went great—better than great." Beth resisted the urge to pump her fists in the air. "I told her I wasn't her pawn and if she sent anyone else out to visit that I would cut off all communication with her."

Sam blinked hard. "Did you mean it, Beth?"

"Every word." She was serious and wasn't willing to compromise. The taste of freedom, the ability to make her own choices, choose her own friends, teach and date whomever she pleased, was an elixir and she wasn't about to risk losing it.

"I'm glad you were able to get your point across, but I don't imagine your mother took it sitting down."

"She didn't," Beth confirmed. "Mom insisted I was ruining my life."

"By associating with me?"

"No, Sam, don't even think that. I surprised her, though. I told her she was right; I was ruining my life."

His frown deepened.

"And I am. I'm ruining the life she planned for me. I insisted that I am going to live the way I want and she could flush her expectations down the toilet." Not exactly in those words, but close enough. Beth beamed him a huge smile, expecting him to congratulate her. "Aren't you going to say anything? This is big for me. Huge."

He nodded but didn't seem to show a lot of enthusiasm.

Their meals arrived and they both reached for their burgers. Beth took one bite, swallowed, and continued. "And that's not all. I found Peter Hamlin, the real Peter Hamlin. I even talked to him and I have to say, he's a piece of work. My aunt is better off without him."

"You're satisfied now?"

She considered that. "I'm thinking on it, weighing my options. One of the receptionists is really chatty and has worked there for nearly forty years." Beth reached for a thick french fry and dipped it in ketchup. "She only works two days a week. I was able to talk to her and learned a little more. While Peter might not be Mr. Personality, I think, given the chance, the two might be able to work things out." She paused and sighed. "Guess I'm the eternal optimist."

Sam didn't look convinced. "If you want my opinion, you'd be wise to drop it."

"I'm thinking over how best to proceed. I haven't made my final decision yet." She took another bite and saw that Sam hadn't eaten more than a bite or two of his burger.

"You feeling okay?" she asked. "You haven't been yourself all week."

He shrugged and leaned forward. "Think it's time you and I had a talk."

"Oh?" This sounded serious. She set the burger down and waited for him to continue.

Sam pushed his nearly untouched meal aside. "I guess the best way to do it is to just say what's on my mind."

"By all means," she agreed.

He expelled a breath. "I think you should consider going out with a few other guys."

Beth stared at him and then leaned back in the booth while she processed his words.

"You aren't saying anything." He looked hesitant and uncertain, which was nothing like the Sam she knew.

"You'll have to forgive me, Sam, I don't have much experience in this. Are you breaking up with me?" Her heart felt like it had sprung up to her throat and wrapped itself around her vocal cords.

"No," he insisted, adamantly shaking his head. "It's just that we, the two of us, haven't been seeing other people."

"True." It took her several moments to sort through her feelings. Her mind filled with questions, the most important of which found a difficult time making its way past the knot in her throat. "Are you telling me you want to date other women?"

His eyes widened with surprise. "Not at all. No way. Besides, I don't date."

He sounded sincere enough for Beth to believe him. It was hard to maintain her surprise and her hurt. "Then exactly what are you saying?" she asked, deciding to let the "I don't date" comment pass.

He rubbed a hand down his face. "I'm crazy about you, Beth, you have to know that."

"The feeling's mutual, you have to know that," she returned, echoing his words. "I don't understand, Sam. This is coming out of the blue and it's mystifying."

"I know." To his credit, Sam looked utterly miserable. "I'm as uncertain and confused as you."

"Can you tell me what brought this on?" If he explained, she might be able to decipher where this was coming from.

"Everything," he said, looking down. "The Kier thing, I guess, then watching you with Matthew and a bunch of other stuff that's been floating around in my brain since you got out of the hospital. You said yourself I was your first serious relationship."

"You are."

"You'll always wonder," he said, as if that was self-explanatory.

"What would I wonder about?" she asked, her dinner forgotten. She gave up all pretense of eating.

"If . . . you know."

"But I don't," she insisted.

"Okay, say somewhere down the line you meet someone else. You might have regrets. Someone better suited to you than I'll ever be."

"Someone my mother would approve of, you mean."

"Not necessarily," he argued.

He was intent and serious, and while he'd shocked her, she couldn't be overly upset with him. It was clear he'd given this matter a lot of thought. She sat for several minutes, struggling to look at it from his point of view.

"Are you mad?" he asked.

Clearly he'd expected her to be angry, and to be fair, at first she had been. "No, a little puzzled, but I think I understand. You want me to date other men to be sure what we have is real."

"Yes." Right away his eyes brightened, as if she'd helped him step out of the fog.

"A lot of men?"

"Sure," he said, but he didn't sound completely convinced.

She mulled it over and then said, "The school is having a Halloween dance and one of the chaperones, his name is Tyler, asked me to go with him. I turned him down, but if he hasn't found a date I'll accept when I see him on Monday."

"Good."

Sam didn't sound overly pleased.

She tapped her index finger against her lips, mentally hashing over other possibilities. "I play the piano for choir practice and Doug Freeman asked me out recently." She'd never mentioned that to Sam. No reason she should.

"Then go out with him."

He sounded like he spoke through gritted teeth.

"Is it considered bad taste to date two men at the same time?" She genuinely needed to know.

"Only if you're in an exclusive relationship."

"Okay," she said, and reached for her hamburger. She paused with the burger halfway to her mouth. "The father of one of my piano students hinted that he was single when he picked up Ricky. I didn't encourage him. Maybe I should. What do you think?"

"That's your decision."

"Right. Guess the more men I date the better feel I'll have about who's right for me."

"Right." Sam's burger remained untouched.

"Question."

"Sure," he said.

"Will I see you again, or would you rather we not see each other for a while? Either way is fine with me. You decide."

"I'd like to see you as friends."

Beth smiled. "Good. I'll look forward to that, then. Being friends, I mean."

His returning grin didn't quite reach his eyes.

"Do you feel better now?" she asked.

"I guess."

"This has been weighing on you all week, hasn't it?"

"It has," he agreed.

"Silly of you, Sam. You should have said something sooner."

The waiter came by with their tab and Beth reached for her purse and took out a twenty.

"I'm buying," Sam insisted.

"I appreciate it, Sam, but as you recently mentioned, you don't date. We aren't a couple, so it's best that I pay my own way." She set the bill on the table, slid out of the booth, kissed him on the cheek, and walked out of the restaurant with her head held high.

CHAPTER 25

Sam

Suggesting Beth date other men wasn't working out anywhere close to the way Sam had expected. The only time he'd seen Beth all week was at the rehab facility. She breezed in at the last minute, after insisting she didn't need a ride. When they'd finished performing, she announced she could play only one night that week. She didn't offer an excuse, but Sam could very well guess the reason. He noticed it hadn't taken her long to take him up on his suggestion.

Friday after work, a week after their initial conversation, Sam found himself at loose ends. He called Beth, not for any reason in particular, just to check up and see how things were.

"Sam, hello." She sounded pleased to hear from him, which boded well.

"How's it going?"

"Good. Real good."

"You up for a pizza? I can stop by and we could watch a movie."

He wasn't sure where the offer came from; he hadn't planned to ask, but now that he had, it felt good.

"Can't, sorry." She did sound genuinely regretful. "I'm finishing up this costume for the Halloween dance. Not sure I should have agreed to go as Dione. Tyler suggested we go as Greek gods, and, not knowing what I was getting myself in for, I agreed. Worse, I decided to sew my own costume."

"Can I stop by?" He felt like a fool needing permission and had no one to blame but himself.

"Of course." She sounded surprised. "You don't need to ask, Sam. You're welcome anytime. We're friends, right?"

Sam arrived less than thirty minutes later and found Beth busy at her sewing machine with yards of diaphanous fabric gathered on the kitchen table.

"I'm sorry I don't have time for a movie tonight, Sam," she said, and sounded genuinely apologetic. "I didn't know what I was getting myself into when I chose this costume. The instructions didn't look that complicated."

"I didn't know you could sew."

"As you can see, I'm not that great at it. I learned years ago in Girl Scouts. My leader was a seamstress by trade and she insisted every girl know the fundamentals." She puffed up her chest and used a high-pitched voice that apparently imitated her leader, causing Sam to smile.

He wandered around her apartment, lost, forlorn, ill at ease, and, in a word, miserable.

Finally, he couldn't remain silent any longer. "So you're going to the dance with that Tyler guy you mentioned." Nothing like stating the obvious.

"Not going going," she returned, as if that explained everything.

Sam narrowed his eyes. "What does that mean?"

She looked up from the table, her hands still braced against the frothy fabric she fed into the machine. "He's not picking me up at the house like it's a date or anything."

"Oh." That made him feel slightly better. Not much, but some. Then he had another question. "Who is Tyler dressing as?"

"Zeus."

"Oh." *Zeus?* Apparently, Tyler had a high opinion of himself.

Beth scooted back her chair, stood, and placed her hand against the small of her back, elbows sticking out as she relieved the pressure in her spine.

"I'm happy to see you taking my suggestion." He'd feel a lot better if she hadn't taken it up with quite so much gusto.

"Me, too," she said, sitting back down and returning to her project. The portable sewing machine buzzed like a chainsaw as she continued to feed the cloth through. "You made a good point."

He was beginning to regret the entire conversation. He'd overreacted and now he'd dug himself into a black hole. One week out and he was miserable and feeling more foolish every minute.

"Zeus," Sam muttered mockingly, thankful he couldn't be heard over the noise.

Feeling like he was more in the way than being helpful, he headed for the door.

"On second thought, you could order us that pizza," Beth suggested, her back to him as she sat at the table.

You'd think she'd offered him a lifeline from the way he reacted. "Happy to." He knew what she liked, sausage and black olives on one half and meat lovers with anchovies on his side.

"I'll pay my share, though, seeing that we're no longer dating."

"The pizza was my idea," Sam insisted. "Let me pay for it."

She stared at him. "You sure you want to do that?"

"I'm sure."

She smiled back before twisting around and racing the fabric through the machine.

"Thirty minutes," he reported, once he'd finished placing the order.

"Great. I'm starving." She shuffled the half-sewn gown onto the table and turned around to face him. "Did you have a good week?"

Here was his chance to tell her he'd been even more miserable than he'd been the week before. The easy way Beth had accepted his suggestion had dented his ego. He wasn't sure what he'd expected, but it hadn't been that. She seemed almost eager to see other men, and that was just plain wrong. He'd imagined there would be tears, accusations, anger. He had to say, this woman was full of surprises. Pride wouldn't let him get anywhere close to the truth. "I'm okay" was all he was willing to admit. "What about you?"

"Busy! The entire week has been hectic. I've had something every night, which explains why I'm putting this costume together at the last minute."

Sam pinched his lips and hoped she didn't notice. If she was going to be dating so much, he certainly didn't want to hear about it.

"I'm sorry to miss our jamming session," she admitted. "I had a meeting with a group of music teachers in the area that night."

So she hadn't been out on a date after all. Sam brightened immediately and his ego slid comfortably back into place. Actually, it felt as if a hundred-pound sack of cement had been lifted from his shoulders.

"Do you remember Jazmine?" Beth asked him. "She was one of the nurses' aides at the rehab center?"

"Vaguely."

"She was one of my favorites. I admire her so much." Beth was excited and nearly rushed the words together in her eagerness to explain. "She's a single mom with two little kids, working hard to make a decent life for herself. She got good news this week."

"Oh?"

"After completing all the paperwork and going through several interviews, she's been accepted by Habitat for Humanity. That means she'll be building a home for herself and her children. A real home with her own two hands. She didn't want a handout, she was looking for a hand up and she got it. When she told me, I swear she was nearly bursting with excitement and joy."

"I know someone who did that," Sam told her.

"Who?"

"Nichole's sister. Rocco and Cassie's husband are good friends. It's a great program."

"From everything Jazmine said, it sounds like it. She asked if I'd be willing to volunteer to help and I said I would."

Beth looked happy and excited for her friend, and when she smiled he found it nearly impossible not to smile back.

"I've never had an active social life before, Sam, and I'll admit I like it."

"It's good of you to volunteer to help Jazmine."

"That's not all I've got going. Doug is taking me out to eat after church on Sunday and then Monday Nichole and I are getting together. I have friends, my own friends, people I choose to associate with. Although"—she paused to inhale a deep breath—"I have to tell you, I don't know what Mom would say if she heard I'm working at a construction site."

Beth continued to chatter away like a magpie at dawn, but all he heard was that she would be seeing this Doug guy she'd mentioned a week earlier. Sam bit down on his back teeth so hard he was convinced he'd cracked a molar.

"And then there's my date with Tyler."

"You're dating Tyler? I thought it was chaperoning the one dance. You mean there's more?"

"He asked me out for next week, too."

Sam's jaw was clenched so hard he feared a thin-line fracture.

"He wanted to take me to . . ."

Sam had to turn away before he said or did something he'd regret.

Beth stopped, and when Sam glanced back she looked at him as if she'd missed something.

"You're right, you are busy these days," he muttered, stuffing his hands in his pockets. A week. All it'd taken was one week: seven measly days. Beth couldn't be accused of letting any grass grow under her feet.

"Everything all right, Sam?" she asked, looking concerned.

Another word about the men she was dating and Sam was going to lose it.

"If you don't mind, I'd rather not discuss the other men in your life."

"Of course, but you're the one who suggested I get more experience, spread my wings, so to speak."

She was right.

Beth lowered her hands on her thighs and released a long, slow sigh. "There's no need to be jealous."

"Jealous?" He laughed as though that was ridiculous. Pride demanded he keep his cool. He was doing his best to downplay his feelings. He'd never dreamed it would be this hard.

The delivery guy chose that moment to ring the doorbell. Sam had never been happier to have an excuse to end a conversation. He would have gladly paid double for their pizza. He gave the delivery boy a healthy tip.

Beth cleared off the table, and they sat down with the open box supported by the back of the sewing machine.

Beth ate her first slice and was reaching for a second when her phone rang. She had it on the table and glanced over and read the caller ID. Her eyes grew wide and she swallowed hard.

"Who is it?" Sam asked, although he wanted to grab back the words. If it was another guy wanting to take her out, then he was leaving. No way was he sitting here and listening to that.

"I don't believe this," Beth cried.

"Someone is bothering you?" Sam would answer and deal with it, if that was the case.

"Unbelievable," she muttered. "Yes, someone's bothering me. It's my mother."

CHAPTER 26

Beth

"Beth," Sam said, concerned for her. "I thought you and your mother had an understanding."

"I thought we did." She wasn't happy to see her mother's name turn up on caller ID.

"You said your piece. You're an adult. You have your own life now and the only way she can take that away from you is if you let her."

Sam was right. "I'm not answering the phone, and if she does decide the only way to talk to me is to fly to Portland, that doesn't mean I have any obligation to see her." What perturbed her was the fact that Beth had made herself clear. She wouldn't put up with any further interference in her life.

"Babe, are you afraid of her?"

He called her babe, and while her heart reacted instantly, she didn't want to show it. "Mom has a strong personality; I'm more like my dad."

"You've only mentioned him in passing. Tell me about him," Sam said, easing back into the chair, comfortable now when he hadn't been earlier.

Beth smiled, thinking about her father, whom she dearly loved. Often in the evenings he would have her play for him when he returned from work. He sat in his favorite chair and listened to her while he read the evening newspaper. Her music soothed him from the stresses of the day. He encouraged her talent and her love of music.

"My dad's name is Phillip and he's a geophysicist."

Sam lifted his eyebrows. "Sorry, but what exactly does a geophysicist do?"

She could remember asking him that herself at one point in her youth and was disappointed when she learned he wasn't a fireman. "He's mostly involved in research. He studies the structure and dynamics of the earth and the solar system. He's quiet and intense and something of a mathematical genius. I never understood how my parents got together. They have opposite personalities. Dad is a loner and Mom needs to be around people, especially those she wants to impress."

Beth appeared to be a nice blend of both personalities.

"If it wasn't for my dad's intervention," she continued, "I might never have been able to break away from Chicago."

"How's that?"

Beth's heart warmed as she remembered the way her father had stepped forward to help her. Phillip Prudhomme was deeply involved in his work and had been emotionally and physically absent for most of Beth's life. He gave his wife free rein when it came to raising their only child. She suspected he had no clue what kind of control his wife had over Beth.

"I managed to save some money," she began, "because heaven

forbid that I should actually have a real job. I played the organ for the church and was given a small stipend, which I hoarded away along with Christmas and birthday money."

"You were going to run away?"

"Ridiculous when you think about it, isn't it? I'm twenty-five, Sam, twenty-five, and had yet to have a life, a real life where I stand on my own, support myself, or have a chance to share my passion for music with others."

He reached for her hand and held it in his own. The warmth she felt from his touch raced up her arm. She'd missed him dreadfully this past week but was afraid to mention how empty her days had felt without him.

"You have a life now," he said, his voice gentle. "And look how far you've come in just a few months."

"Thanks to my aunt. I contacted her and asked if I could come live with her for a time."

"And she agreed?"

"Sunshine told me she'd been waiting years for this phone call. I was determined to leave but felt I needed to tell my dad. I was afraid my mother would make him think my aunt had somehow manipulated me into moving. Sort of an emotional kidnapping."

"The conversation went well?"

Beth nodded. "It was the first heartfelt conversation I'd ever had with my father. All the frustration over the last year when Mom had attempted to marry me off poured out of me. I wanted to teach music, share the classics with young hearts and minds and take on a few piano students of my own. Mom would never approve of that. I poured it all out, and when I finished, I saw tears in my father's eyes."

"I'm going to like your father," Sam said.

His comment produced a smile from Beth. "I know you will. Dad said I didn't need to sneak out in the middle of the night. He would make it so I could leave with my head held high."

"Which you did."

"Because of Dad. I'm not entirely sure what he said to my mother but when he finished talking she'd agreed to stay completely out of my life for six months. He would have made sure she kept away if not for that stupid car accident." Forgetting herself, she added, "That accident was one of the worst days of my life and one of the very best."

"The best?" Sam asked, surprised.

"Well, yes, I wouldn't have gotten to know you if it hadn't been for the accident."

Sam grinned and, seeming to have forgotten himself, he drew her into his arms for a hug. Beth laid her head upon his shoulders and all but sighed at the comfort she felt in his embrace. Neither of them seemed eager to break apart. After several minutes, they awkwardly eased away from each other and didn't make eye contact.

Beth continued with her story. "I suspect Dad was in touch with Sunshine, although she never mentioned it."

"When are the six months up?"

"December."

Sam looked forward to the time he could meet Beth's father and then realized he was counting on the fact the two of them would still be together over the holidays. The thought jarred him, and at the same time the tension eased from between his shoulder blades as he realized that was exactly what he wanted.

Beth connected with her aunt early the following afternoon. As expected, she found Sunshine busy at work in her studio. Her aunt glanced up when Beth arrived. One look and she set aside her brush and asked, "What's wrong?"

"Am I that easy to read?"

"Like an open book, Sweet Pea." Sunshine reached for a rag, wiped her hands, and pulled out a stool for Beth to sit down.

"Sam stopped by Friday evening and we shared a pizza."

Sunshine looked more than pleased. Beth had shared with her their conversation from the Friday before. "I didn't think he'd be able to stay away."

Beth felt worlds better after his visit. "He asked me not to tell him about any other men I was dating."

Unable to resist, Sunshine laughed. "He regrets it already."

"Maybe." Beth wasn't willing to believe it yet. "While he was there, Mom phoned."

"No!"

"I don't know what I need to do to get her to leave me alone."

"Did you answer?"

"No way."

Sunshine approved. "Good girl."

"Can you please tell me what happened between you and my mom? Why is your relationship so awkward?" Even as a toddler, Beth was aware of the strain between the two sisters. Never understanding what had happened, she simply accepted it as something all sisters shared. She remembered she was grateful as a young girl that she didn't have a sister, because she never wanted to feel toward her sibling the way her mother felt toward Sunshine.

Her aunt looked away and a weak smile came over her. "In a nutshell, I loved a man, a special, wonderful man who I thought was my soulmate. I've never felt as strongly about any man as I did about him. He was the sun in my world."

Peter. It had to be him.

"Several men have come and gone from my life since," Sunshine continued, "but there has only been him in my heart."

"What happened?" Beth asked, needing to know.

"Ellie knew how I felt about him and stole him away from me while I was studying in Europe." Her aunt looked away and her eyes grew dim and sad. "He was at fault, too," Sunshine admitted.

"When I returned they were together. I moved to California shortly thereafter. Only a few months later I learned they'd split."

"She didn't love him, did she?"

"Who's to say? Your mother always wanted whatever I had, and in this case it was Peter. I felt betrayed. I was young, angry, and, to be fair, we were all immature. I would have done things differently now, but it's years too late."

"That's when you went to graduate school?"

"Yes," her aunt said, her voice dropping to that of a whisper. "I wasn't in California long before I heard from Peter. He reached out to me, but I was unwilling to forgive either one of them. I couldn't look past the pain of their betrayal."

"What happened to him?" Beth asked, although she was fairly certain she knew.

Her face fell and she looked down at her hands. "He married someone else."

"Oh." Beth hurt for her aunt, who meant so much to her.

"Fortunately, your mother chose well and because she did we have you."

Beth's own heart was breaking just hearing her aunt tell the story. "Why didn't you marry, or have children?"

"I could never love anyone as much as I did him," she whispered, "and as for having no children, one thing your mother did for me that I will always be grateful for is giving birth to you."

Tears filled Beth's eyes.

"The instant I held you for the first time," her aunt continued, "I knew that you were God's compensation to me. I adored you and decided then and there that I wouldn't ever let my sister keep me away from you."

"I adored you, too. Your visits were the highlight of my childhood. I don't know what would have happened if it hadn't been for you."

"I know, and your father knew it, too. Without him I fear Ellie might have kept you from me. I'd like to think she would have let me be part of your life, but I'll never know for sure."

Beth had renewed respect for her father. "This man you loved," she said, carefully broaching the subject. "Have you ever thought about finding him again?"

Sunshine automatically shook her head. "No, never."

"Seriously?" Beth so wanted her aunt to find happiness with this man she loved even if it seemed impossible.

"Seriously," she returned sadly.

Studying her aunt, Beth had the feeling that Sunshine would give anything to talk to Peter again, anything to bridge the hurt that spanned the years.

Right then, Beth determined she would move heaven and earth to make it happen.

CHAPTER 27

Sunshine

Sunday afternoon Sam called Sunshine and asked to meet with her. She readily agreed. She liked Sam and admired him for the way he stood by Beth's side during her lengthy recuperation. She saw in him the qualities of a man who would move heaven and earth to protect the ones he loved. While he might look a bit unconventional with his beard and tattoos, she knew he was solid. As a bonus, Sam wasn't a man her sister could easily intimidate. She wasn't entirely sure what was going on with him asking Beth to date other men, but she suspected she was about to find out.

Sam suggested they meet at a coffee shop close to Sunshine's studio. He had claimed a small table and was waiting for her when she arrived. She purchased her decaffeinated tea and joined him.

They exchanged greetings and then Sam got to the heart of the matter. "I'm afraid I made a mistake with Beth."

"She told me."

He looked relieved not to have to spell it out. "You're a good man, Sam Carney."

"Not the point," he said, clearly not looking for praise. "I care about Beth and now I've dug myself into a hole and I'm not sure how to get out of it."

Sunshine blew on her tea, which was boiling hot. "Did you mention to Beth that we were meeting?"

Disgruntled, he looked away. "No chance. She's seeing one guy or another nearly every night. Every time I think of her with another man, I nearly blow a gasket. It wasn't supposed to be like this. I thought . . ." He paused and rammed his fingers through his hair. "Hell if I know what I was thinking. I was afraid, I guess, worrying that we were getting too involved too quickly. In some part of my head I assumed she'd balk, insist she only wanted to see me. Little did I realize she had men lining up just waiting for the opportunity to date her."

"And now you hate that she's seeing other men."

"Damn straight."

Sunshine grinned, proud of her niece, proud of the way she'd handled the situation. "Then tell her."

"I thought that was what you'd say. Just not sure how to do it."

"And keep your pride intact," she added.

His shoulders slumped as he nodded. "I am a fool."

"Even fools deserve a second chance, Sam. Beth thinks the world of you. If it were me I'd play it cool."

"You would? How?"

Sunshine sipped from the edge of the cup, the hot liquid nearly scalding her lip. "Call her and ask her out, explain that you missed her and hope she'll give you a second chance."

His eyes brightened and he straightened. "You think she'd agree?"

"I can guarantee she will."

Sam relaxed and leaned against the back of the chair. "Then I'll do it. I'll see if she can squeeze me into her busy social calendar."

"It gives me no small pleasure to see her come into her own," Sunshine said. "In only a few months, she's done so much to establish herself—made friends, volunteers to give piano lessons to children who can't afford it. I couldn't be more proud of her."

Sam's smile was wide and genuine. "I realize now how special and wonderful Beth is. I can't believe I nearly let her go because of my own fears." He seemed lost in his thoughts. "Rocco tried to tell me," he said, "but this was something I had to learn on my own."

"I don't think I realized just how special Beth is myself until she moved here. She didn't have a job and was determined to find something that would support her without relying on her parents. She wouldn't accept financial help from me, either. Getting hired as a music teacher has God's fingerprints all over it. The man she replaced had been at the high school for years and decided to retire at the last minute. That was how the position became open. Although untried, Beth's qualifications were impeccable."

"Her students love her."

Sam wasn't telling Sunshine anything she didn't already know.

"She'd only been at the school a couple weeks before the accident, and even in that short amount of time endeared herself to the faculty and the kids," Sam said. "Several of the staff and students stopped by to visit while she was recuperating."

Sunshine swelled with pride. "Like I said, she's come out of her shell and I give a lot of the credit to you."

As he had earlier, Sam brushed off her praise. "Doubt that. Whatever changes there are in Beth are of her own making."

Sunshine was amused by how unaware he was of the strong influence he'd had on Beth's life.

His face tightened. "And if that means swallowing my pride and admitting that I made a mistake, then so be it."

———

After leaving Sam, Sunshine headed back to her studio, where she worked for two uninterrupted hours. She had a good feeling about him and a firmer confidence in the future for her niece. Although he hadn't said as much, she was fairly confident Sam was falling in love with Beth. He hadn't been willing to own up to how strongly he felt about her until it hit him in the face. Truth be told, Sunshine was glad this had happened if for no other reason than forcing Sam to acknowledge his feelings for Beth.

Sunshine was determined not to let her sister pull the two apart. If Beth and Sam eventually drifted away from each other, it would be of their own doing and not forced on them by outside forces.

Thinking about Ellie made Sunshine's teeth clench, and before she knew it the hand that held the paintbush tightened. At that point she knew she was finished for the day.

Ever since Beth had questioned her about Peter, Sunshine's head had been full of long-buried memories, of all the might-have-beens, and the taste of Peter and Ellie's betrayal. She'd been hurt and angry with him, unwilling to forgive him or her sister when she'd moved to California. Her art had become her solace, her escape, her life. Her work was filled with the hunger and thirst of revenge, wanting to lash out and hurt them both for what they had done.

It was her unwillingness to forgive that had driven Peter away. The funny thing was, although there was little humor in it, she did eventually let go of her anger toward Peter. It was harder with her sister, but over the years she'd come to accept that holding on to her outrage was hurting her far more than it did Ellie. They were both hurting. Her sister was left to deal with her guilt. Ellie had never apologized or made an effort to bridge the gap between them and so she hadn't, either. It was time to end this. Past time. Only Sunshine didn't know how to go about it, and so the two remained estranged. Distant and often at odds over Beth. Peter.

Sunshine couldn't think of him without heartfelt regrets of her own. He'd abandoned what he loved most and given in to his father's demands. Sunshine's heart hurt for him, knowing how he would have hated standing in a courtroom, writing briefs and dealing with disgruntled clients. He was meant to work in a studio creating sculptures that would bring light and beauty to the world.

It took the warm winds of California, her own success as an artist, and time for Sunshine to forgive him, but by then it was too late. Peter had married someone else.

As the years passed, she thought about him less often and discovered the grip on the pain he'd caused her had slipped, to be replaced with the memories of the love they'd once shared.

They were both young, ridiculously in love, confident nothing would ever shake the foundation of their commitment to each other . . . until Ellie.

Sunshine cleaned up her studio and returned home and put together a salad for her dinner later with Beth. Her niece's curiosity about her long-lost love had awakened memories she had tried to bury. After all this time, she should know holding them back would be impossible. She might as well have tried to dig a grave in swampland, where the body would repeatedly rise to the surface just as her memories did.

The years had given her the grace to pray that Peter had experienced a good life and that his marriage had been a success. She didn't want him to live with regrets and bitterness. She hoped that over time he'd found contentment and satisfaction as an attorney and that he hadn't completely abandoned his love of art. He'd been so beautifully talented. It pained her to think that all that ability had lain dormant and wasted.

Several times over the years, she'd been tempted to contact him, especially when visiting family in Chicago. Each time her courage had failed her. As much as she wanted to talk to him, as much as she longed to explain that she was ready to release the hurts of the past, as much as she wanted to say all was forgiven, she couldn't do it. She couldn't barge into his life and his family with words that had the potential to start a firestorm for him and his family.

Unable to face Peter, years earlier she'd written him a letter with no return address. At the time it was important she let him know she had absolved him from guilt. She'd needed to tell him she'd found her own happiness and that she would always love him. Thankfully, she'd never mailed it, although she had kept that lengthy missive tucked between the pages of her journal.

Shortly after Beth brought up his name, she'd gone through a chest where she kept her journals, and after sorting through several leather-bound volumes, she found the one with the letter carefully placed between the thick pages. With tears in her eyes, she'd reread it, surprised to find there was more to that letter than words. Between the sentences, woven through each thoughtfully written line, what so clearly jumped from the page was love. A love so strong that even now she felt it tightening her chest and filling her eyes with tears.

That letter as well as any other personal contact had the potential to upset the life Peter had made for himself. Sunshine refused to be responsible for bringing discord or regret into his life, and so she'd never mailed it.

Despite her desire to know about him, about his work and art, she'd never sought him out.

Beth arrived for dinner around six and in good spirits. Right away she mentioned a call from her parents.

"Dad called me back."

"Your dad?" Sunshine asked, immediately wondering if there was something wrong. "Is there a problem at home?"

"No. That was my first thought, too. Dad put Mom on the line and you won't believe this when I tell you."

"Then tell me, Sweet Pea."

"She asked if it would be all right if she and Dad flew out for Thanksgiving."

"Really?"

"And what did you say?"

She grinned sheepishly. "I told them I'd be happy if they did, with one small stipulation. Which involves you."

"Me?" Sunshine repeated, surprised.

"I said they could come, but only if you hosted the dinner."

After her initial shock, Sunshine burst out laughing. "You little devil. I imagine that gave your mother pause."

"I assumed it would, but I was wrong. She said she'd like that."

Sunshine felt like her legs had gone weak on her. "You're joking?"

"Not in the least. You don't mind, do you?" Beth asked.

Without a moment's hesitation, she agreed. "I wouldn't mind at all." It was time Sunshine mended fences with her sister, and it seemed Ellie was maybe eager to look past the wounds of the past as well.

Sunshine placed the huge bowl of greens in the center of the table. "I wonder if your mother is going to recognize the new you."

Beth's beautiful face was transformed by a bright smile.

They ate and chatted and laughed together. Beth was as dear to her as any daughter would have been. She saw in this woman much of herself and all the good parts of her sister. It gave Sunshine pride that she had played an important role in her niece's life, offering her encouragement and small reprieves of independence and happiness.

After they finished their meal, she stood to do the dishes. Wanting Beth to relax, Sunshine shooed her niece into the living room. "Make yourself comfortable," she said. "This won't take any time at all."

Beth went into the cozy room with its art-filled walls but came back into the kitchen almost immediately.

"Sunshine," Beth said softly. "What's this?"

She turned to see what was in her niece's hand and felt all the color drain out of her face.

Beth held the letter Sunshine had written Peter so long ago. She quickly took hold of it and offered her niece a sad smile. "Nothing important," she offered lamely, and tucked it away out of sight.

CHAPTER 28

Beth

Beth had read the first few lines of the letter before she realized what it was and stopped. It was too personal, too private. Yet from those few lines alone she was able to look inside her aunt's heart. Love and forgiveness throbbed in every word. That was when she realized the decision had been made for her. It didn't matter if Peter Hamlin was married. Her goal wasn't to reunite two lovers; it was to help them along the path of recovery from the emotional wounds they each carried.

Monday, during her break for lunch, Beth called the law firm again, hoping to chat with the semiretired receptionist Sondra Reacher.

"Hamlin, Wilkens and Bower," the receptionist answered.

"Oh good, it's you," Beth blurted out.

"I beg your pardon."

"It's Beth Prudhomme," she said. "Remember? We talked earlier?"

"Are you the girl asking about Mr. Hamlin?"

"Yes, that's me."

"I thought I put you through to him once already. Let me tell you he wasn't happy about it, either."

"You did, and I appreciate it. And you're right, he wasn't interested in talking to me."

The older woman made a huffing sound. "That doesn't surprise me."

"I was wondering," Beth ventured carefully, "would it be possible, would you mind talking to me about a personal matter involving Mr. Hamlin?"

Her request was received with an eerie silence until Beth was convinced the line had been disconnected. "Hello?"

"I'm here. I have a question for you, missy—are you trying to get me fired?" the woman asked incredulously.

"No, never—"

"Is this a setup?" she demanded next.

"No, I swear." This wasn't going well, and Beth instantly regretted asking the favor.

"These young girls the firm has answering the phone these days aren't worth near what I am. They know it and have got it out for me."

"I'm sorry," Beth said. "I didn't mean to offend you. The reason I'm asking is because I know someone who knew Mr. Hamlin years ago. Someone he loved and who loved him."

"When was this?" Sondra Reacher asked, lowering her voice.

"Nearly thirty years ago."

"And you know this person how?" she demanded.

"I'm her niece," Beth supplied.

After a short hesitation, Sondra whispered into the phone. "I can't talk here. Too many ears, if you know what I mean. Give me your phone number and I'll call you back this evening."

Excited now, Beth quickly relayed the phone number. "There's a two-hour time difference between here and Chicago and I'm not out of school until three-thirty, so please don't phone until after six your time."

Her words were met with a short hesitation. "Just how old are you, child? You still in school?"

"I'm a teacher."

"Okay, then. You're not underage or anything?"

"No, not at all."

Her voice dipped again. "You do realize this could get me fired."

Beth's hopes did a tumble. "If you'd rather not, I understand and I won't blame you for being cautious."

"My husband would have disapproved, but he's been gone three years so I do what I want these days. That's one of the compensations of being a widow."

"You'd risk your job to talk to me?"

"You gonna tell anyone it was me?"

"No." And she wouldn't. Beth fully intended to keep her promise. She was willing to accept full responsibility for whatever fall-out came from their conversation.

"Then I'll talk. Mr. Hamlin needs help and if this person . . . your aunt, can take that gruff edge off him, then it will be worth the risk."

"Thank you," Beth whispered in gratitude.

"Don't thank me yet."

Beth kept her phone within easy reach as soon as she walked out of the school building. When it rang, Beth jumped with the anticipation of it.

"Hello," she said excitedly, seeing that the area code was from Chicago. "This is Beth."

"I know who it is," Sondra Reacher said. "You're the one who gave me this number, remember?"

Beth grinned at her brusque tone. "I remember."

"Now, what is it you want to know about Mr. Hamlin?" the woman asked, getting straight to the point.

Too late, Beth realized she should have been better prepared. She had a number of questions but wasn't sure where to start.

"Is Mr. Hamlin married?"

"He used to be. He's been divorced now for nearly twenty years."

Twenty years. That was a long time to remain single. "Children?" she asked next.

"Two. Girls, both of them pretty as a picture. One's married and made him a grandfather last June."

Sunshine would love knowing that. "Is he close to his daughters?"

The question was answered with a snicker. "Mr. Hamlin isn't close to anyone. You spoke to him. After the first minute you should have been able to tell he isn't into teddy bears and lollipops. My guess is he'd like to be closer, but his ex is having none of that."

"That breaks my heart."

"Don't know what that woman fed those girls. Can't say for certain, but now that they are older I think their relationship with their father has improved."

"You said you've been with the firm nearly forty years. So you must have been there when Mr. Hamlin came on board."

"I was hired when the senior Mr. Hamlin was part of the firm. God rest his soul. He never made a secret of the fact that he wanted his son to go into law and join the practice. He didn't mention it to me personally, you understand. At the time the office was small and one can't help overhearing conversations."

"Right." That made sense to Beth.

"The younger Mr. Hamlin was determined to attend art school, though. His father refused to finance his efforts and was unhappy when he found a way to enroll all on his own. One time the missus showed up at the office and it was clear she'd been crying. The two of them went into the office and closed the door. I don't know what was said, but it was about the same time as the younger Mr. Hamlin left for art school. I believe the missus backed her son."

"My aunt is an artist," Beth murmured. "That's where they must have met."

"Sounds plausible."

"I'm guessing but I think it was when my aunt and Mr. Hamlin broke up that he dropped out of art school."

"Could be," the older receptionist agreed. "What I can tell you is that as soon as his son switched to studying law the elder Mr. Hamlin was as happy and carefree as a kid on the last day of school. Before long the senior Mr. Hamlin was bringing the younger by and arranging for him to meet Mr. Bower's daughter."

"You mean the two law partners acted as matchmakers."

"It was more than that. Both men made it clear that they expected the two to marry one day."

"Expected?"

"Oh yes. Marriage with the daughter of one of the other senior partners would cement Peter the younger's position as a junior partner. His daddy was all for that."

Beth didn't know the politics of a law office. "But what did Mr. Bower get out of this *arranged* marriage?"

"More than he deserved," Sondra Reacher said with a huff. "Carolyn Bower was and still is a heartless soul."

Beth could only guess what that implied. From the sound of it, Peter had gotten the short end of the deal. Right away her romantic heart kicked in, making it all the more important for her aunt to set matters straight with the man she loved. Like the plot of a book, she suspected that because he was broken-hearted he'd fallen victim to his father's schemes, given up studying art, and married the woman he didn't love. Fanciful for sure but plausible.

"Forgive me for asking this, but is Mr. Hamlin easily . . . swayed by outside forces?" Beth asked, afraid if he betrayed her aunt he might well do it to someone else.

"What?" the receptionist demanded. "No, you have it all wrong. Mr. Hamlin isn't like that at all."

Beth was glad to hear it.

The receptionist asked a question. "Tell me about your aunt?"

"Her name is Sunshine."

Sondra Reacher laughed. "She one of those hippies who doesn't realize the sixties are long over?"

"No, it's a nickname from her childhood. Her real name is Louise."

"There's a famous artist with that same name. Only reason I know is because Mr. Hamlin has a painting in his office by her."

Beth grinned, greatly encouraged by learning this. "That's my aunt."

Another pause. "Are you telling me that Mr. Hamlin was once in love with the artist Sunshine?"

"That's exactly what I'm telling you."

"Now, that's a case for the textbooks. Holy moly. You should have said so earlier."

Beth didn't know why it would make a difference who it was her boss had once loved.

"Did I hear you right when you said Sunshine never married?"

"Yes."

Again there was a pause, but this time it had an entirely different feel to it. Beth could sense the other woman's excitement buzz through the phone.

"Are you telling me you think your aunt is carrying a torch for Mr. Hamlin?"

Beth felt like she was walking on shaky ground. "I can't say for sure, but I'm thinking so." She debated on adding what she'd read in the letter and then decided to go for it. "I saw part of a letter she'd written him years ago. In one of the first lines, she claimed that she would always love him."

"Well, this is a conundrum."

Beth smiled at the older woman's choice of words. "Yes, I'd say it is."

"What would you like to see happen?" Sondra Reacher asked.

That was a good question. "I suppose in my heart of hearts I'd like for the two of them to find a way to be together. I believe that if they were to see each other it might be possible for them to clear the air."

"Not gonna be easy. Mr. Hamlin isn't the tenderhearted young man he once was."

"I got that message when I spoke to him," Beth reminded her.

"Did you know that afterward he asked me to make certain none of your calls came through to him again?"

Beth's hand tightened around her phone. "He did not say that!"

"He did."

Beth could see reuniting the two of them was going to be more of a challenge than she'd anticipated.

"So girl, how are you going to make this happen?" Sondra Reacher asked as if Beth had all the answers.

"I don't know. Do you have any suggestions?"

"Give me a minute to think on it," the woman suggested.

Beth had the feeling it was going to take more than a minute.

"Your aunt doing any art shows in the Chicago area in the near future?"

Beth didn't keep tabs on her aunt's travel schedule. "I don't know, but I can find out."

"You do that."

"What are you thinking?" Beth asked. "Sunshine's paintings have been featured in Chicago art shows a dozen times, if not more."

"Maybe we could convince Mr. Hamlin to attend one of her shows."

"We?" Beth repeated, stunned. "And exactly how do you intend to make that happen? Mr. Hamlin left instructions that he no longer wishes to speak to me."

"Listen, the two of us are in this together. I've spent the better part of forty years seeing that man live in misery. He had a selfish, self-centered wife who divorced him after having multiple affairs. His only joy has been his two daughters who, despite Mr. Hamlin's best efforts, were influenced by their mother. I admire him for all he did to keep in touch with his daughters. If I have the opportunity to bring a little sunshine into his life . . ." She paused and laughed. "I didn't intend that pun, but it's fitting, isn't it?"

"It is."

"If *we* have the chance to help him to be happy, then I think we should do it."

"I agree." Beth's excitement grew with each word the other woman spoke.

"Now, tell me, does your aunt know you're meddling in her life?"

Beth was afraid to admit it. "I . . . I haven't said anything to her about this."

"Thought so. Don't know much about her, but my guess is she's not a woman who lets someone do her talking for her."

"She isn't."

"What made you decide to get involved? Was it that letter you mentioned?"

"No, I stumbled upon that just recently. My aunt said his name once when we were out to eat. It was the look that came over her, and I knew that whomever this Peter was who shared fish tacos with her had been someone special in her life."

"Fish tacos. You asked me about that on your first phone call, didn't you?"

"I did. My aunt explained that she and Peter went to this hole-in-the-wall Mexican restaurant every Friday night and shared an order of fish tacos." Then she had a thought. "Any chance Mr. Hamlin will be in the Portland area?"

"Portland, Oregon, you mean, because if you do, I'm thinking I saw something recently about a conference being held out your way that he was planning on attending."

This was almost too good to be true. "Really?" She couldn't contain her enthusiasm.

"Pretty sure."

"If that's the case, then all we need to do is figure a way to get the two of them together."

Silence followed as they both mulled over the problem.

"Got it," the receptionist cried out, startling Beth.

"You do?"

"Yup. We're gonna do it with fish tacos."

CHAPTER 29

Sam

"Sam?" Beth answered on the second ring and sounded shocked to hear from him. They hadn't talked on the phone for nearly three weeks mainly because he wanted to give Beth the chance to date.

Sam wiped a hand down his face. Knowing she was seeing other men was killing him. He'd stayed away, unable to listen to her talk about the men she was currently dating. It was hard enough to listen when they played together at the rehab center. It seemed she had a date every other night. She'd been friendly and chatty and he'd been forced to smile and listen. Rocco had been right when he'd laughed when Sam had suggested he and Beth be friends. It'd taken these weeks for him to realize they were so much more than that.

This wasn't working, and it was time for him to own up to it. Now it was up to him to set things right. He felt awkward and tongue-tied. "How's it going?" he asked, and then rolled his eyes, thinking he couldn't have asked a less intelligent question.

"Okay. Everything all right?"

"Not really." He swallowed hard and leaned his shoulder against the driver's-side door of his pickup. He'd already put this off longer than he should have.

"Oh."

He cleared his throat. "I was hoping, wondering, actually . . . you know with your busy schedule and all."

"Wondering what, Sam?"

He went for it, rushing the words. "Wondering if you had time to go out with me?"

Silence. Then, "On a date?" Beth asked skeptically.

"Yes, on a date."

She hesitated. "I thought you don't date."

"I don't . . . usually."

"In other words, you're making an exception in my case?"

"Yes."

"Why?"

" 'Why?' " he repeated. This was so much harder than he ever expected it would be. "I've missed you?" The words were stiff, tentative.

"You see me twice a week. Not really much chance to miss me, Sam."

Sam pressed his hand over his eyes. Beth wasn't going to make this easy. "I miss you, babe, more than I thought possible. I was a fool. And afraid of losing my man card."

"Your what?"

"Never mind. Just that I've been an idiot."

"Yes."

He hesitated. "Are you saying you agree with me and that I was an idiot or did that mean you'd be willing to go out with me?"

Beth laughed and it sounded like warm honey to him. "Yes, to both."

Sam grinned. She certainly wasn't holding back. "Have you, you know, missed seeing me?"

She hesitated. "Yeah."

"You have?" He was convinced he heard music in the background, like something out of a Hallmark movie.

"More than I thought I would," she said, echoing his own words.

"What about all those other guys you've been seeing?"

She laughed softly. "The truth is none of them hold a candle to you."

Yup, now he heard it loud and clear. Music, and it didn't come from any radio, either. If he was a peacock his feathers would be in full display. "Thing is, if you date me, then we're exclusive." He was staking his claim right up front, here and now. "No one else but me."

She hesitated. "So you're willing to admit we're dating."

"Yeah, we're dating. Exclusively."

Again she paused, giving him heart palpitations. "Is there someone else, Beth?" he asked. She'd mentioned three or four other men she'd been seeing, but there didn't seem to be one in particular.

"There's never been anyone but you, Sam."

He relaxed, the tension leaving him. "Then we're good."

"We're good. Now, where are you going to take me?"

Sam grinned. "Anyplace you want, babe. Anyplace at all."

They set the time and place for Friday night and Sam hung up the phone feeling better than he had in three miserable, sleepless weeks. He'd dodged a bullet and prevented a self-inflicted wound.

Thursday night it was Sam's turn to host the poker game. The timing worked out well, as Beth was busy Thursday nights at her church's choir practice, where she played the piano. She'd had the one date with Doug, and from what she'd told Sam it would only be the one date. He was a good guy, but they had little in common and simply hadn't clicked.

His poker-playing friends were all married, and their wives generally sent along appetizers and other goodies for snacks. Not being married himself, Sam bought a couple bags of potato chips and called it good. The host supplied the beer, and he'd stacked his refrigerator with a case of their favorite brew, which was sure to last the night. None of his friends were big drinkers, and Sam wasn't one himself. At most he'd enjoy a beer or two.

Thursday-night poker had been going on for about six or seven years now and it was a great way to break up the workweek. Two of the guys were men he worked with at the garage. Alex and Charley had taken to teasing Sam about the new woman in his life. Sam accepted their good-natured razzing. The only one who knew he hadn't gone out with Beth in the last few weeks was Rocco. Thankfully, Rocco had kept his trap closed.

It took Sam longer than it should have to realize all that he'd found in Beth. She was a special woman. He was impressed by her thoughtfulness and how big her heart was. Beth wanted to make everything right for others. He didn't agree with her interfering in her aunt's life, but he kept his opinions to himself. He couldn't find it in himself to fault her for wanting her aunt to be happy. She hadn't mentioned that she followed through with her plans, but it wasn't like they'd been talking regularly.

Since their talk and date, things had been going well with him and Beth. Better than ever, really. He felt they'd both grown in the time apart and come to appreciate each other on a deeper level.

Thinking how well things were going with Beth, Sam cleared off the kitchen table and wiped it down to be sure there was nothing sticky that would mess with the cards. The beer was cooling in the refrigerator, and he had the potato chips in bowls on the kitchen countertop. He reached for one and munched on it and regretted not picking up a couple of those containers of dip.

His doorbell chimed and he glanced at his watch. One of the guys was early. He started toward the front door when it opened and Beth stuck her head inside.

"Hey," he said, surprised to see her and equally pleased.

"Hey," she said, coming into the house. She held a platter in her hand.

"What's that?" he asked, because whatever it was smelled divine.

Peeling back the tinfoil, Beth revealed a plate of chocolate-chip cookies. "I thought I'd contribute something to your game tonight," she said, and, leaning forward, she gave him what he was convinced was intended to be a brief kiss. It didn't turn out that way, hungry as he was for a taste of her.

"I love cookies," Sam said when he broke the kiss off. He reached for one, took a bite, and closed his eyes to savor the rich flavors. "These are homemade?"

"Of course. You think I'd bring you store-bought cookies?"

Sam took the plate out of her hand and set it aside. He then reached for her and brought her into his arms and kissed her again with the same urgency he'd felt a few minutes earlier. She opened to him the way she always did, slipping her arms around his neck and standing on the tips of her toes. It was hard not to get caught up in their kisses. Unfortunately, his poker-playing buddies were due anytime.

When he found the will to drag his mouth from hers, he released her.

"You should have said something earlier," Beth chastised him.

"Said what earlier?" he asked.

"Nichole told me the women supply snacks for the guys on Thursdays."

"They do," he said.

"Am I not your woman?"

Sam couldn't have held back a smile for a million bucks. "Yup. Definitely."

"Then you should have told me."

Sam slipped his arm around her waist and nuzzled her neck as he led the way into the kitchen. He set the tray of cookies next to the bowl of chips. "On Saturday, would you like to—"

"I can't," she said, not allowing him to finish.

Sam cocked one brow. "You aren't going to tell me you've got another date, are you?" he teased. He wanted to remind her that they were exclusive now. He wasn't comfortable with her seeing anyone but him. He thought he'd made that clear.

"No, but I do have plans."

"All day?"

"All afternoon," she corrected, reminding him about her piano students. "I'm volunteering with Habitat, helping Jazmine build her house." She hesitated and then blinked up at him several times, flirting with him. "You could help, you know, make up for all that time we were apart."

"I could, could I?" His Saturdays were precious and he reserved them for working on his cars.

"It's completely voluntary, but everyone says how good you are with fixing things, and I'm sure you'd be an asset to the team. *And* Jazmine would be so appreciative."

"Just Jazmine?"

"Like I said, it's completely up to you."

"If I don't agree, will you ask Tyler?"

A smile twitched at the corners of her mouth. "I might."

"Like bloody hell you will." She had him and she knew it.

"Does that mean you're willing to volunteer?"

Sam had a dozen projects of his own that needed attention. He knew Beth was teasing him when it came to Tyler. He'd never worked with Habitat for Humanity but had heard good things about the organization. "Count me in."

Beth threw her arms around his waist and hugged him close. "You're the best."

"Don't know that I could refuse you much, and you know it."

"I do, and that makes you all the dearer to me."

"Yeah, yeah," he muttered, but he wasn't upset. "Got any other volunteer projects you're conveniently hiding from me?"

She smiled ever so sweetly at him. "A few."

He rolled his eyes. "You free next Saturday? I'd like—"

"Can't."

"Now what?" The woman was making it difficult.

"I'm helping Shawntelle."

Rocco's bookkeeper was one of Nichole's best friends. "She building a house, too?" he asked.

"No. She volunteers at the same place Nichole does, only she's had to cut back because of the baby. Rocco met Nichole for the first time at Dress for Success, remember?"

Sam knew the story well. Nichole had backed her car into a ditch and Rocco drove the tow truck that pulled her out.

"What are you going to be doing there?"

She shrugged. "I'm not sure, but Shawntelle will let me know. I'm filling in for her cousin, who can't make it next week."

Sam wrapped his arms around her and held her close, his heart swelling with an emotion so strong it tightened his chest. Jazmine wasn't the only one building a new life for herself.

Beth was doing the same thing. She was building a life without the restraints and restrictions placed on her by her mother. With this first taste of freedom and independence, she was evolving into her own person. Sam was privileged to witness the transformation.

"I better head out or I'll be late for choir practice," she said, reluctance showing in her eyes.

Sam wasn't eager to see her leave, either.

"Kiss me before you go," he said, finding it difficult to release her. He wove his fingers into her hair and angled his mouth to hers. She tasted of everything that was good, and they were soon focused only on each other. Sam knew he would never grow tired of holding and kissing this woman. He wasn't a man who gave his heart away easily. Never had been. His only serious relationship, before Beth, had been with Trish and he'd been burned so badly he'd avoided falling in love ever since. Everything was new with Beth. Fresh and unspoiled. Two months and already she'd woven her smile, her heart, and her music around his own, binding him in ways he'd never thought to experience again.

They were interrupted by someone clearing his throat. Alex, one of his crew from the garage, stood just outside the kitchen holding a tray of cut veggies.

"Hate to interrupt you two lovebirds."

Beth blushed and hid her face against Sam's shirt.

"We playing poker or not?" Alex teased. He set the vegetable tray down next to the chips. Right away he noticed the cookies and helped himself.

Sam ignored him. "I'll walk you to your car," he told Beth. Then, looking over his shoulder, he told his friend, "Make yourself comfortable and don't eat all the cookies before everyone else arrives."

"You going to introduce me or not?" Alex asked, crumbs coating the sides of his mouth.

Sam gestured toward his coworker. "This joker is Alex," he told Beth. "Alex, Beth."

"Hi," she said, smiling.

Sam steered her out of the kitchen and toward the front door, but not before he saw Alex reach for another cookie.

"Nice to meet you, Beth," Alex called out after them. "Haven't heard much about you."

"He's teasing," Sam told Beth.

"Hey, these cookies are good," Alex shouted.

"There better be some left when I get back here," Sam warned, and they heard Alex laugh as Sam led Beth outside.

He was reluctant to see her go. He'd been playing poker with the guys for years but would have gladly given it up just then for another ten minutes with Beth.

"Have fun tonight," she said as he held open the driver's-side door for her.

"You, too."

She got inside the car. "Enjoy the cookies."

"I have a feeling Alex will have scarfed down the entire tray while I'm talking to you. I'll be lucky if there are any left."

"I'll bake you more," she promised.

"I'll let you."

Rocco and Charley arrived then, and still Sam lingered. His two friends saw themselves into the house.

"Talked to my folks about Thanksgiving," he said.

She looked up with wide eyes. "Are they disappointed you won't be spending it with them?"

"They're fine with it. They're more disappointed in not meeting you."

"You told them about me?"

"Of course, babe." He'd filled in his mother shortly after Beth's accident. His mother had encouraged him, eager to see him settled down and married. She was thinking grandchildren.

"Maybe we can take a day and visit your parents before Christmas."

"I promised them I'd be home for Christmas."

She exhaled on a sigh. "I promised my parents Christmas, too."

Sam hid his disappointment. He'd hoped to spend the holiday with her.

"I'm going to be late for choir practice," she said, but she didn't move to leave.

Neither did Sam. "My friends are waiting."

"Bye, Sam."

"Don't speed," he said, fearing she wouldn't be as cautious as she should be. "Drive carefully and text me when you get to the church, okay?"

She nodded. "Will do."

He eased away from the car and stood with his hands in his back pockets as she pulled away.

When he returned to the house, his friends were waiting.

"Never thought I'd see the day Sam Carney let a woman get her claws into him."

"Yeah, boys, but did you see the woman who possesses those claws?" Sam returned as he reached for a deck of cards.

"Saw her," Alex said while munching on another cookie. "I'd marry her for these alone."

"I get first dibs on Beth," Charley said, reaching toward the plate.

"Like hell," Sam growled.

Rocco slapped him across the back. "Know how you feel, buddy. Been there." Then looking at the other two men, he added, "And so have these clowns."

Sam pulled out a chair and started shuffling the cards. "You boys ready to hand me your hard-earned cash?"

Life was good. In fact, it felt more than good. Beth was his, and while it had taken some time for him to recognize and accept it, he was hers.

CHAPTER 30

Sunshine

It was the weekend before Thanksgiving and Sunshine knew her niece was up to something. She wasn't sure what that little darling had cooked up, but whatever Beth had in mind was sure to be interesting.

"I have a surprise for you," Beth had told her a few days earlier. Her eyes were bright with excitement, and it seemed all she could do not to spill what it was right then and there.

"A surprise?"

"A good one, I hope."

"You hope?" This didn't sound right. Beth was excited and at the same time unsure. Now, that was interesting. "You better tell me what it is."

Beth's eyes gleamed with barely suppressed anticipation. "Sorry, I can't. My lips are sealed. I will tell you that it's one I've been working on for several weeks now, ever since we . . ." Her eyes grew round and she immediately pantomimed twisting a key over her mouth. "I'm not saying another word. All I ask is that you contact me as soon as you're home."

"I have to go somewhere?"

"Oh yes, this is the most important part. Remember that wonderful Mexican restaurant where we ate not long ago?"

Sunshine nodded. "Of course. It's one of my favorites."

"When you arrive, ask for Meghan and she will lead you to your table, and your surprise will be waiting for you there."

The details were certainly specific. Her birthday was months ago, so it was unlikely Beth was throwing her a surprise party. The sale of her artwork had gone exceptionally well in the last year, so it might have something to do with her agent. However, Bill was currently traveling in Europe.

"You sure you don't want to give me a clue?"

"Nope. I can't."

"You say you've been working on this for a long time?"

"Weeks and weeks. The timing is critical. I can't believe we were able to work this out."

"'*We*'? Is Sam involved in this?"

"Nope."

"Anyone I know?" she pressed.

"No. Now stop asking questions, because I'm afraid I might say too much and give everything away."

Whatever the surprise, Sunshine had to admit she was intrigued.

She parked outside the Mexican restaurant and made sure she had her phone charged and inside her purse. Beth made her promise she'd call her at the first opportunity. The doors leading into the restaurant were thick and wooden, carved with cacti that were painted green. She didn't often dine in, but once or twice a month she phoned in an order for takeout. Her favorite was the Ranchero salad, which was similar to a taco salad but without the shell, and, of course, the fish tacos.

As soon as the hostess saw Sunshine, she brightened. She was a bit embarrassed as she didn't know the lovely young woman's name. "Are you Meghan?" she asked, per the instructions Beth had given her.

"I am," she said, flashing her a huge grin. "Your party is already waiting. I've given you a private area so the two of you can talk."

"You know all about this?"

"Oh yes, Beth and I worked together to set it up. The menu is already set, but Alicia will be by to take your drink order."

Meghan led her to the back of the restaurant. It was early enough so that the dinner crowd had yet to arrive. The booths were high, so she didn't see him until she was at the table.

Peter.

Unable to hold back her shock, Sunshine gasped. Her hand automatically flew to her heart, as if to protect it from the jolt of recognition.

To his credit, Peter looked equally stunned. His eyes widened, and all he seemed capable of doing was staring at her in complete and utter amazement.

And not in a good way.

Immediately he frowned and glared at her, as if the sight of her was as unwelcome as it was surprising.

"Sunshine," he whispered after a moment, as if to confirm that it was really her.

"Peter." She slid into the booth for the simple reason she wasn't convinced her legs would continue to hold her upright.

For what seemed an interminable amount of time, all they seemed capable of doing was looking at each other. Peter had changed. He was nothing like she remembered. Thirty years ago he wore his hair long, mostly as a money-saving measure. When he couldn't stand the thick strands flopping down and getting in his eyes, Sunshine had offered to cut it for him and he'd let her. It was an intimate task, and afterward they'd made love. Now he dressed in expensive business suits, his hair was trimmed and neat with streaks of gray. It was thinning, she noticed. His hands. His beautiful hands callused and often nicked and cut were perfectly manicured now. He was a man of the world. It seemed the artist in him had completely vanished.

Sunshine liked to think there hadn't been nearly as many changes in her, other than age. Her thick hair, salt-and-pepper-colored now, hung freely down the middle of her back, and she continued to wear the same long skirts and loose blouses she had while in art school.

"You arranged this?" he asked suspiciously.

"No. I'm afraid this is the work of my niece."

He huffed. "Ellie's child, no doubt. This trick is worthy of her mother. Guess the apple doesn't fall far from the tree."

Sunshine was tempted to defend Beth but had yet to think clearly enough to gather her thoughts. She couldn't seem to stop looking at Peter, yearning for evidence of the man she once knew.

The waitress sauntered up to the table. "What can I get you two lovebirds to drink?"

Peter's head snapped toward the young woman. "We aren't lovebirds, and I'll have a scotch."

Alicia blinked at his waspish tone.

"Make it a double. No ice."

She made a note of it and turned to Sunshine. "And for you?"

Sunshine admired her resilience. "Iced tea, please."

The young woman made a hasty retreat, and Sunshine didn't blame her.

"Was that really necessary?" she asked, keeping her voice low and calm.

"Definitely necessary. We are no lovebirds."

"We once were, if you remember." She hoped the gentle prompt would bring happy memories instead of dredging up the graveyard of their past mistakes and the pain they had brought to each other.

"That was a long time ago." He started to slide out of the booth.

Reaching across the table, Sunshine placed her hand on his. "Please don't leave."

"Why?" he demanded. "So you can remind me that I betrayed you and sold out to my father?"

His words were like a slap in the face. "I would never do that."

"You mean to say you don't want to rub my face in your success?"

His words shocked her. "Peter, no, never."

"Are you sure, Sunshine? Aren't you even a little tempted?" he taunted.

She shook her head, barely recognizing this man as the one she'd loved beyond reason.

"Don't you want to ask whatever happened to the boy you knew? Didn't you ever wonder if I could have supported myself as a sculptor?"

Alicia returned with their drink order and Sunshine wasn't given the opportunity to answer.

Peter nearly grabbed the glass out of the young woman's hand. He drank it down in one swallow and set the empty glass aside.

Sunshine didn't blame the waitress for making another hasty retreat.

Peter's eyes narrowed as he glared across the table at Sunshine. "I curse the day I met you."

The vehemence in his voice robbed her of breath. When she could, she asked him, "Do you hate me so much?" She was barely able to get the words out from the pain tightening her chest. Whatever had happened to Peter over the years had changed him to a bitter, angry man.

"I see your art hanging in galleries and I'm reminded that because of what happened with us . . . my entire life went down in flames. I'd like to blame Ellie, blame you. I can't, though. I was the one who was weak, who gave up everything that was ever important to me. I'm the one to blame."

"I'm sorry for you," she whispered.

"You should be."

Alicia returned with their food. Sunshine nearly groaned aloud when she saw the platters of fish tacos and one bean tostada. It was the same order they had shared on their Friday-night dates.

As the waitress placed the plate in front of Peter, he looked down at it and rolled his eyes. "This is just perfect."

His words dripped with sarcasm.

Reaching for his empty glass, he studied the bottom as if he expected to find something there. He waved to the waitress. As soon as she appeared, he thrust the glass at her. "Give me another."

"A double scotch?"

"Yes," he snapped, as if that was the most asinine question he'd ever been asked.

Seeing how many years it'd been since she'd last seen Peter, Sunshine wondered if he had a drinking problem. They often drank wine together but never more than a glass each. Hard liquor was reserved for parties and neither one of them overindulged—well, other than on a few specific occasions.

"Don't look at me like I'm an alcoholic," he muttered, as if reading her thoughts. "I don't abuse alcohol. At least I didn't until today."

His attempt at humor was weak. "You want to blame me for the way your life has gone," Sunshine said, and it was a statement, not a question.

"I don't blame you for a damn thing," he insisted. "I accept full responsibility for screwing up my own life. It started with you and Ellie. I lost you both and that stupidity cost me dearly. Eventually I caved to my father's demands. It all happened so fast like dominos toppling over on each other. One bad decision followed another. I couldn't seem to stop myself, even knowing at the time this was all wrong for me. This wasn't what I wanted and still I kept stumbling further and further from who I wanted to be."

Alicia returned with his drink. He didn't gulp it down this time. Instead, he stared into the amber liquid as if it held the secrets of the universe. "If I hadn't already destroyed my life enough, I made another tragic mistake when I decided to marry Carolyn. She, you might be interested to know, was the worst of my screwups." He took a big swallow of the scotch.

Neither of them had touched the meal.

"Did you ever go back to sculpting?" she asked, keeping her voice as soothing as she could manage. Anger radiated off him in waves like hot sun against asphalt on the hottest day of summer.

"Never touched it again."

"Oh Peter." Her heart ached for him to the point she wanted to weep. His talent had stirred her. All these years she prayed he had at least found an artistic outlet from the heavy demands of a law career. Instinctively, she realized turning his back on what he loved was the way he'd chosen to punish himself.

Because her throat felt dry and raw with sadness, Sunshine sipped her tea.

"You know what the worst part has been?" Although he asked the question, it was apparently rhetorical. "You'd think it was leaving art school or my divorce or having minimal contact with my daughters. All that should be enough to make a grown man weep, but the worst, the very worst, was knowing you'd stuck with your dreams and became a recognized and highly acclaimed artist."

"You hate me because I'm successful?" she asked, unable to believe he would be so resentful of someone he'd once claimed to love.

"I remember the first time I saw your professional work. It was at a gallery in Chicago. I'd been married to Carolyn for about five years. Even then I knew the marriage was a mistake, but we had one daughter and another on the way. I wasn't completely sure the baby was mine, but that's beside the point."

At the hurt in his voice, Sunshine closed her eyes. "Oh Peter."

"Carolyn and I attended a charity art show and two of your paintings were on display. Not one, Sunshine, two. They were stunning, the talk of the show. The irony was that Carolyn was all over them, talking about them with her friends. If she only knew," he said, snickering.

There wasn't anything for her to say.

"I went numb. I couldn't take my eyes off those paintings. They mesmerized me but not for the reasons everyone was talking about. The choice of color, the shadowing, the technique. I always knew you were talented. Everyone knew you were good. But in that moment, I realized you were quite possibly a genius. I had never appreciated how much."

"Thank you," she whispered, accepting his compliment.

"I hated you then, Sunshine. God forgive me, I couldn't even bear the thought of you."

Sunshine blinked back tears. "But why?" she asked, needing to know.

"Because the emptiness inside me exploded after that. I sank into a deep depression, dreaming of what might have happened if I'd stayed in art school. Every morning I'd head for the office with dread and self-recrimination, hating the life I'd created for myself, hating my father, hating the cheating, lying bitch I had married, knowing she hated me back."

"How could you hate your work; you're a successful attorney." The expensive suit he wore said as much.

"I am one of the finest attorneys in Chicago, and I say that with no pride. Guess I have my father to thank for that. I buried myself in my work. I started winning case after case, exceeding even his expectations, but I didn't do it because I loved the law. I did it out of anger focused at myself, the need to prove I could make something of the mess I'd created that was my life."

"I don't know why you gave up what you love and—"

"Don't," he said, stopping her by raising his hand. "Don't say another word."

Sitting back, resting against the padded cushion, Sunshine wiped a tear from her face.

"You think I'm pathetic, don't you?" he demanded, as if the question was some form of joke. "Maybe I am," he concluded.

Peter swallowed down the last of his scotch. "I don't know what you want to say to this niece of yours. On my behalf, let her know I didn't appreciate this little surprise she concocted. I know who she worked with. My office receptionist told me she found this restaurant online. She actually made the reservation for me. Said it was hard to get a table. What a joke," he said, looking around the near empty room. "Tell your niece that Sondra Reacher will no longer be employed with the firm. I'm firing her first thing Monday morning."

"Beth meant no harm, Peter."

"Perhaps not, but I don't appreciate her intrusion in my life." He slid out of the booth. "I'd like to say it was a pleasure to see you again, Sunshine, but the truth is I wish I'd stayed in Chicago."

With those parting words of bitterness, he walked out of the restaurant.

For a long time, Sunshine remained in the booth, looking into the distance and seeing nothing. When the restaurant started to fill up, she decided it was time to leave.

She was in the parking lot when her phone signaled she had a text message.

Were you surprised?

Staring at the message, Sunshine realized if she told Beth the truth, she'd be devastated. Beth had hoped Sunshine and Peter would reconcile. Her niece was looking for a fairy-tale ending, but that was not to be.

Peter wasn't the man she remembered. He'd turned into a hostile, angry man who had let his resentment burn away a large part of his soul.

While her niece's intentions were good, seeing Peter as he was now had stripped away the memories she'd treasured. While he claimed he accepted responsibility, he was fooling himself. He saw her as the blight in his life, the woman he wished he'd never met.

Rather than disappoint Beth, she texted back It was lovely.

Because she was upset, she drove directly to her studio, but she didn't paint. Instead, she sat in front of the canvas and silently wept.

CHAPTER 31

Beth

Beth knew she should be concerned with her parents' pending visit over Thanksgiving. She didn't trust her mother not to use the time as a subtle way of undermining her life. However, Beth's main concern revolved around her aunt Sunshine. Her aunt had said shockingly little about the dinner Beth and Sondra Reacher had arranged between Sunshine and Peter Hamlin. What she did say was elusive and vague.

"You're looking preoccupied," Sam mentioned as they left the rehab facility. They'd performed well together from the beginning, but over the weeks they had gelled as musicians. "Are you worried about your parents' visit?" he asked.

Beth offered him a fragile smile. "Yes and no. I have no worries about Dad, but Mom concerns me. I don't trust her."

"Don't let it bother you, babe. We got this."

His confidence inspired her. While she appreciated his positive attitude, it was only one of the matters that weighed heavily on her mind. If there was anything to be glad about, worrying over her aunt took her mind off the upcoming holiday.

Instead of having Sam drive her directly back to her apartment, Beth suggested they stop off for coffee. She had some news she wanted to share that she'd learned after her meeting with her fellow music teachers.

Sam pulled into the parking lot at a Starbucks. "Something on your mind?" he asked, and looked concerned. "We're good, right?"

"Better than good," she assured him.

Sam collected their order; he had coffee and she wanted a latte. Beth found a vacant table in the back of the Starbucks.

She was grateful that their spot gave them some privacy. The closest occupied table was three down.

"What's up, babe?" Sam asked once they were comfortably seated. He cupped his coffee with both hands and studied her as if unsure what to expect.

"I hope you don't mind, but I wanted to talk to you about what you told me about your past relationships."

Right away, he bristled. "There's only been one, Beth, and as far as I'm concerned, it's off-limits."

"But I learned something and—"

"Off-limits, babe."

She sipped her latte and mulled over her next move. Sam had said very little about Trish and his daughter. Clearly it was a painful subject he didn't want to discuss, and that disappointed her because she had wonderful news to share with him. Only Sam didn't want to hear it.

"Now, about Thanksgiving," Sam said in a blatant effort to change the subject. "I've met your mother, but this is the first opportunity I'll have to meet your dad. I wasn't going to tell you, but I've decided to have my hair cut and shave off the beard, too."

"Sam," Beth objected, shaking her head. "No way. You don't

need to change who you are for my parents." What she didn't want to tell him was that it wouldn't make the least bit of difference how much Sam altered his appearance. Her mother in particular didn't need a reason to find fault with any man Beth chose to date. Especially one who hadn't been handpicked and vetted by her.

Sam reached across the table and took her hand in his. His fingers gave hers a gentle squeeze. "You're important to me, and while I won't be intimidated by your parents, I want to start off on the right foot with your dad in particular. Cutting my hair and getting rid of this beard is a small price to pay. Truth is, I've been meaning to do it for some time. Your parents coming to town is the incentive I need."

Beth's heart swelled with love and appreciation. "Be yourself, Sam. That's all I want."

He pressed her hand to the side of his face. "Aren't you even a little bit curious what I look like without all this hair?" he asked.

Actually, Beth did wonder. Until now, she'd never given it much thought. The beard was part of Sam. The long hair, too.

Sam squinted at her. "What's up? You're looking at me funny."

"I'm trying to picture you without a beard."

He winked at her and gave her one of his special smiles. "You'll see soon enough."

Beth sipped her latte and sighed, thinking about her aunt. "You did warn me," she murmured, thinking out loud.

"Warn you about what?"

Beth looked up. "That dinner I arranged for my aunt and Peter Hamlin."

"I thought you said it went fine?"

"That was what Sunshine led me to believe, but I think she's not telling me the full truth."

"It didn't go well?"

"I don't think so. When we spoke she said it was a real surprise for them both, but she didn't say it was a pleasant one. I quizzed her about it and all she'd tell me was that they spent time catching up."

Sam studied her as if trying to read between the lines of her aunt's comment. "What were you expecting to happen, Beth?"

That was the same question she'd asked herself countless times since her talk with Sondra Reacher earlier that evening. "I don't know . . . I thought, I hoped, they would reconnect and give their relationship a second chance. In retrospect, that sounds foolishly romantic and a little silly, doesn't it?"

"Not in the least. You have such a warm, generous heart, and seeing them find love again would be natural for you."

Sam was being more than kind when she felt like she deserved to be chastised for stirring up old hurts that were none of her business.

"Are you thinking nothing good will come out of their dinner?"

"Doubtful," Beth admitted. "I asked Sunshine if she was going to keep in touch with Peter and she gave me a sad smile and said probably not."

Beth didn't have a clear picture of what had actually transpired between the two. She knew they'd had ample opportunity to talk and square things away. But it didn't sound like anything of importance had taken place. And she was even more convinced of that after she'd heard from Sondra Reacher.

"What I really wanted," Beth said, clearing her thoughts, "was for there to be healing. I don't know entirely what went wrong between them, other than the fact that my mother played a role in their breakup. But there's more going on than I'm aware of." Her throat grew thick and she swallowed hard. "Oh Sam, I think I might have stirred up a hornet's nest."

Sam stood and took the chair next to her, placing his arm around her shoulder. Beth leaned closer to him, seeking his warmth. "You have every right to say you told me so. You did warn me."

"You meant well."

"I did." Little good that did anyone now, especially Sondra Reacher, who, thanks to Beth, was without a job.

Beth exhaled a long breath with the decision to tell him everything. "I talked to Sondra this afternoon. She's the receptionist I worked with to set up the meeting with Sunshine and Peter."

"I remember."

"Mr. Hamlin fired her."

"What?"

"The first thing he did when he got back was to call her into his office." It was unfortunate that Sondra worked Mondays. Perhaps if Mr. Hamlin had taken a few days to cool down, he might have had a change of heart.

"What excuse did he use?"

"She said he didn't give her any excuse. All he said was that her services would no longer be needed and that she should pack up her things and leave. He had one of the interns escort her from the office." That must have been especially humiliating to the woman who had served the law firm for nearly forty years.

Sam didn't comment, but his arm tightened around her shoulders.

"I was excited for Sunshine and made this surprise out to be something wonderful. After I talked to Sondra I realized that the dinner must have been a disaster and Sunshine didn't want to tell me how awful it was."

Sam kissed the top of her head. "Your heart was in the right place, so don't beat yourself up over it. Move on. I'm sure that's what Sunshine is doing."

Beth wanted to believe that, but she wasn't convinced.

"If nothing else, you gave them the opportunity to set the past straight, and that was a gift all of its own. If it didn't work out, that's not on your head. That rests on the two of them."

Sam's encouraging words helped and Beth was able to sleep that night.

———

Tuesday afternoon as soon as she was free to leave the high school, Beth drove to her aunt's. She found Sunshine as she most often did, working in her studio.

Her aunt glanced over her shoulder and brightened when she saw Beth. "I imagine you're here to discuss Thanksgiving. I ordered a fresh turkey. A little traditional, I know, but that is what your mother would expect. I'd much rather serve Thai, which is what I did last year. I had several friends over and it was a marvelous meal. Best sticky rice ever."

"I want to help."

"I should hope so," Sunshine teased. "Cooking was never my strong suit, and you know your mother. Everything has to be perfect. I don't even have a matching set of silverware. Can't imagine what she'll think of that."

Beth remembered Thanksgiving dinner from past years and the elaborate table settings her mother prepared. They were worthy of inviting Martha Stewart to join in the celebration or anyone from the DIY Network, for that matter. Her mother took pride in making sure every detail of their meal was perfection. The meal itself was catered and the guests were carefully scrutinized and evaluated for their potential usefulness long before invitations were mailed.

Thanksgiving at Sunshine's would be something of an experience for her mother. As for her father, Beth didn't think he much cared or noticed. He gave Ellie free rein when it came to entertaining.

"If you do the turkey and the stuffing, I'll see to the side dishes."

They reviewed the menu and Beth paid special attention to her aunt, looking for any signs of depression or unhappiness. She wanted to apologize for intruding on her aunt's life but was afraid bringing up Saturday would hurt more than help.

"When do your parents arrive?"

"Tomorrow. Around three."

"Are you picking them up at the airport?"

Beth shook her head. "Mom ordered a car service to take them directly to the hotel. She asked to meet Sam and me for dinner that evening."

Sunshine cocked one brow in question.

"I didn't say anything to Sam about it, though. I'll go on my own," she said, feeling uncertain. When he met her mother again and her father for the first time, Beth would rather her aunt was there as a buffer.

"You don't need to worry about Sam."

Sunshine was right. Sam was perfectly capable of holding his own with her mother. He had once already.

"I don't plan to take them to my apartment, either."

"Beth, why ever not? You have nothing to be ashamed of."

"I know," she said. "I'm just convinced Kier made it sound like I live in a shady part of town. For sure it's far beneath Mom's standards, but it's mine and I love it. I won't stand to hear her criticize any part of the life I'm living. Far as I'm concerned, I'm preventing an argument."

Sunshine nodded approvingly. "Smart."

Beth refused to defend her choices. Then, feeling she couldn't ignore what happened with Sunshine and Peter, Beth found the courage to broach the subject.

"Sunshine," she said tentatively, "I have the feeling the dinner with Peter didn't go as well as you want me to believe."

Her aunt picked up her paintbrush and turned back to the canvas. "What makes you say that?"

"Well, for one thing, I heard from my coconspirator that Mr. Hamlin fired her first thing Monday morning."

Sunshine's head sagged as though the news weighed heavily upon her. She seemed to take the news personally. "Did he really?"

"I realize she probably shouldn't have been so free with his personal information. I feel terrible about that." Sondra had been less upset about her dismissal than Beth had.

"Peter said he was going to let her go," Sunshine whispered, "but I didn't actually think he'd go that far."

"Sondra worked part-time and is semiretired. She says she's fine with it. What bothers me is knowing that I was responsible for her losing her job."

Sunshine set aside the same brush she had picked up only a few minutes earlier. "Peter has changed. I barely recognized him as the man I once knew."

"Sondra said he's difficult."

Sunshine smiled. "What Peter doesn't realize is that when we fail to be kind and loving, then we fail to be wise. I fear his life hasn't gone the way he expected or wanted. I wish him well, I do, but he's caught in a net of self-pity and resentment. I doubt anything I might have said would have reached him." She paused and sadness leaked into her eyes. "He doesn't understand that in his effort to penalize your friend, he has hurt himself even more."

Her aunt was wise and beautiful. It stunned Beth that Peter didn't recognize that in her. She was right, he was to be pitied. "Did Peter . . . blame you for what's happened in his life?"

"He said he didn't, claimed he accepts full responsibility. The sad part is he resents my success. While he might be one of the highest-priced attorneys in the city, Peter views himself as a failure."

"But why?" This made no sense to Beth.

Her aunt reached out and cupped Beth's cheek. "I read once that one of the saddest things in life is to die with the music still inside us. There's tremendous talent in Peter that has been long denied. When I knew him, he was one of the most promising artists in college. His work was praised by staff and students alike. His potential was breathtaking."

"And he gave it up?"

"He did. He walked away from it all."

"But why? Why would he do that?"

Sunshine mulled over the question. "That isn't easy to answer. He would like to blame outside factors, but I believe deep down Peter had a terrible fear of failure. His talent came easy for him. I remember how hard it was for him to accept even the slightest criticism. He grew defensive and argumentative."

"You loved him, though."

"Yes, I won't deny that." She turned back to her painting, but not before Beth saw the sheen in her aunt's eyes.

Immediately Beth was struck with guilt. "I'm so sorry."

"Please, no apologies. They aren't necessary. You acted in love, and how could I ever fault that?"

"But—"

"I don't want you to feel bad that the meeting with Peter didn't go well. I'm not the least bit upset. If anything, I'm terribly sad for him."

"You're sure you're all right?"

"Oh yes, very sure."

Beth stood to leave. "I better head to the store so I can get what I need for our dinner." Then, to lighten the mood, she said, "Sam wants to help me with the preparation."

"Does he cook?"

"Not that I've seen."

"This should be interesting," Sunshine said, smiling again.

Beth left then, feeling better than she had when she'd arrived. She had a renewed appreciation of this wonderful, wise woman who was her aunt. Hearing about Peter, she felt a terrible sadness for him, much as her aunt did.

She couldn't let her mind dwell on the attorney for long, though. Sam was hours away from spending time with her parents. If nothing else, this should be one interesting Thanksgiving Day.

CHAPTER 32

Sam

The minute Sam arrived for Thanksgiving dinner, Beth's mother's gaze narrowed in on him like the laser from a sniper's rifle. Ellie dressed with the grace and style of a Jacqueline Kennedy Onassis and possessed the eyes of a werewolf. Staking his claim, he walked directly to Beth, wrapped his arm around her waist, and wished her a happy Thanksgiving.

Beth looked up and he saw the concern in her eyes. Leaning forward, he whispered, "We got this, babe."

Momentarily reassured, she smiled and nodded.

He kissed her cheek, broke away, and walked over to Beth's father, who sat in a chair, reading in the cozy living room. He thrust out his hand. "Sam Carney," he said. "And you must be Beth's father."

"Phillip," the other man said. Putting aside a thick book, he stood to shake Sam's hand.

Sam looked him square in the eyes and knew the two of them would have no problem. Phillip Prudhomme was the picture of the absentminded professor. He was slightly disheveled, the knot in his tie was loose, and his dinner jacket looked large on his shoulders. He needed a haircut, and although he'd shaved, he'd missed a spot.

Having recently shaved, Sam felt almost nude. It would take a few days for him to grow accustomed to not having facial hair. A nice side benefit had been Beth's reaction. When she first saw him, her eyes had grown warm and soft as she reached up and stroked his bare cheeks.

"Well, what do you think?" he'd asked.

"I like it. But then I like you with your beard, too."

Phillip returned to his chair and reached for his book, as if escaping into the written word and academia was where he belonged, where he was most comfortable.

"Good to see you again, Ellie," Sam said, turning to greet Beth's mother.

"You . . . too," she said, and withdrew her hand quickly, as if she were afraid his grip would cripple her fingers.

Beth joined Sam and he wrapped an arm around her waist, bringing her close to his side. His hope was that Ellie got his message. Beth was staying with him. They were a couple.

"Need any help, babe?" he asked Beth. He could see Sunshine busily working in the kitchen. He knew both Beth and her aunt had been preparing food since early that morning.

"Thanks, but we've got everything under control," Beth told him.

"You need anything, all you need to do is ask." He noticed Ellie hadn't gotten anywhere close to the kitchen. She sat in a chair next to her husband and held a glass of white wine, sipping from it occasionally.

Sam took another chair and was about to reach for the television remote when Ellie spoke.

"What was that you called Beth?" her mother asked him conversationally.

"When?"

"Just now. Did you call her baby?"

He nodded. "Babe. It's a term of affection."

"Babe," she repeated, as though amused. Her lips moved, but it looked more like sarcasm than humor. "I find that interesting."

"Really?"

"Well, yes, it's rather ironic."

"Why is that?"

Beth's mother studied him briefly as if she needed to use small words in order for him to understand. "You must know my daughter moved to Portland to show us she could live independently of her father and me. Then as soon as she has her own apartment and a job far beneath her skill, she chooses to let someone call her *babe,* as if she were an infant in need of care."

"Like I said, it's a term of affection," Sam repeated.

Ellie shook her head slightly, as if his answer was beyond her comprehension. "How exactly did you two meet? I assume you aren't one of her charity piano students."

"Mom, you already know how we met. It was a blind date," Beth said, coming out from the kitchen to stand at his side. She sat on the side of the chair and placed her arm around his shoulders.

"A blind date," Ellie repeated, frowning. "Who would possibly think to match up the two of you?"

"A friend from school," Beth supplied.

Sunshine carried out the water pitcher and set it on the table. She shared a look with Sam as though to suggest he not rise to the bait.

Ellie's question was an insult, but Sam let it pass.

"What *friend*?" Ellie asked, as though Nichole should immediately be stripped from the friend list.

"Nichole is another teacher," Sam explained. "She's married to

Rocco, who is my best friend. They arranged for Beth and me to have dinner together."

"The funny part is," Beth said, smiling down on Sam, "when we first met, neither of us were terribly impressed with the other."

Sam swore he could drown in her warmth.

"But then Sam was there at the accident scene," Beth explained.

"He caused it?"

"Ellie!" Phillip laid aside the book and looked pointedly at his wife.

"You know Sam didn't cause the accident, Mom," Beth answered. "Sam was at the stoplight when I got hit by another car. He was the one who helped me most."

"She was hurt," he said, picking up the story. "We didn't know how badly at the time, and I held her hand until the nine-one-one team arrived."

"I don't know what would have happened without Sam," Beth added. "We've been together ever since. He's important to me, Mom."

Ellie nodded slowly. "I've read about incidents like this where someone saves the life of another and then that person feels an obligation to look after the other. Phillip," she said, looking to her husband, "what's the name of that syndrome?"

"What syndrome?"

"You know the one. It's like what happened in Stockholm, only it's when someone helps another and then the person saved feels an obligation . . . or is it the other way around? I don't quite remember how it goes."

"Mom, that's ridiculous."

"I never heard of any such syndrome," Sam said.

"Yes, but Sam, pardon me for being blunt, but you don't look to be an educated man."

Despite his determination not to make waves, he bristled. "I beg your pardon?"

"Oh dear, that did sound rude, didn't it? You'll need to forgive me. I should have put that another way. What is it you do for a living, Sam?"

"Mom, you already know Sam is the head mechanic at the Bruce Olson GM dealership."

Ellie's stare made him feel like he'd crawled out from under a rock. It irritated him, and he decided then and there that he was through playing nice with this woman.

"I left college because I discovered I'm much better with my hands." He looked pointedly at Beth. "Isn't that right, babe?"

Ellie's face reddened.

"Sam." Beth groaned, silently pleading with him. She turned to her mother then and glared at her. "What's with all the questions? You've met Sam. You know him."

"I met him, yes, but there wasn't time to get to know him. You say he's important to you, so I feel I should learn more about him."

Sam didn't believe that for a moment. Ellie Prudhomme was doing her best to belittle him. He loved Beth and would do anything for her, but he wasn't going to allow anyone, not her mother or anyone else, to look and act as if he was dirt under their carefully manicured fingernails.

"Who are your people, Sam?" Ellie asked next.

"My people?"

"Your family," she clarified.

"Mary Alice and Joe Carney."

"The Prudhomme name goes back several generations," Ellie said proudly. "My husband can trace his family tree all the way back to the *Mayflower*."

"My family tree goes all the way back to Ellis Island and then to Ireland," he said. "I come from good people, Mrs. Prudhomme, if that's your concern. We don't have a pedigree, but we have big hearts, determination, and guts. The Carney family is grounded and there's a lot of love. I want Beth to meet my parents and they want to meet her. My brothers and sister, too."

"Just how many of you are there?" Ellie asked, wide-eyed.

"Two brothers, one sister. All married," he answered. "They live in California, near Sacramento."

"How . . ." Ellie paused, as if searching for the right word. "American," she concluded.

It wasn't her words as much as the way Beth's mother studied him. He'd given it his best shot. As much as he loved Beth, as much as he wanted this meeting to go smoothly, he was not going to allow this ridiculous woman to put down his family, Beth, or himself.

"Does anyone object if I turn on the television?" Sam asked, as he reached for the remote to the television. "The Seahawks have a game against the Denver Broncos that starts in about thirty minutes."

"Football on Thanksgiving?" Ellie asked, as if there was something wrong with a society that would allow such a travesty of poor taste to occur on a national holiday.

Sam ignored the question and turned on the TV, changing it to the proper channel.

The time had come for Sam to man up. "Phillip," he said. When Beth's father glanced up from his book, Sam cleared his throat. "Mr. Prudhomme, I want you to know that I love your daughter."

Ellie gave no indication she'd heard, but Sam noticed that the chardonnay sloshed in her wineglass as if she'd jerked.

Phillip considered Sam's words. "Beth is an easy girl to love."

"She's a woman," Sam corrected. "And you're right. She is easy to love. From the day I met her, she's turned my world upside down. She's the most caring person I've ever known. She's thoughtful and wise, generous in spirit, and one incredible person. Just being around her makes me a better man."

Beth stood frozen just outside the kitchen, and he noticed a tear roll down her cheek.

"Mom and Dad," she said, returning to the room. She stood next to Sam and placed her hand on his shoulder. "I love Sam, too."

In all these months, neither of them had verbalized the words. Sam knew long ago he had strong feelings for her. He'd tried to deny it, mainly because giving his heart to another woman scared him unlike anything human. It seemed unfair that he should admit it to Beth's parents before he told her, but it was necessary. Sam wanted it clear where he stood with Beth and that he wasn't going to slink away in the middle of the night because he'd been intimidated.

Ellie looked to her husband and desperately whispered, "Phillip, say something. Surely you recognize this relationship will never work."

Phillip looked from his wife to his daughter and grinned.

Sam reached for Beth's hand. "I don't mean any disrespect, but it seems to me Beth is an adult. She can make her own decisions on who she chooses to love."

"My daughter is an educated—"

"Mom," Beth said, cutting her off. "Sam is right. I love him," she said, and looked at him smiling, "and he loves me."

"But Kier . . ."

"Oh please," Beth exploded. "Kier is not half the man Sam is, and if you don't see that, then I pity you."

Sunshine applauded from the kitchen.

"Stay out of this," Ellie flared at her sister. "It's your influence that's destroying my daughter's life."

"Daddy," Beth said, ignoring her mother. "I'm happy with my life. I can't ever remember being happier."

"That you would choose a mechanic over Kier tells me otherwise," her mother cried, as though she couldn't believe what was happening.

"Kier, Mother?" Beth said again. "What exactly does Kier do? He isn't even employed."

"He doesn't need to work," her mother supplied, as if that was all the qualifications she needed to recommend him. "His grandfather left him a trust fund that has secured his future. You could have everything you've ever wanted."

Beth wrapped her arm around Sam's. "Don't you see, Mom, I already do."

Ellie glared at her husband as if she expected him to leap to his feet and challenge Sam to a duel. "Phillip, for the love of heaven, will you say something?"

Beth's father sighed and smiled at his daughter and Sam. "Congratulations, you two. Now, I've been smelling that turkey roasting for hours. How long before we eat?"

"Phillip?" Ellie cried. "Are you insane?"

"Nope. I'm hungry."

"Just need to mash the potatoes and slice the turkey and we're ready to eat," Sunshine said. "Sam, would you mind carving the bird?"

"I'd be honored." He headed into the kitchen, pulling Beth in with him.

The perfectly roasted turkey sat on a cutting board in the kitchen with a knife and a pronged fork.

Phillip returned to reading his book and Ellie stood in the center of the room as if she didn't know what to do with herself.

Beth began placing food on the table. Sam noticed how she stole glances in his direction, smiling as she moved about the kitchen.

"I refuse to be a party to this farce," Ellie announced.

"Don't be ridiculous," Sunshine told her sister. "It's Thanksgiving. We both have a great deal to be grateful for. Come sit and enjoy the bounty."

"Mother, please," Beth added, gently pleading with her mother.

For his part, Sam was ready to call her a taxi, but Beth might not appreciate the suggestion.

"Ellie," Phillip added forcefully. "Sit down and keep your mouth closed for once in your life. Our daughter loves a good man."

"A mechanic who drinks beer? Heaven help us. What am I going to tell my friends?"

"What friends?" Phillip asked. "Far as I can see, you associate with a bunch of gossip-mongers. Time for you to realize that." Setting his book aside, he stood, hugged his daughter, and shook Sam's hand before he pulled out a chair and sat down at the table. As though paralyzed with shock, Ellie remained standing alone in the middle of the living room. After several minutes, she exhaled, tilted her chin at a proud angle, and joined the others.

Sam thought Ellie was about to break into tears, but she managed to hold herself together. Phillip rubbed his hands and smiled. "Looks like a feast to me. Since Sam is carving the turkey, I'll say grace."

"Dad," Beth whispered, and it sounded a little like a plea.

Ellie closed her eyes. "Phillip, please."

Beth's father waited until he had everyone's attention and then instructed them to join hands.

He bowed his head. Sam did as well, although he had no idea what had concerned both of the women in the other man's life.

"Good friends," Phillip said, "good meat. Good God, let's eat."

Sam grinned. Yup, he was going to get along just fine with Beth's father. He opened one eye and snuck a look at Beth, who was grinning, too.

Thanksgiving had gone as well as could be expected, and Sam was pleased.

CHAPTER 33

Sunshine

Sunshine's Thanksgiving dinner had turned out far better than she'd expected. This was her first experience cooking a turkey, and she'd spent copious amounts of time studying instructions off the Internet. Thankfully, it had baked to perfection and her stuffing wasn't half bad, either. This Thanksgiving was vastly different from years past. It was the first time since their parents' deaths that she had shared the holiday with family.

Correction—shared the day with blood relatives. In previous years, she'd spent major holidays with her artist friends and many were as close as family.

Relaxed now, savoring the silence and the comfort of her own company, she sat in her living room. Almost against her will, her thoughts wandered to Peter. She suspected he'd spent the day alone. Perhaps one of his daughters had invited him to join her or he'd been with friends.

Did Peter have friends? Her heart ached for him, for the bitterness that seemed to eat at his soul. Part of her yearned to reach out to him. She hesitated for fear that would do more harm than good, especially if he was in the same frame of mind as he'd been during their dinner. She was willing to give him a pass for the cruel words he'd said. Like her, he'd been in shock at the trick played on them. In light of their awkward dinner, all she was able to do was send him good wishes and positive thoughts.

Exhausted now, Sunshine headed into her bedroom, intent on reading until she fell asleep. The gathering with Sam and Beth's parents had gone relatively well, she thought, as she undressed and slipped between the covers.

Sunshine saw the way Beth's eyes had widened when Sam declared his love for her to Phillip and Ellie. The look on her sister's face had been priceless. Ellie had been horror-struck, as if Beth had completely lost her mind.

Phillip was Sunshine's hero. She had never fully appreciated her brother-in-law until these last few months. He knew Ellie better than anyone, and while he might not wear the pants in the family, he controlled the checkbook. Phillip wasn't about to let Ellie have her way when it came to their daughter's happiness.

Sitting up in bed, Sunshine reached for the novel she'd been reading for the last several nights. It was a whodunit and she'd gotten deeply involved in the plot. No sooner had she opened the book when her phone rang.

Friends had called on and off all day, but it was after eleven—too late for friends to touch base. She reached for her phone and didn't recognize the number. She was about to let it go to voicemail when she noticed the area code was from Chicago.

"Hello," she greeted tentatively. For no reason she could decipher, her heart raced at the speed of an Indy 500 car.

Silence.

"Hello," she repeated, louder this time.

"Sunshine?"

She sat up straighter. How had she even guessed it could be him? "Peter?"

Silence.

"Happy Thanksgiving." His voice sounded strange.

If her heart was racing, her mind was going at warp speed. "Are you okay?" she asked gently.

"Don't think so."

His words were slightly slurred. "Have you been drinking?"

"You could say that." His laugh was more of a snicker. "You asked me on Saturday if I had a drinking problem."

"I remember."

"Do you remember what I told you?"

"No." Her heart was pounding so hard she could hear the echo of it in her ear.

"I said, and it's the honest truth, I didn't until that day." He snorted with a short-lived laugh. "Had more alcohol in the last week than in the last two years, and you know who I have to thank?"

"Me?" Not exactly a wild guess.

"Wrong. I blame that niece of yours. What's her name again?"

"Beth."

"Right."

Sunshine set her book aside. "Peter," she said gently, "Why are you calling me?"

"Why not? Do you want me to hang up, because I will?"

"How did you get my number?" she asked instead.

"I have my ways. It isn't as difficult as you think."

"Are you alone?" she asked, wondering if he was in any danger.

"Why do you want to know?"

She pressed the phone closer to her ear, unsure he'd like her answer. "I was thinking about you earlier."

"Thought about you, too . . . every minute. Don't want to.

Don't want you in my head, but you refuse to leave me alone and it's driving me crazy."

"You've been on my mind, too."

He barked out a chilling laugh. "You pity me, don't you?"

"No," she answered honestly. "Though I am sad for you. I'd hoped you'd had a good life."

"You're not the only one. Answer me one question. Just one and then I'll hang up and I swear by all I hold holy, which unfortunately is damn little, I'll never contact you again."

"No, don't promise me that. I want you to feel free to call me if you'd like."

Silence followed as if her words had shocked him.

Sunshine bit into the corner of her lip. "What is it you want to know?"

"Why you never married. I don't understand it. Never have. Was it because of me, Sunshine? Did I destroy your ability to trust another man?"

"No, Peter, that's not it."

"Swear it."

"I swear it," she said softly.

"Why, then?"

They'd already had this discussion once, and here he was again needing reassurances he'd not messed up her life along with his own.

"I fell in love any number of times over the years," she said, offering him what she hoped were reassurances.

"Then why?"

Time to own up to him and to the truth. "I had my career, Peter. I got sidetracked with my success."

"And?"

He knew there was more, and Sunshine doubted that she could have hid it from him. "And," she repeated, "I never found another man I could love as much as I did you."

The line went quiet. The only sound was their breathing, which quickly fell into unison.

"You'll never hear from me again," Peter whispered, and he sounded completely sober now.

"Will you do something for me?" she asked, saddened by his response.

Silence again. "What do you want? You who has everything."

"It's a simple request."

"Fine. Tell me."

She held herself stiff. "The woman you fired. Give her back her job."

Peter snickered.

"Is it so much to ask?"

"No."

Sunshine would rest easier now. "She had good intentions."

"Maybe," he conceded.

"Thank you."

"Always thinking about others . . . one of the reasons I fell in love with you."

Sunshine's eyes teared up. "Good-bye, Peter."

She held on to the phone and then she heard the soft click as he disconnected. For several minutes she sat staring into space until she collected her thoughts. She didn't doubt his word. Peter would rehire Sondra Reacher and never contact Sunshine again.

After a while she sighed and reached for her novel.

Friday afternoon, Sunshine met her sister at Portland's Waterfront Hotel. The invitation to lunch was unexpected, although she could guess the reason. Ellie was sure to plead her case in regard to Beth and Sam. The very idea of her daughter dating a blue-collar guy was abhorrent to her sister.

They met in the lobby. Ellie wore a deep blue St. John knit suit and her hair, as always, was perfectly styled.

"Thank you for agreeing to see me," she greeted Sunshine stiffly.

Sunshine nodded. "Of course. You're my sister."

Ellie hesitated, as though the response had shaken her.

"I thought we'd eat here," Ellie said. "I made a reservation and asked for a private table."

Sunshine followed her sister into the restaurant and they were seated right away. They each ordered Caesar salads with grilled chicken for lunch. After the waiter left, Sunshine said, "I heard from Peter yesterday."

Ellie's eyes shot to her. "Peter Hamlin?"

"Yes. It's been over thirty years since we last spoke and then twice within a week."

Her sister looked dumbfounded.

"Peter was in town for a conference," she explained, "and Beth arranged for us to meet. It was a shock to us both." It wasn't necessary to tell her how badly their dinner had gone.

"Beth would do anything for you." Her sister's words were weighed down with sadness and loss as if the love the two shared had robbed her of her daughter.

"She loves you, too," Sunshine reminded her.

Her sister slowly nodded, as though she wasn't completely convinced that was true. "Peter's one of Chicago's most successful attorneys. He's been in the news several times with high-profile cases he's won."

"So I understand." Sunshine didn't mention how miserable and bitter he was. No need for Ellie to know that.

Her sister straightened and looked uncomfortable.

Over the last few days, Sunshine had done a lot of thinking about the past and the role her sister had played in her relationship with Peter.

Ellie spoke first. "I think it's time you and I settled this awkwardness between us . . . I want you to know how dreadfully sorry I am for what happened between Peter and me. I won't make any excuses . . . I thought I loved him, thought we would be perfect together. It wasn't long after you left that we both realized it would never work. He blamed me for ruining his relationship with you, and you . . . you were justifiably angry with me. It was easier for me to get angry back rather than own up to my role in everything."

Sunshine was stunned speechless. Her sister had apologized. She couldn't believe it. "Ellie, I forgave you a long time ago."

"I know," she whispered. "It's taken me this long to forgive myself."

"Oh Ellie."

Something had happened. She didn't know what. The woman sitting across from her wasn't the same woman she'd shared dinner with the night before. There was a complete turnaround in less than twenty-four hours.

"I lost my sister because of what I did." Ellie paid an inordinate amount of attention to the napkin in her lap, smoothing it out with her hand, keeping her head lowered. "And I hurt a good man."

Sunshine leaned forward and teasingly asked, "Okay, who are you and what have you done with my sister?"

A smile cracked Ellie's tight features. When the waiter delivered their salads, her sister looked grateful for the interruption.

"Phillip and I are going through a bit of a rough patch," Ellie admitted with some reluctance, as if it caused her physical pain to say the words. "We've had some heated discussions these last few months. I don't mind telling you I'm lost without Beth. My days are empty. I hardly know what to do with myself."

Her sister's honesty was out of character. All Sunshine felt capable of doing was listening. And an attentive ear was all Ellie really needed.

"My husband and Beth have given me a lot to digest in the last few weeks." Ellie's lower lip trembled. "Phillip was right when he said my friends are shallow. I've come to fear that perhaps I am, too. I have no one that I am close to any longer. I realize I ruined my relationship with you years ago."

"Ellie . . ."

"No, please, let me get this out. What Peter and I did to you . . . There's no way I can undo the damage. If I could turn back the clock I would. You . . . you have a wonderful life. Your paintings are magnificent and you're this huge success . . . and I have no one."

"You have a sister."

Tears welled in Ellie's eyes. "Do I really, Sunshine?"

"Yes, of course. You always have, and the truth is I need my sister, too."

Ellie gestured with her hand as if she didn't know what to say. When she spoke, her voice trembled. "I'm afraid I've lost Beth and my marriage is hanging on by a thread. I feel like I've been cast adrift without a life raft." She dabbed at the corners of her eyes with the linen napkin. "I have no one else." Tears rained down her cheeks and she sniffled in an effort to hold them back. "This is ridiculous. I can't believe I'm admitting this."

Sunshine couldn't believe it, either. She didn't know it was possible to heal her relationship with her sister.

Ellie took a moment to compose herself, squaring her shoulders, straightening. "I expect I've ruined my makeup."

"You always look perfect. You got the looks in the family."

"Perhaps, but you got the talent."

Sunshine smiled but then grew serious. "You haven't lost Beth. She needs her mother."

"I need my daughter, but this man she's seeing. Surely you can see how impossible the two of them are together."

"As a matter of fact, I can't. Sam is good for Beth. Whatever happens in this relationship is up to them. I will tell you that if you push it, you'll only drive them closer together and your daughter further away."

"He loves her," Ellie admitted. "Even I could see that."

"And she feels strongly about him, too."

Ellie's shoulders sagged with defeat. "That was just as apparent."

Sunshine could see how difficult this was for her sister. "Beth is her own person, Ellie."

"She's more like Phillip," her sister admitted. "His mother was a pianist and Beth inherited her musical talent from that side of the family. I miss her something terrible. It killed me to have her move so far away." She sniffled again. "Phillip . . . Oh Sunshine, I don't know what to do. He's so angry with me, and you know Phillip, he's not an angry man."

Sunshine couldn't imagine it, either. "Do you love him?"

Her sister's eyes filled with tears again. "So much."

"What happened?" she asked gently.

Ellie reached for her fork and held it over her plate for several seconds. "Phillip and I disagreed over Beth moving to Oregon and it sort of escalated from there. Then she was in that dreadful car accident and I flew out for the brief visit. I wanted to return, take care of our daughter, but Phillip insisted I keep my word and stay away for the promised six months. He had no appreciation of how hard it was for me to stay in Chicago when Beth was hurting." She still hadn't taken a bite of her lunch.

Sunshine reached for her tea and sipped it.

"I wanted Beth to come home for Thanksgiving, but Phillip made it clear I was not to meddle in her life. I didn't speak to him for three days, and you know what he said?" She stiffened. "He told me those were the happiest three days of his life."

It wasn't a good idea to laugh, but Sunshine was unable to hold back a smile. She didn't know her brother-in-law had it in him. Her admiration for Phillip escalated.

"You sent Kier to check on her?" Sunshine asked.

Ellie nodded.

"Something happened between you and Phillip yesterday, didn't it?" It only made sense, seeing how fragile Ellie currently was.

"At dinner yesterday when I made a fuss over Beth and Sam's relationship, it caused more problems with Phillip. He doesn't like confrontation and ordinarily avoids it until he can't hold it in any longer. Don't misunderstand me. Phillip would never shout or make a big fuss, that's not his way. Once we were back at the hotel, he laid into me about how I spoke to Sam."

"Have you two patched things up now?" she asked.

Her sister went pale and fresh tears filled her eyes. "I . . . I don't know where he is. After our argument, Phillip left the room and he hasn't come back. I've been up all night fretting. I'm sure he must have gotten another hotel room. It kills me that he would go to that extreme. I feel like my entire world is imploding. I've alienated my daughter, and now it seems my husband as well."

Sunshine could see that her sister was a miserable wreck. "You know what you need, don't you?"

"A day at the spa, for starters," Ellie said, and rotated her neck as if to ease away the stress and tightness there.

"No, how about a day with your sister instead?"

"Can we get a massage?"

That did sound heavenly. "I think I can arrange that."

"Can we shop? There are some wonderful bargains. This is Black Friday, you know."

Sunshine shook her head. "I'm not much of a shopper."

"Oh come on, Sunshine. It's time you updated your wardrobe, and I'm just the woman to make it happen."

She couldn't help smiling. Sunshine was telling the truth when she said she missed her sister. While she didn't know what the future held for Ellie and Phillip, she was fairly certain they could manage to be sisters again.

CHAPTER 34

Beth

Beth was pleased with how Thanksgiving went with Sam and her family. They held hands through most of the meal and couldn't seem to keep their eyes off each other. Sam had told her father that he loved her.

Loved her.

Her father had smiled and nodded as if it was understood. Naturally, her mother had freaked out, but that was to be expected. For the rest of the meal everything had gone smoothly, although her mother had remained suspiciously quiet. As soon as the table was cleared, Sam announced he would do the dishes. Beth offered to help while her aunt and parents retired to the living room. No sooner had Beth and Sam gotten the dishwasher loaded when her father announced they would be returning to the hotel. Just the way he spoke told Beth something wasn't right, and she knew whatever it was involved her mother. Her father's eyes narrowed in on Ellie as he steered her toward the front door.

Before he left, Phillip hugged Beth and must have noticed her concerned frown because he whispered, "No worries, sweetheart."

She motioned with her head toward Sam, who was busy filling the sink with soap suds. Her father's approval meant everything, knowing she'd never get it from her mother.

"Good man," Phillip whispered. "He loves you, treats you right. That's what's important."

Her mother dutifully followed him out the door with little more than a brief acknowledgment to Sunshine and Beth.

Because she'd been busy every night, Beth decided to clean her apartment and do a couple loads of wash Friday morning. Sam had decided to work, as he got time and a half. Beth rolled out her vacuum cleaner when her phone rang. Caller ID told her it was her father.

Her dad never called her. Half the time he didn't even know where he kept his phone. Ninety-nine-point-nine percent of all communication came from her mother.

"Hello?" Her answer was tentative. Her first thought was that her father had lost his phone and some stranger found her name in his contact list. She bet he only had three names in his contacts.

"Beth, it's your father," he announced, as if she wouldn't recognize his voice.

"Dad. Anything wrong?"

He hesitated. "Would it be all right if I stopped by your apartment?"

"Of course. Do you need me to come get you?" Beth knew her parents were without a car.

"No. No, I can take a cab, but I'll need your address."

She said it twice and hoped he wrote it down. Her wonderful father could be terribly absentminded.

"Dad," she tried again, nervous now. "Is everything all right?"

"I think so," he told her.

Beth remained unsettled. "Can you tell me what this is about?"

He paused. "I want to talk to you about your mother."

"Okay." That didn't tell her much.

"And apologize for the way she behaved yesterday."

"You're welcome to stop by anytime, Dad."

"I'll be there within the hour."

That gave her time to straighten up the apartment, not that it was terribly messy. She wasn't at home often enough to require a lot of tidying up.

By the time her father arrived, Beth had finished the vacuuming and had one load of wash finished and a second load in the machine. When the doorbell rang, she hurried to answer, opening it wide to greet her father. He had on the same suit that he'd worn the day before and it looked as if he'd slept in it. He needed a shave, too. Her mother would never have let him out of the hotel room in his current condition. Something was up and whatever it was didn't bode well.

"Where's Mom?" she asked.

Her father didn't answer. "I could use a cup of coffee."

"Of course." Beth moved into the kitchen and brewed them each a cup.

"Make mine extra-strong."

"I'll do my best," she assured him, growing more curious by the moment. Carrying both mugs into the other room, she sat down on the sofa next to her father and waited.

He took a tentative sip of the coffee, closed his eyes as though to savor it, and then said, "First off, I want to apologize again for your mother's behavior."

"It's all right, Dad. It was what Sam and I expected. I knew Mom would have a hard time accepting him."

He dismissed her easy acceptance. "I need to apologize to you, too. I've had my head in my work and didn't realize how controlling of you your mother had gotten."

"It's okay, Dad. She knows now I intend to be my own person."

"Yes, I heard about the conversation you had with her recently. She didn't take kindly to it. I thought she was better, but after yesterday, I'm not so sure. I love your mother and I know you do, too. She means well, Bethie."

"I know, Dad." He rarely used the pet name he had for her.

"We had a long talk after we got back to the hotel, and I felt I needed to add my voice to yours. I let her know she was out of line with the way she questioned Sam and that I was disappointed in her."

"It didn't go well, did it?"

He shook his head. "Your mother is convinced you're making a huge mistake loving Sam."

"You don't agree with that, though, right?"

"Don't have a crystal ball, but from what I saw, you two looked like a fine couple to me."

"Thank you, Daddy."

"As far as I'm concerned and I told you mother this, she should get on her knees and thank God you found a hardworking, capable man like Sam. Her thinking is messed up. What's important to her should be at the bottom of the list. And I told her so. After I gave her a few other things to think about," he said, pausing as if to gauge her reaction, "I left the hotel and I spent the night elsewhere."

Shocked, Beth's mouth sagged open and she found herself speechless. "Dad!" This was completely out of character for her father. He wasn't the type of man to make such a dramatic statement.

"Where did you go?" No wonder he looked like he'd slept in his clothes. He probably had and that was why he hadn't shaved.

"I found another hotel down the street. Not exactly the Ritz, but it served the purpose. I had peace and quiet and I didn't need to listen to your mother's endless chatter about you making a terrible mistake."

"Did Mom know where you were?"

"No. I'm finished talking to her. Before I left, I said it was high time she made up with her sister and that the only person she'd hurt was herself; being angry all these years over something that happened when she was young was ridiculous. I told her that if anyone had messed up their life it was her."

Beth could hardly believe her father. This was probably the sincerest, most heartfelt conversation her father had had with her mother in years. She was about to say something more when her phone rang. She was tempted to ignore it until she recognized the number. Automatically her eyes shot to her father.

"It's Mom," she told him. "Should I answer it?"

He looked as undecided as she was. It rang a third time before her father reluctantly nodded. "Go ahead."

Beth grabbed it off the coffee table and accepted the call. "Hello?"

"Beth, it's Mom." Ellie didn't sound right. If she didn't know better, Beth would think she had a bad cold or had been weeping.

"Yes, Mom."

Ellie sucked in a sob.

"Mom, are you all right?" Beth felt she had to ask. "Do you need anything?"

"Yes, but that's not the reason I called."

"Okay." Beth made eye contact with her father and shrugged. She was fairly certain he was able to hear both sides of the conversation.

"This isn't easy for me, Beth." Ellie took a moment to compose herself. "First off, I believe I did a brilliant job raising you. I sacrificed my entire life to take care of you in every way I knew."

Her father crossed his arms.

"But that's not the reason I called. I . . . want to apologize to Sam, but I don't know his phone number, and so I'm asking you to let him know."

Phillip arched his brows and then gave her a thumbs-up sign. He looked rather pleased with himself.

"What would you like me to tell Sam?" Beth asked her mother.

Her mother sucked in a deep breath. "Just that I'm sorry. I was rude and arrogant. Those are the words your father used, and after giving it some thought I realize he's right."

"You don't like Sam," Beth said, pushing the limits, unwilling to accept a token apology on his behalf.

"I don't know him well enough yet. I hope you'll both give me the opportunity to correct his impression of me so that I'll have a chance to do that. All I can say is that if you love him, then there must be more to Sam than meets the eye."

"There is, far more than you know."

"I figured so."

This was huge.

Gigantic.

Bigger than big.

Her mother making this kind of concession went beyond words. Looking over at her father, Beth could see that he was equally impressed.

"There's something else you should know," her mother continued.

"Okay," Beth said, eager to hear more.

"I had lunch with Sunshine."

"Did she call you or did you call her?" It would be easy enough to see her aunt reaching out with an olive branch.

"I called her. We talked and it was good for us both."

"That's wonderful, Mom." Beth felt tears of gratitude gathering in her own eyes.

"We ate at the hotel and then she suggested a massage. No wait,

I suggested a massage and she knew just the person. I felt worlds better afterward . . . or I did until I returned to the hotel room."

"Did something happen at the hotel?" Beth asked.

"Yes," her mother said on the tail end of a hiccupping sob. "Your father wasn't here. Sunshine felt sure he would have returned by now and he hasn't and I don't know where he is," she blurted out all at once.

"You don't know where Dad is?" Beth played innocent.

"No . . . I haven't seen him since last evening after we returned from dinner. He was angry with me and then he left and I thought, I hoped, it would all blow over."

"Oh Mom, I'm so sorry."

"But he's still not back and I don't know what to think. He's never done anything like this before. Oh Beth, I don't know what I would do. I love him so much and I'm worried sick."

Maintaining eye contact with her father, Beth said, "I'm sure Dad will be back to the hotel soon. Don't worry and don't lose hope. Dad loves you."

"I love him more than I ever realized," her mother continued.

Her father widened his eyes.

"Please don't worry," Beth said.

"I love you, Beth," her mother said, a bit less weepy now.

"I know you do," she assured her. "And I love you."

"I might have been misguided, but everything I did was because I wanted the very best for you."

"I know. Now listen, Mom, you need to relax. I'm sure Dad will return within the hour." She looked to her father who nodded, his eyes warm and a bit misty. "And when he gets back, the two of you can talk again," Beth added. "You'll be able to square things with him and you can make a fresh start."

Her mother released a tiny sob.

"Call me if you need me, okay?"

"Okay," her mother agreed. "Thank you, love."

"You're welcome, Mom."

Beth disconnected and set the phone aside. "It sounds like Mom took your words to heart."

Her father seemed ten times better than when he'd first arrived. The light was back in his eyes. He looked as if he'd been informed he had the winning numbers in the lottery. What Beth recognized in her father was hope.

"I better get back to the hotel," he said.

"Let me drive you."

"No, no." His refusal was automatic. "I'll get a cab. I don't want to take a chance of your mother knowing I was with you and over-heard your conversation."

Beth smiled. "You devil," she teased.

Her father laughed and hugged her. "Love you, kiddo."

"I know you do, Dad. Love you back."

He kissed her forehead. Beth contacted a cab company and gave them her address and ten minutes later her father was on his way.

As soon as he was out the door, Beth called her aunt. Sunshine answered after the first ring.

"You heard what's going on with your mother?" she asked with-out greeting Beth.

"Yes, Mom called me just now. I'm still in shock."

"You?" Sunshine said with a laugh. "You could have knocked me over with a string bikini when Ellie invited me to lunch. And that's not all she did."

"I heard the two of you went for a massage."

"We did far more than that. We talked, Beth, really talked for the first time in nearly thirty years. I have my sister back and I couldn't be happier."

"That's wonderful."

"I think so, too, and you're the one who brought us together, the love we share for you."

Sunshine said she couldn't be happier but Beth was the one beaming now.

Later that evening, when Beth saw Sam, she told him the unbelievable events of the afternoon.

"Well, your day was definitely more eventful than mine."

"That's not all," Beth said.

"You mean there's more?"

"Yup. Dad phoned just a few minutes ago and asked if you and I can join him and Mom for dinner tonight. There's a fabulous steakhouse in town he knows about and he wanted to treat us. Sunshine is invited, too."

"That's good news, isn't it?" Sam asked. "I mean for your parents. If they're inviting us to dinner, then they must have come to some kind of agreement, right?"

"I believe they have."

"Do you see what you've done?" he said, holding her by the shoulders, his eyes filled with pride.

"Me?"

"By standing up for yourself, you were able to bring your parents together."

"Maybe." Beth was willing to accept a small role in the improved relationship between her parents.

"Then you brought everything to a head once again when you introduced me. Your mother recognized you weren't going to back down from loving me."

"And I won't," Beth assured him.

"I'd be upset if you did, babe. We got something good, you and me."

"Yes, we do," Beth agreed.

"Now if we're going out for this fancy steak dinner I had better get home and change clothes. Might even put on the suit I wore for my sister's wedding. Really shock your mother; I clean up good."

"I have the feeling it's going to be a much more pleasant meal for us all."

"Think you're right about that, babe." His smile ate her up.

"Could you tell me you love me again?" Beth asked.

"Why? Are you feeling insecure?"

"No, I just like to hear the words."

He chuckled. "Love you, babe."

"Love you, too."

He leaned in to kiss her and her heart swelled with love and appreciation. Sam was going to love her even more once she was able to deliver her Christmas surprise. She could hardly wait.

CHAPTER 35

Sam

Beth had cooked up some kind of Christmas surprise for him and she wasn't giving him any hints. He had something for her, too, but it would need to wait until after the holidays. Everything had been going well between them since Thanksgiving. He was busy with work and the volunteer projects Beth had introduced him to over the last couple months.

Beth was deeply involved with her students at the high school. She took a personal interest in her piano students, especially a twelve-year-old girl named Kameron.

Sam had made peace with Beth's mother and things were good on the home front. From tidbits of conversation with both Sunshine and Beth, he'd learned that Phillip and Ellie were eager to have Beth home for Christmas. Beth had mentioned that her father had signed him and Ellie up for a cruise to the South Pacific as a surprise Christmas gift. They would be sailing sometime in January.

Sam hated the thought of Beth being in Chicago for two weeks. He would miss her terribly. More and more he was feeling confident that they were meant to be together. She'd become a big part of his world, and he couldn't imagine life without her now. Crazy, seeing how he'd sworn never to get involved in another romantic relationship. He'd given up until he'd met Beth.

On Saturday, the day before Beth was due to fly to Chicago and join her family for the Christmas and New Year's holidays, she asked him to accompany her to some piano function. She seemed excited about it, and while sitting and watching kids at a recital wasn't high on his entertainment list, for Beth, he was willing. Truth was he'd do just about anything for this woman and she knew it.

He picked her up around five. When she opened the door, his heart leapt as he was struck once again by her beauty. Whatever he'd done to deserve this woman must have been really good. She was beautiful. She wore a red dress with an angel pin clipped at the base of her throat. In many ways he saw her as an angel.

His angel.

"You look . . . wow." He couldn't find words adequate enough to describe how lovely she was.

As expected, Beth blushed. It was hard not to take her in his arms and kiss her senseless. The temptation was strong but he resisted, knowing it would be hard to stop and they were on a schedule. First this recital and then dinner with Rocco and Nichole at some new restaurant the girls wanted to try. Sam was game for the simple reason that he would be with Beth. In the morning, he'd drive her to the airport and off she'd go to Chicago.

Beth gathered her coat and had the address for the music performance. Her mood was almost giddy.

"Any of these your students?" he asked.

"No, these are more advanced. Kameron should be at this level by next year."

He wasn't sure why it was so important that Beth attend when none of her own students were part of the program, but he didn't question it. She'd made friends with several music teachers in the area and he supposed she was looking to support a newfound friend.

Thanks to Beth, he'd been working with Habitat for Humanity on Jazmine's house and he'd spent more than one weekend with a group of volunteers. Beth often joined him. He'd even managed to involve a couple guys from work. In the beginning, they'd complained, but all it took was one Saturday. Since that time a number of his work crew had become volunteers themselves. Doing something for someone else. Giving back was addictive.

Sam drove to the address for the school that Beth provided. They had a hard time finding a parking spot and barely made it in time. Beth took the program offered at the front door of the auditorium and he followed her inside. Because they were a few minutes late, the only available seats were in the back. That suited Sam fine. He could lean back, close his eyes, and snooze during what was sure to be a long hour.

He had zoned out for the majority of the program when Beth elbowed him in the ribs. "Pay attention," she whispered. "This is the girl we came to hear."

Sam sat up straighter and eyed the young teenager, who must have been around thirteen or fourteen, approaching the piano. She had on a white dress and her dark hair was curled. Sliding onto the bench, she glanced nervously toward the front row.

Sam felt for the kid, who was clearly anxious.

"Oh Sam, isn't she lovely?"

He shrugged. From this distance they all sort of looked the same. He did sit up and take notice when her hands went to the keys. Her back straightened and before his eyes, the teenager was immediately transformed. The girl who had been self-conscious and jittery took on a completely different persona. He didn't recognize the number she'd chosen to play. What he did notice was that the girl was clearly gifted. It was as if she surrendered herself to the music, giving over her heart. When she finished, there was a moment of awe and silence before the room exploded in applause.

Sam applauded, too.

The next student was introduced, and Beth leaned close and whispered, "We can go now if you want."

"We can?" This was an unexpected surprise.

She nodded and stood. They were at the end of the aisle, so their leaving didn't disturb anyone. Sam waited until they were outside before he spoke.

"I thought you said none of your students were part of the recital."

"They weren't," she said, smiling at him. Her eyes twinkled with delight.

"That last girl, the one who played so beautifully, wasn't someone you know?"

"No." Her smile was huge.

"She's someone from the high school?"

"Nope."

"Are you going to make me guess?"

"Actually, I thought you might recognize her but apparently not."

Sam frowned. *Recognize her?* "I know her?" he asked.

"Sam," Beth said, as she placed her hand on his arm. Looking at him, her eyes were full of love. "This is the Christmas surprise I mentioned. That beautiful young girl with that gift for music is your daughter, Luci."

The shock of her words hit him with such force it caused him to stumble back two steps. It felt like a two-by-four had been slammed into his midsection. He was too stunned to breathe, and when he was able to gasp a breath it was followed by blinding pain.

"Are you surprised?" Beth asked, with what he could only guess was expectation.

"How . . . ?" Getting out that one word past the blinding pain tightening his chest was all he was able to manage.

"How did I find her?" Beth supplied the rest of the question for him. "It was sheer luck and a tiny bit of checking. When you told me about your daughter, I asked Nichole about Trish. That relationship was before she knew Rocco, but he'd shared Trish's last name when she asked. Then at one of my meetings with other music teachers, we were all talking about our most talented students. When one of my friends mentioned Luci's name, I asked about her and I figured it out from there. Same name, right age. She's your daughter."

Sam realized Beth had no clue what she'd done. No clue whatsoever. When his chest relaxed enough for him to breathe normally again, he started walking toward the car. Beth had to scurry to catch up with him.

"Are you surprised?" she asked again, still two or three steps behind him. "It makes sense Luci would be musical because you are. You taught yourself to play the guitar, and, Sam, you're good. You're really good. She got that talent from you."

He had nothing to say. Not one word.

"Luci is so gifted," Beth continued. "My friend told me about her and how hard she practices. She's shy, but when she sits down at the piano she feels completely at ease. You saw it when she performed, didn't you? I did. The minute she set her hands on the keyboard she gained all the confidence she needed. It was a beautiful sight. Don't you think so?"

When he reached the car, Sam leaned forward, bracing his hands against the hood while emotion raged through him like a storming wildfire. He had to blot out Beth and her words.

"Sam?" Beth stood at his side. "Did I do something wrong?" For the first time she sounded unsure.

"Get in the car," he demanded.

"But . . ."

"Get. In. The. Car."

She blinked hard. He'd never spoken to her in this way. Still, she hesitated but eventually did as he asked.

Sam remained outside, buffeted by the wind and a light drizzle. He leaned his back against the side of the vehicle and dug the heels of his hands into his eyes. Beth thought she'd given him this great gift when she might as well have taken a scalpel and dug out his heart.

For the first time in years, life had felt good. Just when it seemed that he could move beyond the pain of Trish's betrayal, he was hit in the face with it. Just when he felt he was able to put the past behind him, she thrust it at him like a fast-pitch baseball. No more than a few rows in front of him was the woman he had loved and the child he had lost, and Beth assumed she was doing him this great favor. This was his Christmas gift? The gift she was excited to share with him? Was the woman that insensitive? That oblivious?

He heard the door creak open and Beth climbed out again. "Sam," she whispered, and placed her hand on his shoulder. "Please say something. I feel awful. I thought . . . I hoped. Oh Sam, please believe me I didn't do this to hurt you."

"Don't. Just don't. Get back in the car and stay there before I say something I'll regret."

She slid back inside the car and closed the door once again. Sam paced the area for several more minutes until he felt he could talk. Even then the band of pain around his chest had loosened only enough for him to feel limited control of his emotions.

When he felt he could, he got into the car and started the engine.

"Sam . . . I'm so sorry. I thought you'd want to see your daughter. I didn't do this to hurt you," Beth said, her voice low and tight with concern. "Did I?"

"You think?"

"You know I'd never intentionally do anything to hurt you, don't you?"

He laughed without humor. "I'd hate to think of what you'd do if you were. Another one of your little surprises would probably cripple me for life."

"I thought—"

"Don't say anything more," he snapped. "Don't tell me your intentions were good. I don't want to hear it."

"I wasn't going to say that."

"Good. It'd be better if you said nothing." He didn't want to be cruel, but he couldn't deal with her questions and his pain at the same time. It was all he could manage to hold himself together.

"I'm sorry, Sam. I . . . thought you'd want to see your daughter."

They rode ten minutes in silence.

It came to him as they reached the freeway entrance that he had no clue where he was driving. Dinner with Rocco and Nichole was out of the question. No way could he sit across the table from friends and be sociable and celebrate the holidays. No way on God's green earth. Not with the way he currently felt. He wanted to hit something, plow his fist into a wall or scream in pain and frustration.

As soon as he could, he exited the freeway and headed back to Beth's apartment.

The silence in the car was thick with tension. When he pulled up to the front of her building, Beth looked at him.

"Please say something."

"What do you want me to say?" He couldn't look at her, afraid if he did he would unleash his frustration and anger on her, say things he'd regret. He had the power to destroy her and he wouldn't, couldn't, retaliate with words that would wound her.

"Just something, please. I leave tomorrow and I can't go knowing what I did hurt you."

"Go, Beth, get out of the car. Now."

She placed her hand on the door handle but didn't move. Her head drooped. "I can't leave you like this."

"If you don't get out of the car, then I'm going to tell you what I'm feeling and you're not going to want to hear it."

"I do. I need to know."

"Fine." He whirled around so that he was facing her. "Tell me, in the name of all that's holy, what gave you the right? You can't seem to leave well enough alone. Look what you did to your aunt. You ripped her heart open and jumped on it, disturbing the peace she'd made with her past. And what about that attorney? How do you think he must have felt? Did you see how she was after that surprise dinner you arranged? Didn't you notice the pain in her eyes? Are you so blind?"

"I . . . I didn't know it would turn out the way it did."

"What right do you have to dig up old wounds? And what's worse is that you clearly didn't learn a lesson from the awful mess you created earlier. Oh no, Sunshine wasn't enough, you had to meddle in my life, too."

Beth had gone pale.

"Apparently, you don't have a clue what you've done. Tell me, Beth, did you honestly think you were doing me a favor by bringing up the most painful period of my life and rubbing my face in it? In that messed-up head of yours, did you see any good coming out of reminding me of the daughter I can never speak to, never acknowledge, never know? Are you that insensitive?"

"Sam, I'm sorry, I didn't realize."

"You're sorry? Do you really think *sorry* is going to cut it?"

She hung her head. "I guess it isn't."

"You want to apologize, then start with your aunt and every other life you decided to butt into."

Beth continued to sit for several seconds before she asked, "What does this mean for us?"

"Funny you should ask." Sam tried to calm himself. "I need to think. I love you, Beth. God help me, it's true. But I don't know that I can be with someone who would do something like this. I'm glad you're leaving. That will give me time to think if this is a relationship worth continuing."

She gasped. "Please, Sam, tell me you didn't mean that we're through. I couldn't bear that."

He kept his hands tightened around the steering wheel and found he couldn't answer for several moments. "It's for the best."

"You're angry with me now, I understand that. I'm sorry, so sorry. If you—"

"I don't want to hear it, Beth. Please, don't say anything more."

"I love you."

He refused to look at her for fear of what would happen if he did. If he saw the pain in her eyes, he'd never be able to let her go.

"I thought you'd want to know about Luci."

Sam grimaced at the sound of his daughter's name. It felt as if Beth had reached out and struck him. She didn't seem to understand that apologizing only made what she'd done worse.

"I do mean it."

"I'm not willing to give up on us, Sam. We can work through this. If you feel this strongly, then give it the two weeks I'm away. We both need to think about this. When I get back, then we can talk again. Okay?"

The plea in her voice nearly broke his resolve. At this point he wasn't willing to agree to anything. Tightening his jaw, he held firm. "I'll let Rocco know we won't be joining him and Nichole for dinner."

"If that's what you want," she whispered, tears in her voice.

"It would be best if you went inside now." His grip on the steering wheel was so tight his knuckles went white.

She opened the car door then. "I don't believe you mean it," she insisted. "You're angry with me and . . . and I don't blame you. But I would never do anything to purposely hurt you."

"I don't know what you were thinking, Beth. It's hard to believe you could be this insensitive."

Once outside his truck, she looked back, her eyes pleading with his.

He felt it best to leave it at that. "Good-bye, Beth."

She closed the door and stepped back, and Sam drove off.

CHAPTER 36

Beth

Beth didn't know how she could have been so wrong. Seeing the pain in Sam's eyes when she told him the girl at the piano was his daughter had crushed her. Knowing she was the one responsible for putting it there ate at her like acid. Sam accused her of being insensitive and manipulative, words that had cut deep. Sleeping had been impossible. She got a text message from Nichole wanting to know what had happened that they couldn't make the dinner. Beth left it unanswered. She didn't know what to tell her friend, and in the emotional state she was in, talking to anyone about Sam wasn't a good idea.

When she landed in Chicago and turned on her phone, she saw a voice message. She stopped on the jetway, hoping it was from Sam, praying he'd had a change of heart and wanted to talk. Holding the phone to her ear, she closed her eyes.

Instead of Sam, an automated voice droned on. "This is a courtesy call to remind you of your appointment with Peter Hamlin on Monday morning at nine-thirty a.m."

Disheartened, Beth tossed her phone back in her purse and continued out of the jetway. Weeks ago, she'd scheduled the appointment, never intending to keep it. At the time, setting it up was the only way she'd been able to get in touch with the lawyer without raising a lot of suspicion.

After the things Sam had said to her, Beth felt a need to meet with the attorney. If nothing else, she could apologize and hope he would forgive her. If Peter could look past what she'd done, then perhaps Sam could, too. The appointment had completely slipped her mind and felt like an unexpected gift now. Seeing him would give her the opportunity to apologize and hopefully set matters right.

Monday morning her mother was disappointed to have Beth race into the city first thing until she heard the reason.

When she arrived at the suite of offices, Beth was impressed with the expensive decor. The waiting area was filled with leather furniture and high-end artwork hanging on the walls. She gave her name to the receptionist, who instructed her to take a seat.

"Mr. Hamlin will be with you directly."

"Thank you."

Beth found a chair and drew in deep breaths in an effort to calm her nerves. This appointment was either a very good or a very bad idea, and she was soon to find out which. Up to this point, from everything she'd heard and her own brief experience with the man, it had all been negative.

No more than five minutes later she was escorted into Peter Hamlin's office. He had a corner office with a breathtaking view of Lake Michigan.

He stood as she entered the room and extended his hand. "Ms. Prudhomme," he greeted her, "please take a seat."

She took the comfortable-looking leather chair directly across from his desk.

Settling down himself, he reached for a pad and pen before asking, "How may I help you?"

Her nerve had nearly deserted her and Beth bit into her lower lip. She straightened, gathered her resolve, and started. "I'm here to apologize."

"Apologize?" he asked, frowning.

He didn't recognize her name, which was probably a good thing. If he had, he might have refused to see her. "I went behind your and my aunt Sunshine's back and arranged the meeting between you two. I realize now that by prying into your life I brought you both pain. My hope was that once you saw each other again, you'd talk, sort out the past, and reconnect."

"Reconnect?" He made it sound laughable.

"I . . . hoped you could resolve your differences, that there would be healing for you both." This wasn't going well. "I thought I was helping but clearly I wasn't and for that I'm genuinely sorry."

Leaning back in his chair, he steepled his fingers and stared at her long and hard. "What exactly made you think shocking us both by arranging this dinner would help?" he demanded.

She hesitated, hoping he wouldn't immediately kick her out of his office. "In retrospect, I don't know. This is a weak excuse, I know, but at the time it sounded like a good idea."

His expression remained closed and hard, and an awkward silence ensued. A silence Beth felt obligated to fill.

"It has recently come to my attention that what I did was terribly wrong and caused both you and my aunt a lot of pain. I wanted you to know that I deeply regret my actions and hope that you would be willing to look past my . . . arrogance." This was the short speech she had prepared and practiced on her drive into the city.

Peter continued to stare at her.

"Also, I wanted to thank you for rehiring Mrs. Reacher."

He scowled. "Sunshine asked me if I would, so don't think it was due to any generosity on my part. She's decided to work only on Fridays, as if she's the one doing me a favor."

"Oh." It reflected well on him that he would follow through with her aunt's request.

He looked as if he was about to say something more but didn't.

Not having anything else on her mind, Beth started to stand when she noticed the painting on the side wall. She was in a half sitting, half standing position when she swiveled her attention back to Peter Hamlin. The painting was one of her aunt's. Beth remembered then that Sondra Reacher had mentioned Peter had one of her paintings in his office. It was how she recognized Sunshine's name. Just seeing it she felt a rush of promise, wondering if she should mention it or not. It only took her a second to decide not to bring it up. She'd said what she came to tell him and it was best to leave it at that, although it was hard not to comment.

"I see you've noticed Sunshine's painting," Peter Hamlin said. "It's one of her earlier pieces."

"You've had it a long time?"

He nodded, although he seemed a little reluctant to admit it. "How is your aunt doing?" he asked.

"If you mean health-wise, she's well."

"And otherwise?"

Beth sat back down and stared at her hands. "I . . . a friend told me that my meddling in her life and yours was the wrong thing to do. In my twisted thinking I assumed, I'd hoped, for so much more for you both, but my efforts did far more harm than good." But it wasn't all bad news. "On a positive note," she rushed to explain, "my mom and my aunt have reconciled."

"Because of the meeting we had at the restaurant?"

Beth shook her head. "No. That happened over Thanksgiving, when my parents came to Portland."

"That's good," he surprised her by saying.

"It is for them both. It's time this foolishness between them came to an end."

He grinned as if he found her statement amusing.

Not knowing what else to say, if anything, Beth stood again. "Thank you for seeing me and for letting me apologize in person." He hadn't accepted her apology, she noted. That was on him, though. She'd done her part.

"What you did is forgivable, Beth."

"Thank you." Relief washed over her as she started for the door. "You surprised me."

"How's that?"

"I expected you to demand that I leave your office and have me escorted out."

"But you came, anyway."

"Yes, seeing you was important. It helped that you didn't recognize my name."

"Ah, but I did."

"You did?"

"I was curious to find out what brought you to my office."

That made sense. "From past experience, you probably should have been afraid."

He grinned and Beth had the feeling he didn't find much in life amusing. "Would you mind if I tell my aunt you have one of her early paintings?"

Indecision passed over his features, tightening them briefly. "Sure. Go ahead, if you like. It won't make any difference, but if you feel it would help her to know that I've thought of her through the years, then by all means tell her."

"Thank you for everything." Beth made it all the way to his door before she hesitated and turned back. "Would you mind answering one last question?"

"Depends on what it is."

"You loved her, didn't you? Sunshine, that is."

His eyes grew sad and he nodded. "Always."

For reasons that hit far too close to her own heart, tears gathered in Beth's eyes. She wanted to say more but was afraid if she did her voice would crack. No matter what the future held for her and Sam, she would always love him. If he never wanted to see her again, then she could accept that, no matter how much it hurt.

When Beth arrived back at the house, she found a note from her mother on the kitchen counter.

Out for the afternoon.

Seeing that she had the house to herself, Beth made herself comfortable in her favorite chair, tucked her feet under her, and reached for her phone. Her aunt was probably busy in her studio and would let the call go to voicemail and return it later, which was fine. She was surprised when Sunshine picked up.

"You okay, Sweet Pea?"

She wasn't but not for the reasons her aunt assumed. Beth had yet to tell Sunshine about what had happened with Sam. Deep down, she was confident he would eventually have a change of heart. It was still so new she hadn't dealt with her own feelings and wasn't up to speaking about it, not even to Sunshine. "I'm good. Had an interesting morning, though."

"What's up?"

"Before I get to that, I need to say something." She drew in a deep breath and plunged ahead. "I want to apologize for the dinner Mrs. Reacher and I arranged. We both thought we were helping smooth the path to true love. Yet all we did was bring up old hurts. I'm genuinely sorry. If I could undo that dinner, I would. I hope you know I would never intentionally hurt you. I feel terrible knowing I did."

"Of course you wouldn't, Baby Girl; I know that. It's forgotten. No apology necessary."

Her aunt was more than generous, but then she always had been.

"Now tell me about your morning," Sunshine said, changing the subject.

"You weren't the only one I needed to apologize to," Beth explained. "When I first tried to speak to Mr. Hamlin, the receptionist, not Mrs. Reacher, made an appointment for me in December. I'd actually forgotten about it. Then I got a reminder and decided that instead of breaking the appointment I would go to his office and apologize personally."

"Did he kick you out?" she asked, making a joke of it.

"I thought he would," Beth confessed. "Instead, he saw me. I assumed he didn't recognize my name, but later he told me he had. He accepted my apology and asked after you."

"He did?"

"Whatever anger he felt toward me and Mrs. Reacher has worn off, I think. He was actually calm and almost . . . pleasant."

"I'm glad to hear it."

"He has one of your paintings in his office."

Her words were greeted with silence.

"It's one of your early ones."

Silence again.

"I asked him if he objected to me telling you that he had it, and he said he didn't mind." Seeing how quiet her aunt had become, Beth had to wonder if she'd done the right thing by letting her know.

Beth thought she heard a sniffle.

"Should I not have told you that?" she asked, uncertain now. "I mean, seeing that he has the painting and seems to have had it for a long time says something, don't you think?"

"Yes, I suppose it does."

Beth debated on telling her aunt the rest. "I asked him another question and I'm not sure you want to know the answer, so tell me if you don't."

"What was the question?" Sunshine asked, and it sounded as if she was struggling to hold on to her emotions.

Oh dear, would she never learn? In trying to apologize, she might have made matters even worse.

"I asked Peter if he loved you." She bit into her lower lip while she waited for her aunt's response.

It took her a moment. "Yes, tell me."

"He said *always*." She waited for her aunt to say something more. A long time passed.

Then finally, in a tightly controlled voice, Sunshine whispered, "Thank you, Beth."

Unsure now that she'd done it again and hurt the people she loved, she asked, "Did I do the right thing? Or did I make matters even worse?"

An eternity passed before Sunshine answered, and when she did her voice was thick with emotion.

"You did the right thing."

Beth waited until Christmas Day to send Sam a text. A dozen times or more she'd typed out a few words, needing to reach out to him, hoping he'd had a change of heart. Not hearing from him ate at her.

Christmas morning, knowing she was two hours ahead of him time wise, she waited until she was certain he would be up and about. All she sent was two words: Merry Christmas.

She waited all day and got no response back.

CHAPTER 37

Sam

The second weekend in January, Sam was busy working on a friend's car when Rocco showed up at the house. Sam hadn't stopped by his friend's house since before Christmas for fear of inadvertently running into Beth. Nichole and Beth were tight and he didn't want to risk a chance encounter. It was hard enough not to think about her as it was. Hard enough to push thoughts of her out of his head.

Just plain hard.

This lost feeling was new. Before Beth he'd grown accustomed to the loneliness, filled it with nights at The Dog House, watching sports, and poker nights with his buddies. He found the missing piece of his soul with the music she brought into his life. With her he'd discovered joy, laughter, and most important, meaning. His evenings seemed flat; he looked for things to keep himself occupied so he wouldn't think about her. He consoled himself with the promise that this lost feeling wouldn't last forever. He'd grow ac-customed to life without her soon enough.

"Hey," Rocco greeted, stepping into the garage. He stuffed his hands in his jean pockets as though to warm his fingers. He walked around to the front of the vehicle and looked over the engine. The weather was typical of January, drizzly and miserable. It was a good complement to Sam's mood, which had been dark since the day he split with Beth.

"Hey," Sam returned. He straightened and looked to his friend, wiping his hand with a cloth.

"Haven't seen you in a while," Rocco commented.

"Been busy." Sam suspected this was more than a social visit. Without it being said, he understood Nichole had sent Rocco on a fact-finding mission. Sam had nothing to say, and he'd make sure Rocco knew it in quick order.

"Owen's jar is empty," Rocco said. "He's asking about you."

Sam grinned. "You should bring him by; I'll fill it up for him."

Rocco bent over the car and examined the engine. "You okay?" he asked without looking at Sam.

"Why wouldn't I be?" The question was defensive.

Straightening, Rocco shrugged. "Heard you and Beth split."

"Yeah, well, all good things must come to an end, right?" He placed his hands on both sides of the engine and leaned forward, as if the answers to the questions of the universe were revealed there.

"Not all good things," Rocco countered.

"It was time," Sam said, unwilling to add anything more.

Rocco nodded as though he understood. "Thought that way once myself. Learned otherwise. You two were good together, com-plemented each other. Thing is, Sam, I don't ever remember you being as happy or content as when you were with Beth."

"Appreciate the words, Roc, but not your business."

Rocco raised his hands as if surrendering. "I had my say and as far as I'm concerned, from here on out it's a closed subject."

"Good. Keep it that way." Sam straightened and relaxed. He didn't want to lose a good friend because of Beth. These first few weeks would be the most difficult. It would get easier in time. All he had to do was wait it out.

"Heard Beth's—"

Sam stopped him. "Do me a favor."

"Sure," Rocco said. "What do you need?"

"If you hear of her . . ."

"You mean Beth."

Who else did he think it would be? "Yeah, Beth. If you hear anything she's said or if she's dating again, I'd rather not know about it. Better yet, don't mention her name anytime I'm around. Understand?"

Rocco grinned like he knew something Sam didn't.

"Can you do that?" he asked, letting his irritation show.

"Sure thing."

"Good."

Rocco hung around for another thirty minutes and then took off on an errand for Nichole. When Sam finished adjusting the carburetor on the 1970 Chevy Impala, he fixed himself a bologna sandwich and stood at the kitchen counter, wolfing it down. Funny how even the little things like a countertop in his kitchen reminded him of Beth. He'd stood right here when Beth had delivered the cookies for his poker night with the guys.

He didn't dare let Rocco know how bad off he was without her. It'd been only three weeks since he'd last seen her—three dark weeks—and every day was a challenge. Countless times he'd thought to reach out to her. It took every bit of restraint he could manage to not give in. What held him back was knowing something like what happened at Christmas was likely to happen again. She couldn't help herself. It was part of her nature to fix things. To make everything right. He'd seen it more than once.

What Beth failed to understand was that Sam didn't need fixing.

He didn't need her sticking her nose in where it didn't belong, dragging up the past he was determined to push to the farthest reaches of his mind. After Trish, he'd decided never to trust another woman again. Circumstances had brought him and Beth together and for a time it had been good.

Real good.

He'd let his heart rule his head and it had nearly ended in disaster. He could only imagine what would have happened if Trish had happened to see him at that recital. And worse, far, far worse, was seeing Luci. Seeing his daughter. She was everything he had imagined, everything he'd hoped.

Pain hit him square in the chest and he closed his eyes while his body adjusted to the emotional hit.

His daughter.

His child.

Just thinking about her and his head felt like it would implode. He could never be part of her life. He didn't need to be reminded that his chance of being a father had been taken away from him.

No, letting go of Beth was a protection. Hard as it was, he was determined *to be free of her—this time for good.*

CHAPTER 38

Sunshine

Sunshine had always enjoyed her visits to Chicago and was happy to accept the Lindstrom Art Museum's invitation to display her work. The reception held in her honor was to take place late afternoon on a Saturday. Her sister had agreed to accompany her, and Sunshine could see how well Ellie enjoyed introducing herself as the sister of the artist.

The compliments flowed as smoothly and freely as the champagne. By the end of the viewing, Sunshine was tired and more than ready to return to her hotel room for downtime. Ellie and Phillip had left, and she was about to thank the curator and head out herself when she noticed a lone man remained. His back was to her, but even then she recognized who it was.

Peter.

After a short hesitation, she joined him. Standing at his side she said, "I didn't realize you were here."

He set his empty champagne glass down on the tray provided and smiled. "Your work is breathtaking, Sunshine."

Her paintings had received praise and adulation all afternoon, but none meant more to her than Peter's kind words. "Thank you." She was afraid to say anything more, not knowing his mood. Their past two conversations had left her feeling wounded.

The curator approached and was about to tell Peter the showing had come to an end when she stopped him. "This is a personal friend of mine," she explained.

"Ah, of course. Please, stay as long as you like."

"I appreciate it."

He left them.

Peter stood by her side. "Are you tired?" he asked.

These receptions drained her of energy. Generally, all she wanted to do was return to her hotel room and put up her feet. "A little," she admitted.

"Would you consider dining with me?"

She hesitated, unsure they could spend time together without both of them coming away bleeding and battered.

"It's a simple question," he said when she didn't answer. "Yes or no?"

There was a slight edge to his voice as if he half expected her to make an excuse.

"Yes," she said, not wanting to risk losing the opportunity to spend more time with him even if it did end up bringing her pain.

He grinned then, almost sheepishly. "I know this quaint Mexican place that serves fish tacos."

"Peter." She breathed his name, hardly able to believe it. "Is our restaurant still open? After all these years?"

"Not the same one, a bit different, but with the same owners."

"No." Her fingertips hugged her lips. "Impossible."

"It took some investigating to find that couple. I was happy to learn they are still in the restaurant business."

"I can't believe it. Have you been?"

"No, I decided to wait until you could join me. Will you?"

She nodded, feeling almost giddy with delight.

The curator supplied her purse and coat and then escorted them from the museum. He gushed with enthusiasm and praise along with appreciation as Sunshine walked out the door, embarrassing her with his continuous compliments. When she was with Peter, she was no longer the artist, she was a woman spending time with a man.

Peter led her to a waiting car.

"You have a driver?" she asked.

"The firm supplies one for special clients."

"Am I a client?"

"No," he agreed, "but you're special."

She smiled and squeezed his fingers. He looked down at their joined hands as though shocked. Thinking her touch was unwelcome, she immediately released his hand and pulled her own closer to her body.

The restaurant was in the suburbs and took forty-five minutes to reach. They said little, almost as if they were strangers, which, Sunshine supposed, they essentially were. After all, it'd been more than thirty years.

When they arrived at the restaurant, the driver opened the door for Sunshine and helped her out. She was impressed with the outside of the building, which was a far cry from the hole-in-the-wall place they had faithfully supported in their youth. The original only had ten tables and this place was massive.

Peter approached the receptionist and they were seated right away. Neither bothered to look at menus. They knew what they wanted.

"It's changed, hasn't it?" Sunshine said, looking around at the flurry of activity. The waiter at the booth next to theirs was making guacamole, scooping fresh avocados into a bowl. Another server was delivering chips and fresh salsa.

"We've all changed, don't you think?" Peter asked.

Sunshine could only agree. "Do you ever think back to those days when we pooled our limited funds to share a meal?"

Peter grinned. "I do. I could probably buy every item on this menu ten times over without giving it a second thought now. You, too, I suppose," he added. "But I was a far happier man when I was driving the car my grandfather loaned me and looking under the seat for spare change so I could take you to dinner."

Sunshine looked down at her hands. "I was happy then, too."

"And now?" Peter asked.

Unsure how to answer, she said, "You need to define happiness. I'm content. I enjoy my life and my career."

"Are you ever lonely?"

She shrugged. "At times. You?"

He responded in like. "At times."

"If I were able to reach back in time and change the course of my life, there is one thing I'd do."

"Not leave for Italy because—"

"Not that," she said cutting him off.

Surprise showed in his eyes, and it seemed some of the light faded.

"Not that," she continued. "Italy was a life-changing experience for me, and not for the reasons you assume. The change I'd make is reading the letter you wrote after I moved to California. I was hurt and angry, filled with righteous indignation. I returned it to you unopened. I wish now that I'd been mature enough to put all that disappointment and indignation behind me."

Peter hung his head. "I deserved your anger and more."

"Oh Peter, stop. That was years ago now. We both made mistakes. We both suffered from our stubbornness. I have missed you so dearly through the years and thought of you often. Can we put it all behind us?"

He looked up as though stunned, and she stretched her arm across the table and gripped hold of his hand.

"Your niece said the reason she arranged that dinner for us was so that we could heal our relationship. Healing. Is that possible, Sunshine? After all these years?"

"It is if we're willing."

He smiled then, and it was the smile she remembered from their youth, one that reached every feature. His mouth widened. His eyes sparked with light. "I'm willing," he said.

"I am, too."

The waiter came to their table and they ordered fish tacos, a bean tostado, and because they had a driver, they had large margaritas. They lingered long after their meal was finished. They talked and laughed and then talked some more. It was as though the years evaporated. She learned that Peter had taken up sculpting again and worked evenings on his various projects, finding fulfillment and pleasure in creating once again. By the time they headed back to the car, Sunshine realized she couldn't remember an evening she'd enjoyed more.

The car service drove Sunshine to her hotel. Her flight was for late morning the following day.

"I had a wonderful time," she said, when the car eased under the hotel's portico. The doorman was right there to open her door and help her out.

"I did, too," Peter assured her.

She leaned over to kiss his cheek and thank him, but instead of his cheek, Peter turned his head so her mouth landed haphazardly on his lips. Embarrassed, she started to pull away, but he was having none of that. The hunger in his kiss left her breathless.

"Can I see you again?" he asked.

Her heart sank, weighted down with disappointment. "I'm sorry," she said, wishing she had known there was even a small chance of seeing him. Had she been aware, she would have left her flight open ended. "My flight leaves at eleven-thirty tomorrow."

Peter tapped his finger over her lips. "I didn't ask about that. I asked if I could see you again."

"Then, yes, please, I'd like that."

"Good, because I'd like that, too."

"When?" she asked, needing to know he wouldn't let months lapse before he got in touch with her.

"Is tomorrow too soon?"

"Not even close. I can do breakfast, but it will need to be early, because I need to leave the hotel by nine-thirty and—"

"I was thinking more along the lines of dinner."

"Dinner. I'll be in Portland."

"I know."

"You're flying to Portland?"

"Seems necessary, if I want to be with you."

"But . . ." Sunshine snapped her mouth closed. She had no intention of arguing with him.

"I'll pick you up around seven."

Sunshine nodded. "I'll be ready and waiting."

"I've been waiting for you over half my life," Peter whispered.

"No need to wait any longer," she returned, and climbed out of the vehicle.

Sunshine barely made it back to her room before she collapsed on her bed, happier than she could remember being.

Peter was back in her life, and she had the distinct impression he wasn't going to be leaving anytime soon.

CHAPTER 39

Beth

It'd been a month since she'd last spoken to Sam. Beth had decided if she didn't hear from him in thirty days, then she would reach out to him.

She'd spent nearly that same amount of time in the hospital and rehab center. Each day had felt like a month, but it was nothing compared to January. Time creeped by. She continued playing the piano at the center, but without Sam, it wasn't nearly as fulfilling. When she wasn't busy with her volunteer activities, she wrote music. It helped her pass the time and gave her a creative outlet, although most of the music she composed was fitting for a funeral service.

One night, unable to sleep, she sat in the dark with her iPad on her lap and composed a poem. The words poured out of her so quickly she could barely type them down fast enough.

The Warning Label No One Reads

I fell asleep shaking last night. I wish it was because of the cold.
When I woke my mind was flooded with thoughts of you.
Now I feel like I'm drowning.
I don't want it to be this way, waking up gasping for air.
Crying for however long it takes to pull myself
Back together again.
I let my thoughts, my regrets, get the best of me.
I worry you'll never be able to forgive me.
I'm overwhelmed.
Loving you should have come with a warning label.
The label no one reads.
The warning label that tells me love can hurt.
You can be wonderful, thoughtful, sincere
Or you can be harsh and unforgiving.
Love.
It's the warning label no one reads.

On day thirty, forsaking her pride, Beth drove to Sam's house. His truck was parked outside, so she knew he was home. Sucking in a deep breath to settle her nerves, she approached the front door. With no expectations, she decided she'd have her say and then leave.

When he opened the door, she could tell he was shocked to see her.

"Beth." He breathed her name and then frowned and took a step back as though he needed to put distance between the two of them.

She could almost see the wall go up, blocking her out, which served only to strengthen her resolve.

Sam spoke first. "I thought I made myself clear."

"You did," she assured him.

"Then what are you doing here?"

"I had something I wanted to say," she told him, standing on the other side of the screen door. "It won't take long, I promise." He hadn't invited her inside, and that was fine. Even if he had, she wouldn't have accepted.

He crossed his arms and looked bored. "You've already apologized. Doing it again isn't going to change anything."

"I'm not here to apologize, Sam."

"Fine. Whatever. Say whatever it is and then it would be best if you left."

She cleared her throat, mentally reviewing her prepared speech. "Do you remember one of the first times you came to visit me in the hospital? It was shortly after the accident? I asked you to read me a Psalm from the Bible."

"I remember," he returned, as though bored.

"I fell asleep and when I woke you were still reading. You mentioned that you wanted to learn more about David, the shepherd boy who had composed the majority of the psalms."

"Yeah, so?"

"So," she said exhaling, struggling to hold herself together. "You were amused after reading about David fighting Goliath. You mentioned there were a number of details you hadn't heard before. Saul said if David was going to face off with the giant then he needed to wear the king's armor. You laughed at the picture of this teenage boy strapping on the armor to the point he could barely walk."

Sam exhaled. "Is there a point to this?"

"Yes. I'm getting there. David did his best to do as the king asked, but it was impossible. If you remember, he took off the armor before he faced the giant. We discussed it at the time."

"Yes, I recall all that. So what?"

"So," she said, her lips trembling. "The giant in your life, Sam, is what happened with Trish and your daughter."

He frowned but didn't respond.

"And you're fighting that giant loaded down with body armor. You can't move, you can't love, you can't defeat that giant as long as you're weighted down with this wall you've erected around your heart. I love you, Sam, and I unintentionally hurt you, but you aren't able to see past that because you haven't been able to defeat your giant."

"I've heard enough," he said, and started to close the door.

"Think about it, Sam."

He glared back, unyielding. Seeing her words had no effect, she sighed. "Good-bye, Sam," she said softly, brokenly. "I won't trouble you again."

The door closed and Beth hung her head, breathed in three deep breaths, and turned and left.

A month passed. Beth had hoped to hear from Sam and knew if he had been inclined to reach out, it would have happened before now.

The first Friday night in March, Nichole asked her if she'd be willing to watch Matthew again. She knew it would be a challenge alone but felt she was up to it.

Matthew was awake and crawling around the house, exploring his world when she arrived. Nichole gave her the list of instructions as she had before, and within ten minutes of Beth's arrival, Nichole and her husband were out the door.

"Okay, kiddo," she said, chasing after the baby. "It's you and me against the world." She remembered how watching him the first time had taken both her and Sam's full attention. Smiling, she remembered Sam's response to a messy diaper. They'd had some fun adventures. Despite the fact that they were no longer together, she didn't look back with regret. She'd learned a lot about herself from him and she hoped that in time he would be able to think of her fondly.

Her phone rang and she picked up. "Hey, Sunshine," she said, pleased to hear from her aunt. Sunshine and Peter were quite the item these days. Her aunt had made more trips to Chicago in the last two months than in the last two years. If she wasn't in the Windy City, then Peter was in Portland, the Rose City. Beth was thrilled that the two of them had found each other again. Their relationship was serious, and she fully expected them to stay together. Yes, she'd meddled in their lives, but at least this time there looked to be a happy ending.

"Where are you?" Beth asked.

"Chicago. Peter and I are heading to the theater. I wanted to ask if you'd stop by my place one day next week and bring in the mail for me."

"Of course. You're staying with Peter the entire week?"

"Yes. It's getting more difficult to leave him. He asked me to move to Chicago permanently."

Beth hated the thought of her aunt leaving Portland, and if she did, Beth might move elsewhere herself. Her teaching contract was for the current school year and she hadn't yet signed on for another year. There was nothing to hold her in Portland. It saddened her to think of walking away from Sam, but the truth was it was probably for the best.

"That's wonderful," she said, forcing enthusiasm into her voice. "If you do, I might move back myself. Mom and I are getting along better than ever, and there's nothing holding me down in Portland."

"You do whatever you feel is best," Sunshine advised.

Thankfully, Matthew fell asleep quickly, tired out by all the activity. Beth held him long after he'd finished his bottle. She softly kissed his forehead and mulled over the future. Her teaching contract had been renewed. All that was required of her was to pen her name on the bottom line. It was then that she decided she wouldn't do it.

She was leaving Portland.

——

The following week, the March rains came in full force. Beth waited for a break in the weather and raced toward the faculty parking lot. As she approached her vehicle, she noticed a man climb out of a truck cab and approach her.

Sam.

Her steps faltered and she paused, unsure what to do. She froze, slowing her steps as she walked toward her vehicle, uncertain and struggling with seeing him again.

"I heard you decided to leave Portland," he said, his eyes holding her prisoner.

"Who told you that?" Silly question. Clearly Nichole had been the informant. "Never mind. The answer is obvious."

"I thought you liked Portland."

"I do, but it looks like Sunshine is going to move back to Chicago to be closer to Peter."

"They're together?" He sounded surprised and looked pleased both at the same time.

"Yeah, despite me," she said in an effort to make a joke.

It started to rain again and she placed a music folder over the top of her head as protection. She waited a few uncomfortable moments for Sam to say something more. He didn't. It was silly to stand in the rain, waiting, not knowing for what. She gave him a weak smile. "Nice seeing you, Sam," she said as she hit the remote that would unlock her car door.

"Wait," he said. "Don't go."

"I'm getting wet."

"This won't take a minute." He looked down at his feet and kicked at a rock. "I've been doing a lot of thinking about what you said . . . the giant and David and the armor."

"That's good."

He glanced up at the darkening sky. "Listen, would you like to go someplace for coffee and talk?"

She would more than anything, but she had plans. "Sorry, I can't. I've got an appointment." It'd started to rain in earnest.

His mouth thinned. "An appointment or a date?"

"Does it matter?" she asked. He'd made it clear he wasn't interested in seeing her any longer.

Oblivious to the rain, he held her gaze. "Guess not. Have a good time."

That was it? He had nothing more to say? Beth stared back at him, disappointment stealing over her. With nothing else to do, she slid inside the car and started the engine. The wiper blades automatically went on. After fastening her seatbelt, she looked at Sam, hoping, praying, he would say or do something to stop her. The least he could do was suggest they meet another time. Apparently, that was more than he was willing to do.

With no other option, she put the car in gear and started toward the exit. Her throat was thick and she glanced in her rearview mirror, debating if she should turn back around until she remembered their last meeting. Sam had basically closed the door on her, ending their relationship. If he was serious, if he'd had a change of heart, it was up to him to say so.

She was going only about ten miles an hour when she saw another car approaching the exit at the same time as she was. She stepped on her brake, but it was too late. The other car slammed into the front bumper, jolting her. For an instant, she was too stunned to move.

A minute passed, possibly two, or it could have been longer. Her car door was yanked open and Sam was there. "Are you hurt?"

She shook her head. "I . . . I don't think so. How's the other driver?"

He looked up as if he hadn't thought to check. "I'll be right back."

Racing to the other car, Sam checked with the second driver and returned in short order. "She's fine. She admitted it's her fault."

"I must have bad car karma," Beth groaned. Two accidents within a few months of each other, and neither one had been her fault. She should have been more careful, more aware, but her head had been filled with Sam and she hadn't been paying attention. She felt equally to blame.

The other driver, the mother of one of the high school students, gave Beth the necessary information for insurance purposes so her car could be repaired. No more than fifteen minutes later, the apologetic woman left.

Sam waited and Beth appreciated it. "This is a dangerous way for us to keep meeting," he teased. "You're sure you're not hurt?"

"A little shaken, but I'm fine." And she was. When she'd first been released from the rehab center, one of her big fears was the possibility of another car accident. Her hands shook and she lifted the hair from her forehead. Silly as it was, she noticed that the rain had started to let up. Not that it mattered; both Beth and Sam were drenched. While the accident had shaken her, thankfully the damage to her car was minimal.

"I'm not fine," Sam said, studying her intently.

"Sam. What happened?" Beth didn't realize that he'd been involved in the crash.

"I need you, Beth. I'm ready to take off that armor, ready to move forward. Ready to heal, but I'm going to need help." He paused and seemed to be waiting for her to respond.

Stunned by his words, she could do nothing more than stare at him.

"Would you be willing to stand by me?" he asked gently. "Would you let me love you the way you deserve to be loved?"

She blinked several times, unsure she was willing to risk her heart a second time.

Beth thought about Sunshine and the regrets she had regarding her relationship with Peter. She'd refused to forgive him and waited years to make things right with him.

Sam studied her, his eyes wide with appeal.

"Oh Sam," she whispered, the lump in her throat so large she had trouble talking around it. "Yes . . ." She wanted to tell him how much she'd missed him in the intervening weeks and couldn't speak. When she could, she'd let him know how she'd struggled to fill the giant hole he'd left in her heart.

Groaning, Sam wrapped his arms around Beth and hugged her close, burying his head in the crook of her neck. If this wasn't heaven, then it was pretty darn close. She was wrong. Heaven arrived when they kissed. Beth was starving for want of him. They kissed until they were both breathless, chests heaving, and still it wasn't enough. Rain fell down in buckets all around, mingling with Beth's tears, liquid flowing down her face, her hair little more than wet tendrils dripping onto her shoulders.

Sam pushed the hair away from her face and braced his forehead against hers. "I've been miserable without you. I thought I could do it. Thought I could put you out of my mind. Didn't happen. I thought I'd lost you all over again when you got in the car and drove off."

She'd waited, wanted him to stop her and he hadn't.

"Have you found someone else?"

His heart was in his eyes and she could have drowned in the way he looked at her, the doubt and the regret telling her more than any words he might have spoken. "No. No one compares to you, Sam. No one. Thought you learned that the last time you set me free."

"You had a date this evening?"

"I was helping Jazmine. The house is coming along nicely and I told her I'd stop by after school."

He groaned and then laughed softly before rewarding her with another long series of kisses.

"I should have explained," she admitted, "but I wanted you to tell me why you'd come and you didn't and then I wasn't sure what to think." After all these weeks when she'd hungered for word from him, she'd needed him to explain, to give her something more than simply showing up at the school.

"When you said you had a date . . ."

"I said 'appointment,'" she corrected.

"That seemed like just another word for date, and I immediately assumed I was too late and I'd lost you."

Beth pressed her forehead against his chest. "Guess I have another car accident to thank for bringing us together."

He chuckled, holding her close. "I hope you know how much I love you."

She nodded. "I hope you know . . ."

"I do," he whispered, and kissed the top of her head.

This felt right, Beth mused, snuggling against Sam's warmth, her palm against his chest and his arms around her. She felt the even beat of his heart.

This was what it felt like to be loved.

Warning label or not, she was lost.

ABOUT THE AUTHOR

DEBBIE MACOMBER, the author of *A Girl's Guide to Moving On, Last One Home, Silver Linings, Love Letters, Mr. Miracle, Blossom Street Brides,* and *Rose Harbor in Bloom,* is a leading voice in women's fiction. Ten of her novels have reached #1 on the *New York Times* bestseller lists, and five of her beloved Christmas novels have been hit movies on the Hallmark Channel, including *Mrs. Miracle* and *Mr. Miracle.* Hallmark Channel also produced the original series *Debbie Macomber's Cedar Cove,* based on Macomber's Cedar Cove books. She has more than 200 million copies of her books in print worldwide.

debbiemacomber.com
Facebook.com/debbiemacomberworld
@debbiemacomber
Pinterest.com/macomberbooks
Instagram.com/debbiemacomber

ABOUT THE TYPE

This book was set in Sabon, a typeface designed by the well-known German typographer Jan Tschichold (1902–74). Sabon's design is based upon the original letter forms of sixteenth-century French type designer Claude Garamond and was created specifically to be used for three sources: foundry type for hand composition, Linotype, and Monotype. Tschichold named his typeface for the famous Frankfurt typefounder Jacques Sabon (c. 1520–80).

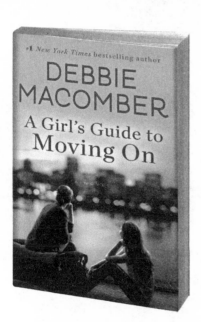
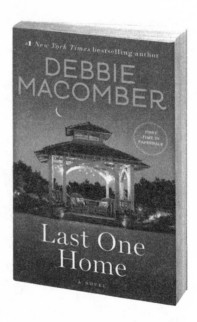

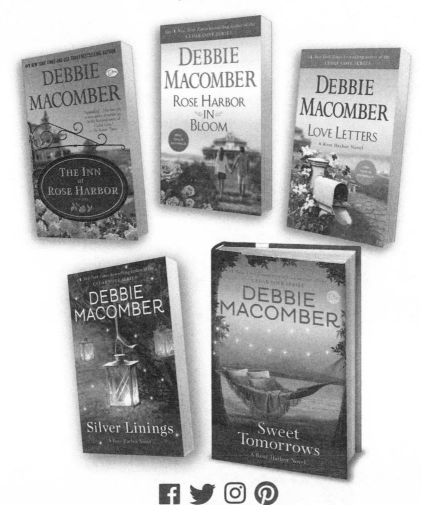

Join DEBBIE MACOMBER
on social media!

Facebook.com/debbiemacomberworld

@debbiemacomber

Pinterest.com/macomberbooks

Instagram.com/debbiemacomber

Visit DebbieMacomber.com
and sign up for Debbie's e-newsletter!